Valentine and the Devil

Terry Hornby

Published by Terry Hornby, 2023.

To my wonderful sons, John and James.

Thank you for letting me tell you stories,

over and over again.

Valentine and the Devil

Ebook ISBN: 978-0-6458491-0-3

Print ISBN: 978-0-6458491-1-0

Electronic Edition published in Australia in 2023 by Terry Hornby

More information may be gained upon contact with the author at hornbywriting@gmail.com

Typeset in 11pt Garamond

Cover design by Amalie J Bech and BookCoverZone

Print book distributed by Draft2Digital

Chapter 1

The devil is not a metaphysical construct. He's a big lump of a bloke, piggy looking eyes, red skin, little horns and a really angry disposition. I'm looking at him right now and he's not happy.

"Look at the size of him, Val," said my companion, "I hope those chains hold."

"Shut your mouth, Wilson," I said, "I don't want them to know we're here." I was standing behind a wall, by peeking around the corner I could see the little tableau, the gypsies, the paying customers. Their campfire light bounced off the walls of the City, they must have just made it in by curfew before the gates were shut. And the devil, he sort of drew the eye.

Pulling back into cover I grabbed the front of the tanner's filthy shirt, "Tell me again, Wilson, tell me about the devil." I slid down the wall into a sitting position and since I'm a big bloke poor old Wilson sank with me. It's not every day someone runs up to say you can pay a copper piece to see the devil. Well, it does happen a lot in the City, just not every day. And this was the first time I'd seen something which really could be the devil. Child of Satan, demon, stuff like that.

It had been a long day and I was tired.

"Where'd he come from, Wilson?" I asked.

The tanner looked at my grip on his shirt and knew I'd never let go. I waved my other paw at him so he could see it, just a little wave but it told him I had a free hand and was more than willing to hit him. He sighed and slumped beside me. I didn't let go, haven't made that mistake since I was a recruit about, I don't know, a couple of hundred years ago.

"You're a mean man, Valentine," he said.

1

"My mum loves me," I replied, letting my head rest against the wall. My grip was still strong, so I gave his shirt a little shake to get the memory juices flowing.

"Look," he said, "I'm coming home and I see their fire, you know how they build up a big burn when they're putting on a show. Heard the music, bells and stuff, thought I'd have a look at some of their freak shows. Last year they had a half woman, half man – split right down the middle, one half a moustache and the other half had a big...," he hesitated, unsure of offending my delicate sensibilities.

"Tit, Wilson, it's called a tit," she had one big breast, I'd seen it on a patrol. Poor woman, parading around for the sleazy types like Wilson. "Stick to the devil, how close did you get?"

The night sky was sprinkled with silver stars, beautiful glints of glittering purity. And I sat with my hand in the greasy folds of a dirty and smelly shirt. Better up there than down here, I thought.

"When I got to the edge of the camp, they were just bringing it out. He had a ring around his throat and three chains linked to it. But strong! Val, he grabbed one of the chains and just yanked it out of the man's hands! Lucky he wasn't dragged into the clutches of that devil monster. I took off. That's when you found me."

He was right about that. I was doing a quick circuit alone - the Night Watch never sleeps and all that - touring around a generally quiet street when Wilson came running down the road like a man on a mission. There I was, a City Watchman doing his rounds, it's night, I'm looking for break-ins and bad guys and what do I see. Some idiot head down and arms pumping and running. From what? I asked myself. Could be a crime. When he came close enough I hit him with my halberd. Just a little tap, barely touched him.

"You didn't have to hit me so hard" he complained.

"Shut up, you big girl, the bleeding's stopped." I thought for a moment, what to do? Better take this up the chain of command to Magic, he'll know what to do. I hoped he would. "Did you see anyone else beside the guards?" I asked. He told me what he knew and when I thought I would get no more I let him go.

Time to see the boss, I thought.

It wasn't the brightest thing I'd ever done, going off alone in Westside, walking the streets of the Thieves' Quarter by myself. Since we were undermanned, as usual, and Magic feels strongly about fulfilling his obligations – never bothered me much – someone had to do this little circuit alone. He had looked at me and said, "Need a volunteer, Val, someone with experience, guts and talent."

I preened until he said, "Since we haven't got anyone like that in the squad, I'm sending you."

"What about this volunteer stuff," I stuttered, "Maybe someone else wants to do it?"

As he turned away, he grumbled "You're a real card, Valentine, now get lost. I've got real work to do."

We had agreed to meet at the Dolphin Fountain Square and that's where I was now, waiting for the rest of the squad to appear. In all honesty I was feeling a trifle edgy, a lone guardsman in this part of the city is like being a new toy. Everyone wants to see who can break you first. To be on the safe side I found a nice dark corner with a deep, black shadow and pulled myself in as far as I could. Standing there with my boots in something soft and rotting, I peered out into the square. If I was lucky no-one had seen me enter. Since leaving Wilson I had slunk from shadow to shadow just like a regular citizen and not like a stalwart defender of the weak.

Unfortunately, my halberd marked me as a guardsman. I considered tossing it away but the thought of explaining how I lost it put me off. The lads would know I had been terrified and, dear friends that they were, they would dump on me from a great height. At least, that's what I would do if it was one of them.

The stupid thing clanked on a bit of stone, the only noise save for the odd crackle of burning materials from the flambeaux scattered around the walls of the square. They didn't really give light, more like they gave shadow, but the illusion was there. If we found them out on our rounds, we reported it and the Lamplighter was docked money. We used to have to light the damn things ourselves before the Lamplighters were formed.

I don't think they'll last as a guild, it's a stupid job. Some sections of the City had Lamplighters during their rounds all night but not here in the grungy bits of our great metropolis. Westside got the one flambeau at the start of the night and that was it, the Lamplighters wouldn't come back after that. Very sensible decision.

But we did, City Watch Guardsman, toiling through the dark and gloomy night, bravely keeping the streets safe. That was me, , making sure no-one came out and pinched the square or stole the fountain. As time passed, I waited and waited for the rest of the squad, my nerves jumping at every sound, nervous as a cat.

I was terrified.

Chapter 2

In the distance I heard the clank of metal and raised voices, this could be bad news. Then I heard Meataxe singing and knew it was the rest of the squad. Since I didn't want to look like a Nervous Nellie I ducked out of my little crevice and sat on the edge of the fountain. It took up the centre of the square and had a nice ledge running around the lip so I draped myself on it, looking all causal and unconcerned. Meataxe entered the square first, probably drunker than when I had last seen him.

He was dressed in the Guard uniform, sensible shoes with fake gold buckles, stockings and cut-off pants which ended just below the knee. The stockings should have reached the bottom of the leggings and made a neat line, complete with a little red ribbon. I say should have because Meataxe had trouble with neat, his stockings were rumpled down around his ankles, the red ribbons were untied and dangling beside the flapping, dirty and stained leggings. Around his neck was our badge of office, a bright yellow scarf, this particular one had only the memory of its original colour. His top was marginally cleaner, a billowing, shiny gold coloured blouse with lovely balloon like sleeves. These were slashed stylishly to reveal his white linen undershirt; it can look quite smart when the Day Watch does its parade.

Not so much us, the Night Watch, especially not Meataxe. He cut a bedraggled figure, topped off nicely by our huge floppy hat, complete with rakish red feather. The hat was a really nice touch, I thought, kept the serious rays of the sun off our tender eyes. Of course, at night it was useless, falling across our already obscured vision and preventing us from scanning high rooftops easily.

"Val!" he exclaimed, seeing me and lurching to one side at the same time. To his credit, he did keep a good grip on his musket. Like most of us, he had some habits burned into the bone. Habits which kept you from getting killed. "There you are! We been look... (hic)...look.. lookin' ev'rywhere for you." He staggered closer and sat down on the ledge beside me. "My ol' pal, Valentine," an arm snaked around my neck as he leaned in conspiratorially, "You know, Val", pause for breath, "you're my bes'...my bes' friend. You know so many big...words...you're so clever and I'm so dumb...." I stayed where I was, embraced by a drunken colleague as he muttered a few more times "Bes' fren, you...Val... my ol' pal...so smart..."

As he continued to breathe noxious fumes I watched the rest of the Night Watch clatter into the square, more noise than threat. Saints above, we were hopeless.

Magic strolled over and asked for a report, most of the squad sat down against walls and chatted, a few dragged out bottles and took some serious pulls. I must have been the only thing keeping Meataxe erect because as I stood up to talk to our corporal he fell into the fountain. Magic just looked at his squad member, floundering in the waist high water, resignedly he said, "Teddy Boy, you and Horse drag that idiot out before he drowns." Turning to me he asked, "Anything worth reporting, Val?" he wasn't really interested, just going through the motions.

I opened my mouth to speak but was interrupted by the clatter of hooves. Those guardsmen near the entrance to the square quickly pulled themselves against the walls, a horse always has right of way if you want to keep the ability to walk. Into the square came about half-a dozen men on horseback, they pounded to a halt at the fountain, steel hooves sparking against the cobblestones.

Us deadly Night Watch personnel looked on dumbly. I sighed and joined the few other guardsmen who at least prepared weapons for defence.

Fortunately, the newcomers were not out to attack us. After recovering from the initial surprise I recognised the Captain of the Night Watch, Lord van Stolberg and his retinue. He was dressed all in black with just flashes of white at wrist and collar where expensive cloth beautifully set off his elegance. The Man in Black, our leader.

"Corporal!" he barked, "Which one of you is corporal?" his eyes swept the square, taking us all in, the drunks, the disorganised, the unready.

Magic didn't look too happy but he pulled himself to attention, "I'm corporal, my Lord".

Another horseman responded, "His Lordship does not use his title while on duty for the Watch, corporal. Please address him as 'Captain Franz'." None of the riders had dismounted, The Man in Black edged forward a little "Thank you, Ensign, that'll do. What's your name, corporal? Is this second Squad?" he asked.

Meataxe chose that moment to lurch erect, spraying water in a wide arc, some droplets pattering off Magic's hat. "Magic!" he proclaimed, "Name's MAGIC!" he repeated before flopping to sit once again in the fountain.

Again, Magic sighed, "My name is Alfort, captain, Charles Alfort," he said, "and yes, this is the second squad." Using his right arm he gestured to us, his command, noble keepers of the peace that we were. The Man in Black followed his movement, eyes taking in our state of presentation. I was reasonably close so I could see his face, waited for the sneer. It didn't come, at least not from the captain.

The ensign spoke up, "Your men are slackers, corporal, bring them men to attention!"

Magic looked at him, "Who'd you be, you're not Watch?" he asked.

"I should say not! I am Ensign Briare of the Household Cavalry and you will call me sir. Now, carry out my orders!"

Before the situation worsened the Man in Black spoke, "Thank you, Ensign, I would prefer the men to stay as they are." Turning back to Magic he said, "Alfort, I know that name." He began to dismount,

"Yes, town in France, very pretty chateau on a hill with delightful woods. Your family, corporal?"

Magic held the captain's bridle, "Not quite, we were poachers in those woods until my dad was hung. Seemed to be a good time to leave." The two men stood together, chatting amiably about forests while Ensign Briare sent off waves of disgust.

The captain spoke again and I eavesdropped shamelessly, "Got an interesting situation here, corporal," he said, "and I've heard your men might be the ones to help." Over his shoulder he called to his escort, "Bring the man forward, Briare."

Two of the riders dismounted and brought a third man with them. On closer inspection, I could see he was under guard, but a light one. He might not even have known he was being policed. Nothing outstanding about him, his complexion marked him as gentry, all pale and wan. His skin didn't look like it had seen hard times so I put him down as one of those rich younger sons who can swan about and call themselves poets. Useless drips.

His clothes were interesting, very fine indeed. A soft gray shirt with what looked like buttons of ivory was tucked into darker gray pants of a heavy material, again this was well made with strange fastenings and bits of metal. But it was his boots that caught my eye. I'm a walker, I don't ride much so I am a fair judge of footwear. His boots seemed enormously supple and shone with a lustre I've only ever seen in expensive leather. He must have had it treated somehow to give it the softness for wearing plus the hardwearing needed for serious walking. And these boots had seen some work recently, they were scratched and scarred but still looked disgustingly comfortable.

Who was this guy?

Magic gave him the once over and asked, "I've never seen him before. What do you want me to do?"

"I understand your squad has a large number of men who speak other languages?" asked the Man in Black. "This fellow," he went on, indicating the stranger, "speaks in a tongue unlike any I have heard. He was brought to Watch headquarters for disturbing the peace, but something about him is odd. Perhaps some of your men can understand his talk."

Magic looked at Captain Franz with new respect. He always told us a good Watchman develops a tingling sense that told you something was not quite right. Seems our leader was a real copper. He pursued his lips before replying, "Could be, we certainly attract the newcomers and refugees to the Night Watch, pay rate's just a step up from gravedigger. I'll see what I can do." He turned and called out a few names, "Guido, Santini, Horse – get over here." He called a few others and then saw me, hovering. "Val, do join us, you have some education." He looked around to see if he'd missed anybody and caught sight of Right Honourable, "Right Honourable, how many languages do you speak?"

The tall, dark-haired man responded, "About ten, dear fellow. Benefits of a private tutor and all that. Having trouble with your tavern conversations, Magic?" He somehow managed to walk over with a lounging gait, casual and regal at the same time. I'd tried to copy it but looked like a constipated pig. When he approached our little group, he went on, "How can I be of service, dear boy?"

My mouth took off without orders, "Magic wants us to listen to this guy speak and see if any of us know his language. Good thing you can speak ten!" I sounded like the new kid at school.

Right Honourable patted me on the shoulder and said, "Well done, Val, excellent summary. As a matter of fact," he went on, "I can understand a few more. And then there are the half dozen I can read. The classics, Latin poets, Hebrew scholars and, of course, the works of Aristotle – all Greek to me." He gave a little chuckle.

"But wasn't he a Greek?" I blurted. I was being a particular doofus tonight.

"It's a joke, Val," said Magic, "Now shut up and listen." He gestured to the stranger but spoke to the Man in Black, "How do you turn him on, Captain?"

"Interesting, this," said the captain, "I think he understands some of what we say but cannot speak our tongue. Knows enough to say, 'yes' and 'no'. Most bizarre." He spoke to the stranger, "Off you go, sir, talk to these men."

We stood in a loose semi-circle around the strange man and he began to gabble in a language I had never heard. Our squad had a lot of foreigners, far more than any other section of the city. If you had no skills in a new town you found a low paying job, but the left overs all trickled down to us. The Second Squad of the Night Watch, on nodding acquaintance with the bottom of the barrel. I can pick up languages easily but nothing he was saying made any sense and, judging by the looks of my fellow Watch, they shared my ignorance.

After a few minutes of speaking, he stopped and started again with dumb show gestures, acting out a message. He stuck his fingers against his head, waved an arm over his head, touched his skin and then pointed at a red stripe on Magic's blouse.

"You're looking for the devil, aren't you?" I said. It just popped out when he put his fingers up, like little horns. Everyone stopped and looked at me, including the stranger.

He nodded with a big smile on his face and said, "Yes! Devil! YES!"

Chapter 3

I told them about the Devil and the gypsies. When I finished the Man and Black gave some quick orders before we trundled out with me up the front, showing the way.

When we reached the gypsy camp the captain just rode on in, he carried his authority in the very air around him.. The rest of us are not so brave because gypsy's can be bad news, especially with the knife. I was walking a little behind the Man in Black and could hear him speaking to the ensign. They were arguing.

"The Archbishop must be told," said the ensign, "I have a duty to..."

"You have a duty to me, Ensign," cut in the Man in Black. "You are under my orders, by command of your Colonel. Now shut up!" He looked over his shoulder, saw me lurking and barked, "Valentine, isn't it? Get up here." I got.

"Go find your devil, Val." he commanded.

I felt alone and nervous. I am used to being alone, but the nervousness came from the high company I was keeping. My halberd weaved a little dance in front of my eyes as I held it at the ready, walking slowly forward towards the tents. Behind me I heard the shuffling of other feet and hoped I was not walking alone.

"Easy, Val," I heard Magic say, close to my right side. Lovely man.

The first two tents were empty but the third held a party, a big party. Lots of gypsies, male and females and lots of drink. As I entered the tent a hush fell, my halberd can have that effect on a small room. It tends to draw the eye, a long ash pole topped by a combination axe and spear, all pointy and hurty.

"Evenin' all," I said, in my best copper voice, "What's all this then?"

A fat bloke untangled himself from a chair, a bottle and a woman, in that order and strutted up to me. The rest of the gypsies in the tent were tensing for a fight, hands disappearing under jackets, no doubt filling with their own instruments of choice. I was feeling no anxiety, this was something I could handle, a bit of violence and mayhem, harsh words and threats – my bread and butter.

I also knew key members of the Night Watch had trickled into the tent and stood behind me, bad men all.

"What you want?" asked the fat gypsy. "We done nothing. No steal."

Magic hadn't stepped forward so I guessed he was letting me run this show, "Where's the devil?" I asked, cutting to the heart of the matter.

The gypsy's face lit up, "Aha!" he exclaimed. "You customers! You want see our devil." He turned to the rest of the tent and babbled. They all relaxed, some smiled, one yelled a comment at us and laughed, the bottles came out again.

Fat boy turned back to us with a face of resignation, "Too late, Mr Guardsman, we not have our devil no more. You can see other good things, what about a half man half woman?" he asked, face alight with avarice.

My interrogation skills had reached their limit so I stood there looking mean at him. Magic tells us to look mean if you can't think of something to say, the bad guys often think you know what's going on and make a break for it. Or fight. Chasing and fighting I can do; clever questions are a bit of a stretch. But I'm learning.

The fat gypsy wiped his hands down his already dirty vest, looked around for inspiration, gazed over my shoulder at my ugly friends and decided to keep talking. "We sell him."

I was running through questions in my mind, trying to work out the cleverest way of asking who bought said devil. Fat Boy beat me to it, "Maestro bought devil."

Maestro, the man who entertained the City, behind me I heard Magic mutter, "Might have bloody known, more work."

We went back outside and told the Man in Black what happened, Magic sent some of the squad off to search the other tents on the off chance the gypsies were lying and had stashed our red friend somewhere. I didn't give much for their chances of finding him, the one time I saw old Nick he didn't strike me as the sit down and be quiet kind of guy. No, if he was anywhere in this campsite, we would have heard a lot of bellowing. Probably why he was sold, so these campers could get some sleep.

Sure enough the reports came up empty, the captain said to Magic, "We'll have to go after him, corporal, bring your squad back into the city as quickly as possible, meet me at the Theatre. I'll ride ahead and see what's what."

"Catch the devil, sir?" asked Magic, "You think this thing really exists?"

"I don't know what it is, corporal, but I do not want to incite a riot. If the Maestro advertises this thing as a real devil, we could have panic. It must be some sort of animal or deformed human," said the captain. I could see he was struggling with yet another problem in a city which threw up nothing but problems. I wondered why he was leading the Night Watch, he looked like he could afford to do better, or worry less.

"Devils exist, sir," said Ensign Briare. "This is a chance for us to demonstrate our faith to the Lord, we find this thing and burn it. That's what God would want."

"You know what God wants, do you, Ensign?" asked Magic. "Got a special message from Him, have you?" Our corporal had a big mouth, and did not suffer fools easily.

"Don't be impertinent, corporal, and keep out of this conversation. It is between your betters." The ensign moved his horse to shoulder Magic out of the way, an old horseman's trick of shoving people around to control the rabble.

Magic is many things, but rabble he is not. He grabbed the bit of the ensign's horse and gently pulled down. The horse's head lowered making the ensign looked like a pimple on a pumpkin and in about as much control.

He stuttered bit, not being used to our little ways, before saying through clenched teeth "Remove your hand this instant, sir, or I shall draw my sword and cut it off." His right hand moved across to the hilt of his sabre.

We all heard a click.

On the other side of the ensign's horse was Teddy Boy, he had pulled the cocking mechanism of his musket into Ready. This was not good practice since it weakened the spring and so was only done just before pulling the trigger. Teddy Boy was not looking at the ensign, nor was he in any way aiming his musket in the rider's direction. He had just cocked his musket and looked out into the darkness around the gypsy campsite.

Then he turned his head and gazed into the ensign's eyes.

The Man in Black stepped into the gap, "Ensign! Prepare to lead the way to the Theatre!" He turned his horse and summoned his escort with a wave, snarling to Magic "Get them back on their leash, corporal." He indicated Teddy Boy, "Put that man under arrest." He scanned the area, getting himself back under control, noticing me, "Keep the stranger with you, Val could look after him; seems to have done a good job so far."

The captain gathered his reins, yelled back to his men "Ensign! Lead the way! See you at the Theatre, Charles" he said to our corporal.

Quick as a flash came the response, "No worries, Franz, see you there." Magic stepped back with a smile and a wave and received a momentary hard look from The Man in Black. Not using his title was one thing, I suppose, but using his first name may have been crossing the line. I waited for a chilly rebuff.

The captain just smiled, winked at Magic and rode off with a clatter and a crash of hooves. We were alone in the courtyard, the Night Watch plus one, my new best friend.

Meataxe spoke up, sobriety beginning to raise its ugly head, "I'm confused, I don't wanna arrest Teddy Boy."

"You're always confused," replied Magic, "and no, Ted's not under arrest."

"But the captain said...," went on Meataxe. I always appreciated Meataxe for the way he asked the questions we were all thinking but were too cool to ask.

"Shut up, Meataxe, and stop drinking." Magic spoke as he walked to the gypsy. "That goes for the rest of you, sober up."

From behind us we heard, "Wanna buy some clothes. Devil's clothes?' asked the gypsy.

The fat gypsy stood beside Magic holding a bundle of clothes. Big deal, I thought. Then I saw the garments, just like the ones worn by our stranger. The gypsy said, "Devil's clothes. Good price, very fair." I lusted after those boots.

When did Satan start wearing leather?

Chapter 4

We put the clothes in a bag and gave it to Meataxe to carry. Because, well, it was Meataxe. At the edge of the campsite Magic had us all gather around him in a loose circle. "This is serious, boys, and we can't solve it with our usual sloppy methods, I think we're in for a big night. Right, we're going hunting for the devil, any questions?" he asked.

Right Honourable spoke up, "You're not seriously suggesting that this thing Val saw is a devil, or THE devil. Much as I support and encourage our comrade," he indicated me with a languid wave, "he is about as reliable as the rest of us. Which is to say, not bloody much. Good heavens, Magic, we're running around like headless chickens on the word of a drunken waster. No offence, Val."

"None taken, Right Honourable," I replied. When he's right, he's right, I thought.

Magic looked at me, "What about it, Val, what did you see?" And it all went still around me.

Great, I thought, I'm the centre of attention. My whole reason for joining the Night Watch was to avoid attention and now everyone's staring at me.

Best to get this over with, I spoke up, "I saw something pretty rough, Magic. And it wasn't human, not maimed, not deformed, not sick or disguised. I don't know what it was but I do know it was really, really angry. And considering we have its clothing then it was standing around naked. Now if you put a chain around my neck and stripped me bare, I'd be feeling a bit peeved, too. This thing was angry, strong and wanting to hurt someone."

Horse chipped in, "If we don't get to the Theatre and this thing gets loose, we'll have a lot of dead people. Our job is to stop them from being dead." That pretty much summed it up for me, too. I've run away a lot, no problem with that, but somewhere in the City there was going to be a need for the Watch. A need for someone to protect others. A need for us.

"No more discussion, we're moving," decided Magic. "We'll have to run to get there, but if we all just hare off through the streets in our normal fashion – yelling and screaming – we'll create a bigger problem than the one we are trying to solve."

That was true. I could picture the scene, people peering out the window at the noise to discover their Watch running away from the City Walls. Their first thought would be invasion by the barbarians, a devastating war followed by looting and blood in the streets. Mass panic would follow. "What are we going to do, Magic?" I asked.

"I've got an idea, been wanting to try this for a while," he said. "Line up three abreast, halberds along the flanks. Front rank is me, Meataxe and Right Honourable. Val, you bring up the rear with our guest and Teddy Boy. We can't march in step but I think we can run in step. Need a volunteer to stay here and look after those idiots already comatose." We looked around at three snoring bodies, Santini said he'd stay and he'd also look after the spare horse, the one our stranger had ridden.

"Form up!" commanded our corporal. We did, a strange sense of purpose seeping into me. An unfamiliar feeling, one I had not felt since those awful days of the siege at Ostend.

Magic had us bunch up shoulder to shoulder, squashed right in. he pushed and shoved until he was satisfied with our formation. We unsheathed weapons, I held my halberd in the ready position, angling across my front with the big head looming over us. Looking up I could see Magic at the centre of the column ahead.

He raised his right hand clenched in a fist. "When I drop my arm, we start running. Keep in step and keep in close. And one more thing," he paused, "NO Talking! No noise, nothing. Watch me and watch my hand – I'll signal when we are to stop. Right, let's do this thing..."

He dropped his hand and we started to run. The first bit of distance was hard, we stumbled, fell against each other, some swore. But bit by bit, we got the hang of it and we increased our speed, faster and faster.

It was one of the most exhilarating things I had ever done. Down the darkened streets we ran, our boots hitting the ground in unison. We were unstoppable. The sense of power grew and grew and became excitement. We were smiling, teeth shining white in the flashes of light.

Meataxe couldn't contain himself, he let out a whoop, a yell of pure joy. "EEEEHAR!!!"

The back of Magic's clenched and gloved fist hit him in the mouth, splitting lips, cutting gums and loosening teeth. I could hear the whack from the back of the column. That dull, moist thud sent a message to all of us - this is serious, Magic is serious. Don't stuff about.

We ran on, silent, grim and implacable.

Chapter 5

We crossed the City, heading to the street containing the Theatre. We were still running in step, still silent. People were getting out of our way. I didn't see any of the sneers normally associated with the Night Watch. There was only shock and awe as we drove our will through the citizenry.

I saw Magic's clenched fist rise in the air and then pump up and down twice. We stopped, some panting but none of us wanting to break the spell we had made around ourselves. None of the usual mutters and grumbles.

Magic called for Teddy Boy and me to bring the stranger. He stepped out of the ranks, turned, and spoke to Right Honourable, "Keep them here, you stand out the front of the formation with drawn sword, wait five minutes then bring them in. Don't run, don't try to keep in step, just move up into the Theatre and find us. Keep it silent, though, that seems to be working. We are looking seriously scary here. Meataxe, you're with me, don't wipe your face, I like the frenzied maniac look. Val, lose the halberd."

I swapped with one of the other men for his weapon, a War Hammer, very useful for knocking down doors and heads. I had a other weapons back in the barracks along with some of the personal armour I had carried with me over the years. But this was the City Watch and they frowned on the psychopathic killer look I tended to acquire when I get fully tooled up. Now that I was civilised, I tended to wear just the Watch uniform. It saved lots of explanations. Not to mention the yelling and screaming from the straights if I walked down the streets looking like one of their nightmares.

We followed Magic up the wide stone steps which formed the grand entrance to the Theatre, home of the most extravagant entertainments in the City. You could see it all here, singers, musicians, acrobats and any weird and wonderful sights. If it made money, it was on the stage, man or beast. I flicked a look at Meataxe, expecting to see smouldering resentment after the blow from Magic. He saw my look and muttered, "Gotta learn to keep my mouth shut, Val. Wouldn't want to miss this."

We put our 'don't stuff with me' faces on and pushed through the few loiterers on the steps. We stepped into a large, covered portico. Down the left side were the ticket booths, at the opposite side to the entrance steps were the tall brass and velvet doors leading to the Theatre proper. In front of these doors were gathered a cluster of moderately well-dressed men looking at us with disdain and suspicion. Not patrons, they were the bouncers, keepers of the peace and throwers out of drunks and uppity guardsmen.

Magic strode to their leader, "Hello, Harris, we're here to see the Man in Black."

Harris waved his bully boys down, "He's inside, Magic. What's all this about?" he chuckled. "You look like you're almost serious?" His cronies smirked. Looking past our corporal he raised his voice, "What happened to you, Meataxe, did the pig fight back?"

He and the others laughed with mouths only, the rest of their bodies expecting Meataxe to lose his temper and start a brawl. He does that a lot. Then they would throw us all out, perfectly justified in defending the theatre against unsavoury elements.

But Meataxe didn't move, even I was surprised. We kept our guard faces up, looking mean. Come to think of it, I was feeling pretty mean right about now. The response caused Harris to rethink his strategy, he looked down at Magic and said in a softer voice, "He's talking to the Maestro. You can go in by yourself. The rest stay here."

Magic turned back to us, he spoke very quietly "Teddy Boy, stay here. When Right Honourable arrives with the squad I want you all inside, understand?" Ted nodded. "The rest of you are coming with me, any questions?" finished our corporal.

"What about Harris, he said you're to go in alone?" I asked.

"Stuff that," responded Magic, and gave the ideal command for a leader. "Follow me."

I took the stranger's arm and, together with Meataxe, we fell in behind Magic. When Harris saw how many were moving, he stepped in front of Magic. "Just you, I said," stated the big bouncer, "these other clowns stay out here."

"You want to force the issue, Harris?" asked Magic, "Fine with me." His hand rested on sword hilt, I readied my hammer, Meataxe hawked and spat. Our new friend, the stranger, seemed to be shaking a little. Can't blame him really.

There were eight of them, all big, all had clubs in their hands. No swords or pistols. The clientele who misbehaved while attending the Theatre only needed a thump, not death. They stood behind Harris, looking quite keen to get into us. I hoped Magic knew what he was doing.

Magic spoke again, "We start this, Harris, and we play for real. I'll kill you without a blink, you know I will. See who I've brought with me?" He nodded back to us, "Meataxe is an animal when he gets off the lease, and we all know about Val. So, either step out of the way or get ready to bleed. Your call."

He started walking forward, we kept pace with him. My bowels were loose, but I was carrying a big hammer and I was just in the mood to use it. If someone gave me grief then I would give it right back. Happy to hit hard and hurt.

Harris stepped to one side. We pushed through the big doors and entered the Theatre. I exhaled.

"Magic," I asked, "what does everyone know about me? What did you mean by that comment?" He ignored me.

We kept walking down the raked aisles to the front stalls. Up on stage we could see The Man in Black with Ensign Briare and his escort speaking with a well-dressed man in evening clothes, a cape and a stylish hat – the Maestro. Magic still hadn't answered me so I nudged Meataxe, "What'd he mean? About me? What about me?" I asked.

Meataxe smiled through his beard and dried blood, "Settle down, Val. Sometimes you can be ... ruthless."

I was astonished. Ruthless? Me? Rubbish, I'm a sweetheart. I confess I was a little hurt, I even muttered to myself, "I'm not ruthless, I'm a nice man." We walked a few more steps and I felt this point needed emphasising. "I am."

When we came to the stage it was to be met by an angry Night Watch captain talking strongly to the Maestro and Ensign Briare, "I want to see this thing, I want to see it now!"

"He is a demon, sir," put in Ensign Briare, pale in the face of our captain's wrath. "We must communicate with the Church over this matter."

"Surely such things as devils fall outside the laws of man," murmured the Maestro, with a significant lowering of the voice over the last phrase. It was only salesman talk, he was probably just trying it on for size, seeing how it sounded for later spruiking. This guy was always talking up his shows, promoting himself and his Theatre.

"He's in my city," stated the Man in Black. "That puts him under my laws. Everyone falls under the law. Everyone. Now get him." He turned away from the group in disgust and saw us, Magic reported and the Man in Black said, "Ah, Charles, well done. You got here in good time."

"Thank you, Captain. We found some clothing at the gypsy campsite. It means this devil creature and our friend here," he indicated the stranger, "are linked."

Chapter 6

The Man in Black took us off to one side, we left the Maestro muttering about interference with the captain's flunkies and giving them some mild abuse. All show, of course.

"Where are these clothes," the captain asked. Meataxe untied the sack from his belt and emptied it onto the floor, not elegant but effective. The boots were amazing, so sleek. This was the first time the stranger I was looking after had seen this gear. He let out a yelp, bent down and pulled up something which may have been a tunic. I had my hammer up in a flash, ready to thump him – was he a devil, too?

Magic waved me back into my kennel. He and the captain, being the two thinkers in the group, let our friend rummage through the pockets of the tunic. It was another beautiful piece of work, soft and supple. Bits of something like thick leather plates had somehow been attached to the rest of the garment. I realised these bits covered the sensitive parts of the body. They could be like fancy armour. The pockets were clever, some hidden behind small pieces of metal that split apart when touched. I thought the denizens of Hell dressed quite well.

The stranger finally dropped the garment back into the pile, he looked a little sad, like he didn't find what he was looking for. He stood up and turned to me, pulling back his hair he revealed his left ear. Inside the ear was a small piece of jewellery, dark in colour and not terribly attractive. If you're going to wear gems and gewgaws then they should be seen, this little thing failed the entire concept of decoration. He pulled it out of his ear, looked at me all sad and shook his head slowly. Pointing to the piece of jewellery, he said, "No."

Communication is not just words, I can read people, understand their moods, and generally guess what's running through their minds unless they are trying to conceal things. Our friend wanted to communicate and I was getting better at understanding him. "I think that thing he's holding is broken," I said.

"Big deal," said Meataxe, "who cares?"

"He does," said the Man in Black, indicating our sad friend. "I really want to see this devil. There's more to this than meets the eye. Strange clothing, I've never seen material like it. Where did these two come from?" He took us all in with a glance, "Pity we haven't any more of your lads, Charles, a show of force might help force Maestro to bring the devil forward. We've only just arrived ourselves," he glanced meaningfully over at Ensign Briare., "We were held by an argument."

He was standing with his back to the entrance so he couldn't see the body of the Theatre, Magic nodded over his shoulder and the captain turned around. Standing along the rear of the seats were the rest of Second Squad. They were spread out with weapons ready, a lot of deadly looking men. All silently standing, waiting to be unleashed.

"Well done, Charles," murmured the Man in Black, a slight smile tinkling over lips and eyes. "How'd you get them to be so quiet? They're quite terrifying that way."

"Just a little something we're trying out, Franz," answered Magic. I could tell he was proud of us. For some reason that was important to me.

Santini entered the theatre and came up to the stage to report. He said he put the drunks on a wagon and sent them back to the Watch House. Right Honourable, Teddy Boy, Meataxe and Horse wandered over. The gang's all here, I thought.

Looking at the stranger I decided to try communicating. I pointed to myself and said, "Val."

He nodded agreement and said, "Yes, Val." Then he pointed at himself and said, "Mendic." Hello, I thought, we're on to something here.

Pointing at him, I asked, "Mendic?" He nodded. This needed checking, I pointed at Teddy Boy and asked, "Mendic?" because perhaps it wasn't his name, maybe the word meant something else.

The stranger shook his head and said, "No." He pointed to himself again and said "Mendic". He pointed at me and said "Val."

We had names. We spent some time identifying each other, to be on the safe side I pointed at Magic and said "Corporal."

Mendic shook his head and said, "No." In a firm voice he stated, "Magic." Well, well, I thought, fearless leader makes his mark.

Again, I pointed at him and asked, "Devil?" I wasn't too sure what his answer would be, I think I was a bit nervous he would say 'yes'.

He said, "No". I breathed a sigh of relief.

Then he pointed at each of us in turn, finally he looked me square in the eye, tapped my chest and said, "You Devils."

"He says we're all devils," commented Right Honourable. "Well done, Val, we'll all sleep much easier tonight." I was confused, this couldn't be right. What did he mean by calling us devils?

A roar announced the entrance of the devil, we all turned to look as handlers with chains and clubs dragged the thing on to the stage. When it saw the stranger, it stopped roaring and very clearly yelled, "Mendic!"

They stood staring at each other for a moment, a short space of time. We stood in a heartbeat of silence. Then the devil lunged against his chains and extended his hands in an attempt to reach Mendic. The handlers hauled back on the chains and a couple of men strode in and hit the horned head with clubs; the devil shrugged off some of the blows but eventually succumbed and sank to the floor.

All went quiet, Mendic was shaking, the devil breathing hoarsely, the rest of us panting with the emotion of the scene. The Man in Black spoke, "Give it the clothes, see if it knows how to dress itself."

I kicked the bundle of material closer to the devil, the boots too. We stood and watched as the naked, snarling beast we thought of as a devil transformed itself into, I don't know, something else. But dress itself it did. Some of the buckles and straps were intricate and could not have been fastened by a wild beast.

We were looking at an intelligent being.

But was it a devil? I decided to ask Mendic. I pointed at the now dressed beast and asked, "Devil?"

Mendic nodded. His posture slumped, his voice was tired as he confirmed, "Devil." This was not making a lot of sense to me.

But he didn't stop there. Pointing at our red and angry visitor he said, "Chayla."

Seems our devil had a name.

The front doors were thrown open again and down the aisle strode three men, two priests and a guard. The first man had a pleasant, open face, the guards were the usual stone faces. When he reached the stage, he walked over to the Man in Black and chuckled, "Hello, Franz. Still keeping low company, I see?" He smiled and held out a hand to greet our commander.

"Well, well, my little cousin," replied the captain, shaking hands, "what brings you out on a dark and lonely night?"

"Same as you, Franz, business. I represent the Ecclesiastical Tribunal in this matter. Archbishop Dominic heard about this devil thing and asked me to look into it." He surveyed the room, spending considerable time gazing at the chained but dressed figure before him. "Certainly looks like a demon. Where'd he get the clothes?" His gaze fell on Mendic, "Hello, who's this? That clothing looks similar to that worn by our horned friend over there. Hmmm...."

We all stood quietly while the priest lowered his head in thought, even the Man in Black was silent.

"I think I need to take both of these individuals back with me, Franz," he concluded. "Please assist with an escort." He turned to leave, authority washing off him in waves.

"Lucius! Wait!" said our captain. The priest stopped and turned back, eyebrow raised in query.

"Lucius," continued the Man in Blac. "There is more to this, there is a mystery here. Surely, surely it is a matter for the Watch, not you." There was a pleading in his voice.

"Come see me tomorrow, Franz," replied the priest, "we can discuss it then. Be grateful there are still good Christian men who speak up when they see potential sin. The church needs stout hearts in the never ending struggle against the evil one, be grateful you have such men with you. Now, give me an escort, please, I want both those individuals brought back with me." It wasn't a request.

The Man in Black signalled to Magic who organised for the transport of the devil and a stunned Mendic. The priest stood at the doors and waited. Finally he exited, followed by most of our men and the two prisoners.

The Man in Black was angry, he spoke in clipped, terse tones. "How the hell did they know about Mendic and the devil?" His eyes fell on Ensign Briare, "You held us up on the way here, Briare. And you seemed particularly keen on letting the Archbishop know of our visitors." He clenched his hands a little before continuing, "Did you inform the clergy?"

"I did not, sir," replied the youth, his voice trembling. He took it well, I'll give him that, he stood his ground and faced the wrath of our captain without a backward step.

"Someone," said the Man in Black, leaning forward to address the young man, "sent word to Archbishop Dominic. How else could he know the gypsies had sold this creature to the Theatre? Those priests arrived shortly after we did. We were delayed. Delayed by you, ensign!"

"I protest, sir, the charge is false!" exclaimed the boy, his cheeks were flushed; perhaps shame, perhaps guilt. No sympathy from me, I just didn't like cavalry on principle. "I sent no word." He straightened himself into an erect and military pose, "I follow your orders,"

"Good, then follow this one," said the captain. "Go away."

The youngster departed the Theatre, his face bright crimson. This time I was pretty sure it was shame.

Chapter 7

After the ensign left, we stood around and tried to come to terms with what we had seen.

A devil who dresses in fancy cloths. A devil with a name. Mendic calling us all devils. But still identifying us by our individual names. The devil recognising Mendic. And speaking to him in their own language.

I had a thought. "Captain," I said, "Mendic called us all devils." All eyes were on me now.

"Thanks a bunch, loudmouth," commented Santini. "Can we just move past that unpleasantness?"

"No," I went on. "I mean he called US devils. He didn't call himself a devil." The tendril of an idea stayed in my mind. I pursued it, "We aren't devils. We," I finished, "are guards." No response from anyone. I plunged on. "Chayla isn't a devil."

"He's a guard!" I claimed.

The Man in Black listened to my reasoning, the way our devil had dressed himself in obviously sophisticated garments spoke a great deal to my case. "What's he guarding?" he asked.

Without thinking I blurted out, "I don't know, maybe he's supposed to guard Mendic." I stopped, I don't know why I made that claim, it just slipped out.

The captain stood for a while in thought and finally spoke. "A stranger comes to our city. Can't speak the language, has an escort. What sort of person does that?" He was musing, talking to himself, we listened. "A simple traveller? No, he wouldn't need a guard. A spy or scout for an enemy? No, why come and seek help from the local Watch when you're in trouble – a spy would avoid contact." He paced back and forth, muttering a little. "What else? Who else goes to strange cities? And why bring an escort like Chayla?"

"What about that Venetian chappie who travelled to Cathay?" asked Right Honourable. "I remember reading his book, 'Il Milion.'" A slight, modest cough, "In the original French, of course." He went on, "Could Mendic be from a distant land? Perhaps a merchant?"

"Possibly," concluded the Man in Black, "but how does this strange creature fit in? Val, you think he's a guard? Possibly, possibly...," He made some decisions, "Val," he commanded, "get back to the gypsy campsite and find out where they caught our red friend. We will cease to call him a 'devil' from now on, it only serves to reinforce his religious credentials and I do not think he comes from hell. Let's go with that name Mendic gave him, what was it again?"

Horse spoke up, "Sounded like 'Chayla' to me." Mutters of agreement came from others.

"'Chayla' it is," said the captain. "Take a couple of men with you, Val. Come back to the Watch House with your report. I have a few people I want to see and then we might all go and call on our friends, the clergy. If he is a trader, we aren't going to do our bargaining position any good by throwing him in jail."

"Or torturing his escort," said Horse, as we left the Theatre.

On the walk back to the campsite I trudged beside Right Honourable. Since he's a self-confessed clever dick I asked, "What's an Ecclesiastical Tribunal?"

He turned a sad face to me and answered, "The Inquisition, Val. The cursed Spanish Inquisition."

The Inquisition.

Mad, bad and dangerous to know. People to avoid.

I was brought up a catholic, my parents believed and for a long time I lived off their faith. They died when I was young, I ran away from home, fled my tutor's beatings. Isolated from my family, I lost their confirmation of belief. They still loved me, I knew that, but they weren't there every week to take me to mass.

So, I didn't go. Just lazy. I was still a catholic, but I don't think I was one of God's pin-up boys.

My walk to the gypsies was filled with memories of long ago, of the first time I came across the Inquisition – The Siege of Ostend, my other school. The place where I learned how to kill.

The Spanish, and the Inquisition, thought Ostend belonged to them, we disagreed. There was a battle nearly every day for three years, not a skirmish, not a minor action, a proper battle. So long, so hard. Our final redoubt was named 'New Troy' by many. A validation of our ordeal. They took the trenches and we killed them. They took the outer works and we killed them. They took the inner bastions and we killed them. We killed and killed until we ran out of city. I heard when Queen Isabella finally entered, to survey her victory, she wept at the desolation. The beautiful city of Ostend was just rubble.

The rank and file, the few hundred of us left from eight thousand defenders, were put on a ship to Zeeland. Our commander, Francis Vere, and his officers got a banquet of Honour from Spinola in recognition of their defence.

No banquet for us, the common soldiers. Just the memory of three years filled with terror, screams, pain and tears. we killed sixty thousand of them during that hell. In the trenches, I found my faith again. It became a hard kernel at my very centre. No churches, no cathedrals, no priests. Just me, God and the days of fear and pain. Now I wore the civilised garb of a City Guardsman, but the beast was till in me. The beast which helped me survive Ostend.

I still retained all the knowledge from my tutor, the sciences, the philosophy, and the books. I could show a calm veneer and bury the violence with alcohol. And quiet, sobbing prayers.

Right Honourable nudged me out of my past, we had arrived.

The Fat Gypsy came out, all unctuous and oily. We started talking, Right Honourable wandered around, he and Teddy Boy had decided to join me for this little investigation. The night was drawing to a close, a long and eventful night for all of us. We stood talking, me trying to find answers, the gypsy trying to sell me things. Around us the camp stirred into motion, figures began appearing over campfires, the smell of wood smoke and savoury aromas drifted between us. My mouth watered, my mind wandered. Dawn was breaking.

With an effort I again asked about Chayla. When Fat Boy shrugged and raised his arms for the umpteenth time I ran out of patience. "Look," I said, "we're the Watch, you know us. It's me asking questions now but the next group out here might be worse than me, much worse. I'm being nice."

He blinked at me, smiled and shrugged. I don't think he believed me. Exasperated I blurted, "The Inquisition has your devil, they will have worse questions."

I didn't expect his response at all. He turned, shouted some commands and the campsite erupted into action, wagons were packed, tents dismantled, people running and shouting. Before my eyes the entire encampment sort of oozed onto wagons which began moving towards the gates.

Right Honourable came and stood beside me. "This is new," he commented.

I called for Teddy Boy and the three of us found Fat Boy. Having run out of patience, I raised my hammer and commanded him to stop. He stood up from tying the bundle at his feet, a piece of rope dangling from his hands. A certain stillness had come around our little tableau.

"Bit of a problem here, Val," murmured Right Honourable from the corner of his mouth. Looking around, I saw a large number of muscular, hairy men gathering behind us. Curvy knives were very popular this year, I noted.

I readied my weapon, ready to do a bit of hitting. My skills at questioning had run their course, I was thinking that now would be a good time to apply my other skill – mayhem and violence. A sudden pressure behind my right ear preceded a brief sensation of pain and shock, very brief because then I fell unconscious. My last thought was a self-accusing mind saying I should have thought this through a bit more.

Big help now, I concluded.

Chapter 8

I came to in the back of an open wagon, trussed up beside my two companions. Dawn had arrived. The sun was shining, birds were twittering, the gentle sway of the wagon reminded me I had been on duty all night and it was way past my bedtime. As I considered dozing off again the wagon lurched over a hole and threw me against a slowly awakening Teddy Boy. Right Honourable snored on, Ted opened one eye, closed it and drew himself into a sitting position with very few grunts. I was impressed.

"You're not dead yet, Val?" he asked.

"Well spotted, guardsman. Any idea why we're still in the land of the living?" I asked.

He shrugged. Ted doesn' t speak if he could avoid it, don't know why. Perhaps he felt he only had a certain number of words to use in life and didn't want to go through them all at once. I made a mental note to discuss it with him one day.

Right Honourable groaned, swore, spat and rolled into a sitting position beside Ted. I was cheered by the amount of groaning and swearing he demonstrated. I gave him a cheery smile, welcoming him to the new day.

Our hands were tied behind our backs, ankles secured by more rope. All in all, we were well and truly captured. "So, what do you think, fellas? Slaves?" I asked.

Ted continued his eloquent silence, Right Honourable said, "Probably. Killing us in the City would leave a bit of blood and mess. Plus, three bodies of the Watch near a Gypsy campsite would mean pursuit. This way we won't be missed for a while. If ever."

Not a happy thought, I was particularly miffed by the assumption that we wouldn't be missed and said so. Surely the City would notice the loss of three of its leading guardsmen? I may have made a comment on this very topic.

"Get real, Val," said Ted.

The wagon stopped in a very lovely patch of shade, the sun making little dappled patterns amongst the leaves of a particularly picturesque tree. Off to one side I could see a small creek tinkling over rocks with slurpy little splashing sounds. It positively beckoned the traveller to come in for a dip.

I was savouring all of these new experiences as I waited for either a quick murder or long enslavement. My last few thoughts of freedom would be in a happy place. I said a small prayer of thanks for the nice morning and quietly pondered the twists and turns of life.

Right Honourable kicked me.

"Wake up, dopey," he said, "someone's coming."

Fat Boy let down the back of the wagon and, with the aid of a few burly types, placed us on the grass under the tree. He stood back and said, "We not kill you. This where we found devil. In water." He gestured to the stream, "Clothes were under tree." He turned and they began to walk away, one of the gypsies tossed our weapons on the ground, placing a knife next to Ted.

"My name is Janos," said the Fat Gypsy as he climbed back on to a wagon. "We Manush Gypsy. We come back to City one day. We not killers." As they drove off, he called back, "Inquisition not good to Manush." And they rumbled away, leaving three trussed guardsmen alone and surprised.

"That went well," I said.

Teddy Boy kicked me. I think he was probably rolling for the knife and his foot slipped. We contorted around, swore a lot, got the knife and freed ourselves. We must have looked hilarious.

I was looking at the river when Right Honourable joined me, Ted had gone off to do a little scouting. Personally, I can't stand the woods, a sentiment shared by Right Honourable. "Thinking of having a little swim, Val?" he asked.

I wasn't. I was standing there pretending I was a hot and tired guard, probably bored. Right Honourable's comment made me wonder about having a swim, the mechanics of it. Take your clothes off, pile them neatly nearby – I looked back at the tree and could see in my mind's eye the image of Chayla stepping back from his gear and heading in for a swim. But he was a guard, and that brought some responsibilities, a sense of caution.

A guard would never leave his weapons too far away. I walked down to the riverbank, squatted on the edge, seeing the stranger splashing away. Turning my head to the left I saw a bush close to the water. It was close enough to hide a weapon, close enough to put a little something dangerous which might be needed in a hurry.

I stepped over to the bush, pulled back the lowest branches and whistled. Right Honourable came over and asked, "How'd you do that, Valentine?"

Under the branches was a belt, and attached to the belt was a pistol.

Ted claimed the pistol, he loves shooty things, I'm more of the hit and thump kind of guy. It was unlike anything we had seen, all dark metal and some other hard substance. But a pistol has a handle, a trigger, and a barrel. Even though we could not see where to put the flint, this was definitely a pistol. Ted pointed the barrel end at a nearby tree and pulled the trigger.

We all expected a bang and flash, possibly a cloud of smoke; Ted was braced for some recoil. Instead, the pistol glowed a bit and a beam of light shot from the barrel and hit the tree. A hole about the size of my head went straight through the tree accompanied by the smell of singed wood. No noise.

Right Honourable and I stood in silence, Ted smiled a very goofy grin and gurgled a little with pleasure. "Cool," he said.

The belt also had a smaller pouch, in which was another of the little black gems which Mendic had put in his ear. I remembered him communicating that his was broken. My brain clicked a bit more.

"Are you saying," said Right Honourable, "that this Chayla devil thing, the one you think is a guard, are you saying he just went for a swim?" I didn't blame him for the consternation. I hadn't planned on spending my day standing in the woods talking about the hygiene habits of hell.

Not knowing what to say, I kept quiet. Ted joined the conversation, "Val's right. Nice spot for a dip. Mendic might have wanted to scout out the City on the quiet. Chayla got bored with waiting, maybe had a snooze then went for a wake up swim. Stupid burke got sloppy."

This was quite a speech from our taciturn Watchman so it carried a lot of weight. We grunted agreement and we moved off to see the boss.

Chapter 9

I told my captain what we had found while glossing over our capture. I may have put a bit of spin on our deductive capabilities.

"Nasty bruise there, Val," he said, indicating my head. Looking at my two companions he went on, "You all seem to have been knocked about a bit." He let the silence drag. "Anything else to report?"

We were lined up, side-by-side, in the little room he uses for an office. Our heads were erect, shoulders back, eyes fixed on the wall behind the captain. We were very proper, very military.

"Fell down the stairs, captain," I stated in my clearest, lower rank, totally innocent voice.

"All of you? Same stairs?" he asked.

"Deplorable workmanship, sir," claimed Right Honourable.

"May also have walked into a door, sir," said Teddy Boy.

"Indeed," concluded the captain. He stood looking at us in silence for a few moments, using the old tricks officers always use to get the lower orders to confess. The steely stare, the pursed lips, the overwhelming sense of disappointment in his men. Totally wasted on the three of us, we've been down that road too many times. He finally gave a resigned groan and I think I caught him with the hint of a smile at our little games.

He sat down and picked up the black gem, "You think this is more than a piece of jewellery, do you, Val?" The captain had long slender fingers, strong and capable, probably played a lot of harpsichord. "Hmm...," he paused in thought before continuing, "I planned on visiting the Ecclesiastical Tribunal this afternoon but now is as good a time as any. You fellows still look remarkably fresh, perhaps you'd care to join me?"

The Man in Black knew some games of his own. We nodded dismally, outsmarted again. No rest just yet for our poor, mistreated bones.

We picked up Magic, Santini and Meataxe in the Watch room and together we set off, the Man in Black walking just like a regular person. I filled Magic in on our adventures with the gypsies. I didn't leave anything out – it was Magic, after all – and he called me an idiot. I agreed with him and we kept walking.

The Ecclesiastical Tribunal was housed in a chunky sandstone structure, all big blocks and small windows. It was enclosed by a high wall which also encircled a large cobblestone area at the front of the building. Entrance was through a small gate in the wall although a larger gate was nearby for carriages and carts. The credentials of the Watch gained us entry to the big yard but we were prevented from moving into the main building by an armed bunch of guards. These were not members of the City Guard, they were the Archbishop's own team.

A message brought Father Lucius out to talk to the captain, the rest of us stood around facing the other guards and trying to look deadly. I don't think we pulled it off, they just looked bored. One bloke even yawned. Just no respect anywhere.

"All I ask, Lucius, is that I be allowed to see the creature. Is that too much to ask?" queried the captain.

"We have been unable to get answers from the beast, nor its master," replied the priest, "Of course, they only speak their own language, the language of demons. The Archbishop himself intends to put them to the question tonight." He paused, looked us all over. I thought he was weighing up our potential as a threat, grim forbidding men that we were.

As his eyes travelled across our party, I noticed a slight flare come to his gaze. He suddenly said, "But Franz, seeing as it is you then of course you can see them. But not all of your men. Perhaps an escort of two or three?"

The Man in Black gestured us over, "Magic, you'll stay here. I want Val with me, and one other."

I spoke quickly, "Teddy Boy, sir. He should come." I had my reasons. My betters looked at me for a moment before Magic nodded agreement.

The three of us set off for the main doors but as we reached them Father Julius said, "Bring another man with you, Franz, just in case." Father Julius himself signalled for Santini to join us. This was quite a liberty, I thought. No-one else objected so I kept my mouth shut, but the Captain's eyes narrowed a little. Magic stood quite steady and watched us enter. I felt better with him out here to back us up - ably supported by a bored looking Right Honourable and a shambolic Meataxe. Still, maybe nothing would happen.

We went through a couple of corridors before eventually finishing up in front of a large oak door in the rear section of the building. Father Julius chatted quite amicably with the Man in Black, people they knew, places they'd been, Stuff like that. I worked out they were distantly related, both from well-off families, they seemed quite friendly with each other; even saw a little smile on the Captain's lip. Apparently, Father Julius was in line for a Cardinal's job soon, fast track up the pay scale for those with important relatives.

Entering this last doorway took us into another, less salubrious place. A large, circular room opened before us, rows of seats enclosing a small platform. Ring bolts were set in the floor around the platform which supported a very sturdy looking chair. Several tables and a brazier were placed in this enclosed area, small and unpleasant looking instruments lay scattered on the tabletops. Unfortunately, I recognised a few of them, devices for extracting confessions under torture – I had hoped never to see them again.

We stood quietly for a minute, none of us were in the mood for any more casual conversation. Finally, we heard a roar followed by the sounds of several blows. Into the room came our devil, Chayla. He was accompanied by Mendic and several unpleasant looking men. I can recognise a thug when I see one.

Both prisoners were exhausted. Mendic was naked and dirty, streaks of soot covered his legs and arms. Burn marks glistened wetly on his chest, his eyes had a look I'd seen before, a look of despair and hopelessness.

Chayla was still bleeding, his fingers dripped blood, red blood, onto the floor; the result of having fingernails torn out. One eye was closed due to bruising. A tight piece of horsehair was around his right thigh, it prevented the wearer from running and caused a great deal of agony. If left on then all blood flow to the limb stops and the leg eventually swells up before undergoing necrosis. It rots while still attached to your body.

I wish I didn't know so much stuff.

When Mendic saw us he let out a cry, "Val!" and tried to walk forward. Each prisoner had three guards and one of these stepped forward to hit Mendic a blow to the back of the neck. The beaten man collapsed with a small whimper. The Chayla creature was reeling, probably a combination of pain and fatigue, I guessed.

Father Julius started forward and commanded the guards to stop. He had gone very white. I think even he was surprised at the sight of the two beaten prisoners. He turned and said, "I apologise for this sight, I detest this sort of thing, it degrades both the victim and those charged with carrying out the treatment. So unpleasant."

Yeah, right, I thought. Then why aren't you standing there bleeding if you're suffering along with them.

"Let them go, Julius," said the Man in Black, "they're not demons or devils."

"Of course, they are, Franz. Admittedly, the man may be an unwitting dupe but the other is quite obviously a devil. Just look at it." The priest had a kind face and didn't seem to bear any ill-will towards his prisoners. I would have preferred him to be mean and cruel, maybe with a sickening little laugh or a twitch.

Mendic was on hands and knees, head down and panting. He started speaking in his strange tongue, his guard raised an arm but Father Julius signalled for him to stop. "Franz," said the priest, "I did not sanction this level of violence, I doubt anyone here did. But just look at them. You've seen their clothing, you've heard them speak."

But the captain wasn't listening to the priest, he had gone down on one knee close to Mendic. After a few moments he stood up and said, "He's a trader, Julius, a visitor. The beast you have been calling a devil is his bodyguard, his name is Chayla. Their job is to make first contact with potential markets and try to line up trade deals. They learned of us through something called the 'Shipping News.' He trades in goods, Julius. Not souls."

The devil, or Chayla, raised his head and spoke, a strange growling sound. The Man in Black listened and the said, "He's hurt, Julius, he's in a lot of pain. He wants that thing off his leg. You must release these two into the care and protection of the Watch. At the very least, they need medical assistance."

Father Julius stood, mouth agape, looking at the Man in Black. "How could you know these things, Franz...?" He moved towards the door, "Please stay here while I consult with... with... Just stay here, Franz."

He turned and left the room quickly.

Chapter 10

"Val," said the captain, "See to Mendic. Santini, you and I will cut that damn thing off Chayla's leg. Teddy Boy, keep watch." I began to move forward but was confronted by one of the prison guards. He blocked my access to Mendic and stood flexing greasy, but quite large, muscles.

The Man in Black faced a similar situation. "Stand down, you men," he said to the prison guards. "We intend to render assistance to these people." He took a step to move around a guard but this man hit the captain a solid blow across the side of the head. His hat flew off, the captain sank to one knee and we all stood, stunned. Someone had raised a hand to the Man in Black!

He slowly stood up, picked up his hat and turned to face the room. "Now listen," he said, very conversationally, "I want to make this very clear to all of us. I am Lord Van Stolberg, Captain of the Night Watch. These men whom you hold prisoner are now in my care." He looked at each of us for a moment, a slight nod, I nodded back. "And the care of my men. Now, we will assist these prisoners, we will remove their shackles, we will bind their wounds and make them safe."

"Stand aside," he commanded. No one moved, the prison guards shifted stance but probably thought six of them could take out the four of us. They were used to beating people up, especially cloaked in the authority of the Inquisition.

"Gentlemen," said the Man in Black. "Do your duty."

I stepped forward with my hammer and hit the first guard a solid blow to the side of the head. His skull crunched and he died on the spot. I continued the movement, pulling the hammer into the second part of the blow. A twist of the wrist with a smooth backhand movement allowed it to slam into another guard's nose, pushing it into the back of his head.

43

I let the hammer go as I hit him and drew my sword ready to face the last, very surprised guard.

Off to one side I heard two explosions Really, really loud explosions; Teddy Boy had pulled out two pistols and shot two of the guards where they stood. A pistol is very noisy and smoky, good outdoors but quite nightmarish in this situation. I had asked for Ted to join us because I know he keeps his hands on the handles of a brace of hidden pistols during tense conversations. Good man in a corner is our Ted.

The final two guards put their hands up and sensibly surrendered. The Man in Black had drawn his sword but stopped when he realised it wasn't needed. Santini was still standing with his mouth open in surprise. Extremely poor reaction time from Santini, we'd have to work on that.

"Santini!" commanded the captain, "Go outside and tell Magic what has happened. He needs to get in here with some men. No, lots of men and pull us out of this mess. GO!" Santini ran out the door, I dropped a large bar in place and turned back to survey our little domain.

Ted was reloading pistols. I took the shackles off Mendic and Chayla and put them on the two guards. For good measure I attached them to one of the bolts on the floor in the centre of the room. The men Ted had shot weren't quite dead but it wouldn't be long, a pistol ball does dreadful things to a man. They'd have a bit of pain before they died but since they had probably dished out a lot in their time I wasn't too worried. I tuned their groans out easily. Years of practice and all that.

I cut the rope from around Chayla's leg and had to dodge a clumsy blow from our new best friend. I guess the poor thing was suffering from a fair bit of pain. A big, naked devil is a scary sight up close, over one huge bicep I saw a tattoo surrounded by some smaller markings. I had my own tattoos, if we all survived, we could swap stories. That was quite a big 'if'. When we'd tided up I asked the captain, "How'd you know, sir? How did you know all that stuff about Mendic and Chayla?"

I had guessed some of it but it was just that, guesswork. The captain had spoken with authority and I was quite sure it wasn't because of my golden tones and convincing arguments.

He pulled back his hair and revealed an ear. Nestled in the ear was the black jewel. "I could understand them both, Val, knew what they were saying. Your idea, really." He pulled it out and gave it to Mendic, the man hungrily inserted it into his own ear.

"Can you understand me?" asked the Man in Black.

It was almost embarrassing to see Mendic and his reaction to these words. He sobbed, he grabbed the captain's sleeve and sobbed, "Yes! Yes!"

There we were, trapped in the bowels of the Inquisition, chatting with an ex-devil in the company of several dead bodies while waiting for someone big and ugly to come through the door and rescue us. Or kill us, depends on who came first.

I sank onto the floor and rested my back against the cool stone wall. Yet again I thought of other careers I could be pursuing, careers which promised advancement for a bright young man, good with languages, comfortable around violence.

Outside a pounding started on the big oak doors, "That's a bit quick for Magic," said the Man in Black. He then made one of the better understatements I've heard, "We could be in a bit of trouble here."

Things were looking grim.

"Where's that little door go?" asked Ted.

I berated myself for overlooking the obvious, Mendic and Chayla had to have entered from somewhere. They hadn't come in by the big doors and now Ted was pointing at a small wooden door tucked behind a rack of painful looking instruments.

Ted and I grabbed Chayla and the Man in Black picked up Mendic. Our captain was one of those wiry guys – stronger than they look and a real problem when you're in a bar picking fights. We entered the next room, shut and bolted the door behind us and moved down the small corridor.

This next bit is not so nice.

Chapter 11

The corridor went between several large cells, more like cages for animals than places for human beings. Each cell had occupants, lots of them. Women, children, a few men. All were hurt in some way. The stink of blood, pus and vomit was fighting a losing battle against the stench of human excrement.

We walked along the silent corridor, no-one sought our aid, no one begged or spoke at all. The only noise was some low sobbing and a few deep, pain wracked breaths. We reached the end of the corridor where it finished at another smaller, door. Placing our injured companions on the ground we turned and surveyed the diabolical scene behind us. I saw my face reflected in the stunned and sickened visages of the other two. We stood, mouths open, shocked beyond comprehension.

The prisoner's eyes had followed us, every face held a mute appeal. Nearest me, on the floor of the cell, was a young boy, no more than seven or eight. He was in a heap on the ground, his limbs and body in that attitude of total collapse. Not rest or slumber, but with the appearance he was sinking into the earth. A look usually reserved for the dead.

But he wasn't dead, a pulse beat slowly in his neck. And his eyes were looking at mine.

I broke that lock. I broke every lock in the room. Some of the women were shackled to the wall, limbs gaunt with deprivation but someone had still seen fit to weigh them down with heavy metal chains. Teddy Boy and the Man in Black moved with me, we exchanged no words, we just tried to relieve the suffering.

We three gathered at the doorway where we had left Mendic and Chayla, I asked "Who are these people?"

The Man in Black answered, "I spoke to some. They're mainly gypsies, Gypsies and Jews." He spoke through tight lips, eyes aflame with outrage.

"They're women and children," stated Ted. "You don't hurt women and children."

Ted had a simple philosophy, protect the weak, be honest, get the job done and stuff like that. I generally skipped the honesty bit.

"Open that door, Val," instructed our captain, indicating the last door. This was at the end of the corridor and would hopefully take us out of this hell hole. "We're getting them all out of here." No objections from us. After breaking the door open, we shepherded everyone into the corridor, the stronger women helping with those in need. I grappled with Chayla's semi-comatose state, dragging him along the corridor. The Man in Black took charge of Mendic.

This left a very angry Ted as the only one available to go through that door first. He opened it with both pistols out and a strong willingness to kill anyone in our way.

Out we went, into another smaller yard, open to the evening sky. Night had cast its black cloak over the scene, even the sun was embarrassed. There was no-one in the yard, probably only used when there was a need to move unpleasant things like bodies, things which the powers that be did not want noticed.

Again, I broke open the lock on the external gate and we emerged onto a quiet side street. We were a rescue party of three able bodied men guarding about forty injured innocents and the foreign merchant Mendic. And a devil, mustn't forget the devil, he was the one that started all this with his desperate need for a swim. What was he thinking? I wondered.

We didn't get far, Right Honourable had been on a stroll around the perimeter because Magic believed in knowing as much as he could about a situation. He saw us, disappeared for a few minutes and soon we were joined by Magic and Meataxe. Together we staggered and weaved our way back to our Watch House, skulking as best we could.

We knew all the shortcuts and the deepest shadows. We'd all hidden in them at some time. I asked about Santini but he had never made it out, another victim of the Inquisition.

Night had fallen across our City by the time we reached the Watch House. When we entered, The Man in Black came over and had a hurried conversation with Magic. Most of the gang took our refugees away for rest, food and bandaging but Magic waved for me to stay where I was. Right Honourable and Teddy Boy stayed with Mendic, they found a seat and just slumped down.

I stood off to one side, out of earshot while they conferred. I thought I was there to run errands and so forth. Get beakers of ale if required. I rather hoped they were required, I could do with one.

There was lots of whispering and darting eyes, their glances roamed the courtyard before Magic's gaze fell on me. I smiled back at him amiably, sending thoughts of ale and pastry. The Man in Black caught his look and they both went silent. I had a small tingle, why were they looking at me?

The Man in Black gestured for me to come closer.

Chapter 12

"Sir?" I asked. I'd lost my hat, my uniform was splattered with blood and dirt. The excitement that comes with action and combat was making my blood sing. Even with all this rattling around in my head, I felt strangely inadequate before our boss.

He looked at me for a while, taking in my straggly appearance, my sweat and general sloppiness. "I know you, son."

"Sir?" No-one knew me, I was just a general dogsbody in a group of flunkies. Magic was keeping quiet, watching our leader deal with me. No help there.

"I watched you over the course of the evening," he said. "You have a brain, Watchman, and you can use it."

"Sorry, sir. Won't happen again."

His mouth twitched. "Listen, Val, I have need of you." His eyes flicked to Magic and I could swear some communication passed between them because Magic nodded. Do people in charge all have secret language? He went on, "We must resist any attempt by anyone to come in here and take custody of those poor, damaged people."

"Certainly, sir," I agreed. "Just one problem. This is the Watchhouse. The Day Watch will gather here before dawn to begin their duties."

"Quite right," he said. "I also believe the Archbishop will send in regular troops. Trained and disciplined men who will delight in the opportunity to come in here. To aggressively enter our domain."

"Aggressively, sir?"

"With extreme prejudice," he said.

"That's the Day Watch and the Army, sir? Extreme prejudice towards us? And you'd like them to stay outside the gates?"

"Precisely," he said.

"Bit of a quandary, sir," I said.

"But we cannot be seen to be in open rebellion," he said.

"Naturally," I agreed. "Er... because...?"

"Because that would be bad," he said.

"Right, sir. Got it. Open rebellion - bad."

He smiled at me, I felt very insecure. Magic had waved over another of our NightWatch team.

"Hello, Max." he said to our newcomer. Max was just another rank-and-file Watchman. He came from the wild northern lands, full of Vikings, reindeer, snow, and sleet. He aways had a big smile on his face, especially during the normal sunny weather the City enjoyed. Something to do with the climate having a minimum of snow and sleet. "The boss wants to talk to you," said Magic, nodding at our captain.

"Yes, sir?" he said.

"Max, I believe you may be able to help young Valentine here," said the Man in Black.

Max looked at me. I looked at Max, he raised his eyebrows. I gazed back placidly, secure in my ignorance of great affairs.

"Yeah, sure, captain." He said, uncertainly.

Our boss pointed at the small gate in our wall, the only way into the courtyard of the Watch precinct. "Watchman Valentine is going to stand at that gate and prevent anyone from entering."

Comprehension dawned on Max. "I see, captain. And you want me to be with him?" His smile broadened. Max enjoyed the idea of mindless mayhem. I think he was dropped on his head as a child. "Perhaps round up a few more of the lads? Won't be a problem."

"Not exactly," said The Man in Black. "The Day Watch does, of course, have every right to enter this courtyard. It is, after all, a shared facility with the Night Watch."

I could see Max was getting confused. This cheered me up, I was not alone, adrift on the sea of what-is-going-on?

"And," went on the boss, "representatives of the armed forces will also be seeking entry. They will have the legal authority to do so."

"Um, right," said Max. He shuffled his feet.

"The Inquisition may also show up," said the captain.

Yessir," said Max. "That's the Day Watch, the army and the Inquisition who we ... let in?"

"Preferably not, Max," said the captain. "No, they must be kept outside."

I thought it was time for me to enter the conversation as a way of showing I existed, "The Inquisition, captain? You didn't mention them before."

"One rarely does, Val," said the captain.

Max took a deep breath, and said, "Okay, captain. We can do it, me and a few of the tougher lads can fight anyone trying to get in." I had to had it to Max, he had progressed from slovenly NightWatch member to valiant defender of the gate. Horatius would be proud. "Especially if Val stands with us and looks mean." What was he talking about? I never looked mean, I prided myself on being the calm one, the chap who just coasts along, getting though each day with barely a ripple. "He can be a terror with a hammer," he finished, smiling at me. I may have to hit him later.

"Ahh," said the captain. "That is the problem. Armed resistance by a body of formed men would indicate rebellion. One lone Watchman standing there on duty would be quite understandable, but more sends the wrong message. We must not give the impression of open rebellion."

"Could it be 'closed' rebellion, sir," I asked.

"Don't be a smartarse, Val," said the boss.

This surprised me, I didn't think the good and the great used such language. Still, I ploughed on, trying to see what was needed.

"Do I understand that you want me to stand at the gate, by myself, and stop the entire world from entering. The entire world being the ones carrying muskets, swords, hammers and other life taking devices? Just me? Little old me?"

Chapter 13

The Man in Black smiled, "I knew you were the man for the job, Val. You're just going to be window dressing. We'll have Max and his squad hidden nearby. All you must do is look fearsome and scary." He scanned me from head to toe, taking in the torn and stained unform hanging off me. "I must admit, your appearance does not quite imbue one with a sense of fright. You rather look like you have been sleeping in your clothes. In a gutter."

Magic chimed in, "I asked Max over because he is one of our recruits from up north. A long way up north. He and his friends still have some of their old gear from their days of ravaging coastlines and terrorising defenceless villagers. Have you ever seen a viking in full kit, sir? Fair curdles the blood. Added to Val's reputation and I feel confident that most wishing to gain entry may have reason for pause.

I wanted to object to this plan but my brain had shut down in effrontery. What did he mean by my 'reputation'?

"We could dress Val up like a berserker, sir," said Max, ever helpful. "Especially if we gave him the traditional haircut." He winked at me, "You'll love it, Val. Totally bald. But we'll keep the beard. And you can borrow my War Axe."

I was definitely going to hit Max later. Possibly more than once.

"Ahh," said the captain. "Perfect, he will look like a rabid dog, one of your fearsome creatures used to terrify young children at night. Excellent idea, Max

The group split up with me being hauled off to that interior of our barracks where I emerged a very short time later in full berserker Viking rig. The haircut had been swift enough to eave a few blood trails dribbling down my skull. Max was very pleased with the effect.

As I moved across the courtyard a stunned silence accompanied me. I felt like a dick and was hoping someone would laugh. Anyone laughing was going to get a full dose of angry Valentine. My face may have shown this because the silence was accompanied by people moving well and truly out of my way.

I stood at the gate and glowered though it, hoping a same damn fool would turn up demanding entry. Preferably alone, but I would accept any number up to a host or horde. I stood with the axe over my shoulder and looked for someone to hurt.

Magic reappeared later and disappeared into the City. Before he left he saw me, did a double take at my new appearance and called me over. "Val," he said, "I've got a little errand to run, shut the gate behind me and stand behind it. Look mean." He paused and gave my appearance the once over. "Shouldn't be a problem for you, love the new haircut. Stop growling at me. Don't let anyone in unless the Man in Black gives the all clear."

"What's going on, Magic, what are we going to do?" I was babbling. We had a courtyard full of people wanted by the Inquisition. Ted and I had killed some of their men and released a host of prisoners, one of which they thought was a devil. They were not going to be happy with us. I saw no way out and said so to my corporal.

"Don't worry, Val, I've got a plan," he said. "Keep them all safe until I get back." He left me standing there feeling a mixture of relief and apprehension. He had a plan. Magic had a plan! But he wanted me to keep people out of the Watch House. How was I going to hold off the army, the Day Watch and the Inquisition.

The Watch House was a tall, solid structure, very square and forbidding. The main entrance to the building led to a large foyer area where we would muster in inclement weather, normally we got together in the main yard and this was where I now stood. The yard was encircled by a tall wall, the only entrance by a set of large wrought iron gates which swung open on a metal track, they were far too heavy to be free standing. One of the gates had a smaller opening which could be used for individuals and was our normal method of egress.

There I stood, looking scary, axe in hand, mind in neutral, bowels aquiver.

Meataxe sauntered over and asked me what I was doing and was I going to a costume party? I told him, he grunted and began to do some serious lounging. After a few more minutes he pointed at someone in the courtyard and asked, "Who's that guy?"

I looked at the elderly man in the yard who was working in a sketch pad. "Painter," I answered, "you remember, he wants to do a portrait of the Watch. He's a mate of the Man in Black. Been back and forth the last few weeks."

We continued to chat a bit more, me getting more and more edgy waiting for the hammer to fall. What was taking Father Julius so long, I wondered? A face appeared in the torchlight, a face I recognised.

"Santini!" I exclaimed, "Get in here!" He ducked in through the small gate and went off to find the sergeant. Before he left, he told me he had become lost inside the Tribunal's building. By the time he found his way out to the front everyone had left. Most of the noise was from the back of the building towards us, banging on doors. Lots of yelling and such like. He took the opportunity to sneak out.

My next caller was Father Julius accompanied by friends, lots of them. They seemed to be burdened with an abundance of pointy things, shooty things and other instruments of destruction. I sent Meataxe off to tell the boss.

The Man in Black came out and I stood to one side while he discussed our situation with Julius. They spoke through the bars of the gate, very polite, very casual. I was terrified again. Or still, I was losing track.

In the edge of the light from the flambeaux the glint of metal sparkled from weapons and armour, occasionally a few horsemen would trundle into the light before being called back. I think the plan was to intimidate us without being too showy. It certainly worked for me, I felt very intimidated.

The Man in Black invited Father Julius in to look at the women and children, the existence of whom the priest was vehemently denying. I wondered if the little guy was on the level, I suppose it was possible for some high-ranking nutcase to give orders and do things to people without informing a front man flunky like Julius. If he was telling the truth then the sight of all the damaged people we had found would cause him to examine his level of belief. I had my own relationship with God. We'd come to terms at Ostend after I worked out that sometimes the church has bullies in high places. Just like most things man makes.

Julius called over one of his escorts, a cavalry officer on horseback, and filled him in. As we unlocked the gate to let in the priest, Magic sidled along the outside wall and slid in behind him. He gave the Man in Black a thumbs up. Oho, I thought, wheels within wheels.

I had to stay by the gate so I missed out on what happened when Julius saw all those we had pulled out of the cells. The cavalry officer stayed on his horse just outside the gate and looked at me like I was less than dirt. I smiled vacantly back at him, happy in the service. His eyes focused on me for a moment and he acquired a look of concentration, I guessed he must be thinking, you could tell by the look of constipation.

"Do I know you, boy?" he asked.

I maintained the goofy grin and replied, "Nuh". After a bit I remembered my manners. "Sir," I finished.

"Been in the army at all?" he asked again, "I've seen you somewhere." I didn't like where this was going, I shrugged a response and turned away from him to look at Meataxe.

"Yes," he concluded, "I have seen you," he muttered, dribbling off into mumbles, "now where was it?" As Father Julius returned, the horseman blurted, "Were you at Ostend?"

Ignoring him I unlocked the gate and allowed Julius to step through. He turned when he was outside and said, in a loud clear voice so all could hear, "I will return at dawn, as agreed. At that time these gates will be opened and all within will submit themselves to the will of the Archbishop. I earnestly suggest that each and every man here examines his soul and seeks forgiveness for offending the Holy Church and endangering their immortal souls. The Church and the Archbishop are God's representatives on earth. Do not, I beg of you, imperil yourselves anymore."

He looked at the Man in Black and made a last comment before turning and walking off into the darkness, "Franz, I will do what I can, but you must submit."

Chapter 14

The Man in Black got us all together; he stood on a crate while we bunched around to hear him speak. "Gentlemen," he was very serious, "I am the Captain of the Night Watch, my duty is to keep people safe." He paused and did something interesting, he looked at us, each and every one of us. I don't know how it worked, he scanned across each face and just for an instant he locked eyes with every individual. Well, he did with me and I'm pretty sure he did the same with everyone else. In that moment it was as if he was looking into your soul, weighing you up as a person, asking if you were worthy.

He said, "I am leaving the City tonight, those women and children you have been tending are, or were, prisoners of the Inquisition. Father Julius has gone to seek reasons why they were detained and why they were made to suffer. He returns at dawn. I do not intend to be here. If you stay, you will be put to the question, I regret having placed you in this situation, it was never my intention. If you wish to accompany me into exile you are welcome. I have secured berths on a ship leaving tonight, but you will never be able to return to the City."

He paused and let that sink in, Meataxe called out, "Is Magic going with you?"

Magic responded by saying, "I am."

"Good enough for me," said Meataxe, "Let's shoot through."

Our sergeant asked a question, "How do we get out of here, Captain? We're surrounded."

The Man in Black started walking back into the Watch House. He called back, "If you want to come then follow me." He entered the building, Magic was one step behind him and I was one step behind Magic.

About then my brain cut in and asked me what the hell was I doing? Poor career move, Valentine, I told myself. The Inquisition is the one that makes the rules, not us. Smart move is to throw yourself on its mercy.

I told myself to shut up.

Inside the Man in Black mounted the front desk, from this height he looked around and saw most of the Night Watch had followed him. He didn't crack a smile or anything. Arrogant mongrel.

I want to be like him when I grow up.

Teddy Boy stood in front of the rear wall of the Watch House, this wall was also the curtain wall for the City. Not supposed to build against it, of course. There should be a clear avenue between the wall and any buildings but with bribable city officials, what are you going to do? We had taken over this particular illegal building from a now exiled merchant. I believe he was accused of bribing city officials.

The Man in Black instructed Teddy Boy, "In your own time, guardsman. Everyone else, please back away." We gave Ted a bit of room, all of us a bit curious as to what he was going to do. He winked at me, took out Chayla's pistol and fiddled with the barrel, then he turned and shot the wall. He shot the wall, the actual wall, but it wasn't the little narrow beam I had seen near the river. No, a wide, cone-shaped beam struck the wall, Ted kept holding the trigger down and we watched.

The wall shimmered a bit and then it just wasn't there anymore. The pistol stuttered towards the end before stopping, he had made a man-sized hole in our City Wall. The city council was going to be really upset with us. Too bad.

Magic had us tie our yellow uniform scarves around our heads, I had fortunately kept this piece of my Guardsman uniform as a memento. Magic reasoned if we got into a fight and the other side were wearing a Watch uniform we would need to know who was on the home team. Fighting the Day Watch would have been fun but I saw his point, we all looked like refugees from one of the Maestro's bad plays about pirates. Meataxe kept saying "Arrr!"

The Man in Black stepped into the gap, nodded to the rest of us and said, "Follow me."

Anytime, I thought.

After about an hour's slow walk we came to a crossroads, our people were half carrying the women and children who were in far better shape than when we had found them. I didn't know what Magic had planned but so far, we were ahead. Even though there were still lots of nasty looking soldiers standing outside our headquarters Father Julius wouldn't come back and check on us until dawn, and everyone knew that there was only one way into the Watch House. One, that is, until tonight, when they would find our bit of redecoration.

The crossroads had some more surprises, a set of wagons, Gypsy wagons. Janos, the Manush gypsy, stood on the back of one waving us over. We loaded all the women and children plus the few men we had found in the cells into the wagons. He chatted quickly with the Man in Black before the little caravan trundled off.

A lone horseman remained, Ensign Briare. He saluted the captain, they muttered a few words together before he turned his horse around and rode back to the city. Magic stood beside me, "Wipe the drool of your chin, Val."

I blinked and said "I thought he was, you know, the one who told the priests where we were. Wasn't he?"

"No," replied Magic, "I found him when I left the Watch House, had a chat. I believed him when he told me he was loyal to the captain. Thought it was worth the risk, asked him to ride out after the gypsies and bring them back. Looks like he came through."

"Bit of a risk, what if he was the informer, we could have ended up walking into a trap?" I said. "How did you know he was on the up and up?"

My corporal put his hand on my shoulder, looked me in the eyes and said, "Didn't."

We stayed that way for a few beats, my mouth going dry at the risk he had taken with us. "Had to do something, Val. Leadership's not all waving flags and marching out the front." He dropped his arm and we joined the rest of the team. "It's also making the bastard decisions."

I was still worried, though. Someone had told the church what we were doing, maybe someone still with us.

By this time, I was seriously impressed with how we had escaped. My poor little brain had been trying to find a way out of our predicament all evening and come up empty. For the life of me, I could not see how we were going to escape the clutches of Archbishop Dominic.

There we stood, about thirty of us, including a trader with his very own devil for a bodyguard. The sight of Chayla had certainly caused a bit of a stir from those in the Watch who weren't with us during the previous night. The previous night! My body reminded me I'd been up and about for quite some time and what was I going to do about it. I thought about the cells of the Inquisition and my body shut up. I could go a bit longer, I'm young and strong, some even say good-looking. Not many, but some.

I had finished up next to Chayla, still lurching a bit from his ordeal and rescue. He was dressed, clean and bandaged, so I gave him a little friendly smile. He growled at me, snarled a little and then relapsed into what I took to be as a very inward looking silence.

When we started walking again, I stayed with Chayla. He staggered so I put my arm out to help. The big mongrel swatted it away, grabbed me by the front of my shirt and pulled my face close to his. We stood that way for a few moments, I got the impression he was memorising my face. Finally, he let go and we continued our cheerful stroll.

We headed into the woods and walked for another hour before stopping at a seemingly random location. The Man in Black stood on a fallen log, faced us and said, "This is it, gentlemen. We go through this little copse and we find the ship, from then on, we are committed. If you want to go your own way, now is the time."

It was Meataxe who voiced the thought uppermost in my mind, probably many others. "Ship? What ship?" he said. "We're inland, the harbour's miles away."

I think I saw a smile on the face of the Man in Black, he just said, "Trust me, there's a ship. BUT if you follow me there is no going back. We leave for good. Right, I'm off, who's with me?" He stepped down from the log and followed Mendic into the copse. My snarly friend gave me a whack in the mouth, friendly like, and stepped after them. The rest of us stood around and looked at each other.

"Anyone have any idea what's going on?" asked Magic.

Now I was worried.

Teddy Boy didn't say anything, he just followed the Man in Black, others trailed after him until there were about half a dozen of us left behind. I looked at Magic, Magic looked at me.

"Got any family?" he asked.

"Nope," I replied. "You?"

Pause, then he indicated the copse where the rest of the lads had gone, "They're all in there. Guess I'll join them." And he stepped into the copse.

While I stood awhile in thought - actually I wasn't thinking of anything, my mind was a complete blank - the other men muttered about families elsewhere and trickled away into the night, taking their chances away from the Watch.

And then there was me, all alone under the stars.

The stars.

"Top day," I sighed, and entered the copse.

Chapter 15

I don't want to dwell on the next part, it's a bit of a blur. After I passed the first few trees I came to a small doorway, I crouched and entered. We were in a dimly lit room with metal floor and metal walls. The door shut behind me, this was followed by a terrifyingly loud noise and the floor rose up and hit me in the backside. I wasn't alone, we were all sitting on the floor which was now bouncing like a wagon in heat. Fortunately, I had strapped my borrowed War Axe to my back, at least it was secure.

After about ten minutes the room stopped bucketing and, not a word of a lie here, I started to float.

Just before I threw up, I got in one really good, long scream.

You know, twenty-odd grown men throwing up in a room is not a sight you want to see too often. Especially when the bits start floating around with the men. Meataxe, bless him, pointed at one particularly loathsome piece of debris and said, "Who ate that?"

When it smacked me in the face, I fainted.

I came to and the room was still. It was very messy, very smelly, but mercifully still. We were all covered in disgusting bits of filth. A door opened and Mendic stepped into the mess, wrinkled his nose and threw up. Do join us, I thought, bit of floor over there not totally covered.

He staggered to the wall behind me, pushed something and the wall slid up. Since I was leaning against it, I fell over. Head first and arse backwards into my new life. Clumsy, ill and smelly I entered my very first spaceship. I was not a happy camper.

From my position of authority I saw, upside down, a whole group of devils. They stood next to some normal people and what looked like a two-legged goat. The goat was talking.

I, sensibly, fainted again.

My next surfacing was in time to see some humans wielding a hose. They were very consciously washing us all where we lay, the water stream pushing us around the room, turning some of the gang over and over. While the high pressure of the water knocked me about, it certainly helped gather my remaining wits. I crawled on all fours over to Magic who looked about as well I did. I flopped down and gave him an accusing look. When the water was turned off, he patted my head, stood up and said, "Come on, you big softie, give us that world famous smile of yours. Let's go and find the boss."

We discovered the Man in Black off to one side, reasonably clean and dry. How does he do that, I wondered. He was talking to Mendic who was holding a bag full of those gems. We were given one each, popped it into our ears and the cacophony separated into understandable voices. Most of the voices came from the Watch, they were all swearing something fierce.

I could feel my self-control slipping away. Wearing my borrowedarmour and clutching a dangerous axe did not help to keep me calm. The whole rig was designed for utter violence and my body and mind were responding.

"Welcome aboard," said a cheerful Mendic.

I punched him in the face.

We were put into a large room full of bunk beds, given some of their strange clothes and fitted with a pair of those beautiful, beautiful boots. My mood was still dark, I noticed people were giving me plenty of space. I suspect I was doing some growling. We each had a chest or locker for our old clothes and gear. I put my now clean armour away carefully and placed the War Axe in an easily accessible position. Max might get them back sometime in the future.

Turning back to the main room, I was met by a small group of the ship people. Some humans and a couple of the goat things with a Tharl standing protectively behind them.

"Something you characters want?" I asked. My fists may have been clenched, my voice was certainly rough.

They shuffled around, the big Tharl sneered and I wondered what was going on. I could feel my body tensing, ready for mayhem. Right Honourable came by and said, "They were curious as to the fearsome warrior in our midst." He smiled at me, patted my head and said, "That would be you, grizzle-guts."

He shut my locker door. "Magic wants you to come back to the realm of the civilised." He bent down and peered into my eyes, "Are you in there, Val? Can we send the nasty man away, please?"

I blinked, took a breath and said, "Yeah. Righto." A few more breaths and the red veil lifted from my eyes. "I'm good."

"Jolly good," he said. "We all feel a bit safer when this stuff is out of sight, mate. And grow the hair back, you look ridiculous."

Mendic told us to get some sleep, we would then be fed and have a chance to talk. So, we did, but I slept with a knife under my pillow. An actual pillow.

The beds were metal framed with a soft mattress, we had sheets - sheets! – and the blankets were of the finest quality. After we woke, we were directed to a large dining hall where there was food aplenty, hot and lots of it, my favourite kind. After the meal we went, one by one, into a smaller room where a pair of humans told us to strip. I was the first in so they learned some of our little ways from me.

Words were exchanged, threats were made and I may have given out a few thumps. Nothing serious, just making new friends. This was fortunate, a less tolerant member of the Watch may have caused them a bit of grief.

When they came too, they explained they were some sort of doctor and wanted to check our health. I promised not to hit them again and let them do their examination. They were very thorough and lucky to remain alive.

While they studied me, I studied them. They had the softest skin I have ever seen, and I've seen royalty up close. No bumps or pox marks, I couldn't even see any scars or lost teeth. These guys must have been really important people, I thought, and considered apologising for hitting them. Considered it, didn't actually do anything about it. It's the thought that counts.

We chatted for a bit and they told me they were just rank and file surgeons, not big deals at all. They did go a bit quiet when they saw my body, I've picked up a few nicks and bumps but, hey, I've still got all my fingers and toes.

The whole experience was a bit of a whirl, I remember bright lights in every corridor with not a naked flame in sight. Their doors were without handles, you just pushed a button on the wall and it opened! And no dirt! Nowhere to be seen! We only saw a few rooms, places to sleep and eat but we were all pretty gobsmacked – it was like living in a palace.

After another fabulous meal – two in the same day! – Mendic took us into a larger room filled with seats facing a little stage, just like the Theatre. We all tried to pick front seats because we thought we were going to see a show. Meataxe was hoping for puppets, we all agreed dancing girls would be too much to expect.

The lights dimmed, we all went, "Ahh!" in expectation, just like a bunch of kids. Onto the stage stepped the Man in Black accompanied by Mendic, several devils and one of those goat things. I was sitting next to our sergeant and he started praying up a storm, bible verses, childhood prayers, anything at all. Behind me a few others were doing the same, Magic was on my other side but he was keeping quiet so I decided to do the same.

The Man in Black started speaking, some of the praying lessened but it never totally went away. He told us stuff, I'd had my suspicions but he just laid it all out for us.

We were in a ship, a big, big ship which didn't sail any sea, it sailed in space, in the sky. He called it a spaceship. Just like the ships back on earth, it was a trading ship. It sailed from place to place and did business. I could handle that, just business, nothing scary here. Mendic's job was to keep up to date with something called the 'Shipping news', a list of new places discovered by someone else. He would then go and visit the new discovery which is where we found each other.

It was all getting too confusing. I was considering hitting something. Or someone, anyone.

To be honest, my mind kept going back to the bit about the ship floating in space. Outside the hull was a lot of empty, a lot of...nothing. I couldn't leave it alone, a deep gibbering fear bubbled inside me. How can we do this? Why don't we fall? What if the nothing that's outside somehow gets inside, what happens then?

He tried to calm us but we were all getting more and more jittery, he was saying that a ship's a ship. We needed one and here it is. Isn't that good news?

Our sergeant couldn't take it anymore. He leaped to his feet and pointed an accusing finger at the devils, "Hell spawn! We are in hell! Look, brothers, look at them! There they stand, ready to leap at us and take our souls to immortal damnation! Rise up, my brethren, strike them down and the Lord may have mercy on our miserable souls!"

I was thinking he was making a bit of sense when Mendic stepped forward and held a little device towards the sergeant. He pushed something on it and I heard a hiss, like air from a balloon. The sergeant collapsed, as if in a faint. Then I joined him.

Chapter 16

I came around a few moments later, still with the knowledge of what we had just heard but for some reason I didn't feel so panic stricken. The sergeant was still unconscious but back in his seat, he was still muttering about devils and hell even though he was well and truly out of it.

I looked around and the sergeant was the only one still out, the Man in Black spoke again. He told us to get some sleep and we would meet again. Most of the lads left looking both nervous and calm. Before I could move he called a few of us back. We sat down again with him, "A few more things, you men have been exposed to more of this strangeness than the rest of the Night Watch. So far none of you looks like you're going mad. The sergeant could lose it entirely. The devils aren't devils, they belong to a group called Tharls, just like we are called humans. And Tharls don't like humans much, especially us."

Magic suggested to us, "Think of them like Huns; you know, another tribe we don't like much, one that scares the daylights out of us." Works for me, I thought. He asked the Man in Black, "Why have they taken a dislike to us? Are we special or something?"

"No," replied the captain, "It's Val."

They all looked at me, I was astonished. "Not your fault, Val, but Chayla has fixed on you as the representative of the humans who caused him pain, he must have seen you a few times during his recent troubles. Bad luck, but that's it. He's a captain in their forces so he pulls a bit of weight."

"We're on probation here, boys," he went on. "They didn't have to take us but now that we're here we have to earn our keep, we have to work." He dropped the other shoe, "and we owe them money for our rescue, clothing, medical treatment, food and board." He inhaled and blew out his checks before repeating, "A lot of money."

I was still mulling over the unfairness of life but agreed when Right Honourable spoke up, "With respect, captain, the reason I joined the Watch was to avoid honest work. It's a bit late in my life to learn some sort of tedious skill."

"We won't have to," said the captain. "This ship is big, imagine a city in the clouds."

"Like one of those stories about Sinbad and the Inscrutable East," put in Meataxe.

I looked at him, "'Inscrutable East'?" You dozy watchman, "What the hell does that mean?"

"Dunno," he replied, "But a fella said that exact same phrase before I went and saw 'The Marvellous Tale of Sinbad the Sailor'. Down the wharves it was, in an old warehouse they were using for a theatre and brothel. Good night on both accounts, I might add."

The Man in Black got us all back on track, "Anyway" he said, "they need guards here, just like in a city, only they're called 'Security' and not the Watch. Tharls make up most of the security teams. We're on trial, there's a little problem of stealing they want stopped and we get to show what we can do. If they like us, we get hired."

"And if they don't like us? Do they put us back where we came from?" asked Magic.

"No. They put us out into space, a bit like sailors cast adrift in a small boat on the ocean. Except there's no boat. And no ocean."

I was so sacred I almost wet myself, my stomach did dry heaves and my mouth tasted like the stable floor.

"We better be good, then," commented Ted.

We were given an observer, a Tharl. We also scored a spotty youth who introduced himself as "Cadet L'On-li", he was going to act as a sort of liaison for us.

Our sergeant was mad, he had gone insane. Every time he woke up, he attacked someone, anyone, even a fellow watch member. He thought we were all in hell and perhaps we were.

Magic was made sergeant and we just needed a new corporal to lead our little trailblazing squad of ace thief takers. He looked at me, raised his eyebrows in a question. I looked right back at him, "Drop dead" I said.

"Come on, Val, you'll love it." He smiled, clapped me on the shoulder and said "Whatever makes you think you have a choice. Corporal." He walked away, chuckling, leaving me with my new squad, a snotty cadet and a dark, ugly Tharl called H'nuth.

I sat in our little hidey-hole, waiting. The hard metal floor pressed my buttocks with total disdain for comfort.

Waiting is boring but safe – I'm a big fan of safe.

"So, what do you think, Val?" my companion said.

Cadet L'On-li was doing a job of acting calm, the slow look, the casual shrug. But the eyes betray excitement. The inexperienced can't really pull it off, you need scars and he had none. I sighed, considered ignoring him but relented, "Yeah, maybe," I said, rubbing my eyes, staring back into the storeroom. "Keep watching."

My companion looked to me like a twelve-year-old, but then I'm bitter and twisted, he was all new and shiny. Eyes wandered around, through the grill, back to me, "How old are you, Val? When did you make corporal?"

Great, I thought, he wants to talk, how sweet. I sighed, "I'm not old, kid, just lived in." Time passed, I could feel him sitting there, trying to think of what to say, struggling to find the right words to have a conversation. Without looking at him I said, "Why all the questions?" I asked.

"Well, I'm twenty-three now," he began, all minty and keen. "I've been in the cadets four years, made cadet officer before joining Security. I was wondering how long it would take me to make corporal. Do you think I've got a good chance of it happening this year?"

Like I care, I thought. When I was his age, I'd lived two lives already. "I think you should do your job, watch that storeroom and stop daydreaming." This kid and I were separated by more than a few years. I don't think I was ever that young.

If I bent a little, I could see through the wall grill into the storeroom. Crates squatting in slabs of darkness, small pools of light glowing on the deck, too feeble and powerless to more than register their presence. The room was all harsh shadows, slow smells and dusty boredom.

An edge of one crate was visible next to the wall. A down light kissed the gleaming edge of a very expensive tool. Sure to catch a good price on the black market running through the ship. Some fool had left it lying around right out in the open.

That'd be me. It was sure to get stolen.

"Val," he said in a low voice, "is it true about the Night Watch? Did you rescue Captain Chayla from death by burning?" A gentle plea was in his eye. I glanced at him, saw the puppy dog stare before ignoring the question and swinging back to the storeroom.

From behind the crate, I saw a hand slowly emerge, pick up the tool and withdraw. "They're in there, tell the Sergeant." I was growling at him now, my patience wearing thin and my people skills needing work. I continued to watch the crate for more movement while my companion whispered into another magic gem. After a brief exchange he leaned and whispered, "Sergeant's sending someone, we're to sit tight." What a surprise.

Shortly afterwards a rough head poked through the hole in the wall behind us, a hole we made last night before creeping in to set up our observation post.

"Whaddya reckon, Val?" queried Meataxe, "Fighting the good fight?" He slowly moved into the room, big, silent, and deadly. Like his smell.

I told him what I'd seen, he grunted and leaned close to mutter. "Magic wants the virgin to stay here and watch. You and me get to sneak and peek. Right Honourable and Teddy Boy will take the doors, Horse's freelance." Meataxe looked at my companion and asked him if he'd heard, of course the kid said yes.

The youngster surprised us as we were leaving by saying, "You know, I really don't like being called a virgin, I am fully trained."

We ignored him, left our hidey-hole and opened the door to the storeroom.

Chapter 17

Meataxe and I crept in, took our time searching, came up empty. We looked at that crate from every angle, pushed it, climbed on top, poked and prodded. Nothing. Definitely no-one hiding behind it or anywhere else in the room. Meataxe checked with all the others, they verified no one had exited the room.

The room didn't have a door or window – who puts a window inside a spaceship? I saw the grill and waved at where the virgin should be. Meataxe sat on a crate and ran his fingers through his beard, "No one here, Val."

He wasn't doubting what I had seen, just saying he didn't understand. Should be a hand here, somewhere. With an attached body. Or at least another exit.

The room had one large loading door and a smaller access hatch, no windows. Crates, cylinders and other odds and ends littered the floor. Walls and floor were metal, a variety of pipes entered and exited the room at odd points.

But of people, not a one. Meataxe was going for the ghost theory, disembodied arms and that sort of thing. I was beginning to believe him even though we both agree he's an idiot. Eventually Magic arrived and got us to go over all the events again. The rest of the squad drifted into the storeroom to listen, our observer, H'nuth tagged along at the end.

"You saw a hand?" asked Magic.

"Yes," I replied, "attached to an arm. Came from where you are standing at this very moment." I pointed to his feet and we looked down expecting to see a disembodied appendage. Some of the men shuffled their boots nervously, we were brought up on ghost stories but Magic is made of sterner stuff. He just kept looking at me nice and even. I hate it when he does that.

Finally, he spoke, "We all know we have a thief or thieves, just like back in the City. We caught them then and we have to catch them now." He stopped before putting some emphasis into his next statement, "This is not a job we can afford to lose."

He paused again and looked around the room, staring at the walls, the corners, looking for a way out of the dilemma. "We're supposed to be good at our job, now's the time to earn our keep. Any ideas?"

We stood silently for a while, looking, listening, smelling, feeling stupid. We use all the senses in the Watch.

"You know, back in the City it was difficult to steal from the docks but one crowd found a pretty clever solution," said Horse from the doorway.

We turned to him as he continued. "They'd fixed up with one of the trading agents to ship a crate of goods and then didn't pay. The rules were, no money, no move. So that crate just sat on the docks. The agent kept it because he was pig-headed and mean. Supposed to contain something useless like baby baskets or something, and he never got around to selling it."

"There it sat during the biggest rash of dock theft in years." He scratched his face and paused, building for effect. Horse loved an audience. "Then I," modest cough, "I discovered their secret and we nabbed the lot."

Right Honourable spoke up. "I recall that incident, Horse. You 'discovered their secret' when you were drunk. You passed out in a garbage pile near the unclaimed crate. Around your comatose, unwashed and undoubtedly pustulant body a collection of discarded rope, sail and other refuse built up. In the morning you were discovered by Teddy Boy, wandering about gibbering. You spoke of witnessing the arcane rites of a secret society, things like 'rising out of the ground' and 'magically disappearing'. Do you recall that epic day, Ted?" he asked.

Teddy Boy was sitting on a small box, not doing much, just being there. "Yep," he said.

Horse took up the tale. "And when I sobered up again, we worked out that ..."

"Magic worked it out," injected Meataxe.

"Yeah, whatever," continued Horse. "Anyway, these guys had put the crate over a tunnel. One they had built earlier for just such an occasion. They'd come out at night and knock over the warehouses."

Meataxe brightened up, "Thassright! We moved the crate, followed the tunnel and got stuck in. Good fight, found a pile of stuff they'd pinched, blood and guts everywhere. Ahh, good times."

Magic brought us back to the present, "Very true, gentlemen, and I do see the similarities but there are a few differences. This is not a sea dock, the floors are steel and cannot be tunnelled into and this crate is.... supposed to be very heavy..." He stopped talking, looked at the crate, slowly swivelled while looking at different points in the room. The vents, the grill behind which we had waited, various dials and pipes running down the walls, he looked at them and we looked at him.

"Well done, Horse," he finally muttered. Horse looked confident, a smile on his face. We knew he had no idea what was going on. Neither did we. Magic does this stuff, that's why he leads and we follow. That's also why we're still alive.

"L'On-li, are there any pipes under this floor?" asked Magic.

"Pipes, Sergeant?" repeated L'On-li.

"Yes, L'On-li, pipes, tunnels under the floor, that sort of thing." Magic gave the youngster full attention. He was making L'On-li feel like the only person in the room who really mattered. Like the youngster was a very important person, like someone worth listening to. Magic was awesome when he did this, made you feel like king of the world.

Naturally, L'On-li fell under the spell and started babbling about ventilation ducts, refuse tubes, energy conduits and other incomprehensible stuff. Some of it would definitely come through the floor.

We're not stupid in the Watch, although Meataxe is from the shallow end of the gene pool. We picked up what was going on. Even though the crate was labelled with symbols indicating it could only be moved by machinery, we all heaved against one side. Grunted, groaned, pushed and swore. Nothing happened, it could not be moved.

L'On-li noticed it. Down at floor level was a small panel. He squatted, flipped up the protective plate to study the worn and dirty buttons. Reaching out he pushed one, he told me later he chose the cleanest because he figured it was the one most often pushed. Good logic.

There was a click. The crate slid away from Meataxe as he leaned against it, he sat down with an untidy thump and a grunt.

Tipping the crate over L'On-li pointed at some strips of metal around the bottom edge "Magnets. The switch turns them on and off," he said. I had no idea what he was talking about, there were so many new and strange words coming into my head. I think we were all surviving by just going with the flow, hoping it might make some sort of sense later. Right Honourable and Teddy Boy nodded like they understood what he was talking about. Probably did, they both like learning new stuff.

Revealed was a manhole. Horse said he knew it all along, Meataxe broke wind.

From here on it was back to the basics for most of us. Moving the manhole cover we climbed in, weapons out. Meataxe led, we took up our usual posts, L'On-li in the middle for his own safety. I don't think he even realized he was being shepherded. We just pretended we were going into a sewer in the City, not crawling around the insides of some huge floating metal thingy, floating in space which was just another word for nothing and.... I got a grip on myself and kept going. "It's a sewer, a sewer" I kept whispering to myself.

Down the pipe we went, eventually climbing into a larger service tunnel. Meataxe carried his mace, the rest of us with swords, hammers and axes. Teddy Boy had a few throwing knives and was trying to get his hands on the new pistols, they called them 'blasters' which seemed very appropriate. Quite sensibly, they were being kept well away from the Night Watch.

We crept towards the end of the tunnel. Meataxe stopped well before the pipe entered another room. Magic snuck forward and conferred with Meataxe, then slid back and whispered, "Big room, lots of small boxes, looks like a storage facility. We'll do this loud and large. Meataxe and Val go in, Teddy Boy - stay at the entrance. Two beats then Horse and Right Honourable. L'On-li stay here and watch our backs, we don't want any surprises coming down the pipe after us. Questions?" There weren't any, "Righto, let's make it happen" he said.

I moved up beside Meataxe, drew my sword and put my left hand on his right shoulder. Magic positioned himself behind me with his left hand on my right shoulder, and then the others behind him. When the last man in the line was ready, he squeezed the shoulder of the man in front. This signal was passed up the line.

We waited, I felt Magic squeeze my shoulder, I squeezed Meataxe. Without looking back, he made a chopping motion with his right arm. In we went.

Chapter 18

Loud and large - not a bad description of Meataxe – means doing a hostile entry with a lot of noise and movement. It usually confuses the opposition. Meataxe always looks confused.

Into the room we erupted, it was reasonably well lit, about the size of a rich man's bedroom. Piles of boxes were spread throughout the open space between the far side door and us. A screaming Meataxe went left. I went right and interrupted a card game, two men and a woman sitting around a small box. Behind me I heard a crash.

I saw the cards in their hands, one had a glowing stick in his mouth – another thing I had to ask about. All were leaning over the box looking at cards. I registered the silent scene, the intent looks, the jumble of coins. They barely had time to react. Using my momentum in the swing I hit the one with the funny stick across the forehead with the flat of my blade. He fell like a sack of potatoes. My dad always taught me to hit hard if you're going to hit at all, I've always found it excellent advice.

Reversing my swing I twisted my wrist so the edge of the blade was foremost. I hit the woman in the neck, separating her head from the body. It bounced off leaving a spray of blood gushing from a ruined neck. Mess everywhere.

I'm not a cruel man but nor am I a complete idiot. She had drawn a blaster and I do not fool around with people who draw weapons, especially ones which can kill me easily. So far, I'm still alive, he who hesitates and all that.

"Stand!" I yelled at the third person. He had risen and was looking around to see which way to run. In front of him was this madman who had just violently decapitated one of his companions after bludgeoning another. Me with the dripping sword. His eyes went wide and he stood very still, slowly raising his arms.

I moved to block his route to the other door, this let me see what was going on at the entry. Meataxe was extricating himself from a pile of boxes, using some inventive language. He had belted around the corner and run smack into a wall, bouncing off and into the boxes. It was always a risk when doing this sort of entry, but reconnaissance and planning rarely affected Meataxe. He was more of your act first, think later kind of guy. Always a delight to hear him swear, not big on repetition but certainly majoring in colour.

Teddy Boy stood stock still, a throwing knife cocked behind his right ear, he was looking at my man and had a big grin on his face. He liked to throw things as well as shoot guns. Multitalented.

Horse moved into the rest of the room, these three were the only occupants but there was still the door in the far wall. The girl's corpse had a tattoo on the upper right shoulder, I'd seen one like it on Chayla, must be a fashion statement, I thought. She was probably looking for excitement, running with the fast crowd.

Magic looked at the tattoo for a long time, pursed his lips and said, "This could come back and bite us." Straightening up he patted me on the shoulder, "Wouldn't be the first time a woman got us in trouble. Come on, let's go."

Teddy Boy and L'On-li tied up our two prisoners, one with the imprint of my blade on his forehead. He was unconscious but fading fast. The other undamaged prisoner looked like he was going to throw up.

I guess he couldn't handle sitting next to a headless corpse in a pool of blood. Sook.

I was beginning to suspect the people on board this ship, traders, humans, Tharls, goats and whatever else lurked in the corridors were not used to real up close and personal violence. Even the normal ship guards. Sure, they could fire their big blasters and engage in a bit of rough and tumble but unexpected mayhem and utter violence on the ship was, well, unexpected.

We, on the other hand, grew up in a world of personal violence and filth, our occupations on that far planet continually put us in harm's way. When we go into a situation we aim to be as violent, aggressive and brutal as we can. Far better for the other guy to be frozen by fear than for one of us to get hurt.

Teddy Boy came over and told us he'd gotten some information out of the conscious guy between bouts of nausea. He said this was just a storage room; their job was to retrieve equipment when asked. The sick guy also told Teddy Boy about the room behind the other door. It was used as a dormitory when things were busy. There could be some gang members having a nap.

Meataxe's shout probably wouldn't have alarmed them since the walls were soundproof and it wasn't a loud yell anyway. We all looked at Meataxe and he said "What? What'd I do?"

We went into the next room using our usual routine and found two other men asleep. The tool from the storeroom was on a small table beside one of the bunks. Teddy Boy put a knife against the throat of one of the sleepers which brought him awake. He became still and quiet after his eyes bulged a little. Meataxe climbed into bed with the other sleeper and snuggled up. The poor sod woke up to find himself face to face with an ugly, hairy man expelling bad breath. Meataxe smiled, the guy made a little gurgling sound in his throat and fainted. Couldn't blame him, really.

Searching the room didn't give us any more information but at least we had stopped this group from pilfering. We also recouped a lot of stolen goods. Since that was our job on this trial run, we hoped we had done enough to stay alive. We needed to be given a job. Ted waved me over to the dead girl, "Seen this?" he asked. He pointed at the tattoo on her arm, up close we saw more detail. A thick line had been overlaid across the tattoo. At each end was a small death's head, it looked like an attempt had been made to cross out the tattoo.

I looked down at the headless corpse of the poor, deluded girl. She may have felt trapped by her family or faction and sought freedom with this gang. She may even have formed a liaison with one of our prisoners. It had brought her to this, a dirty, smelly death in a squalid storeroom. Had she argued with her parents, rebelled against rules and restrictions? However it had happened, she ended up being a thief, living in a den of thieves. She had made a nest far from her birth.

We handed over our prisoners, including one body, to some more Tharls. Then it was back to our big meeting room to see the Man in Black. It's a funny thing about this sort of event, these episodes of violence and terror. They come with an extraordinary intensity of emotion, an intensity which can become seductive.

You don't want to stay too long in those moments or you will lose yourself. Most of us in the Night Watch have learned how to shut the door on those moments, to somehow turn them off. Those who cannot do this usually die or become drunks. Or become something worse, they seek more of the emotion and live in a world of violence and pain.

We treat it as a job, you have to be able to switch it on and off or the adrenaline rush becomes too much. But L'On-li was hyper, he just wanted to bounce around the room and party. Poor kid was full of adrenaline, zapped to the eyeballs. And he wouldn't shut up.

"Man, did you see Valentine! He just whacked that guy across the head..." A bit more leaping and shadow fighting. "Then the big swing into the girls' neck..." He stopped. He was now seeing the girl die for the first time, really seeing it. All the blood and gore, the up close and personal death of another human. The waste of a human life.

He did the normal thing, threw up copiously. Meataxe played a two onto my jack, "Whaddya reckon, Lonely, better out than in?" And so L'On-li picked up a new name.

I looked up to see H'nuth's eyes on mine, no reaction, no sign of any sort. Had we done a good enough job? He wasn't giving anything away, so I did the only reasonable thing and kept playing cards.

That night we stood around the walls of the Main Dining Hall while The Man in Black sat at table with all the movers and shakers, the good and great. In the centre chair sat the big cheese, the boss of the Trading Ship. L'On-li told us he was called the Chief Trader and his job was to maximise profits. Other various folk ran the ship and did sailor sort of stuff, but Trading and making money was the name of the game.

No one was allowed behind the Chief Trader's chair for security reasons. He had his own bodyguard, a squad of giant Tharls.

These guys were recruited from the Tharls on the ship, the dominant population but by no means the only group. Aside from the Tharls there was us, the humans, and about four or five other alien species. It was this variety of life which sent our first Sergeant around the twist. He couldn't cope with the existence of creatures other than humans. It wasn't his fault, he was a product of his upbringing, a man of his times. As were we all. All of us in the NightWatch, we were products of the society of our birth. I was coping, but only just. Whenever it got bad, I went and sat with Magic, he seemed to generate waves of calm.

The old sergeant had tried to rearrange his worldview to accommodate aliens by pretending they were angels or demons, but in the end his mind failed and he went insane.

Chapter 19

Tonight, we were on display, all in our Night Watch uniforms to show off our exotic natures. The uniforms had been cleaned beautifully, I had been able to scrounge up spare bits of uniform and looked vaguely guard like. "No weapons," the boss had commanded and we nodded in quiet obedience. Naturally, we all took this to mean no visible weapons and I was not alone in sliding a few sharp things into various hidden parts of my garish clothing.

We did our best to look like parade quality troops. We did not have any experience in full dress ceremonies but Magic had told us to pretend. We layered ourselves in colourful scarves and whatever flimsy material we could find, I'm sure we looked like brothel guards in a bad play. I was not allowed to wear my armour or bring my War Axe. Magic said I might scare the straights.

As our sergeant, Magic was allowed a halberd for decorative purposes. Tonight, we would find out if we got to stay on board. Or swim in the nothingness of space. Calm thoughts, calm thoughts, I kept telling myself.

I stood at my post behind the Man in Black, looking very grim and forbidding. Across the hall from me was Right Honourable, we stood parade still for the duration. He spotted the change first.

He flicked his eyes toward the Chief Trader who had stopped eating and talking and was just sitting quietly, staring ahead. The Chief Trader is not human, nor is he a Tharl. I'm not sure to which group he belongs. Any species will do so long as you bring home the big bucks for the Spaceship Trading Cartel. I've always liked promotion based on merit.

I slowly moved my head to scan more of the room. I couldn't see anyone else acting strangely. The Man in Black had also noticed, he wasn't giving anything away but he was becoming tense as he watched the Chief Trader. Pretty soon his Tharl bodyguard started making those foot shifting noises and little grunts that bodyguards do when they want to yell and scream but they don't know what's wrong. The Chief Trader was not behaving normally, this started to get freaky.

By now other dinner guests were stopping their eating and talking and were starting to look towards the main chair. At this point the Chief Trader slowly fell face forward into his dinner plate, splashing stew onto the white tablecloth, spilling his wine and generally bringing a downer onto the entire evening.

The captain of the Tharl bodyguard leaped onto the table and pointed the biggest gun in the world at the assembly. Someone else ran to examine the still form and the rest of the bodyguards moved in to surround the Chief Trader. Everyone went very still. We in the NightWatch just stood and watched because we didn't know what to do. What's the protocol for the death of a senior officer on a spaceship? Hmm, let me think, haven't seen a lot of that.

Other dignitaries at the meal had their own private bodyguards, these guys started going for weapons. Hands began emerging from jackets and pockets holding a variety of pistol-like shape. If the Tharls overreacted they might see these as additional threats and then lots of death would be in the room.

The NightWatch stood around in vibrant colours, looking as menacing as a bunch of flowers. None of us had a weapon in hand. Our eyes were seeking Magic, looking to him for an instruction. Things were about to get nasty.

Magic took a step forward and slammed the butt of his halberd into the floor with an almighty crash.

"Still!" he bellowed.

Everyone froze and the NightWatch subtly changed stance. Like hell we didn't bring weapons, we all had them hidden away in various folds and pockets. Nothing big like a sword or halberd, but plenty of things that break bones or aid in blood flow. I was pretty sure Ted would have some shooters. We all stood there holding knives and clubs, lots and lots of knives.

There is a way of standing with a weapon which says you are just a ceremonial guard and another which says you are about to kill someone. The Night Watch morphed from harmless decoration into scary, scary people. A few of the diners and a lot of their guards took notice of us now. Very soon everyone in that room knew we would kill them without a second thought.

The Tharls gathered up the still form and left the room accompanied by some flunkies. Magic dispatched two of our men to go with them because he likes to know what's going on. I was scared and nervous, I didn't know what to do, and I couldn't run away. The most depressing feeling of unease washed over me. This place, these people, these 'things' were all too much, I just wanted life to be normal again.

"Val!" called Magic. "Get the men together, calm them down, stay with them while I find out what the Man in Black wants us to do."

The last thing I wanted to do was look after everybody else, I wanted someone to look after me. On the up side, I had a task, I had been given orders. I yelled a bit, abused a couple of men, snarled at their incompetence, and dragged all the team into a bunch off to one side of the big room. I had Right Honourable and Horse do a weapons check, a nasty one with lots of criticism over dirt and poor equipment. Some of them bitched at me, said I was on a power trip. And we all calmed down. H'nuth had joined us again, our ever-present shadow.

Things started to happen quickly, other security people arrived and started taking statements from all of the guests. L'On-li pointed out the Boss Surgeon to me, he was running in to check on the Chief Trader. He returned and we stopped our interviews while everyone resumed their seats. The Watch huddled against a wall, we listened to the report on the Chief Trader's condition. It wasn't good.

He was dead.

The days passed in a pattern of questions, interrogations and searching. Nothing emerged to indicate the Chief Trader had been assassinated but I could smell a rat. It was all a bit too cute, top politicians and general big wigs do not die accidentally and fall face down in the soup. We all reckoned he had been done in.

I had Cadet L'On-li attached to my squad so I could use him to learn about life on a spaceship. He took a small group of us on little tours and tried to explain stuff, I missed most of it but Teddy Boy seemed interested. Right Honourable and Meataxe loved the box with the little pictures that moved, it was a real hoot to watch these two joined at the hip, a failed aristocrat hanging out with a gutter dweller. Talk about a mismatch.

During one of my solo excursions, I met Chayla and a few of his chums in a corridor. He was looking well again so I went up to say hello, expecting at the least a bit of a thank you.

Standing there, I gave him my biggest smile and said, "Chayla, looking good, my man!" and I gave his shoulder a little punch. I was radiating friendly vibes.

He snarled and hit me big time. Down I went with at least another broken nose, blood pouring over my chest in river quantities. He stooped down over me and spat a few more words out, "You scum! Put me in chains, would you!" He kicked me. "You will pay for all those indignities tenfold, you and your precious NightWatch!" He kicked me again and strode off, flanked by his cronies, I lay there in a lot of pain resolving not to go exploring alone ever again. I wanted cronies, too.

Two days after the big dinner dive we had our normal morning briefing with Magic. My nose was healing nicely, no one gave me any sympathy. They thought it was a bit of a laugh. Not an unexpected reaction from the lads, bless 'em. H'nuth sat beside me, face as expressionless as ever.

"We have a job, bigger than the last one and it gets us back onto proper dirt. We have been tasked with planet side guard duty on one of the Drop Markets, departing in three days. There will be two markets dropped on the planet Gamma 5, we will look after one and another security team will take care of the other. Duty is for a long six-month stretch until the market is retrieved on the ship's next circuit. We'll be joined by another contingent from security to bulk out our numbers." Magic looked around the room and saw my Tharlish companion, "Investigator H'nuth will be joining us for the initial deployment."

We were dismissed and returned to our quarters to prepare our gear. I pondered over who would be joining us, hopefully not aliens. My fragile psyche needed a break.

Chapter 20

Two days later we headed down to the assembly hall for our final briefing before being dropped onto the planet. As the extra security people wandered in we gave them the once over. Who were these guys who had been dumped on us?

After the first few got in, I got a bit antsy. Most of these strangers did not look like newcomers to security. Some looked more like clerks than rough and tough guards although there was one brute of a guy who had hair longer than mine as well as a wide assortment of tattoos and body piercings. We were all in our standard shipboard overalls and all wore the shoulder patch which marked them as members of Security. This shoulder patch was just a round piece of material with a red square in the centre, other sections of the ship displayed a different geometric shape to indicate their work area. We had some interesting lessons from Right Honourable at night about geometrical shapes. I may have dozed. I remembered most of mine from my sadistic tutor when I was young. Very, very young.

The last of the men to arrive was Meataxe. He always had a rotten sense of direction. We grunted to each other. He patted my head. My mates had taken to giving my slowly growing hair a rub every now and then. For luck they said. Annoyed me no end. I followed him into the briefing room. The Man in Black was on the main platform chatting to Magic. Meataxe and I found seats and sat in the back row and the Briefing began. Meataxe nodded off.

Magic paused and took a breath. "Right, now we in the Watch have had some challenges in the past." Lots of nods. "We now have to suck it up and face another one. I'll turn it over to the Captain to fill you in. Someone give Meataxe a nudge."

The Captain took up a stance at the front of the podium. He stood with his hands behind his back looking cool, tall, and erect. The complete man in charge.

"There has been a development in the murder investigation. Enquiries still have some way to go and the First Officer has requested I assist in the investigation. As a result, I will not be accompanying the Watch on this deployment. Corporal Rudolph and a small escort will stay with me. This will necessitate some adjustments to the command structure. Charles will be Acting Captain and also be the Commander of all security forces allocated to this Market. We have discussed other positions; I shall now leave Charles to make further comment. Gentlemen, I have complete confidence in the Watch carrying out this task. To the newcomers to our group I can only say, do your job. Listen to the veterans, solve problems. Don't whine."

Finally, he made to leave the podium. He took a backward step and swept his hat off while giving a formal court bow, the sort he used to give to princes at court. He was saluting us.

Those of us who had come with him from the City stood quietly. The Captain straightened up, nodded to Magic and said, "Make it happen." Then he left.

Stepping forward Magic announced, "Willem, you will take over Squad Two from Valentine. Val, come up here. For the duration of this deployment, you will be assisting me. Your rank will be Acting Sergeant". I stood up, stepping on Meataxe's feet. He winked at me. I moved to the front and took a position behind Magic.

"Welcome to Senior Management, Val," he said.

"Thank you ... Charles," I replied.

Hell's Bells, I thought.

The next day we embarked for the planet. I still had trouble coming to grips with the idea we were in a spaceship and about to visit another planet. I thought it was a big deal if I went to a dance in the next town.

The corridor leading to the docking bays for the Markets was huge, big enough to deal with the amount of trade goods travelling back and forth. The Watch and its attached guards exited the moving room called 'lifts' and joined the stream of personnel moving down the corridor. I recognised the Security shoulder patches of the Tharls heading for the other market. On impulse I followed along behind them.

They all turned off and entered Bay 1, their captain stood at the door, arms folded, looking forbidding. I recognised my old pal, Chayla. With my head only coming to his chest, I spoke to a name tag. Sometimes I do the dumbest things, I don't know what impelled me to walk up and say, "And a very good morning to you, Captain Chayla. Nice day for it." He was unfazed by my most winning smile. "You're the guards for the other Market?" No response, not a twitch.

I tried to peer around him into his Bay but he moved to block my view. This was carrying a grudge a bit far so I said, "Why the attitude, Chayla? Do I owe you money?" I hoped he wasn't going to hit me again.

He unfolded his arms and placed one huge hand on each of my shoulders, leaning down hard he said, "Go away, little man." Then he squeezed, making my eyes water.

I spoke through my fixed grin, although by now it was becoming a rictus. "We rescued you, Chayla. We pulled you out of that hell hole." His fingers felt like iron bars, talk about a deep tissue massage.

He leaned down and slobbered into my face, "I was only there because you humans are so bloody minded and ignorant. You and you irritating band have caused me enough grief. And you, Valentine, have taken something precious from me. Go away and disappear." He turned me around and shoved my back.

It's hard to maintain your sense of dignity when someone way bigger and meaner gives you a hard push. I staggered a bit, gave him such a look, and strode off, harbouring yet another assault on my dignity. Still, an assault on dignity is better than a punch in the face from a Tharl. I know that from experience. And what was that about me taking something precious from him?

My people went to Bay 2. When we arrived, we had another surprise. Standing at the door were two crewmen directing us to Bay 5. I asked them what was going on but all they could tell me was the embarkation point for our Market had changed. They had no other details. Entering Bay 5 I crossed to where Magic stood in conference with some crewmen before the entrance port to one of the huge Markets.

The Markets, what a great idea for trading. You take a whole building, as big as a bazaar and you just plop it down next to your new city, a city full of brand new customers. Do it on a regular basis and everyone travels to meet you. Everyone wins. These things were designed to travel down to a planet and carry a full cargo of trade goods. On landing they somehow changed, I dunno, big doors opened up or something, and they looked like a shop. A really big shop.

Our job was to travel down with the market and protect it until the traders arrived later. They came down in another boat, or ship, or whatever they call the smaller spaceship thingys. H'nuth would drop with us but return on the small vessel which brought the Traders. He was probably not keen on being with us for the entire time. After all, how much observing can one do? In six months, some other big thing came down and towed the market back up into space, back to the ship. I tried not to think about the whole process too much, it made my head hurt and my stomach sick.

While we were on the planet the traders were supposed to, well, trade. And that was how our new world functioned.

It was my job to organize the men and women into some sort of order so we could embark. I asked myself, what does a superb leader of men do in this situation? Answer, I called over the three squad leaders and said, "Get them organized." I had a few ideas, not many.

"Split the newcomers between your squads. Right Honourable, you've got seniority, report back to me when everyone's ready. Teddy Boy, get Horse and join me over with Magic, I've got a little job for you. Willem, keep a special eye on all the extra people, note any we may need to have a quite talk to. Make it happen." Then I turned away and went to see Magic, hoping that the guys could make up the rest because I was out of orders.

"Okay, Charles, what's going on?" I asked, "Give me a few clues here, I'm new at this leadership stuff."

Magic gestured to the crewman he'd been talking to, "Val, this is Technician Wilks, he'll be guiding the Market down for us." Wilks was a slightly built man with a pencil moustache and slicked back dark hair. He wasn't very impressive but he was certainly trying hard to be the man of the moment. We shook hands.

"You're a spaceship sailor, Wilks? Must be a big job getting into your position. Congratulations." Magic had taught us all the finer points of smarmy flattery. Never hurts to stroke someone who holds your life in their hands.

Wilks straightened a little and replied, "It is a big job and a very delicate one, too. No, I'm not a pilot, I work for a living." He gave a little grin like he had made a tough guy joke.

"Throwing one of these Markets down to a planet," he said, "needs someone who can read the instruments properly, not a hotshot with their brain on a joystick." I had no idea what he was talking about. He went on, "There's no real flying in a market, it's more of a controlled fall. Of course, that can be problem if you don't watch the instruments. Yep, it's an important job, but don't worry, boys, I'll see you down safe." He gave us a little finger flick to his forehead as a salute and sauntered away.

Teddy Boy and Horse arrived as I turned to Magic, mouth open in question.

"Okay, you've met Wilks, the ego on legs." Magic waved at the market and went on, "It seems these things are basically foolproof when they are dropped on a planet. He's there to monitor these strange devices and carry out maintenance for the next six months. Then he gets another moment of glory when he calls the booster ship to come and pick us up. He's pretty keen on himself but he's also a bit surprised to get this job, it would normally go to someone a bit more senior than him. He sees it as a promotion."

Chapter 21

Magic looked after the figure of Wilks as he disappeared into the main entrance hatch. "We should be fine."

He did not fill me with confidence. Turning to Horse I said, "Go after that guy, Horse, talk to him, see what help we can give him. Find out what his buttons are so we can push them when needed." Horse grunted assent and lumbered off after Wilks. "Teddy Boy, I want you to find out where we are to be accommodated for this death drop. There's something called stasis couches in the main hall for all of us." His eyes lit up. I think he knew what I was talking about. "Sort them out and be ready to help everyone into place. You're in charge of getting everyone in and settled. Any problems?" Teddy Boy stood a moment and thought, shook his head and moved up the ramp.

Magic said, "Well done, Val, the secret in leading is delegating. I'm going to check out the rest of the market. Report to me when everyone's ready to go." He winked and walked off. I think I had just been the victim of a delegation.

The next hour was awful. Everywhere I went someone had a problem. Where do I store this, what time do we leave, have I got time to go and relieve myself, I want a drink, I feel sick. It just went on forever; there was no point in getting angry, I recognised nerves in the men, especially the NightWatch. When word got around about our method of non-flight there were many who rediscovered an intensity in their prayers. The Corporals were moving around and doing their job but I discovered I was needed, just to be seen. I was learning a lot about real leadership, it's not what you say it's how calm you look.

Finally, I reported to Magic that we were all in and ready. He was having a small talk with Horse and after my report he told me a bit more about Wilks. It seems that Wilks was a bit surprised by the state of the market. It was not in terribly good condition. He found a log in the command centre detailing its history. One of his loves is paperwork, give him a record to keep and he's a happy man. He went through all the entries in the log and concluded the Drop Market was approaching the end of its use by date. Even Markets wore out and when they did, they were generally cannibalized for spare parts and whatever and either jettisoned or used one last time and left on the planet.

Magic had asked if that was the case this time, would the market just be abandoned? But Wilks said no, still plenty of life in the old girl. He was expecting a booster ship to come and get us in six months. While we mulled over this situation one of the ship's officers came up the ramp informing us we were approaching the first drop point. This was when the other market, the one in Bay 1 with my mate Chayla, would be dropped. We would go soon after. Our trajectories would take each market to opposite sides of the planet. Amazing that a small difference in space could lead to such a large distance apart on a planet's surface.

We went into the main hallway and did a final check on the men. I say men but there were quite a few women in the group from the additional people. The members of the NightWatch had tended to cluster together for mutual support and the diffusion of nerves. The others seemed pretty casual about being kicked out into space and flying like a rock. Meataxe and Willem were checking the stowage of gear, Right Honourable was standing near his couch with a fixed grin on his face, trying to look like a leader but his smile was glazed.

Magic went up to the control room to do a final check, I just tried to be visible to all. After about ten minutes the main doors slowly closed and I saw Magic return from his talk with Wilks and make his way to a couch. A voice over the loudspeakers announced our departure in two minutes. I lay on my couch, strapped myself in and felt a need to throw up. My throat was dry, I was sweating like a pig and felt total and utter terror.

We were about to be chucked out of a ship, into space, and fall like a rock to the planet below. What could go wrong? And did I have time for one more trip to a rest room?

Wilks's officious voice came out of little boxes on the walls of the room. "Stasis fields activated." A blue haze shimmered over my bunk. I don't know how it works but apparently it kept anything inside it safe from sudden impact. It wasn't strong enough to withstand massive shocks and it could only cover a small area. Like me. I suspected hitting a planet at great speed qualified as a 'massive shock'.

"Prepare for drop, all checks complete, beginning final count," Wilks was loving this. Another voice started counting down from ten.

The room started to shudder and shake. The loudspeaker announced the drop was imminent. Lights went out, several people screamed, there was a loud bang and my stomach lurched as we were ejected with a great shove from the bowels of the ship.

Before I blacked out, I heard Meataxe call out, "YEAH, BABY!"

I don't think I was out for too long, my eyes opened to a dim red glow coming from a series of glowing panels around the walls of the main room. Turning my head I could see other couches on either side of mine, next to me was Magic. He was just lying there, eyes open, scanning the interior walls. Our couches were nearest the entrance door, by twisting my head up I could see the rows of couches laid out in ranks behind me. All of us had a little blue bubble, the stasis field, to protect us from the worst of the bumps and bangs. It may be good at keeping out physical movement but noises certainly travelled through it. That bang I heard as we left must have been some explosion.

Shortly afterwards another set of brighter lights came on and the place took on a look of normalcy. I was watching one of the red panels when these bright lights appeared. I sighed, becoming calm. As I watched the lights, they began to dim and go out. Farewell calm.

Here we all were, flat on our backs, poorly lit and plummeting towards the planet. I felt a distinct looseness in my bowels.

"Hello, Captain, do you hear me?"

My couch was talking to me.

"Captain, it's me, Wilks. I'm in the control room. Just thought I'd check in and see if you are all well down there." It was Wilks's voice but why was he talking to me?

"Uh, Wilks?" I ventured, "It's me, Sergeant Valentine, I can hear you. How are you doing this?"

"Sergeant! Oops, wrong switch." There was a click and then nothing. I called out a few more times but Wilks didn't respond, he was beginning to annoy me. Turning my head to look at Magic I saw his lips moving so I guess Wilks figured out how to contact him. There was another click and I heard Magic's voice.

"You there, Val?" How he sounded so calm all the time I'll never know. "These couches have got buttons arranged in a triangle formation on the armrest. If you lift your chin, you should be able to see them near your right hand. Push the button at the top of the triangle and talk, that's me."

Finger on the top button I said, "Magic? I'm here. Are we okay?" There was no response until I guessed I had to take my finger off the button.

Magic's command philosophy is, "Tell everybody everything". He told Wilks to turn on everyone's communicator so all could hear our conversation. Wilks choked and made pompous little noises about protocol and military discipline. Then he shut up and did it.

That's how we came to hear stuff which scared us witless.

"Well, everything's in the green across the board," began Wilks. "When we hit atmosphere I'll begin to use the main braking jets to slow our descent. At the appropriate time, when we've bled off enough speed, I'll deploy the parachutes and we'll come to a gentle landing. Just remember to stay inside the stasis couches until after we've touched ground. A common mistake for inexperienced beginners," I'm sure I heard a slight emphasis on these words, "is to unstrap too soon. You will break a leg on the final landing.

"When I say a gentle landing," he went on, "I mean gentle for the Market, not for bodies. Those couches are there to protect you, people, I expect you to use them properly." What a pain.

I understood about half what he was saying, my mind was caught up wondering what he was doing with a green board so I only half heard the rest. If we survive I would have so much to learn and I'm not keen on study. I had a thought, Ted loves this stuff, he could learn it for me and then I'd just pick his brains. Happier with the idea of shirking work I tuned back into the conversation.

Chapter 22

"Wilks, this is the captain, how long before we hit atmosphere, and what can we expect for that part of the ride?" I had the impression Magic knew the answer. He must have been studying but he wanted everyone else to be informed. By this time, we had been out of the main ship for about thirty minutes and I was becoming used to what was happening. Our couches made us feel normal weight but the rest of the main hall had little clouds of dust and loose papers floating about. I remember this was called weightlessness, yet another big word. It was like being in a goldfish bowl while the fish food came down. I hoped there was nothing worse than paper and dust in the room.

We heard Wilks clear his throat and assume his best lecturing voice, "Well, I'll try to break it down into non-technical terms. According to my training and the manuals, the atmospheric entry can be accompanied by significant turbulence which we would feel as a lot of bumps and shakes."

I blurted out, "According to your training! What do you mean training? You've done this before haven't you, Wilks?" Oh great, I thought, we're in a clapped-out piece of junk being run by an idiot.

There was a pause. He went on, "While I have never actually piloted a Market to the surface I have sat in one of the stasis couches in the control room during several descents and I have been privileged to observe the Chief Engineer carry out three landings. I was commended for my work on the simulators and I am quite confident in my abilities. Landing one of these things only requires a close attendance to the instrumentation and the appropriate activation of the descent jets and the final parachutes. There are no decisions to be made since I am instructed to initiate each sequence by the main computer."

"Ladies and Gentlemen, as I said the board is in the green and all is well. We will hit atmosphere in about five minutes and I'll have you on the ground in good shape within half an hour. Feel safe, I've got you covered."

'Safe' was not the word which sprang to mind. I felt like being sick.

There was nothing we could do about it, screaming wouldn't help but if I lived through this I was going to have a long and painful talk to Wilks and whoever had given him to us for this job.

Wilks said, "Entering atmosphere," but nothing happened for a while, a few jerks and bounces. Nothing too extreme, I started to feel hopeful.

Wilks was giving us a blow-by-blow description, "All's well, nothing to worry about. This turbulence is quite normal. Board's still in the green, no problems."

A small pause, then he said, "That shouldn't be there."

Straight away Magic came back, "Give us some details, Wilks, tell us what's going on."

"Uh," he began, "the board's got a red light over one of the bolts securing a hatch cover. Not a real problem, these things are held by forty-six separate bolts, losing one is no big deal. They have a lot of fail-safes and back-ups built into the system." His voice was becoming stronger, I began to feel a little reassured. Silly me. He went on to tell us the bumping was going to get a little worse as we hit thicker atmosphere, he also said he was going to start the landing rockets in about ten minutes.

Sure enough, the Market began bouncing around a lot, like being in the back of an out of control wagon hurtling down a hill. This last analogy made me hope that the ending for the Market and the wagon would be different.

I was watching the hatch cover with the defective bolt so I missed the actual excitement when another door in front of my couch started to creak and wobble.

But I did manage to turn around in time to see it explode outward. I could see the hole it left, a hole big enough for two wagons to travel abreast. I gurgled, and the Market began to dance across the sky.

My mind commented on the now visible sky and achingly clear sky showing the utter blackness of space. I couldn't hear everyone screaming but I'm pretty sure that's what they were doing. I would have done some myself but Magic was yelling at Wilks, demanding to know what was going on.

I heard Wilks screaming, there was a lot of it going around. He yelled, "I don't know, we've become unstable but the panel doesn't tell me what's wrong. The computer tells me we're beginning a slow tumble and I DON'T KNOW WHAT TO DO!" He didn't sound terribly in control.

"Wilks!" yelled Magic. "The main door just blew out! It's not there! Get a grip and help us find a way through this."

"The main door!" replied our crack technician. "No, it's still there! The panel for the door shows it's functioning normally. The seal is still good. There's nothing wrong with the main door!"

Time for me to jump in. "From where I am sitting, Wilks, I can see a great big hole. I really don't give a stuff what your board says, the door is GONE! Now pull yourself together and start thinking or I am coming up there and I will gut you like a fish you useless, puking worm!" That ought to do it, a bit of sympathy to help him through the rough spots.

We could hear him reduce his blubbering and eventually he spoke to us. "Look," he said, "I have to go by this board and it says everything is functioning. The only problem is a faulty bolt in the main hatch. But the computer is also telling me we're wildly unstable and unless we start to reduce speed we'll start to burn up. If that door is open the heat will spread inside and... and we'll probably self-destruct."

His voice cracked a bit, "I don't know what to do!"

The Market was buffeting more and more, I could actually see the air streaming around the edges of the doorway, these same edges that were beginning to heat up. The colour of the sky was fading from space black and beginning to acquire pastel shades of blue. Quite pretty, really.

I felt calmer now. Magic continued speaking to Wilks in a stable, rational voice, "Go with your training, Wilks. If it says we are unstable then we are unstable, get us back under control. If you don't solve this," he went on, "We will all die. Talk to me, together we can think a way through this. Now, what do we need to do?" I held my breath, radiating calm vibes up to the control room, Come onnnn, Wilks...

The choking sounds over the communicator was Wilks, "I'm turning the thrusters on to computer control, that should get us stable. I think. Maybe."

There was no sense of spin but the slow rotation of the sky was visible through the doorway. As I watched the rotation slowed and finally stopped, the sky was definitely blue, the air streaming in was making the side panels glow. I've never seen metal dissolve but that's what the door rim was doing. I mentioned this to Wilks, taking my cue for calm from Magic. "Great work, Wilks, you're doing it, you're saving us. Now, from where I sit, which is really close to that open door, I can see the door panels glowing. I guess that means we're overheating, what can we do about it?" I was using the word 'we' rather than 'you'. Always try to make a problem something which is shared rather than allocating blame.

Wilks just grunted in reply, "Give me a minute." He sounded better now, not so on edge. We were probably still going to die but at least it wouldn't be with him shrieking in my ear.

I planned to do a bit of screaming myself later and I didn't want any competition.

Chapter 23

Lying on the stasis couch and watching the door burn away was the only way I had of passing the time. This wasn't the sort of problem that could be solved by a thump in the ear or a fast exit. I didn't like it at all. Lying helplessly and doing a slow wait for the end is not my idea of coping. I tried to time the rate of burn of the door, little thoughts and calculations crossed my mind, things such as, "At this rate I will be killed by the heat in about eight minutes, unless we hit the ground first, and then I'll just be flat." I'm a real bundle of laughs in a situation like this.

After a few more minutes I noticed other parts of the interior were heating up. The day just kept getting better and better. Covers for the various stalls, normally bolted down, now began to have a slight glow. I would have liked to run around like a gibbering idiot but the stasis couch kept me, and all the others, lying casually in a relaxed position. The stress was bad, I guess I shouldn't have been surprised when one of our new guards turned off his stasis field. He made a wet splat against the wall before being sucked out the doorway. Nice to have a bit of décor to embellish the otherwise drab interior.

Turning off the stasis field meant a quick death at a time of your own choosing and several others tried it. None of the NightWatch took this option. They were either pigheaded optimists or totally lacking in imagination. Wilks came back on and informed us of the next set of events. "The computer has been using all our fuel to slow our descent. We shouldn't be using the engines at all yet but I felt they had to be engaged at this early stage. We only carry enough fuel for the last part of the landing, there is no extra supply for emergencies. It's a requirement of the traders that no unused fuel lands with us, they always calculate exactly the amount a Market will need."

"It's always right because these things don't fail." He must have realized what he'd said, "Until now," he finished.

Magic came back on, "Forget that, Wilks, you've kept us alive so far. We thank you for your efforts. No matter what happens, we know that you've done your best. What's the next step?"

Wilks's response was almost military in its precision, "Thank you, captain, you've helped a lot. Okay, the fuel will be used up pretty soon because they only have a ten minute burn for a normal drop. That time will be up in ninety seconds. After that all we can do is bend over and kiss ourselves goodbye."

"Hey, Wilksy," I called. "Do I detect a note of black humour in your tone? What about the parachute thingys, couldn't we use them?" It's strange when you're in a situation like this, you know, no way out, no hope, gonna die, that sort of thing. You either go nuts or hit acceptance. It sounded like Wilks had hit acceptance.

"The parachutes would be ripped away. Most of the board is red now but I don't know if we should trust it. At least that red light on the main hatch cover has more company ,but we now know that the board is inaccurate. Nope, when the engines cut off in forty seconds we go splat," he replied. Geez, Wilks, I thought, cut out the dark side.

The constant heat and buffeting must have done more damage. We discovered the lights on the board were accurate about the hatch bolts. The cover peeled off and took another three huge sheets giving us a very airy feel. We had a great view of the planet as it came up to say hello.

When this sort of thing happens, you know there's a God. And He's got a sense of humour.

I couldn't help it, I went on a small self-pity journey. The usual stuff, why me? I'm too young to die! And my personal favourite – is this going to hurt a lot? When I caught my breath and was deciding whether to gibber or wet my pants I heard Magic saying to Wilks,

"My timer says more than a minute has passed. Why are the engines still running?"

"Engines! What engines?" I heard Wilks yell. My interest was caught, why hadn't the engines cut out?

"Our engines, you big goose," I shouted, "We can feel them still pumping."

"What? I don't know! They go until the fuel runs out and the timer says we're out of fuel now. Wait a moment, let me check a few things." He sounded a bit calmer, I guess he liked a puzzle. The blue of the sky deepened but we didn't seem to be heating up anymore. The door edges continued to melt slowly and I could see another hatch acquiring the same cherry heat colour. But the interior didn't get that same level of glow. Our stasis couches seemed to be able to keep the dust and debris from damaging us. For the moment we were alive. Gosh, things were looking up.

A blur over my head smashed into one of the still existing walls before being sucked out into the sky. Another person who chose their own doom. Magic came onto all of our channels and used his best captain voice. I guess he was getting a bit tired of bodies bouncing around the room. "This is the captain. You are all now members of the Security group known as the NightWatch. In the Watch we have some customs, one of these is that if we have an issue then we cope, we do not give up and run away."

This was news to me, we used to be very good at running away. I like running away, I was good at it. But if Magic wanted to instigate some old customs, who was I to disagree. He kept talking, "No more gutless wimping out," he said. "Stay in your stasis couches, pray or scream as the mood takes you but stay there. Deal with the problem, we'll either solve it or we'll die. No big deal." What a guy.

Wilks came back on with a puzzled voice, "I don't understand it, Captain, we're supposed to be out of fuel. I've checked the amount we had and it tallies with our drop weight. I don't know what the engines are running on but if they keep it up for another fifteen minutes, we will be slow enough to deploy the parachutes. And if we deploy the parachutes, we might make it down all right. Of course, that leaves us with just one more problem, drift."

Magic sighed and asked the inevitable, "Tell us about the drift, Wilks."

"Well," he began, "we were supposed to land close to a major city to carry out trading. The, er, problems we have encountered have pushed us well away from that landing site. We'll land far from any settlements." I was impressed by Wilks's ability to discuss this calmly. There we were, strapped flat on our backs looking up and at the remnants of the walls and roof of the Market. The wind was a visible force, the whole thing rocked and bumped, from time to time something thumped past. The more we fell the more other objects were torn loose and flashed out the door. This was the environment in which Wilks was now giving his lecture. The guy was becoming very impressive to be able to see all this and remain so cool.

Then I had a thought, "Wilks," I asked, "Where are you located? Are you on the main deck with the rest of us? Can you see what's happened?"

"No, not everything," came a stiff reply. "I'm in the control room, it's a sealed unit behind that door next to the central column. But I can imagine what it must be like out there."

Yeah, sure, I thought. "Good to see you thinking ahead, Wilks. Just for now, though, we'd all take it very kindly if you just focused on getting us down."

"Getting you down is no problem," he went on, "it's the stopping that's the trick!" He burst out laughing.

Time passed. Fifteen minutes, Wilks said, and we might survive.

After twelve minutes the engines cut out.

I wasn't surprised. Another disastrous event seemed to be expected.

"The engines have stopped," came Wilks's voice, "what do you want me to do, captain? If I deploy the parachutes now, they'll probably tear out."

"Deploy the parachutes," came the calm voice of Magic.

There was another jolt as something happened. The Market lurched and, for a brief moment, seemed to come to a halt before falling again. Wilks came back on, "Parachutes deployed but they were torn away. We've run out of options, Captain. The stasis couches will help but it depends where we land. That'll be in six minutes." He paused and then came back on, "Thanks, captain, I'm glad I got to be a member of the NightWatch."

Right Honourable responded with, "Very good, Wilks, you've done your best. While we're saying words of importance perhaps it would be appropriate for me to make a small statement. I cheat at cards. I'm very good at it and I would like to express my deepest thanks to all of you for your generous contributions to my somewhat excessive lifestyle."

After a moment, another voice said, "That's fine, Right Honourable, I've been stealing money from you while you slept for many years."

Chapter 24

There were a few more revelations, generally quite normal until Meataxe spoke about his personal habits. Hey were just unbelievable. When he finished many voices expressed a range of disgust or disbelief, sometimes both.

Magic rode over all of us, "We're not dead yet. God bless." He turned his head to look at me, smiled and gave me the thumbs up. I responded in the same way.

The Market fell with increasing violence towards the planet. Wilks was giving us a running commentary of what he saw on the scanners. Tension mounted.

"We're passing over water, some sort of ocean. Now I see land, it's coming up fast. We're moving across the face of the planet as well as going down, we might hit at an angle. Impact in thirty seconds, there's rising ground, farmland, looks like swamps, leading into hills and mountains."

His voice started to rise as impact became imminent. "We're going down, I can see a field, we might be able to shed some momentum if we slide!"

A moment's silence was followed by a groan, "There's a big mountain up ahead! Oh, my stars! It's huge!!"

Then we hit.

My couch was torn off the floor, smashing into my spine and rolling me into a wall. I bounced with it around the room a few times. The stasis field flickered with each big hit but held. Inside this little cocoon I was safe, the harness kept me pinned tightly to its surface, all I saw was a spinning world. And did it spin.

At one point I was squashed in a bundle with a whole bunch of other guys, Willem and I were face to face for about half a second. II don't know what I looked like but his eyes were bugging out and his mouth was wide open. It was like being on a runaway horse or a ship

in a storm. Up and down, round and around. Once I saw a couch hit
and the field fail, it wasn't pretty. The occupant hit the wall, flattened
out and then was hit by several other couches which just pushed him
into paste. During my bounces I saw other splashes on the walls from
similarly unlucky people.

Then it happened, my couch flew out of the doorway and I
sailed majestically away from the now tumbling Market. The ground
rushed up, slammed into me and I started to bounce along the
surface. This must be how stones feel when they skip across water.
Why do I think these things at the most inappropriate times? On the
second bounce my stasis field flickered and went out.

I was now flying backward in a shallow arc, strapped to a couch,
face up and scared out of my tiny brain. Lot of screaming.

The branches of a tree snagged the couch as it passed between
two of the biggest trunks I have ever seen. The branches were thick
and cushioned the last of my momentum as I slewed to a halt. My
couch was finally still, I was suspended upside down by the harness,
the apparatus under the couch having caught fast on all the greenery.
My face almost touched the ground.

I hit the quick release button in the middle of the harness and fell
onto the wonderful stillness of solid earth. After a moment I crawled
out from under the couch and sat up, panting. My head was still
spinning with the adrenaline of the ride and my body hurt in lots of
new and exciting places.

I leaned forward and comprehensively threw up.

Damn, good to be alive.

After a short time, I felt better. Not good, just better. It wasn't
hard to find the crashed Market, just a matter of following the
devastation and listening for the moans. En route I picked up a few
others who were flung out, all still alive and relatively unharmed. We
came to the end of the forest, it was a fairly definite end since the
trees stopped at the face of a cliff. We turned left and kept walking.

By this time there were six of us moving through the vegetation. We had just about overcome our astonishment at survival and were beginning to think of the future. At least I was, the other five consisted of two newcomers and three old Watch members. These three guys clung together for mutual support. The two newbies were hilarious. Being on board a space ship most of their lives had not equipped these poor fools to the idiosyncrasies of a real live climate. Things like dirt, sweat, strange animal noises and the clutter of a forest environment were giving their worldview a bit of a pounding. After our dramatic landing, their emotional bank account was probably empty.

As we pushed through the bushes, I kept on thinking a real woodsman would have been able to locate a trail. Pity I was not a real woodsman, I'd spent too many days in a city. The wilderness didn't terrify me like it did the ship dwellers but I certainly was not a man of the great outdoors. It was with those thoughts flitting through my brain we came into a clearing and encountered our first casualty. Spread evenly across the cliff face on our right was the remains of one of our people. At the base of the cliff were the bits and pieces of the couch plus a few more body parts. There was no way to identify the body. Think of a balloon being thrown at a wall and you'll have a good idea of what the cliff looked like.

As we stood there looking at the cliff one of the Watch, Guido, muttered in a soft voice, "Saints preserve us..." That pretty much said it for all of us.

There wasn't much we could do here so I kept us all moving. We didn't come across dead more bodies but did pick up two live ones, one was wounded. My friend, H'nuth. Just like me, his couch had failed at the very end but it was after it had hit the rock face, not before. Talk about lucky, this timing meant he did not become a smeary piece of rock art. His stasis field had flickered out only as his couch slid to the base of the cliff. He found himself strapped to a dead weight, his chair, while falling towards the ground. Fortunately, it was a short fall and he came out of it with just a broken arm. Plus a few decent bruises.

Quite lucky, really. I told him that his couch could have landed on top of him and broken his neck or back. He did not seem impressed by my upbeat attitude to his suffering. These Tharls had poor people skills.

This guy was too tough, or too stupid to feel pain. Or both. He still hadn't uttered a sound in my hearing during the entire time he had been observing us, not a word. Not even a moan. He maintained this attitude while we extracted him from the couch and gave him some rudimentary medical treatment. Not a sign he was feeling anything. Not even a thank you. Was this guy tough or what? Wierd.

After about half an hour we broke out of the forest and continued following the cliff on our right. This cliff reduced in height until it hit ground level. We were standing on the edge of a farmer's field, gazing at the massive remains of the Market in the distance. It had clipped our cliff and ploughed across the ground leaving a huge furrow. The farmer was going to be miffed.

The Market finished its journey before it smacked into the foothills of the next mountain. I looked at that far rock face across and pondered what would have happened if the Market had hit it head on, at full speed. Especially with us still in it. I did not think the stasis couches would have coped.

We trudged onwards and could see people milling about outside the downed vessel. I'm certainly no expert but I couldn't see it rising from its present position back to the grandeur of space. It was a dead duck, a very retired Market. There was a fair bit of confusion when we arrived, people congratulating each other on their survival and that sort of thing. Someone pointed me in the direction of Magic, I wandered over and we spent a few minutes catching up.

"Val," commanded Magic, "let's find out where we stand. I'm going to talk to Wilks about what happened. You've got a few jobs. Do a head count and tell me how many Watch and non-Watch survived. We can reorganise if need be. Also, find out our situation with food and water, there should be plenty since this thing was supposed to be stocked for a six-month stay. See to the wounded, bury the dead and get us set up for accommodation. Use the Market for preference. Any questions?" He looked at me patiently.

He'd given me pretty detailed instructions. Not the sort of thing a Captain does to a Sergeant. In the past I've heard the Man in Black just say things like, "Sort it out, Sergeant," and then he'd wander away. He expected his Sergeant to work out what needed to be done and flesh out the orders. Since I was new at this leadership game, I was grateful for the tips.

I stood quietly for a few moments and thought through what I needed to do, I couldn't think of anything else I should know, so I said, "No, I think I'm all right. I'll find the Control room to give you a report when I find out what's what."

His face cleared into a quick smile, "Fair enough," he replied. Magic had interesting rules for the NightWatch, words he hammered into us. Rule number two was 'Solve the problem'. Not 'moan and ask someone to hold your hand'. He went on, "Get the corporals to do all the work, you just stand around and be the one they all report to. Promote people to fill dead shoes, get back to me no later than thirty minutes from now with a report on how you are getting on."

He turned to go and then said "And, Val, you're the face of the Watch. You'll be setting the tone for all the rest. They'll look to you to see how they should be reacting. Be a rock."

Off he went. Be a rock, I thought. Great, I felt like a wet sponge. But then, he's Magic, he knows stuff. Off I went to be rock-like.

Chapter 25

Clambering to the top of a nearby pile of rubble I looked at our sorry state. There were guards slumped around the ground alone, some in silent bunches, others talking in small groups, a few staring at the Market or just gazing into the distance. Some of the Watch seemed to be coping better than others. Right Honourable had a card game going although why anyone would want to play with him after his latest confession was beyond me. Meataxe was pawing one of the females as she lay on the ground, probably under the guise of examining her for wounds. As I watched she threw an arm around his neck and gave him a big, meaty kiss. He must have thought all his Christmases had come at once. Then she stood up, rearranged her blouse and walked off. He sat there like a stunned mullet.

"CORPORALS!" I yelled. "TO ME!" I was interested in who would show up. Right Honourable looked up at me with a pleading expression on his face, I just smiled back and shook my head. He reluctantly threw in his hand, stood up and came over to my rubble pile.

"You're an evil man, Valentine," he said.

Willem and Horse appeared from inside the Market and joined the two of us. I asked them, "What's the story, guys, how are we doing?" I was looking over their heads and could see some of the people turn towards us. Lost people always look for guidance.

"Place is a mess," began Horse, "we need to get ourselves organized." He turned back to the scene behind him and gestured at the numb survivors. "Got some injuries need looking at. Willem and I have been looking for medical gear but so far every locker in there is empty, even the ones in the sick bay."

"What do you mean?" I said, my voice raising a little. "The Physicians and Apothecaries must have supplies in there somewhere, we've only just left the mother ship. Willem, if you haven't found the herbs and bandages then you can't be looking in the right places. You've just got the job of Chief Apothecary. Get back in there with a few guardsmen and find those medical supplies. Then track down anyone who can help you and get them working on the injured. I want to know how many and how bad in fifteen minutes. And look after H'nuth - Right?" He looked at me, swallowed and nodded.

"Make it happen," I said. Off he went, yelling for Watchmen he knew and pointing to some of the newcomers.

I turned to the other two. Right Honourable took a piece of grass out of his mouth and commented, "What do you want us to do, Sergeant?" He was smiling but I think he was relieved things were happening.

"Horse, do a head count. Gather everyone together and see if you can work out who lived and who died. I want definite answers so give me three categories, those alive, those dead because someone saw them die, and those missing. Some of the missing will be dead." I thought of our cliff wall with the body splat on it, "but until we know for sure we assume the missing might be alive."

"Right Honourable, send five more reliable guardsmen to me so I can give them jobs. Your task is provisions and quarters. Get some people to dig out the food stocks and start thinking about where we sleep tonight. Put us all in the Market until we know how safe this place is." I had a thought, "Horse, when you do the roll call see if anyone is comfortable in the woods. Maybe some of the Watch were farmers or trappers, they could help us out here." Most of us were city boys, we didn't like the wild. Our jungle was smelly drains and dark alleys, our animals were murderers and men of violence. The forest was some place in which we did not feel comfortable.

Right Honourable asked, "What will you be doing, Val, where will you be?"

I sat on the hard mound and replied, "I'll be right here, gentlemen. Being a rock." They looked at me strangely for a moment, turned and strode off to their tasks.

Our overalls have got these pockets, some on the torso, others on the legs and arms. Normally they're empty but before we embarked, we were taken to a big supply room and given lots of neat stuff. We were told what went into each pocket and instructed in the clever way all the odds and ends were stored. Most of us treated it as a new set of toys. I found a medical kit in one of my leg pockets. There was also a sewing kit, lots of little packages, which I would look at later, and a small clasp knife. I liked the knife best of all, it was beautifully made from high grade steel.

Now I just had to wait. I stood up and put my hands on my hips, gazing meaningfully at the slow progression of order. Anytime someone caught my eye I gave them a "Don't stuff me about look", no smile, no recognition. When I did it to Meataxe he grinned and gave me the finger. Such disrespect.

Now I wondered if we could eat.

Teddy Boy, Santini and three other NightWatch showed up to do my bidding. I checked their pockets, we all had a similar load, I was especially pleased to see the medical kits. These men had also boarded the Market with some form of personal weapon. I had my sword and I'd noticed others had their preferred instrument of mayhem, Teddy Boy showed me a pair of blasters. I sent four of them off to do a quick scout of the area, told them to split into pairs and report back in half an hour. Ted stayed with me.

The corporals reported their progress, the news was bad, we had nothing. Not a thing, nada, zip, bupkiss, cupboard was bare, zilch. We had no food, no water, no medical supplies, no provisions of any sort.

Right Honourable commented, "Correct me if I'm missing something here, Val, but this strikes me as rather odd. Shouldn't we have some food seeing as how we, and others, were supposed to be down her for six months? You know, eating and all that."

Horse gave us the personnel roll. We were down to seventy-nine survivors. These included three severely wounded who would not last the night since we had no physician, twelve walking wounded who would eventually heal, and the rest fit and well. Shaken but not stirred.

I told Willem to gather everyone's medical kit. He was to set up a station with help of any who knew some of the healing arts. Horse gave him a list of people who were called 'medics.' He said they were better than witches but not as good as a physician. Another new word for me.

Right Honourable was still working on our accommodation, I had no suggestions and did not know what he could accomplish. Fortunately, there was rule 2, so I just said, "Right Honourable, get it done." He opened his mouth to speak, thought a bit and then shut up.

Turning to Horse I said, "We will need food. Sort it out, use anyone with field experience but get some people out hunting and trapping. Find water, have a meal for us by nightfall."

I gave Willem my first aid kit saying, "I'm going to brief Magic, see if he can give us any clues. Boys, I don't know how you're going to solve your problems, but I need you guys to step up. Get the job done. Any last questions or comments?"

Not one spoke, but they sure looked worried. As I left I said, "Suck it up, guys, if you look like death you'll infect the others. Look confident, look in control. If you're worried or scared then bury it deep."

This leadership stuff wasn't so hard.

I signalled for Ted to accompany me as I set off to find our new captain and hoped that, once again, he would be able to get us out of another mess.

We eventually found the control room and discovered Magic sitting quietly as Wilks did things with the main panel. A bunch of lights were flashing and he was working at what I had learned to be a thinking machine. Yes, in this world they had machines which could think.

Every now and then he would curse or exclaim in astonishment and write in his notebook. An interesting man was our Wilks, when I first met him on the boarding deck, he was a pain, and I still thought of him as a slightly pompous individual. Yes, I know he probably saved our lives but I just couldn't warm to the little twerp. I'm just a bigot.

Magic waved me over, I brought him up to speed on our supply and personnel situation and then told him what I'd done about it. He mulled it over and filled in the blanks, "Wilks can't raise the mother ship, our radio malfunctioned when we lost the main door. He's finding all sorts of anomalies in our records but no mention of the removal of our supplies. According to the computer it's all still in the stowage compartments."

He paused and thought a minute, "Teddy Boy," he began, "go and have a look in the main holds. Make sure the Trade Goods are there, here are the keys." He handed over a small plastic card which, when slid through the slot near the door, would unlock the secure rooms. This was a big call by Magic, the punishment for playing around with Trade Goods was more than for murder. It was money, after all.

He came back in half an hour and reported all trade bays were empty.

We were sitting in a crashed Market containing no supplies and no Trade Goods. It had no reason to be here.

I found that strange.

Chapter 26

Wilks solved our water problem. Every Market had a water purification/extraction processor built into the roof. Wilks said it was solar powered, whatever that means. We wouldn't die of thirst.

The patrol groups didn't report any hordes of angry natives approaching seeking redress over the alien invasion. Only one small human looking creature was making its way towards the crash site. Magic suggested it might be the farmer, probably checking on what had ripped his crops apart.

"Who's going to talk to Mr Angry Farmer, Magic?" I asked, looking for guidance. "Pretty sure we haven't got anyone to speak his language."

"That's not a problem, just get him talking and we'll soon have translation ability," said Wilks.

I must have looked perplexed because Magic explained, "It's the ear gems, Val. By the way, they're not gems at all, some sort of made-up substance so don't try selling them or making jewellery for any girlfriends. They're called Translator Beads. Let them hear enough spoken language and they'll be able to translate it into one that suits the wearer."

"Let them hear enough language, huh?" I sounded sceptical. "What, have these little things got ears?" I took mine out and looked at it, no ears.

Wilks said something in another language which I missed, I replaced my translator gem and said, "Sorry, what was that?"

"I was saying that once one of the Translator Beads has made the translation it transmits this facility to all the others. It would take me too long to explain how these things work, sergeant." Wilks was on a roll, "Quite frankly, you don't have the technological background to understand most of what goes on around you."

I thought about hitting him, but decided I hadn't been insulted. "You're right, Wilks, let's just call it all magic," I commented.

He choked a little, "You will not!" he croaked, "It's science!"

"Whatever," finished our new captain. "The point is, Val, the best way for us to understand this bloke wandering towards us, is to have him do all the talking. Who do we have who can keep their mouth shut and think, as opposed to keeping their mouth shut and daydreaming?"

I turned to Teddy Boy and said, "You're our man, Ted. Go down and let him rant at you for a bit." Our taciturn comrade eased his way out of our conversation and sauntered down to the perimeter to meet yet another alien being. Never thought I'd be saying that.

That left Magic, Wilks and me in the control room. "Right," Magic said," we're not traders, explorers or soldiers. We're coppers, and this whole crash stinks of a set up."

"Beg pardon?" I asked.

"Wilks, tell us why we crashed," instructed Magic.

"What can I tell you? We nearly died because of this piece of junk. If it wasn't for my quick thinking and insights we'd all be dead. Dead!" Wilks was not one of those people who can let things go. "I don't know what happened or why, I just want to get back to the mother ship and be safe. This isn't my area, I'm a technician not a, a," he seemed lost for words, "a pilot!"

When he stopped Magic just kept looking at him. I took my cue from him and stayed still. We sat. Magic seemed quite content for the silence to go on, he didn't fidget or display any sense of impatience, he just sat, waiting. This was some learning curve I was on. By shutting up we filled the gap with quiet, it drove Wilks nuts.

"The door blew off!" exploded Wilks, then he went silent, when he spoke again he sounded more rational. "The Market came unstable during the descent. At the time it came unstable you told me the main door blew off. It did not, repeat, did not register on the big board. According to all the diagnostic programs the main door was still in place. The only malfunction that was registering was a defective bolt on one of the main hatches. Later, before these hatches blew out, the big board registered multiple failures of the restraining bolts securing these hatches."

He ran his fingers through his hair destroying any last vestige of the well-groomed young man who had boarded this structure a few hours ago. "This stuff is not supposed to malfunction like that."

I put my hands in my pockets and leaned against the door, "Maybe it didn't malfunction. Maybe everything that happened was supposed to happen," I said.

"Don't be ridiculous, destroying a Market would be a major breach of Regulations," said Wilks. I could hear the capital 'R' in his voice. He went on, "It's unthinkable!"

"Let's assume someone could sabotage the drop. What would they have needed to do, for us to crash the way we did?" asked Magic.

Wilks pondered a moment, "This particular Drop Market wouldn't have needed much, the log indicates it was almost at the end of its useful life. Removing a few more bolts, cutting some cables, pretty easy for anyone to do it. Just about any damage would be enough to compound its already poor mechanical state. And if," he was getting excited, "if you stopped any preventative maintenance on the Market it would be a death trap, an accident waiting to happen!"

"Some accident," I said. "So why are we still alive?"

Magic asked Wilks, "On the way down you were surprised at the amount of fuel we had left, you seemed to think we should have used it all up. What was going on there?"

"I don't know. Fuel is expensive," said Wilks. "I can't see how, or why, anyone wanting to crash the Market would put in extra fuel. Unless....wait a minute, you said that there was nothing in the storage bins, no food or supplies."

I nodded. "And nothing in the big warehouse rooms, no trade goods, nothing."

Wilks turned back to his desk and did strange things with his thinking machine. After a few moments he spun around and stated, "We did have the right amount of fuel, IF we had the right weight!" He sat back looking triumphant, Magic and I stared back with no understanding of what he had said.

"And that means...?" I asked.

"It means, sergeant," he used his best patronising voice, "that if we were fully equipped for a proper Drop, all the food and supplies plus a huge amount of trade goods, if they were all on board then we had the right amount of fuel."

"Well, gee whiz," I said. "That's just keen."

"You still don't understand," he paused for a big sigh, raised his eyes to the ceiling. "Because we weren't as heavy as expected we had more fuel to burn. More fuel to burn means that we were able to lose a lot of altitude before the engines ran out. It saved our lives!"

"We can assume," put in Magic, "that whoever wanted us dead was in a position to take supplies and trade goods but not tinker with the fuel. That sound right, Wilks?"

"Very well put, captain," replied our technician. I may have to hit him some more.

"Who could do that?" I asked, being the muggins again.

Wilks pondered, "No one from the Flight Deck. Either someone from the Traders or Security, they are the only ones who could access the trade goods. The sabotage could be anyone."

"I wonder if it's linked to the Chief Trader's death?" asked Magic.

"What about the Man in Black, why did he get separated from the rest of us?" I asked. Could our old captain be mixed up in this murderous scheme?

Magic tapped a finger on the console, eyes unfocussed, "I don't think Franz has a crooked bone in his body. I reckon he stayed behind to keep investigating. Maybe he and the First Officer agreed to a deal. Franz keeps digging but the rest of us have to keep working."

"Fair enough," I said, "but why send us on this job, why not just let us get on with more of our security stuff, like we were doing?"

Wilks was squirming in his chair like he a schoolboy. He even put his hand in the air, "I know1 I know!" he said, waving his paw around.

Chapter 27

"Yes, Wilks?" asked Magic.

"I saw the original orders, there in that pile of papers beside your hand, captain. The squad assigned to this Drop was pulled recently, the orders were amended. If you look," and he stood up to riffle through the documents, finally coming up with a paper, "you can see where the NightWatch has been written over the original squad's name. AND," he gave us all a significant look, "the actual Market was changed. We only got put on this heap of scrap at the last minute, remember how we were told to go to a different bay?"

Magic studied the sheet, I peered over his shoulder. "Who's allowed to do this, Wilks? Who can change these orders?"

"The change could only have been made by anyone from Security, any senior officer, that is," said Wilks.

I had a thought, "What about the supplies and Trade Goods originally meant for this Drop Market. What would they be worth?"

"A lot," answered Magic. "Think about it. We chased that little group over petty theft. I'm pretty sure stealing everything in a Market qualifies as more than petty theft. It would be a major crime. Be worth big money."

"Do you think the Chief Trader knew about it?" asked Wilks.

"If he did then we certainly have a motive for his murder," I said.

"But the theft would have been discovered. The moment we landed and opened up we would have noticed the missing goods!" said Wilks.

"You're missing something, Wilksey," I snidely commented, quick to point out my fellow man's flaws.

"We weren't supposed to land," said Magic. "Whoever took the Trade Goods also sabotaged the Market. If we all died there would have been no witnesses. Even if follow up searchers came down and discovered missing goods it could be explained away. Perhaps the local population got in some heavy pilfering."

"A pity we haven't got some way of contacting the ship," I said. Magic asked Wilks about such a device.

The technician squirmed. "Somehow, er, the radio was, er, destroyed shortly after that first jolt. I'm a professional so I declared an emergency to the mother ship, then the radio broke down. As far as they're concerned, we were heading for a disaster. "

"What did you tell them in that last message?" asked Magic. I filled in the blanks and guessed that a radio lets you communicate over distances.

Wilks leaned over to the computer and tapped a few keys, "I can play it for you, It's a pretty basic message. The sort of drill we practice over and over again." He pushed a final key and his voice came over the small boxes in the wall.

"Arrr!!! We're exploding!" came a high pitched version of Wilks's voice. The man could talk and scream at the same time. "Something's wrong! Help! Help! Out of control!" There were a few more screams, Wilks looked faintly embarrassed.

The voice continued, "Emergency! Market Five declaring an Emergency. A really big emergency! We're going to crash! No fuel, Market destroyed! We're going to dieee!!"

The recording stopped. We looked at him.

"Very professional, Wilks," I said.

Pulling us back on focus Magic asked, "You say the radio stopped working at that point. What happened to it?" The man asks slow and easy questions, he has a gift.

"Well," Wilks looked over our heads, his eyes took on that reliving the past gaze as he spoke his thoughts aloud, "let's see. I gave the call, we were being bucketed around a lot, my hand flopped about and hit some switches. Oh." He stopped. "I think I must have done something because when my hand crashed into the radio there was a flash and it just stopped. Whoops."

He had a sheepish grin on his face, a face I considered pushing in with some force. He says 'Whoops' after destroying our only chance of contacting help. How much of a doofus was this guy! What a dork! What a total and utter waste of space!

Magic interrupted my little internal tirade by making a good point. "Are these radios so fragile that they erupt inside when hit by a fist? I see no mark where your hand dented the panel. Surely it would take a considerable blow to impact the internal workings. I mean," he went on, "these things are meant to drop with the market over and over again without damage. Are you sure it was you who caused the malfunction?"

Wilks spun back to the radio and pulled out one of the side panels. He strapped a light to his head, turned it on and peered into the innards of the machine. Looking past him, I saw a tangle of wires and bits of exotic materials. I didn't have a clue. After a moment his hand reached into a toolbox, picked up something fiddly which he inserted into the now dead radio. Slowly he pulled out a lump of melted gunk. It was embedded with bits of wires and other weird stuff.

"Aha!" I exclaimed. Frost flowed from Wilks to me, the village idiot.

"This," he lectured, "is the fused remains of a critical component. Interestingly, it is also the piece that is most isolated from vibration damage. So," he went on as I stifled a yawn, "the question is, how did it become this rather unattractive lump of refuse?"

Take me now, God, I thought.

"I suspect the answer lies further in the bowels of this machine. I shall conduct a very detailed examination of the situation." He sat back with his all his old pomposity restored.

"If it wasn't an accident then it was deliberate," I stated. Enough of this tap dancing. "Hell's Teeth, we were sent out do die! "Someone in the Trader's section, or Security. Or both." I ticked off points on fingers. "He rigs the manifest to show all the Trade Goods are on the Market but quietly slips them into his own storage areas. Chief Trader finds out about it so he's killed. We are conveniently handy so we get pushed onto the Market Drop. He also throws in some other deadheads, probably evening a few scores. Gets rid of all the incompetents."

I looked at Wilks and smiled, he didn't quite get it yet. He was one of the incompetents. I felt better.

Magic had one final zinger, "But why choose us, the NightWatch? No one knows us well enough to want us dead." He looked hard at me. "Val," he accused, "what have you done?"

I stammered and blathered before he finally grinned, "Chayla, dear old Captain Chayla, our local devil. Works in Security and he hates you Val."

I groaned. It made sense.

At that point Teddy Boy signalled to us that he had arrived with his farmer. Magic told Wilks to keep going over the data and examine all the malfunctions and try to come up with some clues.

We left to meet our visitor. Just what we needed, another alien, angry at the Watch.

Coming downstairs we encountered two strangers, not one. Both were dressed in rough work clothes, one obviously older than the other. Teddy Boy was outside the entrance to the Control Room. The older stranger was keeping very still, large eyes gazing about at these newcomers to his domain. He was leaning on a thick staff and did not seem at all put out by being in the middle of a crashed spaceship.

The other, younger visitor was not as wrinkled but still had a very physical presence. Instead of standing and gawping like his elder he was moving slowly towards the area where our wounded and damaged personnel were gathered. This area had become the focus for Willem's medical treatments, it wasn't a pretty place. Lots of moaning, blood and the stink of fear and pain. Right Honourable and a few others were moving among the injured trying to give what relief they could.

Into this site of misery came the young alien. He was about the same physical size as me but had arms that could bend iron bars, his legs were of the sort that implied a great love of walking with heavy weights. Nothing was going to push this guy over in a hurry.

As Magic and I emerged this youngster bent over one of the injured and tentatively touched the crewman's arm. He showed a great gentleness, and I was struck by his sense of care and wonder. The young alien stood up and moved to another prone patient where he squatted and again reached out a gentle hand.

He stopped before making contact, paused and slowly straightened up. Standing in the middle of our sufferers, his face reflected anguish, he was desolated by their pain. Fair enough, so was I.

Chapter 28

Magic looked at the old guy and started speaking. He used low soothing tones like he was talking to a cow. The old guy certainly smelled like one. After a few phrases he stopped talking and held out his hand in a gesture of friendship, palm open, no weapons. The old guy looked at it and then held his hand up to shoulder height. He used it to point at our crashed Market and then turned to encompass all of the debris, mess, dirt and destruction we had caused. He turned in a circle to fully ram home the fact that we had really messed up his paddock. I sensed he was telling us he was not happy.

The younger guy was back on his knees trying to bandage a broken arm, he seemed to know what he was doing so Willem left him alone. Magic had picked up on the old guy's displeasure but he was at a loss what to do. I guess it's hard to say, "Sorry I smashed up your back yard but we're sort of dying here," when you can't speak the language.

I was watching for their reaction upon first seeing H'nuth, our resident devil. He was sitting on a pile of salvaged rods, observing us all as usual. They saw him and both stopped moving to stare at the big Tharl. He was worth a good stare. H'nuth, like all Tharls, was red of skin and big on muscle, he was well over six feet in height and built like a small mountain. He wore a weapons harness from which hung a blaster and a large knife. His clothes were our standard overall covering arms and legs except for one missing sleeve due to our recent crash. It allowed for the display of well-defined muscles. Ihe only had the one facial expression, stone cold neutral. I guessed he wasn't a big hit at parties.

The two natives dragged their eyes away and just continued as if H'nuth was another person, albeit large and ugly. I was impressed, not even a ripple of reaction. This was in stark contrast to how Chayla was greeted back on Earth. If the opportunity arose, I was going to ask one of them why they were not more excited by seeing a scary alien.

Eventually the old guy started speaking. Or screaming, I couldn't tell which. His voice rose and fell in an ululating wave. Our Translators Beads got in the occasional word, we could tell he was not a happy camper. All in all, he was telling us he was upset about the destruction to his pasture, plus the fact we seemed to have cleaned up some of his breeding herd. The translators really kicked along when he started swearing.

When he ran out of steam, which took a while and duly impressed most of us, he thumped his stick in the ground and turned around. Yelling a word of command to the younger guy he stumped off back the way he had come. The young guy glanced up at his elder but continued his ministrations. Without breaking stride, the old bloke yelled sharply again. The young alien quickly stood up and ran after his elder, the old guy not even looking back. Quite the charmer.

We all stood and watched them leave until Magic asked me to check on the troops while he went and had a think. We needed him to have a think, a good one.

I spent the rest of the afternoon walking and talking, no one else died but Willem was pretty upset about his lack of skill and the pain it was causing folks. I've seen him stick a six-foot spear into a guy's kidneys, twist it, pull out the messy end and never even blink. But he got cranky when stupidity caused unnecessary grief. He did say the young alien had done a reasonable job with the bandages. Must be all that practice with the old guy's animals.

We spent the night huddled around some fires. We'd moved what wounded we could into the shelter of the wreckage while Willem stayed with the more serious ones. I don't think he slept a lot that night. Wilks came and sat by me as we gaily sucked back as much water as we could hold. Nothing else to drink, unfortunately. Nothing to eat, either. Our foragers were out of luck but hoped they might be able to find something if given time. Unless we solved our little food problem whoever had sabotaged the ship would accomplish their goal.

Even if by some miracle we found food and survived we would not be returning to the ship. Given the tone of Wilks' last transmission they had probably written us off for dead. Couldn't blame them, really. This world was going to be our new home. Whoopee.

We had a few country boys in the Watch so we could get some food eventually but not enough to keep us all going indefinitely. I took great pleasure in telling all of this to Wilks who hadn't quite realized the precariousness of our situation. Living on the spaceship all of his life, he had never considered what might happen if the food ran out. No trouble with losing oxygen, or power, or being hit by a comet, but no food was never considered. Unheard of, at least by him. Poor old Wilks.

Needless to say, he was a delight to listen as he blathered to about our plight. The NightWatch characters who had observed our little exchange commented on my cynicism and lack of compassion. Meataxe thought I should have talked about cannibalism. He's a treasure.

Later, I saw Wilks walking around with a clipboard, making an almost continual flow of entries. I asked him what he was doing and he said, "Completing the paperwork, the captain asked me to ensure all of our records are up to date and all appropriate entries have been made. It's usually a task set aside for the mission commander but he felt I was more than qualified to do it. This leadership experience will be very good for my next performance interview. Do you think the captain would mind if I referred to myself as part of the leadership team? The records have to be signed by a member of management."

I think he was in denial. We weren't returning to any ship. I hesitated and decided against kicking him while he was down. "Nah, that should be fine, Wilks, you go ahead," I told him. He gave me thumbs up, no idea why, and strode off. The Man of the Hour.

Next morning, I sent someone to relieve an exhausted Willem and told Horse to take Wilks for a walk. Horse wouldn't wind him up like Meataxe or some others but he might give him a thump if he became too annoying. Good learning curve, I thought. Going in search of Magic I found him sitting on the dirt berm around the crash site gazing into the distance. I hoped it meant he was lost in the intricacies of some plan to get us out of here. I would have settled for just staying alive.

I plopped beside him, made my report and asked for any instructions. He never said a word, just raised his hand to shade his eyes, looked into the distance and asked, "Hungry, Val?"

Yes, I was hungry. He pointed, and in the morning glare a cart could be seen approaching our poor settlement. It was pulled by a small, hairy quadruped about the size of a goat with our young alien visitor from yesterday walking alongside it. As he got closer, I could see he was grinning and waving something in the air, something that had a very bread-like air about it.

We took him into the campsite where we distributed the food his cranky old relative had given him. Bit by bit our translators were acquiring his language so we were able to work out he was fascinated by us and had convinced his uncle – at least that's as close as the translators could put his relationship with old misery guts – to give us aid. He had dazzled the old boy with pictures of trade and what we might offer, us exotic folk from the stars.

He was a good kid and Right Honourable dubbed him Smiley because he had a mouthful of stunningly white teeth.

In the NightWatch, good teeth were not common, Meataxe used to have breath that could strip paint. All that changed after our medical inspections after our arrival on the ship. We all sat while one of their physicians stuck his hand into our mouths. So gross.

He banged and clattered around for a while, replacing some teeth and polishing the rest. When it was finished, we would walk around smiling at anyone who would notice. Dental hygiene, it's for me. I still had most of my original teeth and they were currently all clean and sparkly. But Smiley outshone us all. His teeth were pure white and matched his size, everything about this boy was big. Right Honourable said he should be able to eat an apple through a fishing net.

We all liked Smiley, his upbeat approach to life was infectious. He came each day with food and stayed all day. In the afternoon we let him select whatever we had that he thought his uncle would take in exchange for more supplies. Bit by bit we built up a small reserve of food as we traded away parts of the broken Market.

Magic said he had a plan but we needed to get to a larger settlement to kick it off. The only obstacle being we had no idea where such a settlement might be. Smiley was no help, we'd quizzed him through sign language and mime games and discovered he was confined to the farm. His uncle used him as free labour in return for food and board. This was fair enough since that was the normal situation in my home country. He was even lower on the food chain than the youngest son. he had no hope of bettering himself but didn't mind. He liked his family and the farm. One day his uncle would die and he would continue to serve the oldest son. They all liked Smiley and saw him as no threat, just a good worker. Both sides had a good deal.

Then we came along and Smiley started thinking about the big wide world.

It was while I was performing a particularly clever mime for Smiley to ask, "Where Big Village?" when Teddy Boy wandered over and suggested giving him one of the spare translator beads. We had a few of these, retrieved from the odd dead body, most of them still worked so we gave one to our country cousin to wear for the duration of his little visits. He returned it each evening when he left.

Chapter 29

After about a week his uncle came with him on his daily visit, he made the trip to see what Smiley found so interesting. All he saw was a dirty bunch of people with a poor attitude. We could understand him well enough although he, of course, had no idea what we were saying. I guess Smiley hadn't told him about our translators so we were able to easily pick up on his sarcastic asides to his nephew when he made scathing comments about my parentage, discussed the size of Meataxe's backside and commented on the rough head of Teddy Boy.

Smiley stood with a frozen grin on his face until we gave the old guy a translator. After a few words it must have occurred to him we knew what he was saying about us, especially me. "Wanna fight?" he asked, looking at me. The guy was only up to my shoulder with skinny little arms and legs, but no shortage of guts. I had no desire to see them.

"No, you're too big for me," I replied.

The old guy smiled and said, "Idiot." After that we all grinned and Magic started asking questions about the nearest big town. Still no luck. There was a village about a day's journey away but a few more questions revealed it was in no way a big town.

The old man made a suggestion. "Go to the mountain," he said.

He went on to tell us of a monastery nearby. It would have some residents who might be able to help us with directions to a large town, we could even hope for a map. The only downside was that it housed a community of priests. I twitched a little.

Magic turned to me, "Val," he said, "get over it. You stay here and look after things. I'll take a squad and go visiting."

"Don't worry, Captain Magic," interjected Smiley, "I'll stay and help." He turned and babbled to his uncle, way too fast for our translators to pick up. Whatever he said caused a reaction because his uncle's face turned bright blue as he built up a hefty head of steam. He was about to really let rip when Smiley flashed his big pearly whites and informed us all, "I'm joining the Watch!"

No worries, I thought.

Next morning, we mustered in front of the Market waiting for Magic to say a few words, Smiley arrived with a sack containing all of his worldly goods. He stood at the back fitting the translator in one ear while the rest of us shuffled into a crowd. The ship's people, those thrust upon at the last minute, attempted to form a proper drill company but the rest of us successfully destroyed any sense of order.

Eventually Magic emerged and climbed on to a handy pile of rubble. "This is how I see it," he began, "We're stuck here until we die." Not one for sugar coating a situation is our Charles There were a few murmurs and some of the newbies made loud noises of disbelief. He went on "It looks like we've upset someone back on the ship. I don't know how we did it and I don't know who we did it to, but someone up there wants us dead. The Market was deliberately sabotaged and was meant to crash on entry. All the doors and ports should have blown off. We've discovered damage to every hatch and panel. For some reason they didn't all blow and Wilks was able to bring us down safe. "

A heavily muscled and scarred crewman from the ship called out, "This is safe? We got no food and no hope. How do we know it wasn't just an accident? What if that idiot Wilks just pushed a few wrong buttons and that caused the whole problem? How do we know this was sabotage?" He got a few grunts of agreement from his henchmen, men of low brow and large smell.

"How do we know?" asked Magic. "Well," he went on, "what's our mission on this planet? What is the sole purpose of the Market?"

"Sell stuff," yelled one of the crowd. Others called out "Trade goods" and "Make money".

"Yes", agreed Magic, "to sell Trade Goods. Now don't you find it a little unusual that this Market, this place for doing business HAS NO TRADE GOODS ON BOARD?" This caused quite a bit of confusion and many side discussions broke out. The NightWatch guys tended to stay out of it because we trusted wherever Magic was heading. But the regular crew people were grappling with the concept of a Market with nothing to trade. Sort of turned their world upside down.

"Another thing," continued our leader. "The entire NightWatch is here but since we needed more personnel, we were joined by additional security guards. Quite frankly," he leaned forward a little as he finished off, "some of you new guys smell of troublemakers or incompetents. I don't think you were real volunteers. I think maybe you were encouraged to join us."

"Encouraged, hell," called out one of the bruisers, "I was told to join you lot or I'd face charges." Other similar comments emerged from the more gruesome members of the newcomer brigade. These were, to my mind, balanced by the rest of the unknowns who had a collective look of a washed out, insipid bunch of colourless no-hopers. Yes, I know I'm cruel. It's part of my charm.

Magic quieted them down and went on. "As I was saying, I believe we were supposed to die. We didn't. I intend to keep on living. Now, to do that we need information on where we are and the location of the nearest large city. Let's face it, we all need a city. None of us can carve a living out of the wilds, although I'm not too sure about Meataxe, he'd eat anything". This wasn't exactly a joke, I'd seen this character eat stuff which I'm sure was passed over by rats.

"Our current hosts," a nod to Smiley, "have been unable to assist us in directions and I feel we must leave soon before we exhaust the current generosity. I have been told of another settlement up in the hills, it seems to be some sort of monastery. Tomorrow I will leave for this site to find a map or a guide to a town. I will be taking some

NightWatch and many of you ship people with me. This will give us a chance to get to know each other. The rest will stay behind with Val and you will gut the Market for all transportable goods. We will need all the assets we can acquire. Val, you and I need to discuss weapons and who goes with me. Any questions?"

A few hands went up, mostly from the meek and mild bunch, none from the NightWatch. "Good", responded Magic, he ignored the raised hands, stepped down and suddenly the meeting was over. The questioners stood open mouthed, still with hands raised. I could see they felt betrayed. Life's tough. I joined Magic.

"Who will you take out of the newbies?" I asked. "We've got two main groups, the thugs and the wimps. You can have one or the other or a mixture."

"I intend to take most of the softer group in order to toughen them up." Magic was big on the beneficial effects of experience. "We'll add in a couple of the thugs just to spread them out a bit but I plan to leave most of the rough nuts here with you. Squads one and two from the NightWatch will accompany me. I can get by without the Corporals, the veterans will keep everyone in line so you keep Horse and Right Honourable, plus a few other reliables. Keep Meataxe, probably not a good choice for our first meeting with priests. That should give you a chance of maintaining order. We may need another corporal eventually, make L'On-li the number two in a squad where he can learn the ropes. Keep them all busy, work them hard, rip that Market apart and sweat them into a team."

Magic paused and watched me as I took in what he said. He was taking about forty people with him, since most of them were our guys, he was probably going to be all right. Still, I was worried about his plan to take so many unknown people and said so.

"Not to worry", he said, "I'll use Stomach and Large as my enforcers, that make you happy?"

Stomach and Large were big men, monsters, in fact. They looked about the same size, each with enormous guts hanging over their belts, arms the size of my head, thighs I just don't want to think about. Stomach was just fat, impossible to knock down because his brain was, I believed, too small to find in a fight. Large, on the other hand, also had a huge gut but it was mostly muscle. He used to be a stevedore on the docks where everything was loaded by hand. Individually they were quite imposing but together they were terrifying. Magic would have them stand around while he questioned a suspect, they cracked their knuckles and such like. Usually worked.

If these guys were going with him then all would be well. Which left just me and the majority of the hard cases. I planned on working them to exhaustion most days and then getting in some form of training. Keep them busy, keep them tired. At least, that was the idea.

Chapter 30

Next day they set off. Smiley had given Magic directions. The trail was quite visible from where we stood so we thought he should have no trouble. The plan was for him to return in a week when we would have a meeting to discuss our next move. Knowing Magic, I was sure he had already planned the next move but would allow us to think we all had a say in it.

Smiley wasn't keen on going with them and stayed with us. I gathered he didn't like the people who lived in the monastery, felt they were too judgmental. What, a priest making you feel bad? Tell me about it.

He stood beside me waving at the brave lads and lasses as they trudged off. I could tell the space dwellers were going to do it tough, some of them had very poor co-ordination even for a walk, tripping over roots and knocking themselves against branches. Creatures of the wild, that's us.

I turned back to my depleted command. About thirty faces gazed at me. I could feel a few evaluating my leadership skills. None of the Watch would be against me but I could see old Scarface muttering to some of his cronies out of the corner of his mouth. The cronies chuckled. I walked over.

"Hey, Gorgeous George, take yourself and your friends into the market and start stripping out everything not bolted down. Then break the rest off and bring it out, too. Teddy Boy, you're in charge." Walking away I could feel Scarface building up to a challenge, there was the sound of movement.

Later Meataxe told me Teddy Boy just walked up to Scarface and stood right in front of him, nose to nose. Teddy Boy didn't look threatening, he didn't even have a visible weapon. He didn't do much of anything except stand there looking calmly into Scarface's eyes. No threat, he just stayed very, very still. It's a great technique, too many people feel they have to embellish it with a tough guy attitude or talk. Teddy Boy does it just right. Scarface moved off.

I was going to have to sort that one out before too long.

We spent the next three days methodically stripping every piece of metal out of the Market and organizing it into portable bundles. There was an abundance of rods. Predominantly light, strong pieces about five foot long but a bunch of smaller sections as well. Looking at them gave me an idea for training so once we hit the fourth day and there wasn't much left for us to do in terms of destruction, I set up my little plan.

"Oh, please, no", groaned Right Honourable, "Not quarterstaffs! I hate the stupid things."

"Yes, quarterstaffs, "I replied. "Tool of the underprivileged. Weapon of the masses. The original blunt instrument and a first class training tool. And you, Right Honourable, get to lead the instruction."

He picked up a suitable length of rod and twirled it about effortlessly. "Why me?" he asked. Good question. I'd given this some thought, a new experience for me. The haughty attitude of Right Honourable would send the thugs around the bend. Then, when one snapped, we could deal with it. Get it out in the open so to speak, that's what I told him. I really hoped it worked.

H'nuth sat watching us with his bandaged arm. I had seen him around the campsite from time to time, looking, never talking to anyone. It was unnerving to come around a corner and see him standing there, watching. He was in for a treat now, I thought.

The men and women picked up their chosen bits of metal and began twirling them about. The untrained crewmen tried to copy the Watch in their warmup routine and, one by one, thumped themselves on legs and head. Much swearing and cursing was had by the team, all good fun. Eventually Right Honourable strolled out to the front and began drawling out basic drill movements. Meataxe did the spins and twirls with a grace and ease which took on the air of showing off. Doing his best to upset the spacers.

After a couple of hours of staff work Right Honourable took us all on a run, several laps around our campsite, and then he produced a bundle of rags which he tied up into a ball. The NightWatch cheered up immensely as they began a rousing game of village football, all running, kicking and good-natured abuse. Village football consists in two teams, usually a whole village each, trying to carry, kick or throw a ball across the opponent's line. No real rules, weapons are frowned upon. It's hard, fast and rough and will always end up with bruises and possibly broken bones. The spacers looked on in amazement and gradually got drawn into the magic of just playing. Even Wilks ran around trying to catch the ball, kicking, missing, falling over and making an absolute goose of himself. I was beginning to like the little twerp.

Eventually all but Scarface and about eight of his ugliest mates were the only ones not playing. They deliberately stood off to one side and sneered at the children playing games.

We ran out of steam and struggled back to the campsite where we collapsed after drinking copious amounts of water. After half an hour of deep panting we began to be able to think rationally so I gave the signal to Right Honourable. He mouthed some decent obscenities at me, then called the troops back to quarterstaff training. By the close of day all of the men and women were exhausted, they lay on the ground and panted. We ate and fell asleep, a good day's work.

Next morning, we started again. By mid morning the complaints coming from Scarface and his group were beginning to lose their magical charm and become real pains in the neck. After the break they stayed on the ground and refused to return to the exercises. Everyone was watching to see how it unfolded, this was it, I thought, the moment of testing.

I stood up and wandered over to where Scarface sat, surrounded by his cronies. Standing there, looking down at him I smiled and greeted them all with a cheerful hello.

"Ready to get back to it then, lads?" I asked. Dead casual, I was.

"We're not goin' back to those stupid exercises." Scarface slowly stood up, his followers joining him. All of them standing and menacing little old me. The rest of the newcomers were on the exercise field, the regular members of the Watch stayed wherever they happened to be, sitting, standing, or just lying on the ground. They weren't too worried. I suppose they thought I could handle it. I hoped they were right.

I squatted down and pulled a blade of grass out of the ground. Putting it in my mouth I said, "Well, you see, that could be a problem. Not to me, no, I really couldn't care less what you do, what with you being so ugly and all." I couldn't help myself. "But, you see, I've delegated the authority for this training to one of the Watch and," I waved Right Honourable over, "I expect my men to do as they're told."

I stood up and turned my back on Scarface and began to walk away. Over my shoulder I said, "Do your job, Right Honourable."

"You heard our commander," he began, "back to work." No one moved, I turned and watched. Right Honourable went on, "Ahh, I see." He pointed at Scarface, "I am giving you a direct instruction, guardsman, move yourself, you horrible little man."

Scarface crossed massive arms across his chest, drew himself up to his full height and said, "We're leaving. We'll take a share of the supplies and make our own way in this godforsaken world. You have no authority over us." He nodded his head at some of his followers and they took a step towards the open doorway of the Market.

"Actually, I do," replied Right Honourable, placing himself between Scarface and the Market. "You were seconded to the Watch. You were placed here as members of our command. Magic left Val in charge and he has delegated authority to me, I intend to carry out his orders because we, in the Watch, know the importance of discipline and obedience."

This was a bit hard to swallow but I kept quiet, so did the rest of the Watch. Hello, I thought to myself, what's happening to us. We suddenly have long established customs about discipline and obedience? What's next, a work ethic? And Magic telling everyone we just get on with the job? Not the old Watch, that's for sure.

But maybe we weren't the old Night Watch anymore. Maybe we were becoming something different. Something better. We were becoming a variation, the NightWatch.

Right Honourable continued, "You men are to remain motionless." To Scarface he said, "You are a troublemaker. I do not like troublemakers. My instruction to you consists in the direct order to immediately and rapidly comport yourself in such a manner as to lend credence and respect to appropriate authority. To that end you will now move to the site heretofore used as a training field and prepare yourself for the next set of orders. Failure to carry out my instructions will carry some inevitable consequences."

The group of rebels were trying hard to follow what Right Honourable was saying, I had to go through his words a few times in my head to pick up the gist of it. He was a bit of a menace when he really got going. Scarface unfolded his arms and drew a huge knife, probably from a sheath behind his back. He lowered himself into a fighting crouch and told Right Honourable, quite colourfully, that he could go away and perform obscene acts with his mother.

"Mmm, how very articulate you are. Now, I feel I must warn you," responded Right Honourable, "if you attack me with that knife, I will kill you." This caused a bit of a sensation amongst all the non-Night Watch. Threats to kill someone should be yelled or screamed, not just mentioned in the same tone as discussing the weather.

Scarface weaved his way forward, knife making little patterns in the air. Right Honourable glanced at me and I nodded. "Right then," he said, "let's go." Out of the corner of my eye I could see H'nuth taking it all in, he hadn't jumped in with advice or countermanded my orders.

It's lonely at the top.

Chapter 31

A knife fight is a very particular sort of dance. Most people are not keen on knives because the sense of being cut is so very real. A man will handle being shot or hit with a blunt object, but the thought of having one's flesh sliced open and peeling away gives most people the heebie-jeebies. The major part of a knife fight is the fear, the very reasonable fear, of being cut. Good knife fighters know this and work on maximizing that fear in their opponent.

Scarface glided forward, weaving the point of his blade around so Right Honourable would be aware of exactly what was in store for his flesh. He even embellished it a little by muttering little phrases like, "slice you good...cut your gut and watch your stomach leak .... Slash your pretty face." Stuff like that.

I do not like knife fights.

The thug circled around, making a few tentative cuts and slashes. Right Honourable dodged and weaved but did not have the fluidity of his aggressor. He was unarmed. I kept my face blank and hoped I'd figured this right. My stomach was knotting and my backside clenching.

After a few more fakes and feints Scarface made a decent low stab. Right Honourable did the unexpected, he stepped towards the blow. He extended his left leg towards the blade while crossing his arms at the wrist. He thrust these crossed arms towards the knife hand, trapping it. He was now in control of the blade, unfortunately the blade had moved far enough to reach his outstretched leg and a wide cut opened on the outside of his thigh. The knife did not lodge in the leg. Blood gushed out, it looked quite messy.

Right Honourable swivelled his hands, now grasping Scarface's extended knife arm by the wrist. He hadn't moved his left leg at all, the blood flowed freely into his boot. This is the thing to do in a bad fight, accept the cut and hope it's not a crippling blow. Scarface was taken by surprise, expecting his opponent to automatically retreat from the stab. For a heartbeat he was still. Most people when they are cut, pull back. It's the normal reaction. It isn't normal to step into the blade. It isn't normal to leave your leg all bloody and messy.

It quite took Scarface by surprise.

Right Honourable pushed his wrists out to the left, taking the knife arm with them which removed the blade from my team mate's leg. More blood. At the same time, he stepped onto his left foot and brought his right knee into Scarface's groin. There was a little moan of pain from the rebel's lips but he kept his grip on the knife. Right Honourable continued the move, stepping behind Scarface while twisting his knife arm behind his back. The human arm is not made to bend this way. There was a very audible snap as his arm popped out of the shoulder joint. He dropped the knife.

Still keeping a grip on the damaged arm, Right Honourable used it as a lever to shove his opponent to the ground where he lay on his back, moaning with pain. That arm would be putting him in a world of hurt.

There we all stopped. Right Honourable stood over his fallen opponent, breathing heavily, droplets of sweat trickling off his chin. Blood ran down his slashed leg as he straightened up and drew in huge lungfuls of air. Scarface lay on the ground making little mewling noises, his arm bent at a very wrong angle. The knife lay ignored on the ground near his head.

I was watching the rest of Scarface's cronies, as were Meataxe and Teddy Boy. There was some murmuring, one stood up but none moved to interfere. To them it looked like the fight was over but I knew it wasn't. Right Honourable had asked me how far to take the fight. With my nod, I had instructed him to go all the way. Bad men do not go into a dangerous situation like a knife fight and then shake hands and make up, I wanted everyone to see Right Honourable in his true light. He is a bad, bad man.

The tall Watchman bent down, retrieved the knife and knelt over Scarface's prone body. He grabbed the fallen man's hair with his left hand and tilted his chin back exposing the throat. I could see Scarface's eyes, wide with panic. Some of the rebel crew made questioning noises over this, wondering what was going on. After all, the point had been made, to them it was the normal way of establishing the pecking order. Big fight, loser eventually recovers and acknowledges all commands of the victor.

Right Honourable pushed the blade under the man's chin, up into his brain. Scarface's body shuddered, his legs twitched, his bowels loosened. He died. There was a dreadful stink.

Willem moved over to Right Honourable as he knelt beside the corpse and started to treat his wound. From his kneeling position the victorious Watchman spoke to the remaining rebels, "I am quite prepared to kill each of you."

My turn. I stood up, "Meataxe, get the drills going again. Pairs this time, I want one veteran NightWatch against one of the newcomers." I looked over at the shocked rebels, making direct eye contact with each of them. "Any man who draws a weapon on us outside of a drill is acknowledging they want to fight. We do not fight pretty. Now get over there."

A few moved over immediately then the rest slouched across, I kept my stone face until the drills started. Willem took Right Honourable off to our makeshift medical area for treatment, I'd get a report on the damage later. I hoped it wasn't too bad.

Looking over at the drills I saw Wilks with a newer NightWatch member, both looking totally hopeless. I called them over. What a surprise, the guardsman was my old comrade, L'On-li, from the stakeout in the supply room. "Lonely!" I exclaimed. "Good to see you again! Got a job for you two." They both looked at me warily, expecting some awful task. Putting them out of their misery I said, "Bury the body."

Wilks said, "I feel sick! Look at all that blood. No, I'm a technician, not a guard. I don't really come under your authority. The regulations are very clear on the chain of command. You need written authorization for me to leave my duties in the Market. I'm not going near that mess." He indicated the body with one shaky hand.

"Is that so?" I asked. "What about you, Lonely, any qualms about following a direct order?" My voice was low and calm, I'd been down this road before.

Lonely stared at me, his face didn't look anywhere near as young as when we first met. Old eyes stared back into mine, "No problem. I'll stick him in the ground." He grabbed the fallen man's arm and began to drag him out of the campsite.

"Well, Wilks," I began, quite cheerfully. "It's just you and me now. Tell you what, you run along and help the kid and I'll only be mildly cross with you. Disobey me again and you'll see me upset. Now just between you and me, you may want to think about your future. Remember, I'm the man in charge now." I smiled at him, dropped my voice and put an arm around his shoulder in a brotherly embrace, "What do you think? Follow orders, or what? I've got another knife here somewhere."

My voice was still very calm, even looking at him I had not resorted to any mean glares but my eyes give me away. I was ready to beat the living daylights out of him then and there, no problem, no anxiety, no worries. He saw it, paled a little and scurried after Lonely.

They scraped out a deep hole, rolled the body in and covered it with dirt and rocks. Wilks only threw up twice but he dry retched a lot as he shovelled. Even Lonely was running out of patience with our technician. Finished, they reported back to me and just stood, not asking to return to the group, just waiting. I realized that one or both wanted to say something to me.

"What's on your mind, fellas?" I asked. Polite.

"What happened here?" asked Lonely. He gestured behind him at the campsite, the grave, the fight area and even waved at where the rest of the men and women were still drilling. His eyes looked like they were ready for the next bit of growing up, Wilks's didn't but, hey, life's tough.

"What did you see?" I asked, very softly.

Lonely turned his head from side to side and blurted out, "I saw Right Honourable kill a man. In cold blood. He didn't have to. He'd already won the fight."

I took a breath, "You saw Right Honourable doing his job, boy. You're in the Watch now, this is what we do."

"I thought you were just security guards. But each time I'm with you someone dies. Dies violently." Poor kid was looking confused now, he wasn't crying, he wasn't even close but I could see he was hurting.

"Look, Lonely, a guard is alone. A guard never has any friends in the population because everyone thinks we are after THEM. On patrol we are always outnumbered. Always. Do you think it's reasonable that a force of thirty men could police a population of thirty thousand? In the City we patrolled the worst areas of the city and did it in the bad guys' hunting time - the night. How do you suppose we did that?" He stared at me. I think he followed my line of reasoning but I wasn't sure.

Wilks had no idea, "You can't just kill people," he murmured, sulky and resentful. He plopped himself on the ground.

Without looking down I said, "Shut up, Wilks".

I kept eye contact with Lonely, there was hope for him, I thought. "When we get into trouble, and that's regularly, we have no one to depend on except each other. There are never any reinforcements ready to bail us out. We either get out of it ourselves or we die. Before the Man in Black and Magic came along the average life expectancy of a guardsman was two years. In the NightWatch it was two months. After Magic arrived, we only lost a handful of men in three years, and they were all novices. Now, why do you suppose things changed?"

He was thinking, I'll give him that. "Better training?" he ventured.

"That's partly true, but not the sort of training you mean." I gestured over to where the rest of the squad was having a break. "That sort of training is essential. You have to know how to fight. BUT," I said, "Magic showed us that when we fight we fight to the end. We don't fight fair, we don't fight with honour or decency, and we don't fight pretty. We fight with brutality. When we fight, we spill blood and guts, we make sure screams, pain and suffering happens around us. We mess up the streets and cause utter bloody havoc. No one wants to see us get mad because everybody suffers. You get that, Lonely." I shut up and looked at him.

He stared at me for a while, tilted his head back to look at the sky. We all stood there very quietly for a while and then Wilks, from the ground, commented in a thick voice, "But he was already beaten. You'd had your blood and pain. Why go that final step and take a life?"

"Do you know why, Lonely?" I asked the young guardsman.

He dropped his eyes to gaze at the top of Wilks's head. "Because he was a threat. He instigated a minor revolt by the way he acted and by the way he encouraged everyone around him to act. We couldn't just lock him up. His arm would have healed and he would have been the focus of a group of bitter, resentful people. And he pulled a knife on Right Honourable."

"You don't know what might have happened in the future!" said Wilks. "You can't predict how Scarface would have acted after the fight! He might have changed. He might have smartened up and ... and..." He rose up to face Lonely, letting his anguish flood over the young man. Wilks was almost incoherent while Lonely stood like a tree in a storm.

"There is no way that you could predict his future behaviour!!" Wilks screamed.

"We can now," replied Lonely, "he's dead."

Chapter 32

Right Honourable was not wounded too badly. Smiley seemed to know which leaves and gunk to put on cuts and abrasions. He made up a foul smelling poultice for the leg. Although we were aliens it seemed worth a try and Right Honourable felt he would be able to move around after a day's rest. With him in the medical area were a few more wounded, all of whom could travel for short distances. The rest of our injured had either recovered or died. Smiley was not happy with us over the fight, I don't think he approved of violence. Was he with the wrong group or what?

In the early afternoon Magic returned to camp with a wagon and a half dozen strangers.

Priests. Oh, yay.

I filled Magic in on the events of the last few days, he asked about Right Honourable and his ability to travel. We went over to see the wounded man. He was sitting on a makeshift chair reading some poetry and looked the image of a wan and colourless youth, all floppiness and languid hands. Bored poet seeking meaning in the world. He is such a liar, the man is a drunk and a gambler. He assured Magic he could travel and although he treated me with feigned indifference, he made sure our commander was well aware of his true status.

As we were leaving Magic told me to get everyone ready for travel the next day, there was a village about eight hours travel from our campsite and he wanted us there by the next night. We would leave as early as possible in the morning. I called the squad leaders together and gave instructions. I wanted four squads plus a command squad.

Right Honourable, as Senior Corporal, would be with squad 1. I also gave him all of the remaining rebels and bunch of our more thuggish veterans. If the rebels hadn't learned their lesson by now then the rest of the squad would sort them out. Or kill them.

Squad 2 would be commanded by Horse. We filled the squad up only with veteran NightWatch. This would be my 'go to' squad.

Willem would be in charge of the wounded as well as squad 3, I attached Smiley to him. Smiley seemed to have some sort of gift with healing and he wasn't afraid of getting in my face if he thought someone needed more treatment. I didn't like it much but it was certainly effective, made him a good advocate for healing. Willem had a slightly gentler touch than me when it came to dealing with the troops so he could probably give Smiley a few tips on surviving my meetings.

I also attached Lonely to squad 3 and padded it out with the more competent newcomers, the ones who looked like they might be able to make it with just the normal routine of training and abuse. Lonely would assist Willem and hopefully pick up some leadership clues. After a short chat with Willem, I left him to take on the task of training Lonely as a potential squad commander.

Stomach and Large formed a command group with Magic and myself. They were big enough for someone to be able to spot in case a decision had to be made. After some thought I stuck Wilks and H'nuth with us, couldn't think what else to do with them. Teddy Boy tagged along to look after Magic.

That left a bunch of useless troopers. These were the ones who had successfully dropped their weapons every training session, tripped over their own feet on the hike with Magic and generally had trouble finding their backside with both hands. I could see why we got them from the rest of the ship's company. As scattered individuals they would have been a real nuisance and a source of continual frustration. Putting them all in one group brought them into their own success story as walking disasters. This squad would be a nightmare to run and would need the right person as leader.

Meataxe was just the man. He had all the compassion of a dead sheep and would keep them in line purely by sense of awe at his personal habits. These guys became squad 4.

We'd never had four squads before or even a command group, I was looking forward to seeing what a stuff up I could make of this dog's breakfast. After telling the squad leaders to have everyone ready to move out early next morning I went to find Magic.

I was missing something, I had a tingle in my thief-taker muscle, a sense of unfulfilled patterns. I stopped enroute to where Magic had a command tent and scanned the area, what was it? People were clustered in groups, talking, cooking. Smiley and Willem moved through the wounded. All seemed normal as ever. But I wasn't being watched. It hit me, where was H'nuth? He was always somewhere, watching us, and I generally found him watching me. No pressure on my command decisions, I liked working under a microscope.

Where was our alien?

I did a quick circuit and found drag marks leading into a wood, these marks were made by something heavy, possibly a Tharl's boot heels. I called some nearby guardsmen over to me and sent off messages before following the tracks at a run. Entering a small clearing revealed a sad tableau, H'nuth was unconscious, arms bound and head back exposing a very vulnerable neck. Kneeling beside him, head down and facing his bound victim was Santini.

I worked it all out in those few steps. Santini. The man who had used the spare horse to ride to the Tribunal and inform them of Chayla's existence. The man who had led Father Julius to the Theatre. He had never tried to help us when we were trapped in the cells of the Inquisition. Instead he had again found the Archbishop's men and led them to us.

Santini, poor trapped man, trapped by a belief that unbelievers and demons should be killed. Rocking back and forth over H'nuth's exposed neck, the throat ready for a knife. The knife was on the ground, I had arrived in time to see Santini hold it above H'nuth's neck, shudder and throw the blade away. Now he sobbed, begged forgiveness from God for not executing the demon.

Magic arrived as H'nuth's eyes opened. Santini looked at his captive and said, "I'm sorry." He stood up and raised his arms to the heavens and repeated, "I'm sorry."

Archbishop Dominic had gone too far when he sought to kill women and children. Santini was a god-fearing man but he knew it was not right to murder innocents, to kill the helpless. This was Santini's last attempt to follow a ruthless stricture, and he failed. He failed to kill. He rejected the thinking which said his God sought the death of someone just for being who they are.

Santini's God believed in love and tolerance and, in the end, so did Santini.

Magic had some of the veterans, his friends, take him away. He needed is friends now. He needed us and we would not leave him behind. I untied H'nuth, looking for a reaction but again found none. No anger, no resentment. He moved his good arm and legs to restore the circulation, massaged a new lump on his head and returned to the campsite to do some more watching.

I made a judgement, no consequences for Santini. The past was done, finished. In a fight we helped each other and Santini needed our help as he fought his doubts, his questions and his guilt. He was one of us again and we would not leave him alone.

I found Magic talking to Smiley, figured they were talking about me because Smiley gave me one of those 'here he is now' looks and stopped talking.

I had great faith in Magic and he didn't let me down, he came right out and said, "Val, Smiley's been giving me his opinions about the wounded and a few other matters. I'd like your response on them. He feels the wounded need more time to recover, the journey would slow their healing. There is also some suggestion that you have little regard for the total welfare of some of the men, and especially the women, under your care. Has Smiley spoken to you of these issues?"

"The wounded will definitely suffer on the journey." I began, Smiley looked a bit surprised at my admission so I went on, "But they won't die. We have to get out of here and we have to leave soon."

Magic turned to Smiley, "Will any of the wounded die during a one-day march?" he asked.

Smiley stood quietly for a while before replying, "None will die but you are causing them suffering, there is never a need for senseless pain or cruelty." Gutsy guy, this. I was impressed by the way he stood up to me and said his piece. For all he knew I might have been a vindictive sort who would make his future life a misery. But I'm all sweetness and light.

"We're going to have to disagree on that one, Smiley," I said. "Sometimes there is a need of pain, and tomorrow is going to be one of them. You care for them in your way and I'll do it mine. As for cruelty, perhaps you better explain that."

"You showed no emotion when that scarred man was killed. I saw no evidence his death, or the fight, caused you any distress. I am still unsure why he was killed, it seemed so unnecessary. There must be other ways of taking the men forward without resorting to such extremes of callousness, brutality and what I believe to be cruelty."

Sweat formed on his upper lip, perhaps he was anxious over my reaction. I must admit I wanted to flatten the sanctimonious fool but I knew Magic was doing all this for a purpose. I needed to learn how to handle this level of confrontation without sticking a sword in someone's guts. He's such a peach, is our Charles.

"Scarface made his own choices, Smiley." I said. "He started the fight. And he pulled the knife. I have no intention of discussing the rightness or wrongness of it with you or any other man here except my captain. As for my reactions, they are my business," I continued.

"I'm not going to bleat and whine over suffering or death I cause. If I didn't think it was right, I wouldn't do it."

I turned to Magic, "Any time you think I'm not doing my job just let me know and I'll step down. With great pleasure."

Magic looked from me to Smiley and asked, "Had a fair hearing, Smiley?"

Smiley stared at me for a while and then said to Magic, "I trust you, captain." He turned to me and looked at my stone face. "But you're a hard man, Valentine, mean and ruthless."

I wasn't interested in his opinion of me, but I sensed saying this out loud would not be a good thing. Besides, I am so a nice guy.

When in doubt, change the subject, so I asked, "What's with the priests, Magic?" Smiley left us and returned to his patients.

Chapter 33

"We've got a job, Val. Escort duty, we're taking the clergy and a wagon to the nearest big city."

"That's great, Magic, really happy for you," I said, sarcasm dripping from every word. I don't think he noticed. "Why do they need an escort? Especially a big one like us. Do the farmers get a bit uppity sometimes?"

"It seems there is a bandit group operating in the area, nasty pieces of work." Magic kept talking, "The monastery was just tossing up if they should send to the capital for help when, hello, here comes the NightWatch. So, I got us the job, in return they'll feed us a bit and show us the way."

"You're kidding me, right? Who, in their right mind, would hire us? We're not exactly locals." I felt this was a compelling argument.

He grinned at me, "I may have glossed over a few of the pertinent facts to our new employers. I may have even extolled our prowess as guards. Let it go, Val. We're on a good thing here, come and meet our employer." We wandered over to the wagon, this gave me a good chance to study these characters up close.

The leader wore one of our spare translators, I didn't notice anyone else with them and later Magic explained he only gave out one, didn't want to be too free and easy with our gear. The leader's name translated as Father Dexus. He didn't introduce us to the rest of his band but when I looked them over I had a hard time believing they were in holy orders. The priests I used to hang around with were generally dressed in rough clothes or utter finery. These guys wore armour. The two biggest had back and breastplates, arm and leg armour as well as helmets. They both carried very decent looking swords as well as something that looked like a throwing axe. Two others had more pliable leather armour, all black. They sported small swords with handles of other weapons peeking out of various gaps in their harness. I decided not to upset these guys.

The last fellow was the runt of the litter, he seemed to be low man on the totem pole. He had a small buckler and sword but mainly just hung around Father Dexus as a flunky. He reeked of subservience.

Father Dexus was a real piece of work. He didn't smile, he barely spoke. As we approached the wagon he stood up and gave me the once over. I think I failed. Magic introduced me as his second-in-command, Dexus looked disappointed. I smiled and shuffled my feet. He made me feel like a naughty schoolboy. Priests, eh? What are you gonna do?

The grown-ups chatted for a while, eventually I drifted away to check on preparations for the next day. All seemed well so I turned in for the night. Things were going so well.

Next day Magic designated as our Sabbath, we gathered and he read from one of the Bibles we had brought with us, a beautiful translation which had been sponsored by the English King James. Then he gave a sermon on the prodigal son and said we were a bit like him, we had to find our way home. We finished with Santini leading us in a couple of hymns, all good stuff.

Wilks, Smiley and the new recruits joined us, Magic decreed that everyone in the Watch attend Sunday Service. We might have lost access to our priest when we joined the spaceship but we didn't lose our faith. It gives me something to hold. I guess Smiley was really rocked, he just stood there with eyes bugging out. He loved the prodigal son story, maybe identifying with the lost soul.

Then we set out. The two agile priests were scouts and guides, the two heavy guys just strode beside their wagon and made sure we all kept our distance from the Holy Artefacts. The rest of us humped a great load of stuff from the Market, anything that could conceivably be of use. Even Magic carried a load, he believed in leadership by example which really got up my nose. It meant I had to lug a bunch of junk on my shoulders. So much for rank having privileges.

The only exception was a duty squad who would be our roving guards for the journey. Each squad would rotate through this role, swapping loads and responsibilities. All except for our pig-headed leader who probably wouldn't bother to take a turn having no pack, he would just do it all. That meant I had to do the same. Love that man.

We were three hours into our journey with Willem's squad on guard duty when we met the bandits.

Bandits! What a joke.

We had finished a rest break and reorganised roles so Horse's squad was fresh as Duty Squad. The site we had chosen for the stop was on a low hill, just off the main track. The road continued on down the hill and disappeared into a forest. This place screamed ambush to the lads so we decided to rest and think about things before sticking our heads in the noose. Father Dexus told stories about bandits appearing by magic, destroying whatever was their target then vanishing into the wilderness. Sounded spooky.

Smiley didn't have a lot to add, mainly because he just hated being around the priests. Father Dexus seemed to bring out the worst in our newest recruit. He was rude and uncooperative whenever they were in contact. During the break I decided to investigate a bit further so I dragged him off to help me visit the wounded.

While we examined Right Honourable's slashed leg I asked Smiley why he was such a pig-ignorant, selfish, ill-mannered lout with Dexus. To his credit he got all embarrassed and apologised. It seems that, in his youth, Smiley asked his local priest, not Dexus, a few questions about their religion. Nothing unusual in that, sooner or later everyone must come to terms with his or her own belief. Or lack of it.

Well, it seems Smiley was ostracised by his community on the priest's instigation. No one was allowed to talk to him until he begged forgiveness for his doubts and accepted the authority of the priest without question. Sounded like a real sweetheart, full of love and compassion. Smiley's religion didn't have just the one God like us, they had about seven and none of them were big on compassion. They were, however, very definite about obeying authority. This priest took those precepts to heart when he laid into our boy.

My observation of Smiley's character led me to think he does not take a lot of backward steps. The way he stood up to me in front of Magic took guts so I could imagine him just hammering question after question at this poor little village priest whose only response was to yell, "OBEY ME OR ELSE!" I don't think he and Smiley ever really hit it off after those conversations.

We had a recruit who distrusted religion, priests and the concept of unthinking obedience. He would have fitted nicely in the cells of Archbishop Dominic.

Having sorted all this out I indicated to Smiley he needed to show respect and courtesy to others, especially our employers. I further pointed out that I would take a dim view of any continuing displays of rudeness on his behalf and made my point all the clearer by talking about honour, integrity and that sort of stuff. By the time I had finished he was looking at the ground, shuffling his feet and carrying on like an embarrassed teenager. He swore he would mend his ways. I love it when my heart-to-heart talks have that sort of effect, makes me believe in the essential goodness of human nature. Other people's nature, not mine.

Magic thought there might be something unpleasant waiting for us in the forest. He discounted all the tales of suddenly appearing and disappearing villains and just assumed they were the typical murderous types who leave no one alive. That tends to slow the population down a little. He asked Dexus to send his two scouts into the wood for a look around and pulled the rest of us back over the reverse slope of the hill where we sat and waited.

The scouts returned to tell us of an overturned wagon blocking the road inside the forest. There was no one alive in sight but they did see a body carrying a few arrows lying near the front seat. Smiley wanted to rush in and check for any wounded, a natural desire and one we felt would get us killed. The scouts also told of smelling horses nearby – at least their equivalent of horses. These guys were good.

It seemed to be a trap, anyone going into the forest would see the wreck, stop and then be attacked. We couldn't go around the forest, it was too big. So, we had to take the road. Given we were a big party carrying many weapons, there was a chance we would be seen to be too much of a challenge and allowed to pass unharmed. After all, there were more than seventy of us.

Admittedly, when I cast my eyes over the gang, they did not look very intimidating. The newbies were all moaning about walking so far. The extra gear we carried made us look like pack animals. I would have bet a stiff wind could have knocked us down. If we took the risk and were ambushed, we would be easy meat.

Magic gathered his squad leaders and we had a yarn, eventually coming up with a plan which might let most of us live. He climbed onto the cart and told everyone about the wagon and about our chances of being attacked. "To survive we must invite attack and then fight it off. I am confident we can look useless, but to survive the attack will mean going into the forest with your head ready. Fight to win, fight to protect the person beside you. Do not run, do not let others down. You new people will be scared, that's alright, I will be scared. But fight, just keep hitting until there is no-one left to hit. We will lose some people."

He finished with a rousing call to arms, "Life is hard."

Chapter 34

We rearranged our marching order after dumping the packs with the wounded on the reverse slope. If we survived, we could come back and get them. Willem went into the forest first with his squad, mostly NightWatch. Even among our veteran comrades I knew we had some dead weight for this sort of a fight.

We're city people, not soldiers. We can take on a mob, a rabble, even an armed gang. We're particularly good at unarmed civilians. Fortunately, we would not be met by a disciplined army, we would be met by thugs and killers. We could handle thugs and killers. After all, that's what we were. On a good day.

Slowly, we inched along the path until we got to the wagon. The females in our party, about twenty of them, had pulled their hair out and unbuttoned blouses until they looked all harmless and inviting. We had them in the centre with the artefact wagon and the rest of us front and rear. It didn't take much for our group to resemble a small merchant caravan, complete with hangers-on, important traders and a few guards.

I was watching the back path with Stomach and Large so I missed the front ambush. But I was perfectly positioned to see the riders who hit us from behind.

They had been hiding well out of sight and came charging through the trees to meet the path some distance behind us. There they reformed into a cohesive bunch and charged down the path towards our little band of heroes, and me. They were riding on things with four legs and big teeth. They made a lot of noise, screaming like something out of hell. I guess that was how they unnerved their victims, I've done it myself, a blood curdling scream sometimes makes your opponent freeze for a moment or just run away. It probably works well on farmers and normal travellers. Didn't worry us a lot.

Stomach and Large carried halberds, useless in close confines but nobody liked to argue with these guys over their choice of weapon. So, down the path came this bunch of ratbags, screaming and hollering. Stomach and Large readied their weapons, I drew my sword and Wilks wet his pants. He didn't run away but I could tell he was scared.

Large swung his weapon in an arc that smacked into the right-hand rider's head, pushing him off the horse and neatly into the lap of the centre rider. He hung there for a second, scrabbling for a grip before sliding beneath all the various flying hooves. The centre rider was distracted by this and didn't get himself under control until he found my sword busily chopping off his leg. He lost all interest after that.

Stomach was too lazy to swing his pole arm. He just lowered it into the chest of the left hand animal and ground the butt. The rider couldn't stop in time and impaled his mount neatly onto the upthrust weapon while he sailed over all our heads. He was greeted by the ladies and a whole lot of sharp things.

Large had reversed his weapon and lunged forward with the lance head on the other end. This pierced another rider's shoulder, Large just left it there. The weight dragged the screaming man to the ground. All around me was confusion, sweat and fear.

A close fight like this is hard to follow, it's generally just flashes, fleeting impressions. I saw a face shatter under a quarterstaff. My sword blocked a downward slash from a rider before I pushed his foot out of the stirrup and heaved him out of the saddle. His mount stamped and trod on something soft. Wilks was screaming with fear, I saw Large with a fixed grimace on his face as he hacked and slashed. Stomach picked up an injured bandit and threw him at another rider.

We killed and killed, we killed mounts and riders, we hit anything which might be a threat. Stomach grappled with a bandit who had thrown himself from his mount on to the big man, Stomach bit his ear off and then wrenched his head into a snap before the bandit could use his daggers. The big man's eyes blazed with frenzy. I wasn't going anywhere near him for some time.

Then it was over, at least our little part of the fight. Wilks stood sobbing, Stomach clubbed at fallen bodies in a rage screaming, "Mongrels! Mongrels!" Large was looking around for other enemies, eyes blazing with the fighting madness. My sword carried a lot of blood, it was splashed onto my chest and face. I don't remember any of the spray. My back ached, my throat was parched, sweat poured into my eyes and every muscle throbbed. On the upside I was alive.

I told Large to look after the rear while I moved up to the head of the column to see the dead and dying.

As I came up, I saw the big priests hacking and slashing. They weren't too concerned over who got hit which allowed them to keep a small space around them. I stayed out of range. They were positioned near the wagon, cutting down anyone who came near. I hoped the injured Watchmen near their feet were not their victims.

My own rage was still up. Approaching the front I saw hurt, pain and confusion writ large. The bandits were vicious, dirty, wild-eyed killers. Their commander had seen he had taken on too much and was trying to extricate what was left of his band. This had caused the fight to slow a little. A lot of our newbies were on the ground, hurt or exhausted, some of the bandits were filtering away from the rear of the fight. In between those on the ground and those trying to flee was still a lot of violence. A bandit stuck a knife into a woman's belly before taking a blow into his mouth, spraying blood and teeth. Willem finished him with a blow to the back of the head. Some newbies were still fighting, screaming beside the NightWatch veterans, side by side.

We would have won eventually but a lot of our guys would be dead, the big difference was the priests. The pair with the armour were good but it was the little scout priests who were fighting above their weight. They would dash in and slash or stab then leap away, sometimes spinning and kicking. I saw one of them leap in the air and kick a bandit right in the jaw, his neck snapped back with a loud crack.

I punched my sword into a kidney, attacking from behind has never been a problem for me.

I stood and swayed a moment and had a close up view of one of the leather priests in action. With one hand he grabbed a bandit from behind and with the other drew a dagger across his throat. Blood gushed out of the neck as the priest swung his victim around. The corpse washed all those nearby in blood spray before the priest pushed the body onto another bandit. This guy stood frozen in horror as the dead man flopped into his arms. The priest then slashed his face open. He wasn't dead but his wound showed teeth and muscle before he stumbled into his comrades, screaming through the nightmare.

The ferocity of the priest's attack was appalling, he incapacitated as well as killed. I've seen and done rough stuff myself, but these guys took fighting to another level.

All the ambushers started to waver. We needed one more push at them. I hit one in the back and tripped another. The fight was at a delicate balance, they were ready to break if we could keep them off balance. The bandit chief was still mounted, screaming at his men. They might regroup at any moment.

Then his head disappeared into a red mist, the entire skull vaporised, leaving the headless corpse in the saddle. The horse bolted. Teddy Boy had brought out the old equaliser. After a moment's pause the rest of the bandits turned and ran, some on foot, others mounted.

The aftermath of the fight was just clean up. The priests slit throats of the wounded bandits, I guessed this was their version of last rites. We had lost two veterans and eight newbies. We counted four prisoners and twenty-three bodies. Willem patched up our wounded, made a couple of rough stretchers for those who couldn't walk. Smiley trudged back and forth, giving me the odd accusing stare. We sent people back for our bags. Father Dexus took charge of the prisoners and said he would question them. I did not envy their position.

Turns out the wagon was also a victim of the bandits, the body with the arrows was the driver. Probably happened a couple of days ago, the overturned wagon was such a good roadblock the thugs left it there and attacked anyone who came along. I guess they would have run away from regular guards in uniform but we didn't look too threatening. Quite understandable, but I felt vaguely insulted. It was the wagon with the priest guard which was mighty tempting.

We patched up, had a brief rest and kept on. Magic visited the wounded and generally put himself around the place. Seems that every time someone looked up they saw him talking nearby or just trudging alongside. I couldn't be bothered. I'll never be a great leader.

Nothing much else happened for the rest of the day, we entered the small village as dusk settled. The scouts had gone on ahead and prepared our arrival, we had hot food and more medical treatment waiting for us. That evening Magic called a meeting of all the people to tell us his great plan.

He told us we were going to walk halfway around the planet to reach the other shuttle before it was picked up in six months. Well, colour me surprised, you could have heard a pin drop. That was quite a stroll he was proposing.

"If we don't make it," he said, "then we are no worse off than we are now. Think about it, we make the trek and learn about the planet. Knowledge is always useful. This is a chance to make it back to the ship, it may not work but at least we'll have given it a shot. Any questions?"

A hand shot up, "How do you know where to go?"

Magic indicated Wilks, "He knows. Tell them, Wilks."

Our technician cleared his throat and spoke up with a great deal of importance, "The locations of both Markets were in the computer. I downloaded a survey of the planet and used it to indicate where to go. When we get close our Translator beads will guide us the rest of the way." He sat down.

Magic asked, "Anything else?"

Another hand, this time from one of the newcomers who had backed Scarface in the fight, "Who died and made you God?" He looked around expecting sniggers of support, must have been surprised when people edged away leaving him in a small circle. "I mean," he gulped, "maybe someone else should be calling the shots. Just saying, that's all..." his voice trailed off.

"Yeah, could be," said Magic, "But they're not. I am. All right, that'll do for now. Val, set up sentries."

I'd been expecting this so had a roster in mind already. I called the squad leaders over and gave them the good news. They just nodded and went their ways. I'm getting better at this stuff.

Chapter 35

That night we had a chance to relax in real huts. It doesn't sound like much but, hey, we were getting desperate. We'd crashed onto a planet, survived blood and mayhem, trudged through the countryside infested by bandits only to find we had a planet to cross. Call me small minded but it seemed we were all feeling a little stunned. That night the lads and lasses let it all out and partied like there was no tomorrow. Could be true.

I took the opportunity to chat to a few of our journey companions. The regular Watch were fine, just argumentative and drunk, pretty normal. The newcomers were getting better at blending in, the useless ones, male and female were dead. We were left with the competent and the lucky.

A big fight always pulls people together, the thugs had stood beside Right Honourable, shoulder to shoulder. One died. I still didn't like them much but I could accept them. Come to think of it, there were still a few veterans I didn't like too well, but they did their job and that's all anyone can ask.

What to do with Santini? Did he still want to kill H'nuth? I found him in earnest conversation with Teddy Boy and that was a surprise in itself, Ted was helping the sad and lonely man come to terms with his actions. They invited me to join them and I listened while Santini unburdened himself, he was looking for forgiveness from someone, probably God. He was damaged, but if Ted was willing to stand by him then so was I. We'd watch him, but I think he felt better. He still had a fight to win, one with himself and his inner demons. H'nuth was safe.

The females had all stuck together at the start for mutual defence. They didn't need too, but they liked being a group. I had a delegation that night, bit of a Boy's Own dream, really. Eight girls asking to see you alone. We stepped into the gloom between two huts, thoughts of fantasy flickering through my brain but no such luck. The girls said they all wanted to be in the same squad, very polite and wanted me to consider it. I don't think I was swayed by their charms when I sent for Right Honourable. He thought it was a brilliant idea so he got them. Squad one was now a mix of veterans, eight females and a couple of the thugs. I moved the other thugs in with Meataxe, a match made in heaven.

Wilks was a lousy, boring drunk. He told endless stories about how wonderful he was. Lonely was interesting, he sat on a small stool outside his hut and watched the giant campfire we built. He had a small smile but didn't seem to be opening up, I sat beside him and tried to chat before realising he was totally mulleted. Insensible with alcohol. I thought it was a neat trick, being able to sit smashed without collapsing.

Being older and wiser I declined all offers of a drink, it really hurt to turn them down. I knew Magic was probably relying on me to keep some sort of self-control and be ready for the unforeseen. For me, staying sober was quite unforseen. Authority has its downside.

I came across H'nuth on my rounds, he was alone again, as usual. Time to take the bull, or devil, by the horns, I thought, so I sat down beside him in the dirt. Together we gazed out at our little clan.

"Evening," I said, waves of comradeship positively flooding out of me. All I got was silence. I turned to face him and ended up staring at a profile, he hadn't even given me a glance. These guys were ugly up close. "How's the arm?" I asked.

It was as if I wasn't there, he just kept looking at the girls and boys hooting it up. The light from a few campfires flickered shadows across the craggy and vaguely terrifying visage of this strange, strange person. And that's when I realised it – I had stopped thinking of Tharls as a type of devil, I now considered them to be people. Very different people, but still people. Ugly, scary people.

"You're a pain in the neck, H'nuth," I said. "Crack a smile or something, willya!"

Success! His head turned to face me with all the deliberation of an aimed cannon and a very similar effect on me. "How'd you be, sport?" I managed to croak.

"Valentine," he said, and then shut up.

"You don't say much do you, H'nuth. Are you angry with me too, like Chayla?"

"Different Lord," he replied, turning back to face the party.

Trying to keep the words flowing I asked another insightful question, "Whaddya mean?"

Without looking at me he showed me the bicep of his broken arm, a big, big bicep. At first, I thought he was just bragging – I sure would be – then I had a closer look at his muscle. By the flickering light, I saw a tattoo. It was in the same location as the tattoo on Chayla and the dead girl but was of a completely different design. Was there a pattern here? Risking further rebuffs, I told H'nuth about the other tattoos, especially the one on the girl. He didn't move, could have blinked a couple of times but I might have missed it.

When I finished, I looked at him, hoping for a response but saw only his hooked nose in full profile. About the time I decided to give it up as a bad job he spoke, "The tattoos indicate which Lord we serve, each Lord rules a separate clan. I don't hate you, I'm just doing my job."

"What about a line through a tattoo, a line with little skulls on each end?" I asked, thinking again of the girl.

He shrugged, "Crossing out a clan mark means the person has denied the clan, has moved away from its values."

"You realise someone on the ship has tried to kill us? Kill you too?" I said, pushing the self-preservation angle.

"Probably only trying to kill you," he said. "I'm collateral damage. They'll pay a fine to my Lord, no problem."

"Terrific," I said. "Couldn't be happier for you." Sarcastic pause. "Aren't you even a little bit ticked off that someone tried to kill you? Just a tad, just slightly angry?"

"No," he turned to me again, "My clan follows the Path of the Stoic. Accept everything, live without expectation." He turned back to the fires again, our very own party animal. I left him then, wallowing in his own personal belief system, what a ball of fun he was going to be for the next six months.

The noise gradually subsided, about midnight the only noise was from a few groups of die-hard talkers. I did a slow circuit of the village, poking my nose into dark corners, talking to sentries, upsetting a few amorous scenes and satisfying myself we were safe.

I recognised Meataxe's feet poking out of a dark alley and stepped in to give him a once over. Flat on his back, mouth open and snoring loudly, he lay in a puddle, probably his own fluids. I decided against looking too closely. As I stood there, gazing at my comatose companion of many years he broke wind. God bless him, I thought, and left him to his slumber.

Time for me to get my head down. Around the village were low fields, some hedges and fences. A small wood sat off to one side, cut off from the rest of the forest where it looked all glowy and pretty. I wandered over to these trees after snagging a blanket from another inert form. It was quiet as I nested, looking towards the warm glow of the village, so calm, so.... I dozed off, the next thing I knew it was morning.

I trudged back to the slowly waking village encountering a very smelly Meataxe enroute to the river. It seemed even he couldn't handle his delightful odour.

Smiley was standing in the centre square, slowly turning in a circle, gazing at the small collection of huts with a look of awe on his innocent face. Santini was earnestly chatting to him, I overheard something about 'your immortal soul'. Walking up I asked "How's it going, Smiley? Get a good night's sleep?"

He blinked, seemed to see me for the first time. "Val, "he said, "isn't this just an amazing sight." He indicated the spread of the village with one outstretched arm. "Such a city!"

Turning I looked at the rude collection of huts, small animals clustered in and around doorways, the smell of many unwashed bodies. Poor Smiley, he'd spent his life on a farm or out in the backwoods, he thought this place was a major metropolis. "Yeah," I replied, "quite a place." We moved off and sat, basking in the morning sun.

The priest's wagon stood regally in the middle of the street with two of the guard priests around it. I was willing to bet one of the sneaky ones was tucked around the place, ready to ambush anyone foolish enough to try for the treasure.

As the three of us sat in companionable silence the little priest, the flunky, stuck his head out of a hut sniffing the air. Catching sight of us he withdrew his head and re-emerged with three bowls of hot food, bringing them over to us. I was very grateful for the warmth and something which would stick to my belly. Smiley was dumbfounded, speechless and stunned. This little priest was shaking up his world view, showing consideration to others and actually giving away food. It's always good to have your prejudices jostled. Santini got up and walked off so I invited our new friend to join us and he quietly sat down.

I took the opportunity to ask them about H'nuth. Smiley did some translating. None of the natives, including the priests, had reacted as we had on earth when they first saw our red devil. The little priest told me there were other races on their planet, occasionally individuals from other species moved into different areas for trade or just exploration. They just assumed he was from somewhere else out of their area. I guess they were right, too.

"What's in the wagon?" I asked, more to make conversation than any real interest.

The little priest's face took on the look of reverence people get when they're about to speak of significant things, his voice dropped a level as he said, "The Holy Artefacts."

His tone dripped with reverence.

Chapter 36

"Good for you," I replied, still monumentally uninterested. The conversation dried up again so I attempted another verbal sally, "So, what do you do with them? Take them on a tour from place to place every now and then?" My left boot was particularly interesting. I waved it back and forth, watching the sun glint off the dried mud. Boredom threatened.

"More than that!" the little guy stated, a bit of vigour in his voice. "We take them to the Capital for the Portal Ceremony! Each year we open the Great Path!" He gave me a meaningful look, even Smiley nodded a few times, agreeing that this was a big deal. Yawn, big deal, I thought and drifted off into silence, conversational gambits exhausted.

Not long after this short break I was dragged off to one of the outer guard posts. Willem was waiting with a very grim expression. At his feet were two still forms, dead watchmen with their throats cut. We had a problem.

I instructed Willem to question everyone and find out what happened, Smiley and Santini joined me as I poked around the campfire. I was looking for some way the killer could have crept up on the guard post. I was stumped. From where it was situated, they had a clear view across the fields, no obstacles, no cover for a bandit to sneak up. The guards were two of the newbies so I didn't really know them, but they couldn't have fallen asleep or slacked off. I had tasked one of the older veterans to regularly do the rounds. Still, they were part of my team and I had a responsibility to them, a responsibility to find out why they died.

A small thought wafted through my mind saying that I should have been doing more checking during the night rather than sleeping. I argued with myself, with that inner voice full of criticism, the one that never shuts up. Okay, I said to it, next time we just do not sleep, we roam around all night after being on top of things all day. Not a problem, no sleep for the next six months. Where do I go to resign?

Both bodies lay on their backs, no sign of a struggle, knives still in scabbards, quarterstaffs leaning against a wall. Santini and I sat down and *looked*, there is a difference between looking and *looking*. You have to go a bit cosmic and do what Magic calls 'centring yourself'. We both sat there, trying to see a clue, a motive, anything at all. After 30 minutes we called it quits, compared notes and went our separate ways. I did ask him to check the village to see if anything was missing.

I dismissed the notion the two guardsmen had fallen asleep. They were in Willem's squad, he checked things and doing the round of the guards was a big thing to check. When I asked him, he told me he had indeed been by the post several times that night and on each occasion the guards were on the ball. I was alert to any unspoken criticism from him about my role but didn't sense anything. Willem was too busy beating himself up over losing two of his squad. Inner voices again.

Someone was good enough to sneak up on two sentries. Not one but two. Whoever it was had some serious sneaking skills. Time to brief Magic, he gets the big bucks.

Next day we set off on the next leg of the journey, the long, long journey Magic had set up for us. Some of the lads moaned, I felt like doing a bit of moaning myself, but it's probably another of those things we don't do in the Watch anymore. By long tradition.

I missed my slack and idle days.

Walking is boring, I mean really, really boring. I enjoyed the first day and some of the second but by the time day three rolled around the charm had begun to fade. My legs hurt, my gear chafed where it rubbed against my lily-white skin. The worst part was that I had to hoof it backwards and forwards up and down the line of march checking on the state of play. Magic just strolled in front of the wagon expecting me to give him regular progress reports. I was so loving this job.

None of us were in great physical shape after shipboard life but bit by bit we reacquainted ourselves with the ways of a long march. Even back in the Days of the City we had little need to do prolonged excursions like this but the sheer hardness of that life made us tough. None of us liked it much.

The newbies were another case entirely, they were a hilarious mess. Soft, complaining, moaning, whinging. Did I say they were having trouble coping? Magic and I decided to slow the pace a bit more after day three while they sorted themselves out. Some had huge blisters. Meataxe had performed his special kind of baptism for their boots, urine makes new boots pliable and allows them to mould to the walker's feet. He didn't let on what he was doing when he took the newbie's boots out of their sight. It does work, honest. Just stinks. We made these volunteers walk in their own unique group until the smell wore off.

By the end of the second week most of the noise had died away as people realised that mummy wasn't going to come and make it all better. Funny thing about a problem, once you realise it won't go away you have to do something to fix it. Magic's second rule. Crying doesn't seem to work.

Wilks continued to be an idiot. Much as I appreciated his work in landing our flying coffin, he was not a man I could warm to, he was just so fussy. He came and complained over any insults or slights, he never gave anyone any slack or let things slide. Something in his makeup prevented him from taking any shortcuts. If the rules said do it this way then that was the way he always did it. And if there were any gray areas his brain sort of shut down. He was a bundle of fun to be around.

Some of the female newbies really did it tough and tried to charm some of the men into carrying their loads. We didn't stop the practice since it made for an interesting learning curve for the volunteer porters. As they struggled under double loads and pleaded for help we just told them they had made the choice to carry double. Put up with it or do something about it. Pretty soon all the loads were returned. Quite a bit of blue language from the ladies, lots of insults about manhood and gentlemen and stuff like that.

Teddy Boy infuriated one of the women when she called him worthless and unkind. He agreed with her and kept walking.

Week three came and went, we lost a couple to sickness. Passing through a small village, Smiley negotiated for a small people powered cart, we put the sick and injured in this but even so some died. We buried them and kept walking. Magic had us pick up the pace again and we stretched out, pacing ourselves against the time limit for the next shuttle return.

In all this time we didn't have any more attacks, no more midnight murders.

I spent a lot of time talking to the little priest with Smiley. He told us to call him Father Dale, all priests apparently have names beginning with D. It's a religious thing. After the death of one of the newbies we gave the little guy one of our translators and conversation became easier.

I really wanted to learn how they did that strange fighting stuff, the flying kicks and leaping about. During the ambush these wiry priests had used their hands as weapons, hitting with the edge of their hand and doing awful things to a body. Father Dale said they all trained in it and he would try to teach me. He admitted his level of skill was low and nowhere near as high as the guards, he told of how they could break thick branches with a single blow.

Every day I went through his exercises, my spin kick was becoming particularly good. The various patterns he had me learn gave me a sense of peace as I moved through the forms. I had to concentrate on each step and place my feet and hands in specific locations. I found the whole technique somehow calming and satisfying. Plus I got really good at it.

Each evening this session would be interrupted by some detail which seemed to need my attention and I had to run off. I learned new ways to throw an opponent around with hip and shoulder movements, as well as learning how to fall. Like, I need practice in falling down?

Right Honourable started quarterstaff lessons again when we decided the newbies were tough enough. The days passed. It was so boring.

Each night we talked around the campfires, bit by bit our minds acclimatised to the enormous changes in our lives. The walk was a healing time for us in more ways than one. We talked about the City and things we missed or remembered. The regular members of the spaceship crew told us of their life, of living with aliens every day, of coping with machines which kept you alive. Teddy Boy soaked up any talk on technology. Not me, like a lot of the others I just let it wash over me. Santini preached a lot, he gave comfort to many and never pushed. We trudged on this strange and wondrous journey.

After two months we entered quite a large town and Magic ordered some rest days. The priests had also requested this pause while they did priesty things at the temple. Lots of significance was attached to the journey. Their wagon contained religious artefacts of great significance, something on a par with bits of the True Cross, and the local people needed to have a look at the precious goodies. I saw Dexus give back his Translator bead to Magic, it was like watching someone wash their hands after handling garbage.

We found a reasonable place for us to stay, sort of an inn but different. I can't explain it any better than that. It was big enough for all of us and had space in the yard for any assemblies we needed. We wouldn't require the stables for horses but we put our little wagon in one of the stalls and all had an early night. Next morning, I went in search of an animal to pull the wagon. I volunteered Smiley to accompany me as we went searching for a place to buy a beast of burden. Magic gave me some trade goods for finances.

We came back after an hour with something big, black and omnivorous. It had bad breath and could pull a house down if harnessed right. Smiley was in love with the huge animal so he picked up another job, he was now responsible for sick people AND animals. Entering the yard with the creature from the black lagoon, Right Honourable told me that we had another murder scene.

This time it was two veterans of the NightWatch.

Chapter 37

Right Honourable preceded me up the staircase to one of the bedrooms of our inn. The people I passed were all reasonably subdued and moved about quietly. As I started up the stairs Magic saw me and said, "I'll be up in a minute, Val." Right Honourable held the door open allowing me to enter first, I saw two small cots against the walls and two large bodies on the floor. Both bodies had been mutilated.

"This is pretty bloody grim, Val," murmured Right Honourable. I stood aghast at what I saw, mess and blood are not unknown sights for me but even so this was out there. Before me lay what was left of Stomach and Large. Both bodies were lying on their backs, hands by their sides. A long slit had opened up each corpse from the chin to groin with the sides of the cut pulled apart. Intestines and organs were trailing out of each body cavity, they looked to be arranged rather than merely tossed out. The two men were still fully clothed with the cuts made through the layers they had been wearing. The organs of each corpse were pulled to opposite sides so that, as they lay closely side by side, it looked as if some careful person had meticulously arranged everything to be symmetrical. Perhaps the killer was tidy, whoever it was they were certainly efficient. Efficient and bloodthirsty.

Large had only one sleeve of his overalls, the other was hanging loosely from a few threads, it looked like it had been torn off. I noticed the piece holding his shoulder patch was missing.

Magic entered behind me, "Let's all just stand here for a bit and look, everyone", he instructed. "What do you see?"

"You're joking, Magic," muttered Right Honourable. "It's bleeding obvious what we see, two of our biggest and toughest laid out like old clothes. We didn't hear a thing, didn't see anyone, didn't have a clue what was going on. Sainted Fathers! How could this have happened? We were all downstairs, all nearby...we should have heard ...we ..." He waved his arms encompassing the room and finally lapsed into silence.

I felt the same way, a sense of shock. It was bad enough the killings were messy but to do them under our very noses seemed inconceivable. "How could someone do this to Stomach and Large?" I asked, "And do it so quietly?"

"LOOK," commanded Magic.

"I see an open window," said Right Honourable.

He was right, of course, the only window into the small room was open to the outside world, its shutters latched back against the exterior walls. I started to cross the room to look for ropes or ladders but Magic stopped me. "Be careful, Val," he said, "walk around the bodies, don't touch or step in anything. I don't want the scene disturbed until quite a few of us have had a good look at what this room has to offer."

Right Honourable turned to Magic, "This is a pretty sick thing to see," he said. "Stomach and Large were our friends and deserve a bit of decency. How about I just throw some of those blankets over their bodies? And maybe Smiley and I should make them look a bit more, I don't know, more like ordinary dead bodies rather than leftover toys from some sicko. Come on, Val, give me a hand." He started forward but Magic spoke again before he had taken a step.

"No, Miguel, don't touch anything. If we LOOK at this scene, we might be able to work out what happened. Remember our training; Look, Think, Guess." Magic asked me what I could see from the window. Not much to report, no ladders, ropes, drainpipes. Other buildings were across the street but no clues there either.

"You better now, Miguel?" asked Magic and when Right Honourable nodded he was told to go downstairs and brief everyone on what he had seen. He was then to send the squad leaders upstairs to view the scene. Right Honourable turned to leave and collided with Father Dale who had quietly entered the room behind us. The little priest gave a yelp of pain as Right Honourable's boot squashed his sandal. He quickly pulled himself into one side of the doorway while the larger squad leader clattered down the stairs.

"May I enter?" he asked, showing just head and shoulders around the doorway. I looked to Magic for permission and, on his nod, gave Father Dale a Translator Bead.

Magic replied, "Please do, Father, but I would ask you not to touch anything until my men have had a chance to look at the scene."

I stood leaning against the window sill and watched the little man as he took in the grisly sight. His body was still, frozen like a bird watching a snake as he observed the two bodies. His eyes roamed over the entire scene, moving from point to point, pausing before moving on.

He took a step in to the room and asked, "Do you know what lies before you?

"Pretty much," I responded. "Two of our men were butchered. Two of our strongest and toughest. Someone surprised them so well they had no chance to cry out or fight back."

"How do you know they didn't fight back?" asked the priest.

I shifted my weight onto the other hip, "Because there's no sign of a scuffle. These two guys don't fight neatly, or they didn't. They're big and they're messy. The beds are still in one piece, there's no blood splatter, weapons are against the wall, nice and tight like good guardsmen. No, whoever got them did it quickly, probably a poison."

"No, not poison,'" he answered. Stepping carefully between the two bodies he reached into Large's stomach cavity. Before Magic could cry out the little priest straightened up and held up a bloodstained hand, in it glinted a long silver pin. "You will find a pin like this in the body of the other," he said. "They are used to assist in the ceremonial draping of the victim's entrails when a *sarengo* is performed."

The scene was almost obscene, this little man standing daintily between two huge bodies, guts everywhere and the bloody hand holding the pin at his side. I watched a trickle of blood run down one finger, onto the pin and drip onto the floor. Splosh.

"What's a *sarengo*?" asked Magic. "And why would my two men be killed this way?" Some of the other squad leaders and H'nuth appeared at the top of the stairs to witness the little priest in his macabre court. Smiley's face appeared over their shoulders, I saw him give a little gasp and say, "*Sarengo!*"

"A *sarengo* is the ritual killing of an infidel," said Father Dale in a flat voice, "a non-believer. A person of less worth than the worms which crawl in the earth. To gain forgiveness for their lack of belief the victim is disembowelled, all inner organs are pulled out and placed on one side of the body. This allows the cavity to fill with peace and harmony. These pins are used to arrange various organs. You may find more holding some of the further body parts in their pattern."

The little priest delicately stepped back towards Magic and said, "The pins are then used to pay for the burial." He opened Magic's hand and dropped the stained piece of metal into the outstretched palm.

Magic stood nonplussed for a moment before speaking, "Val, stay here and be a Watchman, find out what happened." He turned to the others on the stairs, "I'm taking Father Dale with me downstairs, the rest of you stay here and do something useful. Listen to Val." He took the priest's arm and moved towards the stairway; the squad leaders stepped aside, allowing the two to leave the room.

I looked around the room and saw no hope or help in any face. Willem, Right Honourable, Horse, a few others and Smiley all looked at me expectantly. I said, "You know what to do, Look. Then we will tell the story."

We stood looking around the room, no one moving or speaking until Smiley asked, "What are we doing?

Teddy Boy surprised me by answering, "We're looking with our eyes. Then we're going to close our eyes and look with our ears."

"How can we look with our ears?" asked Smiley.

"It means you listen, dopey," replied Willem. "Then you look by touching, by smelling, by any way you can. Magic calls it 'LOOKING'. Then we try to work out what happened, that's the 'tell a story' part. You try it, now shut up and give us some peace."

The room remained silent as we stood, turned, shifted our weight. Slowly some of the lads began to move around the room, touching various bits and pieces of furniture and other odds and ends. I turned to the beds and looked under them, patted the mattress, lifted them up and shook. I sat on the bed, closed my eyes and listened, trying to get the sense of where this room fitted in the world.

Teddy Boy called softly, "Val."

He was squatting beside Stomach's head pointing to where it rested on the floor. Except it wasn't on the floor, there was something thin under the back of the skull. I nodded to Teddy Boy and he gently pulled the head forward and pulled out a small stone tablet. It was covered with carvings. I saw Smiley's reaction when he saw the object as he stood behind Teddy Boy. His eyes widened and his mouth made a little "O" of astonishment.

Reaching out I took the stone from Teddy Boy and held it up to Smiley, "What is it?" I asked.

Smiley, eyes fixed on the tablet, responded by saying, "It is a Dedication Stone." He scratched an armpit and went on, "Given to a newly baptised baby."

"Keep looking," I said.

Garments rustled as the other occupants of the room made small movements. Being still and quiet allows you to train your other senses. Magic spoke of telling a story, the story of the crime. By using the clues we picked up at the scene we could each tell our own story. They often conflicted but we understood the scene better after trying to retell the tale. I sniffed the air, felt the movement of air on my cheek, there was an odd odour, something sweet and very faint.

I tried to see what had happened in my mind. Opening my eyes, I said, "Let's tell the story. Willem, you go first."

Willem stood near the two weapons that those big men had wielded with such effectiveness. He rubbed his hand up and down the shafts and began to speak. "They came in and put their gear down, placed their weapons against the wall."

"How do you know?" asked Right Honourable, moments before I did. This was also standard practice for us. Ask questions, be able to back up your statements. That was why we rarely invited Meataxe into these discussions, he tended to claim bizarre situations, vampires, ghosts, conspiracy theories. Sometimes he was right.

"This is where they always put their weapons in relation to their sleeping positions, said Willem. "We all do, I know Val puts his sword on his right side, Teddy Boy keeps a dagger near his head. This is where they put their tools. Seen them do it a thousand times." He stopped speaking and leaned against the door jam, folding his arms.

"Right,", I said. "We agree, they came in, no problems. Anyone else?" We talked back and forth. Leaving out all the disagreements, wrong turnings and implausible scenarios a story emerged.

Stomach and Large had entered the room, racked their weapons. Then they lay down on the floor and waited for someone to come in and cut them up.

This story had a few holes in it, try as we might, we couldn't think of a good reason for the men to do this. Even if they were poisoned or drugged, they should have staggered, made a mess. No, they had just neatly stretched out between the bunks. And why would the killer take a Security patch?

One of the younger squaddies came up the stairs, Magic wanted me. I told the team to keep thinking, Willem was smelling his hands. Down the stairs I went with Smiley, he was looking a bit the worse for wear. H'nuth tagged along.

Magic was sitting at a table in one corner with Father Dale. Both men looked quite solemn. Not all that surprising, I thought.

"Val," said Magic. "Bit of bad news. The Father here has been telling me of an attempted robbery on the building holding those artefacts we brought from way back in the mountains. It appears the priests who did all the guarding on the journey have been taking a break, turning the job over to some of the local constabulary. Earlier tonight the rostered guards looking after the things were found all dead."

He looked at me and waited.

Chapter 38

I'm never sure what he wants when he does this. He's not an idiot and he doesn't normally treat the men like idiots. So, he was stopping there for a reason. I had a quick think. Robbery, valuable things knicked, Father Dale comes here and talks. Got it! I thought, they want our help in solving the crime.

"Do you want me to take a squad over there and lend a hand?" I asked, "This isn't our town but we might spot something." I stopped and looked at them, Father Dale wasn't lighting up like I expected. I was showing keen, leaping to volunteer, lend a hand and all that stuff. "What else?"

Magic indicated by a gesture he wanted the little priest to speak. Father Dale slowly opened his mouth and said, "The guards were killed by a single blow to the head. Blows delivered by a lot of force," a further pause. "Probably delivered by someone with great strength," he looked embarrassed.

The squad leaders had come back downstairs. They moved through the room checking on all the Watch. The sick and wounded, male and female.

I got it. "Upstairs we have two dead guardsmen, both strong men, capable of killing with one blow, especially if they used those huge weapons of theirs." I sat back and shifted my gaze between the two men.

"Thing is, they're dead," I thought for a moment. "But you're here now, Father Dale, warning us." Pause. I got it, "We're being set up."

I turned and looked at Magic, "We're in trouble. We make two groups, one to stay and take the heat, the other to find out what happened. Who goes?"

"You," he said, "I'm too old for running around. Take Smiley as interpreter, Meataxe as a personal guard, Teddy Boy is good anywhere and you might as well take Lonely and give him some experience. Anyone else?"

I turned and yelled to Teddy Boy to get those people assembled at the back door and then begged, "Just as long as you keep Wilks, I'm happy."

There was a pounding on the front door, it had been shut, I noticed, with the locking bar in place. "That'll be the local coppers come to make their enquiries," said Magic, "Righto, I'll keep Wilks with me, he can keep a record of all the interviews. Would you believe he's been setting up a filing system while we've had some down time? You might need at least one other veteran NightWatch. Pick someone and go. We're probably going to be under some sort of house arrest for a wee while."

Passing Horse, I told him to join us. Moments later we were out in the street, skulking along the back roads to the main part of the city. We're good at skulking, it's a useful skill when you're all alone in a nasty part of town. Often the good citizens are looking for someone with a uniform to vigorously discuss political issues. The discussion usually involves pickaxe handles and large boots. Most of us have had these conversations, we were keen to keep repeats to a minimum.

Meataxe took front position, Horse brought up the rear. Teddy Boy took charge of Father Dale and bundled him off to the front to show the way. I stayed in the middle with the more useless members of the group, Lonely and Smiley. I told Lonely to look after Smiley hoping both could walk without falling over their own feet. It kept them busy and might even do some good. I'd be happy if they could just walk quietly. We'd have to teach them skulking later.

As we moved down the side streets, I trundled up behind Father Dale to ask about the deaths. "So, Father," I asked, "What's with this *sarengo* stuff? You seemed to know what was going on the minute you saw those bodies."

The little priest puffed as he kept up with our longer stride. We were on the main road through town now and Meataxe was setting a cracking pace. "The *sarengo* is the ceremonial killing of a non-believer. I ... I don't know why someone would choose only those men to kill, I mean, you're all unbelievers!" He stopped and stuttered a little before continuing, "I don't mean you should all be killed, the *sarengo* comes from an earlier time in our land's history when some awful things were done in the name of God. Thankfully, those times have passed."

"Not quite," I said. "Some nutter still felt strongly enough about it to fillet Stomach and Large." We walked on for a while, slowing as we entered the central area of town. The main civic building would be here somewhere. Meataxe signalled us towards a side street. When I came up I saw what had caught his attention, the cart that had carried the artefacts was just outside the side door of one of the main buildings. A guard stood in front of the door, obviously both watching the cart and keeping the non-paying customers out of the temple.

Father Dale's words made me think. Why had the killer chosen those two particular men to pay the ultimate price? Stomach and Large would not have been the easiest of victims. Surely some of the newbies would have been a better choice. He could have gotten more than two. Presuming it was a 'he', and who sent him? I asked Father Dale, "If the killings were ceremonial would the killers have some sort of sanction, like official executioners. Who would give this blessing? And were women ever involved?"

"Women! Oh, no, no, never women!" responded Father Dale, quite vehemently. "After the unbelievers were identified a priest would delegate the task of killing to a worthy member of the congregation. It was an honour to be so chosen. A woman! Dear, dear, me. Never a woman. Oh, no..." He trailed off. My question about women had really set him off. As we stood there I could still hear him muttering, "A woman, fancy that, no, no, no ..."

Meataxe had begun to slink towards the inattentive guard. He enjoyed creeping up on things, just his little way. He stopped directly behind the still unaware guardian of the door and lightly tapped him on the shoulder. I've seen him do similar things like this over and over again. The person jumped in fright and Meataxe had a good laugh. We kept telling him to cut it out but he never did. I told him one day it would end in tears.

The guard felt the shoulder tap and instead of leaping in surprise as Meataxe expected he dropped to the ground, balanced on his hands and kicked backward with both feet. The man's boots punched him solidly in the stomach and chest lifting Meataxe off the ground. He hit the wall and slid to the ground with eyes bulging, mouth forming a little "O". He struggled for breath before slowly slumping to one side, tears trickling down his cheek.

I told him, one day....

Chapter 39

Running up, Father Dale reassured the guard we were friendly, I examined Meataxe. He still had a pulse but I think some ribs were damaged. His face slowly turned purple as he struggled for air. At this point Smiley, to my way of thinking, performed an action worthy of heroic status. Shoving me aside he pushed Meataxe's head back and began to give him mouth-to-mouth resuscitation until the downed man began to splutter.

He lay on his side, coughing and clutching his ribs in obvious pain. We all watched and waited until Horse, leaning against the wall said, "Get up, you big girl's blouse." Meataxe slowly dragged himself to his feet with Smiley fretting around him. No sympathy from the rest of us.

Teddy Boy asked Meataxe, "You finished? Can we get on now?"

Grimacing, Meataxe muttered, "Yeah, no worries."

As we moved past him, I patted the injured man on one shoulder, enough to make him wince and said, "Told you. One day you'd sneak up on the wrong guy. You big dill."

When we entered the building Father Dale took us through a couple of smaller rooms until we came into a large chamber. Standing around a central altar-like table were a group of the locals plus the contingent of priests and fighters who had come with us from the monastery. Father Dexus seemed to be in charge. He saw u, pointed a wrathful finger at Father Dale while and shouted, "You! What have you done?"

Father Dale dropped to his knees and bowed his head. The big cheese advanced on our stunned group, lashing Dale with his tongue, "How dare you? By what right did you leave this holy place and go to those unwashed heathens! You were seen running into their building ahead of the soldiers. Soldiers I had sent! And now you bring them here to attack us again! Get to your quarters and do not leave until I speak to you!" The little guy bobbed up, did some sort of curtsy to everyone without making eye contact and scurried out like a whipped puppy.

The rest of us stood there like kids caught doing the wrong thing, we just felt guilty. Dexus certainly had presence, I stood there feeling ashamed until I realised I hadn't actually done anything. So I spoke up, "Hang on a second ..." I didn't get very far because I remembered that none of these characters had one of our Translator Beads, not a lot of point in talking to them since Mr Important had just sent our key translator off to his room. I realised Father Dale still had his Translator Bead but any further thinking was cut off by the Chief Priest's continuing rant. It's hard to think any coherent thought while some loudmouth yells in your face.

Fortunately, Smiley again came to our rescue. He started explaining what had happened, I Dexus cut him off abruptly, "Be silent, peasant! You demean this room with your presence. My guards will take you to the prison where you will join the rest of your unholy rabble."

Guy was a real winner.

"Why are you doing this?" I asked, Smiley translated, "We have done you no wrong. Is this the thanks we get for giving you safe escort all these weeks! What has happened? Tell me, if my men have erred, they will be disciplined. But I must know what has taken place here."

"You 'must', unbeliever! Who are you to talk of 'must'?" He ran his eyes over us, more guards filtered into the room, no chance of fighting our way out. "Some of your vile company dared to interfere with our sacred stones! Fortunately, the Gods looked down and were angry at this sacrilege. You were stopped before completing your desecration." He crossed his arms and looked very stern and righteous.

I'd seen plenty of wacko priests in the City so I wasn't too fazed by the Abbot's intensity. Smiley and Lonely wore terrified grins, Teddy Boy and Horse had on their neutral guardsman faces, Meataxe was down on one knee recovering from the thump he'd received outside.

But my job was to defend my men, so I spoke up. "How do you know it was one of our company?" I asked. "We could have taken the relics anytime when we were on the road, why would we wait until now?"

"The workings of an unbeliever's mind are a mystery to those of faith. I care little for his reasons," he beckoned to one of the soldier-priests that had walked with us from the monastery, "I only know it was one of you filthy scum."

The soldier-priest stepped forward and held up a shoulder patch with the Security emblem, "This was found near the sacred stones."

"That's a piece of our gear," I said, "Can you show me where it was found, exactly?

"I could," said the Abbot, "but I see no reason to indulge your whims." Turning to his men he instructed, "Take these thieves back to the rest of their filthy company. Imprison them all."

"Wait!" I yelled but he kept walking, leaving the room. I've handled this well, I thought, Magic will be impressed.

Telling Smiley to keep up the translation I called out again, "Why did you send someone to kill my men? Why the *sarengo*?"

Dexus stopped and turned, "What did you say?" he asked.

"Two of our men were killed last night," I said, "Father Dale says it was done as some sort of religious execution. He called it a *sarengo*, the killer was sent by a priest. Was it you? Did you authorise an assassination?"

Dexus instructed our captors, "Hold them here, I will speak to Father Dale". He left the room in a bit of a hurry, eager to browbeat the little priest, no doubt.

Each of us had our arms pinned behind us by two other soldiers. We didn't struggle although Smiley wasn't too happy. Horse and Teddy Boy stood quietly, Meataxe dribbled a bit, saliva flowing over his beard. Gently standing on a guard's toe, he slowly increased the pressure while looking at his man with a little smile. Living up to his name, I thought, mad as a meataxe. He'll get thumped again.

I wasn't too worried about the veterans but Smiley and Lonely were new to this sort of treatment. I watched these two carefully. Lonely was keeping an eye on Teddy Boy, copying him. Fair enough, I thought, can't go too wrong following our Ted.

Smiley was more of a worry. He was chafing under the restraining arms and might end up doing something foolish. I needed to interrupt his thinking, derail any urges he was gathering. "What can you control, Smiley?" I asked.

He looked at me, "What?"

"I said, 'What can you control?' Standing here, as we are, what can you control?" I asked again.

He stopped fretting over being a prisoner and started fretting over my words, "I don't know what you're talking about. I'm not in control of anything. We're all trapped. We need to do something!" He finished on a strong note, voice slowly rising.

"Listen to me," I said, and then repeated. "Listen to me. Generally, we cannot control what happens to us, life doesn't ask our permission, stuff just happens. This is one of those times, we are not in control of this situation. We are outnumbered and outclassed. You've seen these priest guys fight. They'd knock the stuffing out of us without breaking a sweat. We don't control the situation, but we can control something."

He'd stopped fidgeting and was listening to my words carefully. You had to hand it to Smiley, he might come from a poor cow farm but there was a real brain behind those teeth. I don't know how smart he really was but I suspected there was still a lot of gas left in his tank.

He thought for a while, looked at the other Nightwatchmen, noticed Lonely watching Teddy Boy and said, "They know, don't they? They know about control."

"Yep," I said.

"They're controlling themselves," he said.

"You got it," I said. "When we can't control what happens to us, all we can control is how we deal with it. Now it's all very wonderful getting angry, having a little tantrum or just sulking, but that doesn't change the situation. Teddy Boy and Horse have been watching and learning how this mob operate, seeing how they stand, where their weapons are, walking patterns, stuff like that. It might help if, and when, we need it. But probably it won't. One thing is for sure, if we lose control of ourselves, we don't help the situation. We just add to the problem. Do you understand?"

Smiley looked into my eyes, he tensed and relaxed. Before he could reply we heard a loud scream from somewhere inside the complex. We all jumped, prisoners and priests.

Father Dale burst into the room yelling, "The Abbot's been killed! Help! Help!"

Chapter 40

Some other head bozo told our guards to bring us along, so we all trundled down a few more corridors until we came to a squalid, dirty room. One for Father Dale, no doubt, just the thing for a priest at the bottom of the food chain. No door, most of us had a chance to peer in and see the body of Father Dexus stretched out on the floor. Robes all askew; tongue sticking out, eyes bulging and face a nice shade of blue. My guess was strangulation.

Father Dale babbled the whole time. Essentially, he said some masked character jumped them while the big cheese was giving him a right old tongue lashing. The last thing the father remembered was seeing a boot fly towards his face and thinking, "That shouldn't be there." When he came to, he found Dexus on the floor, dead. He took off looking for help.

And came to us.

I was able to ask Dale some questions in a quiet moment while all the priests and various soldiers ran to and fro. He still had his Translator Bead in place.

"All black, dressed all in black," he responded when I asked for a description of the murderer.

"Any weapons, did you see the colour of his hair, any scars, any way to identify him?" I asked, another thought struck me, "Are you sure it was a man, could it have been a woman?"

The little priest pulled out of his funk and looked at me with a real intensity, "A woman? No, of course not!!" he seemed astonished at the question. "I didn't see much, Father Dexus was quite cross with me, I was kneeling in front of him while he, quite rightly, upbraided me for my lack of faith in his authority. My head was down, looking at the floor in my humility and shame. He collapsed in front of me. I looked up and saw this black garbed figure, it even had a black scarf and mask, then he kicked me. When I woke up the good father was as you see him, I was terrified, ran out and found you."

He gulped, looked at the body, shuddered and said, "I must seek out the Senior Priest for this temple and beg forgiveness. My sin has brought the wrath of God upon this place." He moved off very quickly, too fast for me to ask any more.

This was not going as planned. I hummed and grumbled a bit, trying to think of something wise to do. Be the rock, I thought, be the rock.

Nothing. I had no idea. Which was just the right time for Horse and Teddy Boy to roll up and ask for instructions.

"Sure," I said, "Okay. This is what we'll do ..." I paused and went on. "Right. Horse, I want you to, uh..." I ground to a halt.

"You've got no idea, have you?" asked Teddy Boy.

"Not a clue," I said.

"Come on," said Horse, "Let's go back and look at the crime scene. Pretend we've discovered this while on City patrol. Get our heads back to being NightWatch and not just puppets." He headed off to the room and the corpse.

Teddy Boy moved off after him, I mumbled, "Yeah, right, good idea," and joined them.

It was a good idea. I appreciated Horse coming up with it. I had to tell myself it was alright not to have all the answers, we were a team and anyone could come up with a good plan. It didn't have to be all me. Thinking back, someone always came up with an idea, a way forward. Maybe when I thought I was being an inscrutable rock other people thought I had run out of ideas and just got on with the job. Maybe I should shut up more.

I joined the others and we LOOKED at the scene. Horse knelt beside the corpse, I could see him sniffing, feeling the robes, listening. Closing my eyes, I tried to focus on what was happening outside the room, get a picture of the past. Noises in the hallway, snatches of conversation, shuffling feet, clank of metal, swish of material. Further off some chanting, nothing else.

When I opened my eyes, I saw Teddy Boy had lifted the body onto its side and was examining its back. Horse had grabbed Smiley and they were running interference with the priests and other onlookers outside the room who thought we were being disrespectful. It's amazing how being businesslike and looking like you know what you are doing gives people confidence. Horse moved with deliberate precision and knowledgeable movements, he looked like someone investigating, not a ghoulish onlooker.

The three of us made eye contact, nodded to each other and went into a huddle in one corner. Smiley stayed with the crowd, keeping them calm. Meataxe had fallen asleep in another corner, mouth open, slight dribble.

"What do you reckon?" I asked.

"Dunno," said Teddy Boy "Looks like he was strangled, face shows all the signs and there's a mark around his neck."

"Rope?" asked Horse.

"Probably a scarf" said Teddy Boy. "Smooth bruise, no rope burn or fibres in the wound. Couldn't see anything else, no knife wounds or other marks. I reckon he was strangled from behind. Dale was lucky not to have followed him."

"To kill one and leave the other means it was a targeted killing, Dexus was the intended victim. It also means that the murderer only kills those he intends to, loose ends and witnesses don't bother him," I said.

"Or her,'" said Horse.

"No," I said, "Dale was clear on that. He says it couldn't have been a woman." I told them about my conversation with Dale and his belief the killer of our two men also could not have been a woman.

"You realise Dale had to be kneeling in front of Dexus while he was strangled," said Teddy Boy. "You say he didn't notice anything, Val, anything at all?"

"No, Dexus may have been finished off after Dale was knocked out, little guy was in la-la land for a while. This guy in black is pretty slick," I said.

"Reckon it was the same guy? Kills Stomach and Large and then comes over here to do in Dexus?" asked Horse.

"What's the link?" asked Teddy Boy.

We paused and had a think about that, "Can't see one," I said. "Except they're all dead. But the shoulder patch links our killer with he attempted robbery. This is all very confusing."

A priest waddled over to us looking like he'd had one too many trips to the buffet. He huffed, "I am the Senior Priest for this temple. You may return to your quarters, the other members of your group have been released."

"Pardon?" I asked. "Released? Why? Aren't we still under some sort of arrest?" This seemed a bit unusual.

Smiley and Meataxe joined us. Smiley had one of his big tooth-eating grins. "They don't think we killed Father Dexus!"

Well, duh, I thought. "So, who did?" I said, "Do they have any ideas on that?"

After the fat priest asked Smiley to translate my words he turned and said, "We believe it was a sectarian assassin, one sent to disrupt the smooth passage of the sacred relics on their journey to the capital. This killer would also have been responsible for carrying out the *sarengo* on your two men. This young man," he indicated Smiley "has put forward convincing arguments about the attempted theft. We now believe the killer tried to shed blame onto your company. Please leave now, we have much to do."

He instructed Dale, "Return with these men and ensure they are ready to start the next stage of the journey, I want them to leave in three days time." He fixed Dale with a glare, swept his eyes over the rest of us before leaving the room. All the other hangers-on went with him leaving my little crew standing around the slowly decaying corpse of the Father Dexus.

Love that old time religion.

Chapter 41

"Who's the lard-butt?" asked Meataxe after the room cleared.

"Senior Priest of this temple. Please, we must go," said Dale moving to the doorway, doing his best to cajole us out of the place.

We had one more look around and left the room, trundling down the corridors back into the original altar chamber. Dale crossed straight to the exit door and beckoned us on. We sauntered through, looking around at everything, there was no one else in the chamber, the artefacts were somewhere else by now. Somewhere safe, I hoped.

Teddy Boy and Horse took the long way around the room, walking along the edges, looking at the ground, up and down each wall. Meataxe rested against the altar. I stood in the centre of the room slowly turning to scan the entire chamber, grateful Meataxe hadn't actually sat on the altar. Small mercies.

Dale fretted and signalled for us to go. I didn't want to cause the little man any more stress, after all, he'd already had one good kick in the head today. I signalled to the others to head off.

I couldn't see anything unusual in the room, no scraps of garment or a dropped item which might be a significant clue. In fact, the whole room was very clean, not a mark on the floor, no dirt, no mess, nothing. Outside I asked Dale about the state of the room, why it was so clean. "After the attempted theft the room had to be reconsecrated. That entails a ritual scrubbing of all the walls and floor," he said. So much for any clues.

We walked on, trudging through the day traffic of the town, sharing viewpoints and ideas. I sent Meataxe on ahead to let Magic know what had happened. His idea of a run was an asthmatic trot but at least it got him out of my hair.

"Who found the shoulder patch?" asked Horse.

"The priests found it while they were cleaning the room after the attempted theft," said Dale. "Father Dexus was telling me about the theft, before ... before he was killed." He stopped speaking for a moment and then carried on. "He said he knew the thief was one of your company. I don't know how he knew. I must confess I kept thinking of your men, the ones we found dead with the Dedication Stone."

I walked on in silence, we all did. Each of us was considering the implications of the stone. It was a brand. But it was a brand linking a priest to the killings. Had Stomach and Large gotten involved with someone from the church? Had they fallen out and been killed? Those leather clad priests might be capable of taking one of the big guys down, perhaps both. But not in silence, not Stomach and Large.

Tramping on we moved into the street leading to our inn, we got back around early afternoon. It seemed a long time since Smiley and I went off that morning to buy a beast. Meataxe had indeed arrived ahead of us and Magic came out to get a report. The others went off to see to their squads while I ate and described what had happened.

At the end of my report Magic said, "Good job, Val. I'm curious, what was your plan before Dexus was killed? You say you were being sent back under arrest to us and then ..., what was that bit again?"

"Yeah, well, I didn't exactly have a plan," I admitted. "We were gone for all money before I asked Dexus about the *sarengo*. That's when he bolted off to give Dale a hard time. He seemed to be angry the little guy was talking about temple business with us unbelievers."

We sat on a bench outside the inn, stretched our legs out and relaxing. "The *sarengo*, eh?" mused Magic. "What's the big deal with that?"

"Bit of a mess, all of it really", I said. "Do you reckon the same guy killed Dexus as well as Stomach and Large?

"Could be. You didn't you see any links between the two scenes?" asked Magic.

I told him about the Dedication Stone, it was the first he'd heard of it. It was a link with a priest but how Stomach and Large figured in it all wasn't clear. The shoulder patch was significant, it certainly linked the killer of our two men with the attempted robbery. We must have targets painted on us, every group we meet tries to kill us or pin some crime our way. Not for one moment did we think that Stomach and Large had tried to steal the artefacts. As we spoke one of Willem's squad members ran up. He had gone with Willem and a couple of others to buy more supplies for the next stage of the journey, nothing vital just a few odds and ends. I expressed mild surprise since they didn't have a translator with them.

I know Willem, he likes to bargain. One of his favourite stunts in the last few weeks had been to engage a local in some form of barter using sign language. Of course, he would use his bead and know exactly what the seller was saying but he never let on. To the poor slob trying to make a deal he appeared like some brilliant negotiator, able to understand the worst sign language. He always got a good trade.

After we were all released, he decided to try this stunt at one of the local markets. Shouldn't have been a problem really, after all it wasn't Meataxe trying to buy alcohol. Willem was cluey and sensitive to moods. I asked his squad man for a report.

The guy gulped, he was one of the newbies from the ship, and said, "As we walked, Willem got slower and slower. By the time we got to the market he was staggering. He wouldn't come back, said as long as we're here we should try to buy something. We had him leaning against a wall, he didn't look well. Some of the people were pointing and talking, we got nervous." He stood before us, all dirt, sweat and worry, floundering on, "We didn't know what to do!" I didn't like where this was going. "We hustled him into an alley, out of sight," he finished.

Magic groaned, sure as eggs someone had seen them go into that alley. "Were you followed into the alley, maybe by a few men, offering to help?"

"Yes!" said the newbie, surprised, "How did you know? And they did want to help, they kept asking if Willem was alright and could they do anything. They even offered to take him to a healer."

I stood up and signalled to Horse to join us, "You didn't let them take him, did you?" I asked.

"Willem must have heard us talking, he jerked away from the men and pulled out his sword, he was waving it around in front of him. I think the locals felt threatened! Some of them pulled out little clubs to defend themselves against Willem. It got all messy, they accidentally hit some of the other guys in the squad. I think a few got hit quite badly but I'm sure it was an accident." The newbie was fretting quite a bit by now.

I told Horse to get a squad ready and do it five minutes ago, he ran off yelling. I turned back, "Who else was with you, any old NightWatch?" Please, please, I thought.

We had sat the newbie down, he gulped down a drink before answering, "No, there was just Willem, me and five other guys from my squad. When the clubs came out, Willem grabbed me, told me to run all the way back here for help. He'd used his sword to wound one of those men who came to help! Why did he do that? He was staggering and yelling! More men came in from the other end of the alley. They seemed really angry, lots of yelling. I don't think Willem should have stabbed that man or even drew his sword."

Smiley had joined the group, I told him to get his gear and come with us. We might need a medic and probably a translator.

"Did you see any edged weapons, knives, swords? What's the last thing you saw?" asked Magic.

Horse and his squad were all assembled. I had a quick look, all old NightWatch. Good. "Um", started the newbie, "I saw Willem get hit and go down. I didn't see any knives. No swords." He looked at his drink and went on, "I'm a coward, aren't I? I should have stayed and helped Willem. When he was hit, I should have gone back."

He turned pleading eyes to us, looking for salvation.

Not from me, not yet.

"On your feet, sunshine," I said to him. "Show us were all this happened. And we move at the run." I grabbed him by the collar and dragged him over to Horse, "He'll show us where to go. Use that formation Magic taught us when we left the gypsy campsite, do you remember it?" He nodded. "Let's move," I finished, "no violence until we find the bad guys."

Chapter 42

I had my sword out as we ran, it clears paths quite nicely. None of us said anything, the newbie wanted to babble but I told him to shut up and run, he'd need his breath. I ran alongside him, Horse on his other side, then the rest of the squad. We ran in step, close packed and swaying, moving as one solid mass and the whole thing was dead quiet except for the sound of boots hitting the ground.

People got out of our way very, very quickly. They ran into doorways, they pulled each other into alleys. Eyes widened at the sight, crowds evaporated. Down the streets we went, the newbie very quickly picked up on the mood of the run and shut up. He even started running in step with me, complete with the sway. Occasionally he would point to a corner and we would enter a new street. The streets emptied, up ahead I could see where it entered the market. Stalls nearest our exit point were rapidly losing customers when they caught sight of us. The newbie indicated an alley on the right, this was the one in which he'd left Willem and his mates.

Holding my hand over my head I clenched my fist, pumping it twice, pointing to the alley. I ordered scouts ahead into the alley and a cordon around this end. I sent some other guardsmen down to the other end of the death trap as blockers to give us security.

The scouts and blockers ran past me and disappeared around the corner. By the time I arrived they had found where the fight had taken place. Not hard to see if you know what to look for, blood on the ground, a fallen quarterstaff.

Oh, and the body, that was a bit of a giveaway.

It was one of ours, his throat crushed. Probably his quarterstaff on the ground. I had a look and found a bit of hair matted on the end. Looked like he had given someone a good thump before going down. Another patch of blood was in the centre of the alley, the newbie said it was about where Willem had stuck one of the attackers. Sucking in great gulps the newbie cried, "But we shouldn't have attacked them. We were in the wrong. They just wanted to help us."

I said to Teddy Boy, "Find where they've gone. Must have a base nearby, a place to keep their catch." He turned and set things in motion, various members of the squad left the alley in pairs and looking dangerous. To the newbie I said, "Look, kid, they were the bad guys, right? No one goes into an alley just to help a bunch of strangers, not in the real world. And it doesn't take a bunch of armed men to go into a dark alley just to help a sick man."

"What? Of course, people do that! And they weren't armed. They only had those little club things." We attacked them, it was Willem who drew his sword. He shouldn't have done that." The youngster was confused now, upset we didn't understand it was all our fault.

I was watching both ends of the alley and only half paying attention to him. "Those little club things were to knock you out. A group of men coming at you in an alley, armed with those 'little club things' means one thing – they were recruiters."

"Recruiters?" he asked, "Who would they be recruiting for?"

"For anything, you moron!" I let my exasperation leak out, "Slaves, army, navy, anything at all. None of it good. Willem knew, and that's why he drew his sword."

"But they didn't have their clubs out until Willem drew his sword. If he didn't do that everything would have been alright," wailed the newbie. I glanced at him before looking back to the alley entrance. Two of the men had just entered with Smiley and were talking to Horse.

"Yeah, right, kid," I said. "Good Samaritans always come at a guy when he's armed with a sword. Only wanted to help? Wake up and smell the roses, he drew his sword to get them to reveal their intentions. Genuine helpers would have stopped and probably backed off a little, maybe even tried to talk. These guys just drew weapons and kept coming. I don't know what made Willem sick but you better be really grateful he wasn't too far gone to save your hide. Without him pushing you back to us you might have disappeared. As it is we might not find them at all."

Horse signalled me over before gathering the rest of his squad. As I left him sitting all sad and alone, I said to the newbie, "Now just shut up and pull yourself together. Deal with your problems but keep them to yourself." Before leaving I finished with, "Get on your feet and stop snivelling." I continue to be a real sweetheart.

Teddy Boy told me his men had identified a recruiter's building. Smiley had talked to some of the locals, they told him of a warehouse not too far from this alley. The men were slavers. Damn, I hate slavers.

They would linger outside taverns at night and pick up drunks. Probably only did it in the more unsavoury districts, the local citizenry didn't feel obliged to stop it. May have felt the sort of person picked up by the slavers was better off out of circulation. Stay away from decent folk and it was like a self-cleaning service they provided for the city. The slavers probably encouraged this belief by good PR and a lot of bribes. At least that's the way I would have done it.

The warehouse wasn't much to look at, a big building, and separate from other structures. No roofs to creep across, no common walls to dig through. It stood all alone. Good planning rather than accident, I thought. The front door was guarded by a bunch of tough looking customers including a little guy in a chair, whittling. Horse and I were peeking around a corner trying to find a way in without much luck when I felt a hand on my shoulder and caught a whiff of Meataxe's breath.

"Whaddya reckon, Val? We go in and get them?" he asked.

I turned around and saw Magic with a few more veteran NightWatchmen. "Who's minding the store?" I asked.

"Don't worry, Val, Right Honourable can look after things," he said. "What have we got?" I told him. He scratched his chin and asked me, "Got any ideas?"

"Not a one," I said.

"Me neither", he said. "Let's gather the troops and see if we can come up with something." Horse placed a couple of men to keep an eye on the building while the rest backtracked a short distance to form a loose circle around Magic. Time for a planning session. "Righto," he said, "Willem and a few of the lads are in that building. Probably. Could be long gone, could be dead. We don't know anything about the place or how many are in there. Anyone got any ideas?"

"Yeah,'" said Meataxe, "Let's just march in there, kill a few and bring the boys out."

"Thanks, Meataxe. Any other ideas?" asked Magic.

A few suggestions were made, sneak around and find an open window, dress up like women, put sleeping draughts in their food, we went on and on. Finally, Magic held up a hand and said, "Enough, we're off in fantasy land now. Anyone got a clever idea?"

Silence.

"Yeah, me neither. Righto, it's up the guts," said Magic. I'm sure I wasn't the only one who let out a resigned sigh. This was just going to be hard work, I thought.

He went on "Val, you'll do the front, take five men. Horse, you're second wave with another ten. I'll keep the remaining men with me. Smiley, you're not coming, you stay here with you, you and you." As he spoke he pointed to one other veteran plus two of the newbies. "Guido," he said to the veteran staying behind, "you get back to the rest if it all falls apart. Tell Right Honourable he's now acting captain. You can be Sergeant."

"Yeah, no worries, boss," replied Guido. He leaned against a wall and watched the rest of us get ready. I made sure Meataxe was in my five, it was his idea, after all.

It didn't take us long, Magic said, "Off you go, Val."

Chapter 43

I'm a hit first and talk later kind of guy, not strong on any sort of tactics. Having said that, I would much rather avoid a fight and am more in favour of Magic's clever ideas and sneaky plans. All of us are, I don't think anyone in the NightWatch, including Meataxe, actually looks forward to these sorts of situations. Occasionally someone will join the Watch who does have this gung-ho sort of attitude, the sort that likes the glorious charge into battle and the taking on of all comers. We tend to get out of their way so they can get killed as soon as possible. They're just dangerous to be around, pick fights in bars when they're sober, swagger a lot and have loud mouths. I like to think that we are just a little bit more subtle.

Normally, but not today. Today was not a day for subtle.

I looked at my men. We all nodded a greeting at each other before I said, "Let's go." Gripping our weapons, we took off at a flat run around the corner, no yelling or screaming. I intended to keep my screaming for later. You never know when you're going to need a good scream.

There were seven guards, all armed with cudgels, a few swords and knives. No spears, bows or projectile weapons that I could see. Thank goodness for that. They hadn't woken up to us at first, one of the reasons we weren't yelling. Most people have a mental picture of an attack and men running silently isn't one of them. But eventually their brains worked it out and they grabbed their implements of destruction and prepared to meet us. One of them, the little guy, had ducked back into the building, alerting others, no doubt.

I used my momentum to duck under a blow and kept running into my assailant. Or maybe I was his assailant? Not sure, anyway, I hit him with my shoulder and stomped his face while he was down. I wasn't fooling around. I pushed my booted heel as hard as I could on his neck and ruptured something bad there. He grabbed his throat and writhed a bit, then went still.

Something whacked me on the left arm, not too hard but enough to make me glad I used my right hand for holding a sword. I swung this particular sword up to block the next blow of the cudgel, rolled my wrist over his hand and plunged the sword into his eye. The point of a sword will always beat the side of a club. Bit of eye splash, sword got stuck so I let it go. The falling body pulled it out of my hand.

Meataxe had deliberately dropped his sword just as he reached two men in the initial charge. They, of course, were watching the sword and not the man. As their eyes followed the sword to the ground, they left themselves a bit vulnerable for a moment. Meataxe didn't slow his first rush and was running at some speed by the time he reached the guards. He slammed into them and they all went down. Again, they made a mistake by trying to retrieve their dropped weapons. While they scrabbled about Meataxe bit the tip of one's nose off and then rammed his tensed fingers into the other poor sod's eyes. He lost complete interest in the fight. The one with the bitten nose clapped a hand to his face, screamed, saw his attacker and screamed some more. Meataxe was coming at him again while chewing on the nose, letting a bit of it be seen. The man's nerve snapped. It can't have been a pretty sight seeing our boy looking at you with a mouth full of blood and an eye full of crazy. He very sensibly ran off.

One of our men was down, two bully boys continued to club him. He was curled up protecting his head but he couldn't prevent the odd blow hitting his kidneys. That would kill a man, albeit slowly and painfully but dead's dead. Meataxe and I ran over to help but we never got there as the next little part of our drama unfolded. Reinforcements for the bad guys had arrived from inside the warehouse and were streaming out the door towards us. We joined our other two survivors as they held off their original guards.

Meataxe and I were down to our knives, we each hit or stabbed a man in the back

Our actions must have seemed a bit insensitive to all of those nasties coming out of the building because I heard them scream in outrage. We moved back slowly, edging around the side of the warehouse. We were yelling our lungs out by now. Shouting encouragement, giving warnings and making as much noise as we could. They weren't rushing at us, thank goodness, since we were well and truly outnumbered. Bit by bit we stepped backwards and bit by bit they followed, spreading out until they stood between us and any hope of escape.

The gang now stood facing us with their backs to our entry alley. The alley in which Horse and the lads were waiting. We encouraged the trapped rat look by slumping our shoulders, drooping the arms and generally looking disheartened and defeated. Trapped we were, cut off from all hope.

The little guy pushed forward and stood, hands on hips, "Wha's wrong wid you guys? You wanna be dead? Fools. Thin' you jus' come at us an' we run 'way? We don' even know youse! Man, we's gonna hafta hurt you bad. But we talk wid wun of you, we ask a cuppla questions." He pointed at one of our guys and went on, "I pick you, man, we jus' ask you a few t'ings 'bout dis an' dat. If 'n you lucky, we les you die quick. Res' of you fools, got no use." He glanced at his men, "Kill 'em".

That was the best time for Horse to lead his ten men into their rear. They had also charged over at a silent run and with us making all of that noise they were able to get right on top of the gang before anyone knew what was happening. Our boys mainly went for crippling or incapacitating blows. The human body is quite resilient and to put someone down can take a bit of work. Since we were still outnumbered the lads fought dirty, kneecaps are a special favourite.

I grabbed Meataxe and indicated the little snot who had been making all the threats. As soon as Horse's men arrived, we headed for the short and by now nervous thug. He stood for a couple of heartbeats gawping at this sudden disruption to his day and then bolted. He tried to make his way through the press of fighting but that's a good way to get hurt, sure enough some bozo got him a lovely backhander with a club. He staggered a bit and by then I had one hand on his hair, I pulled backwards. Meataxe grabbed him by the throat and squeezed.

The rest of my little band had followed me and were keeping most of the melee at a distance. I wasn't too worried about the outcome. Although outnumbered we had started with surprise, I could tell these bully boys didn't know a lot about serious fighting, fine at beating up the helpless but not so good when faced with proper bad men.

This crowd did not have the benefit of prior knowledge, so they fought in the old-fashioned style. Big hits, body blows, and head smacks. Nothing really lethal, nothing which could stop us for more than a heartbeat. Their men went down with eyes poked out, shattered kneecaps, mangled testicles and smashed elbows. As many blows as possible were done when the opponent wasn't looking. Knife cuts hit the inside of thighs, aiming for arteries. Groins are another good target, even if missed it makes the defender pause for thought.

Then it was over, just a lot of broken and pain-wracked bodies on the ground with survivors standing amidst the carnage.

Smiley and the non-engaged personnel started treating our wounded. We all had lumps or bruises, two had broken arms, one a busted shoulder. We sent these back to Right Honourable with a small escort. Three of our men were dead. We left the slavers where they had fallen until all of our own were looked after, another lesson for them. I stepped over one bruiser holding a shattered kneecap, he was yelling at us, swearing revenge along the lines of, "I'll hunt you down! I'll kill you! You'll wish you'd never messed with me..." I stopped, drew my knife, put the tip behind his ear and pushed it hard. His body shuddered, heels thrumming the ground for a moment.

Extracting the knife from the now dead body I stood up and surveyed the other fallen, "Anyone else?" I asked. My men just kept moving around and tending to their duties, ignoring this little scene. Those on the ground went very quiet, no more threats.

After looking to our wounded, Smiley started on any slavers who could be saved. We even moved a couple into the shade. One asked, "Who are you guys?"

Meataxe ruffled his hair, gave him a big smile and said, "We're the NightWatch. Be a good boy now or we'll come back." The guy didn't know what Meataxe was saying, of course, but he flinched anyway.

Teddy Boy exited the building and came over to me. "Magic's inside, ducked in as we hit them from behind, only a couple of guards left in there, they're both dead. Willem's alive but unconscious, others are fine. Place has three large rooms where they keep prisoners, two rooms are pretty full, last one's empty. About a hundred people all up, women and kids as well as men. Captain's thinking about what to do with them. Who's he?" he asked, indicating the little guy.

"Don't know," I said. "He was giving us a bit of lip before you arrived but he's minding his manners now. Seems to be good at running away when there's a brawl on, not keen on the personal touch."

We went over to where he was tied to a post. We'd stripped him first because it's very hard to feel in control when you're sitting down naked. I poked him with the toe of my boot, pulled out my knife and gave him a meaningful look. He just about soiled himself on the spot. Smiley was moving past our small tableau and said to the little guy, "Tell them all you know, they kill easily," then he kept moving.

Chapter 44

"Hey, man, you don' wanna hurt me none," said the little weasel. "Whatcha wanna go and come on all gangbusters for? You wan' someone, you coulda jus' walked up and buy 'im. Take any of 'em, we don' care, take 'em all. Hell, we in the business a sellin' people. Look at the mess you made, man we are gonna be in some deep trouble when word gets out. Jus' lemme go, man, I ain't no threat to you." He spoke with a strange accent but we could follow most of it, I gave him back his clothes and untied one arm so he could get dressed.

Magic came out with Willem on a stretcher, Teddy Boy untied our pet slaver so we could take him with us. We made our way back to the tavern, I sent someone ahead to alert Right Honourable. Before leaving, we set the rest of the prisoners free but stuck all the gang members in the cells where they could look after each other. Or not, their choice.

As we walked, I had Smiley stay with me and the little runt to translate our chat. "You said we could have just walked up and bought our men back. Is that what happens around here?" I asked.

"Sometimes, bro. We grabs lotsa folks and if'n the guy we grabs got friends or fam'ly den they jus' swing on by and pick 'im up. All sweet," he said. "Yo' wanna tell me who youse guys are, 'cause I don' wanna be around anywhere yo' is for the near future."

"Why's that?" I asked.

"Naw, man, I say an yo' jus' get all mad again and like as kill me like yo' kilt Sanjy back there. I ain't sayin' nuthin' to make yo' mad, no way, man. Yo' a crazee man" he said.

It took me a couple of moments to work out what he was saying, then I went on, "Listen, Shorty, I'm the nice guy of this bunch. Tell me what I need to know and I promise I won't hurt you. Hell, I'll even let you go as soon as we're done. No charge."

The little guy looked at Smiley and asked, "He tellin' it true? You won' whack me jus' fer tellin' yo' bad stuff, stuff yo' really don' wanna hear?"

Smiley is incapable of telling a lie, I know because I am a very good liar and I can pick guys like Smiley. They are good to play cards with. The little slaver must have felt the same because he believed it when Smiley assured him I would keep my word. Not true, of course, I'd kill him in a second if it was needed. Smiley doesn't know me all that well yet, still thinks I'm an honourable man. Ah, youth.

Anyway, the little runt opened up a bit more after this character reference. "We snatch people and then sells 'em, open business, no secrets. Sometimes people come to us and sell members of their fam'ly, no problem, bro', we take 'em all. Like I said, if'n we snatch someone wid a bit a backgroun' – you know, money, or lotsa friens – we led 'em go. Easy. Plenny a' times someone comes up to der fron' door an' buys back a guy. Or dey come wid a whole buncha backup, or da boss jus' says to led 'em go. No problems, no one gets hurt. It's a business, afta all. I'm onna fron' door to do that sorta sellin', thas what I do, man, I'm just a salesman."

"Back up a little," I said, "why should we be worried about the next few days?"

"'Cause yo' didn' do business, bro'. Hell, the amount a' pain an sufferin' youse guys did back there jus' gotta mean somthin' gonna be done. Boss'll come and take youse all down, he gotta. Man, you really messed up bad. If'n the boss don' do somethin' then the next time we put the snatch on someone we might have another little fight. An then a lotta people gonna get hurt, lotta good folks, lotta customers, mos' like. So, yo' all hafta die or go 'way." He looked at me a bit anxiously, obviously still a bit concerned that I was going to do him harm.

He went on, "But he prob'bly won' do a full on brawl, they other guys willa tol' him how mean youse mothers are. Hell, man, yo' don' fight like decent folk. Pokin' a man inna balls! What sorta fightin's that? An' you musta put four or five guy's eyes out! They been made good as blind now, what yo' wanna do that for? An I fo' sure seen you and that big ugly guy stab a man inna back! Inna Back! Not fair, man, no way. So youse prob'bly be havin' a little visit from one a' them silent killa guys like the priests use. Then we see what's what. Yes, siree, we surely do at that."

This did not sound good.

We had arrived back at the tavern by now and everyone moved off to heal and mend. Right Honourable set guards everywhere while I conferred with Magic. Willem was beginning to come round, no wound on him, he was just asleep. This did not make sense. Even though he was groggy he was sure he had not been hit, he just fell asleep in that alley. Fell asleep!

Smiley was taping my ribs, I had taken a blow during the brawl. Never felt it at the time but now it was giving me trouble. He seemed preoccupied so I nudged him a little, asked him if he had anything on his mind. "Is 'Teddy Boy' his real name?" he asked.

Where'd this come from I thought, "No, his father's name is Ted, so we started calling him Ted's Boy but that was too hard, changed it to Teddy Boy."

"That's it? That's the reason you call him 'Teddy Boy'?" He looked mildly offended. "Doesn't he have a real name?" I will never understand how a person's mind works. Here we were, all banged up from a big fight, under threat of some dreadful death and the thing uppermost in Smiley's mind was a nickname. Go figure.

I pulled my overalls back into place over the bandages, wincing a bit. "Yeah, it's Michael," I said, "But where's the fun in that?"

He repacked his gear, looked at me for a moment and said, "I don't understand you guys."

I winked at him and joined Magic at one of the outdoor tables. We had to put it all these pieces together.

From what my runty little friend had said we could be the target of a retaliation strike from the slavers. If we were not confronted over our actions it would diminish their standing in the community, their business was based on threats. But he also said we would not be faced with another gang fight, but an assassin. Magic had him brought over.

"What's your name, son?" Magic asked, Smiley translated. All the squad leaders except Horse were there, as well as Wilks and anyone else who was interested. Veteran NightWatch were wisely asleep. I leaned against the wall and shut my eyes for a moment. Sheer bliss.

"Who you, ol' man?" No answer, I guessed someone was keeping Smiley quiet. After a space the slaver went on. "I ain't your son, granpa!" More silence. Even with my eyes shut I knew what was happening. The men would be sitting or standing around the table, all looking at the slaver. No hard stares or mean looks, just faces expecting an answer. Magic would be sitting closest to the runt, being patient was a great virtue of his. We could do this for any amount of time, wait until we had an answer.

A chair shifted, I could smell the closeness of people overlaid with the peaceful sensation of sunshine warming us all. Before I drifted off to sleep I heard, "'S 'Lucky". They call me 'Lucky'," it was murmured in a low tone.

Opening my eyes I watched Magic continue the questioning, "Lucky, what do you mean when you spoke of a 'silent killer like the priest's use'?"

"These priests got some badass dudes, do their killin' fo 'em. We done it once, putta hit onna bigshot army freako. No way we coulda got 'im, he tryin' to cloz our biz down but we the ones tha' cloze him down! Yeah! Motha came in here and threw 'is weight aroun'! We the big engine in this town!"

'Lucky' the slaver had worked himself into a state of excitement, his eyes blazed and some of the swagger had come back into his posture. He finished his last statement and threw us a triumphant glare, probably expecting us to fade away in terror. Instead of collapsing into subservience we kept up the same deadpan routine. On the scale of threatening people, he ranked a little above a puppy. A sick puppy.

When there was no reaction he sat down again and went on, "Well, boss wen' an seen a guy, priesty guy. And this guy musta seen another guy 'cause nex' day army dude wake up dead. He was inna barracks, had alla his big ol' soldier boys protectin' his ass! Heh! An he lyin' there chewin' on his own sword! We hadda killer guy write onna wall wid blood, he make our sign, man! Everyone know, don' mess wid us, baby! No way! No How! An now, you all gonna get it! Oh, yeah, man! You picked the wrong town to mess in!"

We all continued looking at him, no reaction. After a moment he sat down again and muttered to himself. Magic spoke again, "Did you see the killer? How do you know the priest organised it?"

Looking up the slaver blinked. By now he was must have felt he was dealing with a bunch of granite rocks. We hadn't argued with him, no counter-threats, we just weren't impressed by a little runt slobbering at us. "No, I didn' see anyone, no one did, man. Thassa point! Boss tol' us he saw the priest. C'mon, gimme a break. We all know them priests got guys who do this sorta stuff, them assassinin dudes. They dress all inna black and can walk thru walls! Thru walls, man! An' they kill ya jus' by lookin' atcha! They be freaky dudes." He was sitting back in his chair, slumped in resignation. I guess he realised he was in the big leagues now and he was only a bit player.

Magic asked him a few more questions but we didn't learn anything new, the slaver was taken away. Just for fun I had him chained to Meataxe.

Chapter 45

"We are back in the good books of the temple," said Magic. "Our contract has been extended to escort the artefacts on to the capital. The clergy is very concerned about this black-clad killer, and from what we have all heard they have a reason to be concerned. I have no idea how these events are linked. Unless anyone has any better ideas, I think the best place for us is away from here. Anyone care to comment on that?"

Right Honourable spoke for all of us, "When can we get out of this place?"

"We have to wait another couple of days before we can leave," answered Magic. "During that time, we could be attacked at anytime by these slavers. Or this assassin Lucky mentioned. Any ideas?"

I had one, "It seems to me that the slavers are keener on business than violence. If we can find a way for them to keep their rep without us dying maybe we can buy some time, at least until we're ready to move."

"Go on," said Magic.

"How about we meet with the boss," I said "Use Lucky as a go between, and put a deal to him. We move out of the city tonight, as if we are scared and we're running away ..."

"Which we are," said Right Honourable, "both scared and running away."

"Too right we are," I said, "but we see if we can buy his permission to come back into the city in two days to pick up the artefacts before heading off."

Magic asked the big question, "Why would he agree to that?"

"He's a businessman. It will cost him money if he has to hire assassins. And we'll get some of them before we go down. More expense. So, we put it to him that we will be saving him money by camping outside. Plus, we'll throw in some of our own funds to buy him off." I sat back, looking to see how the proposal went.

Some hours later I was sitting at another table in another inn with Smiley and Horse. Lucky sat next to a rather corpulent, over dressed man who was his boss. I was wearing my most winning smile as I started to negotiate our way out of this mess. The slavers had agreed to meet and discuss my plan. My head hurt, I am not used to having a plan.

After some initial dickering the boss slaver came out with, "Bottom line is, you owe me big. You say you want to avoid problems? Well, you should have thought of that before sticking your nose into my business. I'll let you buy your way out but it won't be cheap and it must be public. The money's no good if I still have to re-establish my authority after what you clowns did."

Horse wore his expressionless face. Smiley looked back and forth between me and the boss. I could tell I was losing any edge in the deal. He was treating me with barely concealed disdain, as if I was trying to buy the cheapest thing in the store. And I had no idea what to do.

"Can we get off the blame game," I said. "Do you want to deal or not? If we're going to fight let's fight, if we're going to deal then let's deal. But please, can we move it along." I paused before continuing, "So, what do you want us to do and how much will it cost?"

The boss looked at me, then down at his fingers. He played with a couple of big rings on his fingers before saying, "Alright, here's what you're going to do. You're going to come to the market tomorrow at noon with a whole heap of money or trade goods, I don't care which. You will hand them over to my representative in front of anyone who cares to watch. Since it's the busiest time of the market there will be lots of people to watch you grovel."

This was fine, eating humble pie wasn't going to kill anyone, it might even keep us alive. I figured why not? We dickered over the amount with Smiley's help. The final figure was steep but it was better than being dead. I stood up and said, "We'll see you tomorrow" and started to leave.

"Sit down, we're not finished yet," he said. "You think that's all it takes, just money. No, you have to do something else, nothing big, nothing that's going to cause you any real problems but it will reinforce my position in the town."

I sat. "What?" This was not looking promising.

He leaned forward and shifted his weight from cheek to cheek before leaning back again. "You're going to the capital, right? Taking the Sacred Artefacts for the ceremony?"

I nodded, so much for secrecy. "We're not going to steal the artefacts for you, forget that!"

"Please," he said, "nothing like it. No, I merely want to add to your little convoy. Since you're already heading that way, it shouldn't be a problem. I want to send one of my best men to the capital to conduct a bit of business. If he travels with you then I can be sure he'll arrive intact."

Sounds reasonable, I thought. "Okay, we can add one more to the group. That all?" I asked.

"That's all, he will have couple of men with him to ensure his safety at the other end of the journey but they won't be any problem. Oh, I'll send along a few trade goods just to set them up. Good, we're done." He signalled for some drinks and opened his arms expansively, a smile beaming from his face.

Thank goodness for Horse, he had spotted a potential problem, "What sort of trade goods?" he asked.

The boss gestured casually for more drinks, "Hardly anything really, a wagon with a few women for sale, possibly a cook or two. I couldn't say exactly until I've sat down and thought about it."

The drinks arrived. He made a fuss of giving each of us a full cup. I didn't touch mine, just let it sit on the table. So did Horse, Smiley squirmed. The boss realised there was a change in the atmosphere. He asked, "Something wrong? You were quite eager to get on your way before. You're coming out of this well, you know." He paused, "Oh, out with it, what's happened?"

I asked, "Do I understand this right? Your 'trade goods' are people, they're slaves?"

"I would have thought that was obvious, what's the problem?" he said.

Picking up my drink I took a sip while watching the boss, "What do you think, Horse," I asked while keeping my eyes fixed on the boss, "Is the NightWatch ready to become slavers? Buy and sell women?"

Horse's expression hadn't changed the entire negotiation. Maintaining his stone face he said, "When Hell freezes over."

"And there you have it, ladies and gentlemen, the voice of the people. Listen, pal," I leaned forward, "we went to a bit of trouble to get our man out of your hands. We are not going to help you do that to other people. We'll take your representatives, we'll take a wagon load of garbage, and we'll even take dopey there." I pointed to Lucky before continuing, "But we will not be taking any slaves." I sat back, had a drink and then waited to see what would happen. I felt I had just killed the deal.

"You'll take 'dopey', will you?" the boss mused a moment, gazing at our little pet slaver. "Fair enough, take him with another man and we'll call it square. But you pay for their food and you organise a wagon for their needs. Done deal."

"Uncle! You can' sen' me away, 'Mum'll have a fit!" We all turned to Lucky, he was looking terrified. "C'mon, Uncle, quit jokin' aroun'. This ain't funny."

I stood up, shaking hands with the Chief Slaver I said, "Agreed." Turning to Lucky I grinned, "See you tomorrow, and don't forget to give your uncle a goodbye hug." We left the meeting, all happy except for one spoilt brat who was off to see the world.

Back at the inn I met with Magic, we began to plan for the trip. Right Honourable would take the trade goods and money to the market the next day and make the payment. He asked for Smiley to be interpreter and Teddy Boy as backup. No problem. Teddy Boy had used his time well and all our gear was in good shape. All we had to do when the time came was pack up and go. Our wounded would eventually recover or die, everything possible had been done. We ended up that evening sitting around in the main room talking over the weird stuff that had been happening.

Wilks asked if life was always this haphazard in the NightWatch. I left him with Meataxe as an answer.

Chapter 46

Right Honourable and Willem joined me. "We were thinking," he said, "what if whatever made Willem sleepy was used on Stomach and Large? If those guys were given a knockout anyone could have killed them. The way Willem tells it, he was semiconscious. He might only have picked up a small dose. If those big guys had a full belt, it's possible someone came in the window and did them in. Could have entered anytime during the night, taken their own sweet time about it."

This was a grim thought but after thrashing it around I felt it was possible. The big question now was, what did Willem do that gave him a dose of the knockout drug? I asked that very question. Willem responded, "We were all in the same room together. I must have done something different to everyone else. I didn't eat or drink while in the room, it must have been something I touched or smelled."

Right Honourable came up with it, "The weapons. You ran your hands along the shafts of their pole arms."

"That's right!" agreed Willem, and I did smell something different on my hands after I'd done that. Damn, should have mentioned it! There must have been enough left to make me groggy, full strength could easily have put the big guys out."

"But how did it get there?" I asked. "Stomach and Large weren't in the habit of leaving their gear lying around."

"With all the movement in when we arrived someone could have done it. A customer, one of the staff, anyone. Probably someone in the city already, someone who knew we were coming." Willem seemed to be on the right path. "We'll have to watch our gear very carefully, especially whenever strangers are about," he finished.

This small city had not been good to us We had two murdered, more dead in a brawl and others wounded. There was a masked assassin running around killing priests and we had upset the local crime syndicate. On top of it all we were going to lose a lot of our funds. And the church was barely tolerating us. Our work here was done.

Next morning, we went to play out the little scene with the slavers in the market. Right Honourable was our front man, he walked into the market where some of his squad lay out a blanket, then he had the rest of his men bring out our trade metal plus some other bits and pieces until we had the bribe all sitting pretty. We knew the amount because Lucky had stopped by last evening with another slaver, this one looked way more serious than Lucky and a whole lot meaner. He seemed to be a very capable organiser as well as a first rate thug. I decided to walk carefully around him.

There we were, a blanket full of goodies on the ground, Right Honourable standing all proud and tall, his hands by his sides. Smiley stood beside him to translate, Teddy Boy was just behind these two, arms folded across his chest.

Shortly after noon the boss arrived with Lucky in tow, just late enough to show all concerned who was more important. I couldn't care less, pride kills very quickly. They were backed by about a dozen assorted thugs. We had kept our men back so Right Honourable and Smiley were on their own, except for the lone figure of Ted behind them.

The boss spoke in a loud voice, "Well, cur, have you come to make amends for your behaviour? Why should I not kill you where you stand?"

And so it went, Right Honourable made lots of obsequious noises, the slaver made him look small. There was a point where the slaver seemed to decide to kill Right Honourable on the spot. He gave the order then changed his mind, told his men to wait. He did a little dumb show of thinking it through. At least, I hoped it was just play acting because if he decided death was the answer we had no chance of saving Right Honourable. The rest of the men were well behind me, out of sight. We could get revenge but not stop the deed.

I was thinking I had not put enough planning into this. For some reason I didn't consider a double cross. Stress set in, I chewed my fingernails, ran my eyes over the situation, trying to come up with a plan on the spot. We were too far away, what a fool I had been!

Then I had a closer look at Teddy Boy and relaxed. Right Honourable had specifically asked for him, I hadn't given it a thought until I saw his folded arms. It meant his hands were hidden inside his jacket. Knowing his affection for things that go bang I was pretty sure Teddy Boy had a blaster tucked away under his armpits. No one was going to get close to Right Honourable without becoming very dead. At least, that was what I hoped.

Anyway, it was all a show, no double cross, no violence. After about an hour it finished, we had swapped a bundle of good stuff for Lucky and the mean looking guy who came to the inn last night. We got the raw end of the deal.

As Teddy Boy walked past me, I caught his eye and raised an eyebrow. He patted his jacket and gave me a little smile and a nod. Not a man to mess with is our Ted.

Back at the inn we introduced Lucky and the mean guy to everyone. The mean guy's name was Wallace. He made Lucky nervous just by standing beside him. I liked Wallace already.

Father Dale panted through the doorway, robes flapping, forehead beaded with sweat. Poor guy, everybody's flunky. Magic signalled me over, I was getting pretty good at knowing when to look at him in case he gave a signal. I had thought he and the Man in Black had a secret signal system, they always seemed to turn up together when there was a problem. I was realising it was because Magic kept his eyes open. I had better learn to do the same if I was going to be any good at this job.

Dale was out of breath again, but managed to deliver his message. What a surprise, the news wasn't good. The priests had decided to move everything a day early, they wanted us to go and get the artefacts. No problem there, I thought, we were set to go. Then he dropped the other shoe. No-one was to know we had the stuff. The priests wanted us to pick it up real quiet and slip away. They apparently had a tip-off that someone was thinking of making a snatch for the goodies - we all thought about the black assassin – and they wanted us to throw a loop at everyone else by sneaking out a day early. Not a bad idea.

Magic sent me with Willem's squad to get the gear. I was happy with this, Lonely was shaping up well as a second in command and a lot of the others were either veterans or competent newbies. Horse's men were still recovering after our little dust up with the slavers, plus he needed the other squads to help get things moving quickly. Smiley stayed behind but this was no big deal since Dale could translate if needed.

We moved quickly through the streets. Shifting a sizable body of men without anyone really noticing is tricky but we came up with a few ideas and decided to try them out. We split into twos and threes, separated from each other by a short distance. We used both sides of the street and the middle to saunter along, occasionally we changed our outer garb so we did not look too uniform, hats on, hats off, reverse coats, that sort of thing. Then a couple of the boys would yahoo it a bit down the centre of the road while the rest of us snuck along the walls. People will always turn and watch a couple of yobbos talking loudly, maybe even having an argument. In this way we crossed the city quickly and without a lot of folk aware it had happened.

We again arrived at the side street where Meataxe had made a fool of himself with the guard. Dale told us to wait a minute while he went and smoothed the way. He disappeared into the building after speaking to the soldier priest on duty, this guy then followed him in. Moments later Dale reappeared and told us to come in. "The priests have pulled everyone out of the room but they can only keep people away for a few minutes," he said. "It is most important that you are not only speedy but also very quiet. Not a sound. We are not telling all of the guards, we want them to spread the word of its disappearance. Confusion will be sown in the ranks of the unbelievers who would desecrate our holy shrine."

Certainly confusing me, I thought. The whole plan stunk of a set-up, like they wanted to frame us for stealing the artefacts. The priests might be on the up and up, the deal might be genuine but I was worried. No point in asking Dale, he was in it with us like a sacrificial lamb. Since there was not much choice we went ahead and took the lot.

Some of the lads packed the stuff into the travelling chests which were nearby, others stood on watch near doorways. Dale hopped from foot to foot in anxiety and successfully made us feel nervous. Lonely gave the okay and we started out back through the way we had come. I came last with Dale. We passed a few closed doors hoping they stayed closed. The men with the chests were almost on tip toes in their efforts to keep quiet.

At the doorway we paused while Willem peeked around the corner, he gave the all clear and out we went. Going back to the inn was different than the trip to the temple. The men carrying the chests needed to be guarded so we had two small knots of bodies, one around each chest. There was another bundle rolled up around a staff, this was the Sacred Banner, another big deal. Fortunately, it had its own leather carry case. Willem put it over his shoulder like a spear. We took our time, easing through the intersections, waiting for any groups of people to disperse before we moved on. I sent Lonely to tell Magic all was well, Dale stayed with me. He was a nervous wreck, trying to look in all directions in case a rush of thugs erupted bent on sacrilege.

To calm him down I asked him about the black clad assassins. "They are a sect, an outlawed group of warrior priests," he told me. "They are feared by all, it has even been known for lesser priests to don the black garb. The mere sight of one of these vile murders is enough to quell rowdy elements."

"Are they such a big deal?" I asked.

"Oh, dear me, yes," he said. "The 'Black Ones', as they are called, see others as unbelievers and so worthy of punishment. There was a dark time in my church when it was ruled by an extreme sect. People would disappear from the street, fathers taken from their homes, children snatched from a mother's arms. The Black Ones were the militant arm of this fanatical group, monsters all. A few remain, despoiling our communities until hunted down. They have many techniques for causing pain. For them, suffering is the only legitimate penance for an unbeliever. Therefore," he finished, "they slowly torture their prisoners to death. The more suffering the victim undergoes, the closer thay come to God."

What a bunch of winners, I thought.

Chapter 47

Upon reaching the inn our conversation was cut short by the final preparations for leaving. Magic told me to detail someone to look after our guests, Lucky and Wallace. Someone who would make sure they didn't get lost or run off, someone who could make sure they were looked after.

After a quick think I sent for my favourite technician to give him the good news. "Wilks," I said, "I need you to be at the top of your game here. Very important these two, very influential, they will require someone with a high level of personal skills as well as significant diplomatic training. Have you had any such training, Wilks?"

"No, Sergeant," he said, "I've only had the basic courses in teamwork and leadership." He stopped for a thought before continuing, "But I would like this job, it would certainly add to my resume. I'm looking for that next step in the promotion ladder; I think I'm ready for more responsibility."

Yeah, sure, I thought, more responsibility, just what he needs. I went on, "Look, Wilks, don't mess about here. You're going to have to make some decisions on the fly and sometimes cut a few corners. Do you think you can do that?"

He looked at me with slight confusion before saying, "I don't think it will be necessary to 'cut corners' if things are done the right way. I am keen to do the task but I will need some support and training as we go. I'll run any decisions by you just to make sure I'm on the right path."

This was about as flexible as he was going to get, good enough for me. "Right, Wilks, you're now Senior Liaison Officer for our visitors. Go and see what they need, keep them out of trouble, look after them." Thinking we were done I stood up.

Wilks remained where he was, still sitting. "Just one thing, Sergeant," he said. "Is there a time allowance for this duty or is it entirely salary?"

I stopped and looked at him, "What?"

"Well, being a liaison officer will take time, time away from my other duties. How will we cover that?" he asked.

My brain ran in circles for a while, "Wilks, you're a Drop Market Technician without a Drop Market. What other duties are you talking about?"

"I have been keeping the records of goods traded and so forth," he said. "I've completed all the required forms for loss and/or damage to the Drop Market, I've been logging all relevant incidents into our Market Log. I thought I should bring it with us, Magic agreed I should keep these tasks current. When we get back to the ship there will be a full and complete record of what has happened. It's all been filed, each day I update and cross file. This all takes time, Sergeant, and then there are other duties which you have given me, assisting the squad leaders. I assist with the food and then there is the care of the sick and wounded with Smiley."

He stopped and looked quite exasperated, almost overcome with his workload, "I don't see how I can fit any more into my schedule, there are only so many hours in a day and I don't want to let anyone down by not being properly organised. The medicines are constantly in need of examination, bandages are forever going missing. As for the food, well, it's a miracle we have gotten this far with people just helping themselves. There's no roster, no distribution plan.... I'm not blaming anyone but sometimes Willem ..."

I jumped in quickly, "Okay, hold on, I can see you've got a huge workload there." Hells bells, I thought, how has this guy lived so long? "Tell you what, I'll get someone else to assist Smiley and Willem, you stick with the record keeping and the visitors."

He stood up with me, "But I'll need to train my replacement. I had no training at all when I took on those jobs and it was quite difficult. You know, Sergeant, the NightWatch really needs to look at its Induction Program. I'm not surprised we have communication breakdowns when so many of the new people have little idea of our culture and the way we do things. Perhaps you could have some regular meetings with me and the others where we could discuss various points? Shall I set up an appointment diary for you?"

This guy was out of control, "I'll get back to you on that, Wilks, just get started on the liaison. I've, ...er ... I think Magic is calling me." And I actually ran away.

I haven't run away from just one guy in a long time.

We snuck out of the gate about midday and set off. Given that we may be leaving some cranky people behind us Magic was willing to accede to a request for a forced march. When I say "forced" I mean we had to use the metaphorical whips and clubs to get the little caravan to move at speed and when I say "march" I mean nothing of the sort. We can't march. We can barely head in the same direction. But we walked quickly. Extremely quickly.

We did this for two days and two nights, pushing on at a hellish rate. Brief pauses, long days of marching and short nights of sleeping. Magic had us up before dawn each day. We ate cold food when we eventually stopped after dark. It was so very, very hard.

The evening of the third day descended on our rather disorganised collection of crack guardsmen and women. We made camp in a small bend in a river, Magic had relented and let us make camp before it got dark. He felt we had put enough distance between ourselves and any pursuit to have at one full night's sleep. We had just crossed over a nice little bridge, our camp had a good overview of the ground we had covered behind us.

Due to us being on a small rise we could actually see our back trail for some distance. Meataxe and I were standing chewing something inedible and gently arguing about how far we could see behind us in the gathering gloom. Bets were laid, money changed hands.

"I can see the road where it disappears into the woods about two hours march back," I said.

He squinted and said, "You're hopeless, Val. Look past the woods, see where the road comes out and goes into the hills. I can see that road, clear as day."

I peered. I could see the road, but the far end of the woods was completely invisible to me in the gathering gloom. We had crossed some hills before coming down into this valley but I couldn't see any part of our track. "There is no way you can see that far. It's too dark", I said. "You are just a lying, ill-bred little man."

"There is much truth in what you say, o great and wise leader," he said. The camp had started to quieten down, guards were posted, a gentle, collective sigh seemed to come from behind me as everyone settled in for the night. "But in this case, as in so many others, you are greatly mistaken," he said. "It's there, just a little, faint line running up the slopes. Oh, there are some lights. Someone's coming down the mountains in the dark. Must be keen."

This worried me. Why would someone be travelling over such dangerous ground in the dark? I sent a runner to find Teddy Boy, he has great eyes.

It was full dark by the time he arrived and listened to the situation. He stood looking into the night for a while and then said, "You owe Meataxe a drink, Val. There are lights out there and they are moving down those hills. I think we better tell Magic" He was right. We sent for the boss.

Standing around in the dark we discussed options. Magic, me, Teddy Boy, Right Honourable, Willem, Meataxe and Lonely. "Could be anyone," said Willem, "could be normal travellers."

Right Honourable countered, "At night, down a hill? Who's in that much of a hurry?"

We were standing on a very gentle slope, dew on the grass, the river giving soft slurping sounds channelling over rocks, the stars sparkled in a beautiful velvet sky. The seven of us stood watching the approaching lights, an occasional breeze ruffling our hair or gently kissing a cheek.

"They're after us," said Teddy Boy.

"I reckon," confirmed Magic. "Good spotting, Meataxe."

The big man gurgled with pleasure before pretending he was shrugging off the compliment, "No worries, boss."

"Righto, boys, what do we do?" asked Magic. We moved into a bit of a huddle. I guess we were the brain's trust.

Lonely spoke first, "Why don't we find a good, defensible spot, like a small hill with some boulders. We could put up barricades, wait for them to come to us."

Meataxe snorted, "You been hearing too many stories, Lonely. We don't do organised fights. We're more sneaky bastards."

Lonely bristled. Meataxe just spoke his mind, there generally wasn't much on it. Lonely tried a command tone, "You know perfectly well my name is L'On-li, Lance-Corporal L'On-li. I outrank you, Guardsman Meataxe. Do you even have a real name? I also think you underestimate our fighting skills. I am sure we could give a good account of ourselves and send those ruffians packing, whoever they are."

"Yeah, whatever," replied Meataxe.

We continued talking while Lonely stood dumbfounded at this gross breach of discipline. Horse leaned over and whispered something in his ear, Lonely's face turned red before he eventually regained his composure. He took a breath, let it out and rejoined our planning session.

The thrills of growing up in the NightWatch.

Chapter 48

Magic told Meataxe to rouse the camp, get everyone ready to travel. The untidy watchman walked off, thus preventing Lonely from making a bigger fool of himself. "More ideas, gents. We have to move but where do we go?" Magic asked.

Right Honourable chipped in, "Might as well keep going to the capital, Charles. It's two weeks normal travel time journey from that last city. I reckon we've done the equivalent of five days travel already. We could probably do the rest in four more days of hard march. Don't know if the lads and lassies are up to it, though."

"Why don't we stand and fight?' suggested Lonely.

No one answered him. We were ignoring him but being polite about it. Willem said, "Be good to slow those guys down a bit. I reckon I could destroy that last bridge pretty quickly."

"Going to do your Horatio at the bridge impression, Willem?" asked Right Honourable.

"Hardly", the other man answered, "It's wood, I'll just burn it. Reckon Meataxe'll give me a hand with that. What do you reckon, Charles?" Magic agreed, sending him off. He told Right Honourable to lead the march since it was his idea.

Lonely again spoke up, "Hey, I had an idea! What about what I said. We could stand and fight!" No one answered him as we moved off to our various tasks.

There were a lot of moans and complaints from the camp, but things slowly came together. Smiley came over to protest about the treatment of the wounded. Shortly after him came Dale, anxious to find out what was going on.

"Ted," said Magic, "take some people who won't trip over their own feet. Find the road. Leave markers for us. We'll stop for a rest about midnight."

Lonely was looking frustrated, upset over the poor reception we had given to his suggestion. Magic said, "Look after him, Val. Tell him."

So, I told Lonely a bit more about the Watch, "We're brawlers, mate. Thugs with a badge. Think of all of the times we've had to fight. In every one of them we fought dirty. We hit from behind, we run away, we gang up on anyone alone. We'll even kick a man when he's down. That sort of fighting we are good at."

We walked back to the slowly evaporating campsite. "A lot of us have been in an army of some sort," I said. "But the reason we're not there now is, well, it didn't work out. Some deserted. Just ran away. We're good at running away. And that's what we're going to do now."

The bridge had started to burn nicely, Meataxe was running around whooping like a kid and waving burning brands in the air, probably trying to write his name. I put my hand on Lonely's shoulder and gently squeezed. "Get your squad together. Travel with the artefacts and banner. Your job is to get your men through this alive, not to fight battles. Your people come first. Look after them, see to their needs. To survive this, we have to reach the capital. Alive. Not die while fighting. Even if it means losing the artefacts, we get to the capital. Get your people there, that is our job. Do you understand?"

His squad had drifted over to us looking for instructions. I raised my voice a little and said, "Listen to Lance-Corporal L'On-li, he'll tell you what to do!"

I left them to stumble back on to the path. To stagger, fall over and get up again. To follow after the NightWatch along a dark and lonely road. How terribly poetic, I thought.

We hoofed it through the night, through the forest and finally out onto a great, dark plain. The road stretched ahead of us, shining in the night, I asked Smiley how we could see it, he said all major roads had a faint glow after a few hours of starlight, it helped country folk find their way at night. Something to do with the way they treat the soil when making a road, starlight activates some germ or something. Neat trick. This planet didn't have any moons to shine down but the path ahead of us glowed as if a full moon was smiling on all of us.

Magic let us rest for ten minutes every hour and after thirteen hours he finally called a halt. We had walked all day and into the next night. As evening fell, we just lay down and slept, and when I say we I mean everyone else except me. Being Sergeant meant I had to walk around doing leadership stuff. All I wanted to do was lie down and die, my body ached, my legs throbbed and I felt like throwing up. But walk I did. Guards were set, corporals put on roster before I checked in with Magic.

Then I lay down and evaporated under the twinkling stars. I was sick of walking, sick of being stuck on a mud ball planet trying to kill us. I even entertained some positive thoughts about life aboard a clean spaceship surrounded by lots of nothing.

Meataxe was shaking me, "Val, Val, walk up, dammit!" I knew it was Meataxe by the amount of drool raining onto my face. "We got a problem, Val, there's someone in the camp!"

I rolled over and dragged myself to my knees. What had he said? Someone in the camp? Of course, there's someone in the camp. My sleep drugged brain wasn't finding anything unusual about it, after all, weren't we all in the camp? I think I may have giggled.

"Val!" said Meataxe, "Get a grip." He was whispering in a very loud voice directly into my ear with a breath that could kill a brown dog at ten paces. I shook him off and rolled upright. Meataxe pulled me back down into a crouch. Looking around I tried to see something different about the camp. Nothing, all was quiet.

He pointed towards one edge of the camp, it all looked fine, everyone was asleep. Just bundles of sleeping bodies on the ground. The guards were moving in their pairs, pairs on duty after a hard day means a big chance they'll keep each other awake. For the life of me I couldn't see anything amiss. "What is it? What did you see?" I whispered. My whole body ached.

Then one of the bundles moved. It crawled a short distance and stopped.

I pointed at it and looked a question at Meataxe, he nodded. That moving bundle was what had caused him to come and wake me. I was didn't think this was a prank. Given my state of fatigue, if it was a joke there would be murder done by me. So, ergo, there was something about the moving bundle which bothered Meataxe. What? I watched as it moved and stopped again, it was now well and truly inside the boundaries of our camp. As I crouched, gazing at the shapeless mass, I tracked its future path; it was heading for the wagon containing the artefacts. Big surprise.

Righto, how to handle the situation? I looked at Meataxe, he had dozed off so I pulled his beard. I was very satisfied when he came awake with watering eyes. "Saints Above, Valentine! Fair go!" he said. I pointed at the blob and then at the artefact wagon so he got the idea. Looking him squarely in the eyes I shrugged my shoulders, no idea what to do. I was out of clever solutions. In fact, I was out of any sort of solution.

He paused a moment and then started gesturing with his fingers, giving off hand signals. I looked at him, his eyes agleam in his own world. He had a plan, Meataxe had a plan and wanted to tell me all about it. His hands danced as he communicated the grand strategy for dealing with our intruder.

I had no idea what he was saying.

I stood up, grabbed a nearby heavy cudgel and walked over to the hump. I hit it very hard about where the head would be. I'm a big lad and was out of patience, I put a lot of resentment into the blow. There was a solid thump and the lump went still. Meataxe ran up, "What did you do that for?" he asked. "You said you didn't know what to do? What about my plan?" He sounded quite put out.

I put my arm around his shoulder and said, "Shut up, Meataxe. I was too tired, you lost me after the double pincer movement and the belly crawl. I'm sure it was a great plan but I'm knackered. Come on, let's see what we've got." I pulled the blanket off the hump as Horse came up with a couple of men. He was the corporal on duty and had a lamp. We all had a good look at our catch.

"The assassin!" one of the men gasped.

Chapter 49

Sure enough, lying at our feet was someone in black, complete with the black headgear Father Dale told us about. Was this the killer of Stomach and Large? What was he doing here? My brain couldn't think in a straight line, it kept going around in circles. Eventually Magic arrived with Dale and some others for company. Most of the camp remained snoring, a condition I thought would be pretty useful right about now.

Dale knelt down and rolled the body over. It was a body, a dead body. I must have hit it a bit too hard. Ah, well. Magic turned to Dale and asked, "Is this the man who attacked you and killed the Abbot?"

"I cannot tell," said Dale, "it could be." His hands were exploring the various pockets and folds of the black garbed corpse. A few of us exchanged glances over these actions. Horse went off to double check the guards and add a few more, Meataxe squatted down with Dale and also started going through the deceased's clothing. Dale may have been searching for clues but Meataxe was just rifling the dead for any lootables. Old habits and all that. "There are more than one of these Black Ones," said Dale. "This could be the one that attacked me but there is no way of knowing."

"What's he doing here?" I asked, trying to look on the ball.

Meataxe said, "Hey, he's all wet, he's soaked through and through. Even his headgear. I bet that's how you got to him so easily, Val, he probably didn't hear you." I was a bit put out over this and muttered something about my stealth skills and cat-like reflexes but no one took any notice.

"Settle down, Val," said Magic, "I think it was a combination of his muffled hearing and your decisive and rapid action which brought us to this point. A more elaborate plan may have been too late to stop him before he wrought untold havoc."

While looking at Meataxe I grinned and gloated, "Untold havoc, eh?"

"Yes," said Magic, "or just dumb luck." Meataxe coughed a laugh which I felt was disrespectful of those in authority. Magic continued, "In any case, here we are. And what have we got?"

Dale stood up holding a small black pouch and some knives. "They generally carry poisons or sleeping potions in these pouches," he gave the pouch to Magic. "I cannot find any weapons other than these knives. But then, his whole body is a weapon." Whoopee! I thought.

Right Honourable had been lurking on the perimeter of our conversation, he does a lot of lurking on the edges of conversations. Probably why he is so well informed. "Can we surmise that he probably swam the river and then sought to delay or attack us?" As he spoke, he was scanning the area of the camp, looking for threats. "Would he not have expected to be apprehended? But he came on nevertheless."

That was scary. "You mean," I said, "he was on some sort of suicide mission? He was going to stop us even if he had to be caught? That doesn't sound like these guys."

Magic neatly punctured my bubble, "What sort of guys are these, Val? Do you know them?"

"No," I blustered, "but no one just ... runs in ... accepts capture ...or death." This was not going well. "Do they?" Fatigue had caused my brain to go on holiday but it chose that moment to return. I could think of a dozen occasions in Ostend where someone had sacrificed their own life for the benefit of others. I went on, "Look, perhaps you could just forget I spoke, I'll be quiet now."

The stars still shone down on our little group, gathered around a dead man. We stood in the darkness. A single lantern flickered on the ground, casting shadows into the gloom of night. Behind me, behind all of us, the rest of the camp slept on, oblivious to danger. Exhaustion takes a big toll.

"Wake 'em up," said Magic. "Let's move."

And on we trudged along the bright-lit ribbon of road. It softly glowed under our feet, its beauty lost on each of us as we concentrated on the back of the person in front. Step followed step, numbness had set in, we walked as if dead. Cresting a hill, I am sure the whole thing would have looked beautiful from above. A beautiful clear sky, the hills debouching onto a large plain with the shiny road slinking off into the distance. And there we were, coming down the hill as a series of small dots against the brighter road, fleeing the unknown.

Total rubbish, of course. I wasn't watching from some lovely aerial spot, nor was I sitting and looking from a position of rest and peace. A peace gained by a nice relaxing meal followed by a few good whiskeys. No, I was head down and tail up dragging myself up and down the column. A column of lucky, lucky people who had had a few more hours of sleep than me. A few more hours! Even one hour! My brain couldn't cope with the difference, a whole hour of sleep, what I wouldn't give for that opportunity. And were they grateful? Did they leap about and cavort in a spry fashion? Ingrates. They moaned, they whinged. They bitched at me, they muttered at poor planning, they sneered about running from shadows! How dare they mutter! I'll give them mutter, I'll...and then my brain came back and saw what was going on and told me to shut up. On we walked.

And walked.

At some point the sun came up to say hello but we kept walking. We drank water on the move. Anyone needing to relieve themselves meant leaving the column, dropping your drawers and doing the deed while the rest of the column walked past. No one looked, no one made funny jokes or gave a snigger. We were too tired. We knew we could be the next person to squat and strain.

I had most of the corporals at the rear keeping stragglers up. Ensuring those dropping off to one side to perform the necessary business didn't fall asleep while mid-deed. It happened a few times. I'm sure life takes on a certain charm when you're woken up after falling asleep with your pants around the ankles. Even worse if you happen to slowly fall over and lie in your own filth. Such is the glamourous life when in the NightWatch. We kept everyone moving by threats, kicks and shoves. But did we get any thanks? No, ah, the fickleness of popularity.

Somewhere around the middle of the day we stopped and fell over. Magic came and got me for a talk. I hated him.

We wandered off to one side and he said, "How are you doing, Val?"

"Absolutely marvellous," I said. "Couldn't be better. Can I die now?"

"Not for a bit," he said, "Look over there." He pointed off to one side and there was a small hill. Just a little hill. And up on the crest there was a deserted farmhouse, a tumble-down ruin, ready for some lovely little event.

"Oh, no," I groaned. "Not the hill, come on, Magic, no, no, no."

"You'll be right, Val," he said, "I'm going for help, we're all stuffed, we won't make another day like this. I'll even take Meataxe and Smiley with me. Just the three of us. We might even have a picnic."

I groaned. "Not a Last Stand, boss. Not another one. I can't take it, we're all wrecked." Standing in front of him I couldn't believe he could look so fresh. It wasn't fair at all, I thought. "How do you do it, Charles? I mean, I'm trying as best I can but I'm dead on my feet. You stand there looking bright and chipper. I don't know how you do it. Are you, are all real leaders just made of special stuff?" I think I swayed to and fro at that point.

He looked at me, he gave me that complete openness that only happens between people who have suffered together, who have overcome great pain and hurt and still came out the other side. His shoulders slumped. His face sagged. "Mate, I hurt so much. I don't want to play any more. I would volunteer to be hit on the head right now, I just don't want to keep on doing it. This game is too hard. I want to stop." He took a deep breath, straightened up. "But I can't."

He put his hand on my shoulder and looked into my eyes, "We can't." He leaned into the first word.

"Yeah. Righto... okay ... let's do it," I said. "I take all of us up the hill, form a defensive line in between the snores, and hold out until you come back with reinforcements. That about it?" I looked around at the rest of the company, they were all lying down, most were asleep already. I noticed some of the veterans had taken up some guard positions. The corporals were distinguishing themselves by still being mobile. I was impressed. "Do it now?" I asked.

"Yeah," he said. "Listen, I spoke to Dale, he says these assassins, these 'Black Ones' would be in whatever group is chasing us. Makes sense, we've already caught one of them – hail to you, O Mighty Slayer – so the following bunch of chaps may well include others. Kill 'em, quick, Val, they are bad news. Unfurl the great banner so they know you're there with the artefacts. Suck them in and kill them. I'll be back, with help. Just stay alive. Keep the men, and the women, keep them all alive, Val. I'm relying on you, you are the only one who can keep the NightWatch alive."

No pressure then. Good, I hate pressure.

Chapter 50

The corporals and I got everyone up the hill. No point going into the farmhouse, all that was left of the building was a few half walls, no roof. We assembled in a small yard enclosed by the remains of a low stone fence. We let Dale carry and unfurl the great banner. He stood over the chests containing the artefacts and planted the pole firmly in the ground. Not quite the heroic image. He was skinny with knobbly knees, sandals with a torn and stained robe. Still, he was having a go, can't ask for more than that.

We waited, the day dragged on, people slept or drank or ate. Most fell back asleep. Some sat having quiet conversations, probably not really listening but just to hear a friendly voice. I gathered the squad leaders for a planning session, Teddy Boy had put a few veterans on lookout duty so we had a bit of peace in which to think our way out of this mess. "Anyone got any bright ideas? I asked.

Lonely spoke first, a regular Mr. Keen, "Let's arm everyone, spread around the perimeter and be alert to the first attack. I could have a group ready to run and plug any gap, we could build another set of barricades in the centre and that could be our last redoubt. If we get overrun, we pull back into that and just hang on. My group would be the 'Flying Squad.'" His eyes shone, they actually shone.

There was a pause while we all stretched legs, looked into space and tried to think of alternatives. Right Honourable gave the decision, "Yeah, righto. Not a lot of choice, is there. Let's go with Lonely's plan. Better still, stick Dale and that banner in a very visible spot, let the bad guys see it easy. Might make them just a bit overanxious." He lay on the grass, resting on one elbow, tired but not spent.

Teddy Boy gave the final call, "Magic will see us right, he'll come up with something."

We sat together in silence, enjoying the company and the small interlude of peace. Overhead the sky was a lovely blue; I sat on a boulder looking out at my company, the people for whom I was responsible. Again, I felt tired to the bone, the other leaders were all shot, they had hollowed, deep-set eyes. There was no banter, turning a head seemed to take a lot of effort. "Well, we're it, boys. All those folks over there, all our people are depending on you. We've brought them here, they need us to bring them out alive. How you react, how you fight, how you look, how you talk – they will do just the same as you. Do it right. Lead them. Encourage, help, bully, but never give up. Never let them think we've had it."

I don't know where the energy came from but I found myself getting to my feet, face ablaze with emotion and will. "Damn it," I said, "we're the NightWatch! We do not roll over! We've come too far. We're a better, tougher bunch than we were back in the City. Do you understand? If they come up that hill we're going to kick their teeth in!"

The men stood up and moved off, quietly patting me on the shoulder as they passed by. They were staggering and tired, not heroes at all. They were filthy, haggard and smelled bad. Thieves and murderers, liars and cheats every one. My best friends.

Around mid-afternoon we spotted the first people in the distance, a small group of runners who stopped when they saw the banner. Some stayed where they were while one turned around and ran back they way he had come. About an hour later a larger body came into sight.

We certainly had a good vantage point for viewing, the little hill we were on was one of several dotted across the plain, ours was the first in a series of such hills, the rest strung out behind us, no trees just rolling grassland. Some of the Watch who came from farms said they probably raised the equivalent of sheep or cows with all this grass. That would explain the lack of fences and the sheer openness of the place. The road entered the plain off to the south from where we had come. It passed by our little enclave and then weaved its way between the hills behind us before eventually disappearing.

I thought our position was pretty good, unless the attackers had cannon but we'd seen no evidence of that level of technology. As I got a better look at our pursuers, my heart sank and didn't stop until it hit my boots. The oncoming bunch were not a raggle-taggle bunch of vengeance seekers, not just an organised mob of citizens. There were a lot of them and they seemed to be wearing some sort of uniform. It was the army. Light glinted on metal, lots of armour and pointy things. They were formed troops. Oh, joy.

On the other hand, a sick man waving a dead cat would have been able to overrun our position. Manned as it was by people at the end of their rope.

At least, I thought they were ready to roll over and die until I did my rounds. Whatever the corporals were doing and saying, it was working. The veterans on the wall were immovable rocks, big, horrible, ugly men ready to cause great amounts of personal damage. The women who had joined the watch and been with us for a while had the same look. A look which could be described as stern and resolute, but bitter and twisted would be more accurate.

Lonely had his 'Flying Squad', these were most of the newcomers armed with their quarterstaffs. Willem, Horse and Right Honourable were scattered around the perimeter while I stood with Dale in the centre with his banner. Also with me were Wilks and our guests, Lucky and Wallace. Had they ever joined the wrong crowd. We'd given them both Translator Beads for the duration of the trip. Lucky looked like death warmed up but Wallace appeared both competent and reliable. He still didn't smile a lot.

As we waited for the oncoming crowd, I studied the little group near me. Dale looked nervous, a bit worried but not panic stricken. Lucky sat on a chest with his head in his hands, probably asking what he had done to deserve being stuck with us. Wallace just leaned against the now empty wagon, flipping a knife into the air over and over again. The biggest surprise was H'nuth, he sat next to Wallace, matching him trick for trick with the knives. And they talked occasionally, actually talked to each other. New best friends, no doubt.

Wilks was writing in his logbook, good to know that future generations would be able to read of our glorious struggle. I had put all the wounded somewhere in the battle line. I reasoned if you were conscious you could hit someone. Or at least trip them up by letting them fall over your bleeding body. I believe I had said as much to them in a little inspirational speech. They had responded by asking me to perform unnatural acts on animals.

If you're going to die, I guess it's best to do it with your mates.

Chapter 51

The mob marching up the road caused me a lot of concern, mainly because they were marching. I dislike trained and drilled troops. They stopped at the bottom of the hill, did some to and fro stuff which was all very pretty to watch before finishing all lined up ready to come and kill us. My team were definitely the underdogs in the coming competition but at least they would be a bit more rested. I knew that because I could hear most of them snoring. Amazing, isn't it, here we were faced with imminent doom and they all, or nearly all, had fallen asleep. Poor little tykes, I thought, have a nap before the big bad man comes up the hill and sticks a sword into you.

There must be some way out of this, but I could not think of what it might be. Any time now these troops would march up the hill and roll right over us. And then I had a thought, why? Why are these guys chasing us? Haven't we been doing the will of the authorities, or at least the priests? And surely the army came from the authorities? Perhaps it was all just a simple misunderstanding? I was becoming quite confused and my head was hurting.

Where were Meataxe and Magic? Wouldn't any help they found be the same as these guys here, the regular troops? This was all too hard, so I asked Dale, "Why is the army here? I thought we were being chased by a bunch of assassins. These guys look like a whole different problem?"

Dale just kept staring at the assembled multitude, and by the saints there were a lot of them. His gaze was fixed, his mouth open a little, I could see the wind ruffling his hair as he stood silhouetted against the blue sky. Couple of nice clouds up there, too. Finally, he spoke, he said, "They shouldn't be here..."

Well, that helped a lot. He thought they shouldn't be here. What did that mean? Should someone else should be here? These guys should be somewhere else? What? I looked from Dale to the solid ranks below, ran my eyes over my sleeping throng and came to a decision. Up I stood, moved through the comatose bodies, over the wall and down the hill. About halfway down the hill I stopped, just stopped. And sank to a sitting position on the now warm grass.

This was neat, I thought. A bird flying above would see this mini-army assembled at the bottom of the hill ready to charge a bunch of supine bodies cuddling the remnants of a stone wall, the banner of some God fluttering in the breeze. Sitting on the ground smack between the two of them was a mighty warrior, in this case, me. Please, don't let me fall asleep, I prayed.

From where I sat, I could hear Right Honourable speaking to me, asking if I was alright. I didn't turn around but gave a little wave with my hand so they would know I was hearing them. From the ranks below a lone figure detached itself and moved up the hill towards my position. As he got closer I could see that he was dressed in black, from head to toe, even a black headpiece including a piece of cloth across the face.

How good is this, I thought, I found the bad guys right off.

The figure stopped just below me and unwrapped the cloth from around his face, and he was a she. Hello, I thought, this is new. "I didn't think you were allowed to be females," I asked. To this individual my words would have sounded like so much gibberish. Silly me, I had left the only translator up at the camp.

"Do you understand my words? Nod your head if you do," she said.

This was clever. I nodded. "I command this force," she said. "Do you have the artefacts?" Again, I nodded. "You stole them" she added.

I shook my head vigorously. "We didn't steal them. We were acting under instructions from the church," I said.

She stood quietly. We looked at each other. "We want them back," she said. "We will climb this hill in one hour and get them.

Any resistance will be met with extreme force. We will kill you, every one of you. Do you understand? You may, of course, return them. Your lives will be spared." I was impressed by the quietness of the tone, she didn't rant and rave, she just told it like it was. Of course, I didn't like what I was hearing but she was a great public speaker.

I nodded, stood up, turned around and headed back up the hill. When I got there the corporals and Dale rushed over to me asking what was going on. I told them. In one hour the army would climb the hill, kill us all and take the artefacts. We stood in a little huddle, I had half stepped down from the wall and the rest were clustered around me in a small knot. Dale said in a slightly astonished voice, "You spoke with one of the Black Ones!" I hadn't told them the leader was a woman. I felt Dale would take it kind of hard.

"Who gave you the instructions for us to take the artefacts from the temple?" Horse asked Dale.

The priest looked at me for a moment before answering, "It was ...," he paused, "It was one of the Deacons, he told me he was delivering the message on behalf of the Senior priests."

"What's a Deacon?" I asked.

"You know them," he said. "We had several with us on the journey, they helped guard the artefacts."

"You mean those warrior priests in the armour with all the weapons?" asked Right Honourable.

"No," said Dale, "they are what they appeared to be, monks with special training. They are charged with temple security and things of that nature. No, the Deacons were the other priests, the ones who fought without armour."

"Those guys!" exclaimed Lonely. "They were amazing, they just kicked and punched and ... oh, my, they were Black Ones!"

"No! I knew them all well," replied Dale. All Deacons receive that level of training. Only a few are asked to go on and become assassins. And how the Black Ones are recruited I do not know."

"Fair bet they come from the ranks of the Deacons," said Right Honourable.

"Again, not necessarily," said Dale. "The Black Ones hide their mastery of the fighting arts, or so it is said. They could be anyone, perhaps even someone not associated with the temple." He stopped and looked around at all of us. "Perhaps a mere farmer, or labourer"

I jumped in then, "Do you mean Smiley? Are you suggesting he could be a Black One?" This was crazy. And then I thought, maybe it wasn't. He was well placed to keep an eye on the doings of the monastery where we first met the priests. In fact, it was Smiley who suggested we go there. We all thought he was very switched on for just a farm boy. By the saints, perhaps he was one of the Black Ones? And he had gone off with Magic and Meataxe. We might be facing a situation where not only help was not forthcoming but both of our comrades may well be dead.

Willem said, "We thought it was just a bunch of thugs after us, perhaps with a few Black Ones. But these guys are regular army. Val, is the leader a Black One?"

"I don't think so, just dresses that way," I responded. "Maybe we've been running from just the one guy. And we've killed him. I think we've been had, gentlemen."

They say that when big events arise, a great man will also arise to lead people. I was not that man. I think I swore a bit and then sat down and held my head, moaning.

It was Teddy Boy who pointed out the obvious, "Why don't you and Dale just go down there and tell them what happened? Give them back their precious artefacts." I saw Dale begin to object but he didn't come out and say anything.

Ted's idea might work, I thought. Shortly after this we wandered down my little slope and sat at the halfway point. I had Ted come with us and quietly bring his gun, or guns. Guns in the plural would be a lot better. I was beginning to like the idea of guns, lots of guns.

The black clad one detached herself from the throng and strode up to join us. She had a little entourage, two military looking figures and one of the more traditional looking warrior priests in armour. They stopped a short distance in front of us but realised this gave us the height advantage so they slid uphill to sit down at our level.

Then they waited for us to say something.

Chapter 52

I leaned back on one elbow, nudged Dale and said, "This lady is the leader of our new friends, how come she is a female and a priest? Anyway, speak softly, Dale, so these nice people don't feel the need to kill us." Then I leaned back onto the softest grass I have ever felt and put my arm over my eyes. This was heaven. "Poke me if a fight breaks out, I may doze off," I said.

Lying in the dark I heard Dale say, "You are the leader of this band of heretics?" Oh, good, I thought, a positive opening. I moved my elbow so that I could peek from under my arm. "Why do you seek to thwart the will of the Holy One?

My small sight picture did not include the female leader but it did cover the military types. They stood stone-faced but their eyes flickered around, not missing a great deal. I heard the leader say, "You are mistaken, father. Dale, isn't it? You are wrong on many accounts and perhaps your errors have led you into unsafe doctrines."

"You dare!" spluttered Dale. "Who are you, a female," the word came out with great distaste, "to speak to me so?" This was a new Dale I was hearing, he wasn't the scared little runt of the early days. Looking after the artefacts must have given him some backbone.

I heard the rustle of paper before the woman went on, "Here is my warrant from the High Priest. It charges me with the rooting out of the apostasy known as the 'Black Ones'. I have been tracking one for many days. You take too strong a tone with me, priest. I represent the interests of the church in this matter. If you feel more inclined to argue then you may take the matter up with this gentleman behind me. You may have heard of Captain Britlar."

She said this with such relish that I had a closer look at the military type who had nodded his head. I also heard a deep intake of breath from Dale, "Captain Britlar, is it really you?"

A deep voice rumbled back, "Indeed it is Father Dale, the High Priest has released me from my normal duties and sent me searching our lands for these criminals, the 'Black Ones'. I assist this investigation. I do not lead. We follow the orders of my lady here. If you are wise, you would do well to follow my example." This guy hadn't made any change in his stance but I didn't doubt he knew which end of the sword went in first. He went on, "I recognise you, Father, do you still doubt our credentials?"

A spluttering noise came out of Dale as he said, "No, no, of course not. You are the Captain of the High Priest's guard. I know you well ... have seen you many times... I am very confused." Looks like we might live after all.

"Tell us, Father, why did you assist these criminals in the looting of the temple?" she asked. Nope, I thought, we're all going to die. Criminals, eh?

"These men are not criminals," said the wonderful little priest. I loved him so. "I was sent to them seeking help to take the artefacts on the last leg of the journey to the capital. I was told we had to do this quietly since there were rumours another attempt was to be made to carry out this outlandish theft. There was also some unpleasantness with the slaver's guild which further complicated things." Dale had resumed his subservient tone, although I could tell he was not too impressed about treating a woman as his superior.

"Who told you these things, Father Dale? Who sent you on this mission?" asked the woman. Good question, I thought. Sounds like we were set up and I would be keen to know who was involved.

"The Deacon I met said the orders came from two people. They were the Senior Priest and ...," he paused and sidled a little away from me. What's going on here, I thought." The other was," he went on, "the leader of this band, a man known as Magic."

Well, talk about surprised! I leapt to my feet, made a grab for Dale and ended up doing a decorative face plant after Captain Britlar did something clever involving hips and arms. I felt a sword at my neck and yelled, "No, Teddy Boy! Stand down!"

The captain helped me to my feet after I promised to behave. He exchanged a few words with Dale who told him what I had said to Teddy Boy. He looked at me, said he was intrigued, "It was my sword at your neck yet the man you first thought of was one of your own. Interesting. Why would you tell him to stop doing whatever he was going to do? Don't you find that fascinating? What was he going to do?"

"He was going to kill you," I said. Dale translated and there was a little riffle of excitement through the group. I know how to stir up a party.

Except for Britlar, he just gave Ted a five second look and said, "Indeed?" Ted hadn't moved at all, just stood there with his arms folded, one hand in the jacket. He gave Britlar a little smile and a wink.

"Can we get on?" said the lady. "Father Dale, the Senior Priest was found dead in his rooms. He had been seen alive at evening devotions which was some hours after the discovery of your theft. When we found the artefacts missing, he gave no indication it was by his order, he instigated several searches himself." She paused and sat easily on the ground. "Why did he not just say he knew where the items were? When I arrived in the town I was informed of the event, by the time I came to the temple he was already dead."

She faced Dale and demanded, "Who was the mysterious Deacon, Father? Did you recognise him?"

"No!" the little priest shook himself angrily. "He was not anyone I know!"

"What about the ones who came with us from the mountains, was he one of them?" I joined in.

"I said no! Are you deaf, Unbeliever?" he yelled. There was a moment of stunned silence before he went on. "I'm sorry, Sergeant

Valentine, I apologise for my tone. All I can say is that I did not know the Deacon who gave me those instructions. I did not believe Captain Magic would do such a thing, but it was what I was told."

The lady said, "Well, that's settled. Now, let's talk about those artefacts and how much suffering you wish to endure before they are returned."

Rolling over on the grass and looking at her, I unzipped one of my pockets. I fished out an item and held it out to her. It was a Translator bead. She took it and, following my mime directions, placed it into her ear.

"Hello," I said.

Any female with the talent to be put in charge of Britlar and go against some entrenched sexism was my idea of a tough chick. I wanted to be in her good books, opening communications was a way to show her I was one of the nice guys.

Her eyes lit up quite pleasingly with the discovery of our technology. She said, "I can understand him, Captain Britlar. How sweet." Britlar just grunted. She went on, "Where is this magician?"

"Pardon?" I asked.

"Magic, where is he? Why is he not facing me himself? Is he a coward to hide behind one such as you?" she asked. I wasn't sure what she meant by the 'one such as you' crack but nevertheless we kept talking. She wasn't thrilled to learn Magic was not in camp but cheered up a bit when we said that the artefacts were up on the hill, right under the sacred banner.

So, up the hill we went. Britlar summoned up a squad and soon the whole bunch of us stepped over the low rock wall of my glorious last stand. Spread out before us was the fighting NightWatch, ready to make a valorous last stand against insurmountable odds. Every one of them snoring gloriously.

We stepped over the sleeping bodies, "They've had a long day" I said. Britlar shook his head in disbelief. Arriving at the sacred Banner I let Dale show the chests containing the artefacts.

He opened them up and, sure enough, they were empty.

Chapter 53

There was a bit of commotion after that. Dale seemed especially agitated, poor little guy. When he opened the first chest, he had this huge grin on his face. He threw the lid back with a great flourish of both ownership and reverence. He stared for several seconds at the empty chest and I could see his brain telling his eyes to go back and check again. Gradually realisation dawned, he ran from chest to chest, throwing them all open and exposing some very decorative linings.

That Magic, I thought, he's up to something. Anyway, Captain Britlar didn't see the humour in the situation and treated us all with understandable contempt. I didn't mind, contempt can't kill you.

"So," he said, fingering his newly acquired Translator Bead, "your leader has left you here to buy him time while he makes good his escape." He paused, said something to one of his aides who went scurrying off down the hill. He went on, "He has left you to die."

Right Honourable coughed, "I rather hope not" he said.

"Do not worry," said the lady, "we don't kill innocents. We leave that for fanatics like the 'Black Ones'. We will question many of you but you will not be harmed".

"Say," I said, my brain going off into random locations. It does this when I'm tired, "I've got a question. What's a Portal Ceremony?" They all looked at me, where did that come from?

"I don't think you quite understand how this works," said the woman. "I ask the questions and you answer them." We sat and talked for a while, she asked each of the squad leaders a few bits and pieces while Captain Britlar had lots of soldiers rip apart our goods. By this stage, of course, most of the NightWatch were awake and sitting back observing the goings on.

Watching the soldiers go through the small wagon used by Lucky and Wallace was worth a show. Lucky strutted and preened, expostulated about being treated like a criminal. Stated how he should be shown the respect due to a merchant. Stuff like that. Wallace and H'nuth sat against a wagon wheel, both chewing something from a pouch. Wallace didn't seem too worried.

Lucky went right off when his personal wardrobe was investigated. He had a few implements involving leather and handcuffs which we all viewed with a certain amount of mirth. He rounded on his audience, ready to let fly. I saw him glance at Wallace who shook his head. Lucky shut up.

Wandering over I sat beside Wallace, we'd given him a Translator Bead earlier. I asked, "How's it all going for you, Wallace?"

He chewed, "Can't complain."

"Lucky all right? Not too put out by our little escapades?" I liked this guy.

He looked at me, stopped chewing and said, "Like I care." Went back to chewing.

"How does this work, Wallace? Are you his boss or what? What's his story?" There wasn't anything else to do and Wallace looked like the sort of person with a few stories. He was heavily muscled, large arms and shoulders. Tattoos were keeping the scars company.

"Nah," he spat something vile onto the grass. "He threw his weight around a bit too much back in the city. Somethin' had to be done about the little loudmouth. Otherwise his Uncle was going to call on the *Deathsman*."

Sounded unpleasant. "What's a *Deathsman*? Some sort of standover merchant?" I asked.

"Killer," he said, spitting another noxious stream.

I said, "He was going to set a hit man onto his nephew?" Possible, I knew some Italian families back in the City who didn't mind knocking off the odd close relative. Glad I'm not a Medici.

"Not anymore, you guys gave the boss a better option," he said. "I'll take him to the Capital and enrol him at Military School. Or kill him." I looked at him, was he joking? Probably not, he didn't strike me as the type of guy who went in for light comedy.

We sat for a while in companiable silence. Wallace spoke again, "Them patches are pretty special, eh?"

"What?" he'd jolted me out of a nice daydream, something to do with beds.

"Them patches," he repeated, touching my shoulder badge with a stained thumb. "I see everyone makin' sure they got their patch nice and visible. Wanna go into a fight knowin' who they are." He looked at me, eye contact, direct stare. "Good team, too. Gutsy bunch."

For some reason I felt a warm rush of pleasure at his comments. He rolled one sleeve back and showed me a tattoo of an imprisoned skeleton. Beneath it was a dagger. He pointed at the skeleton and said, "My patch. My people."

Well, I thought, this is different. I'm comparing unit insignias with a slaver. You don't see a lot of that. I pointed at the dagger and asked, "This part of the badge?"

He rolled his sleeve back down. "Nah" he said, "That's me. *Deathsman.*"

He was the mob's hit man. The people you meet in this job, never ceases to amaze me. He went on, "Why's your patch dark? Some of them are dark like yours, others not, they're light. What's all that about?" He'd stopped chewing now. We were sitting talking like old friends.

I explained about the NightWatch, told him where we came from, it took a while but we weren't going anywhere. I'd noticed the shading too, sometime during this long walk all those who came with us from earth had darkened their patches, including me. I don't know how it started but it felt right, the newcomers hadn't done it yet and again I wondered why. I talked all this through with Wallace, it was good talking to someone outside the chain of command, it allowed me to unpack some of the stuff in my head.

"They don't think they're with you yet," he said. "Be interesting to watch them, see when they decide they're good enough. See when they darken their patch."

He was making sense, I talked about flags and insignias, and how we used them on earth. "I understand," he said. "It's important. Anyone hurts someone wearing our sign, it's an insult to all. Even Lucky, useless as he is, he wears our mark."

"Hang on," I said. "You just said his uncle was thinking about having him killed!"

"S'different." He stood up, wiping his hands on his pants. "If we do it, it's family. No problem. But if someone else kills one of our own, well...," he pulled a hand across his throat while making a cutting sound. He looked across at Lucky, shook his head and finished, "Useless twerp."

This seemed like a good point to leave, I heaved myself to my feet and waved goodnight. He gave me a smile showing lots of stained teeth before moving over to intimidate Lucky some more. H'nuth tagged along with him.

Wallace made me remember the girl I had killed back on the ship. She had a sign on her arm, some form of tattoo. Magic had commented on it, thought it might come back to us since she was from an important family. If we had upset someone powerful it might have been a reason for revenge. Pulling out a pad and pencil I sketched the tattoo, you learn how to remember signs growing up in my world.

By nightfall it was obvious we didn't have the artefacts. In fact, we didn't have much of anything after the soldiers had ripped apart our gear and tramped our supplies into the ground. My complaints didn't get a very positive hearing. Captain Britlar just redoubled his efforts to be unpleasant and the lady ignored me. Eventually we were left alone, in the dark, cold and hungry. On the positive side, we were still alive.

Next morning, we were woken by a tired and cranky bunch of soldiers. We were told to get on our feet, gather our gear and start walking. Since we were tired and cranky ourselves there were some interesting exchanges and a few blows. Nothing serious, soon we were on our way, now we were hungry as well as tired and cranky.

I trudged along beside the lady who led this band. She was still dressed in black so I asked her what it all meant. "Nothing too ominous," she said, "this is very close to the garb of the 'Black Ones', I find that by wearing it I get a bit more respect from the citizenry."

"What happened to the Black One you said you were chasing? I asked.

"He joined you," she replied.

"He did not!" I said. "We don't have any Black Ones, unless he's in disguise." I had forgotten my own discomfort by now. The thought of one of those killers in my company was not attractive.

"Calm down, Sergeant Valentine. We found his body back at your last campsite," she said. I was feeling better now. "He had been killed by a blow to the head. What happened," she went on, "did you have a falling out of thieves?"

One track mind, this girl, "We're not thieves," I said. "That body you found wasn't a part of our group. He came into our camp one night. We found him and killed him. No big deal." Very modest.

She raised her eyebrows and said, "I find that hard to believe."

"That's a shame," I responded.

"He was a Black One! They can move like smoke and are just as hard to catch," she said. "Also, we found only his body, what about the people he killed?"

"What do you mean, 'the people he killed'?" I asked.

"The ones he took down before he was felled," she said.

"Ah," I said. "Those people. Well," I paused. "He was killed as he was creeping into the camp, didn't really get a chance to fight back."

This time it was her turn to pause, "Are you telling me that someone in your group was able to creep up on a Black One and land a killing blow? Unbelievable! Who is this paladin?"

I gave a modest little shrug and answered, "That'd be me".

Long silence. Long, long silence. Finally, she muttered, "Unbelievable."

Chapter 54

On we walked, conversation seemed to dry up after this little interchange. About midday we were groaning again so she called a halt. Once again, my people just staggered off the road, fell over and lay comatose. Some took food, all drank copious amounts of water. We would have to find a source of this wonderful stuff by tonight.

The members of the lady's company, especially the soldiers, had been a bit more organised in their meal set up. Little fires were soon glowing, metal pots bubbled over flames surrounded by interested groups of soldiers as well as growing bands of freeloaders from my people.

Our stopping place was quite lovely, the road wound in and out between low hillocks, small clumps of trees were scattered around where we sat or lay. Grass swept over all the land, up and over the hillocks in a gentle layer. In this idyllic picture the road emerged from between two of the low hillocks. I hadn't set a guard, mainly because we were probably prisoners and I don't think that's allowed.

Captain Britlar hadn't put out any pickets either, but I figured it was his business how sloppy things got. There we sat, moaning and whinging, trying to scab a meal. A few were sleeping, judging by the snores. Just us, in our quiet little meadow between the hills.

The sound of something in full gallop had barely registered on our consciousness when from between low mounds and down the road ahead of us pounded a horse. The rider was at full stretch over the neck of his mount, riding like there was no tomorrow. We watched him, conversation ceased, food paused on its way to mouths, and we all just looked. About halfway along our little picnic area the rider realised he was not alone, pulling back on the reins he brought his animal to a very spectacular halt. Lots of dust and sweat flying in the air.

Then stillness, we formed a very quiet tableau. Must have seemed a strange sight, us all scattered on both sides of the road, some with boots off, sitting, standing. Finally, someone spoke, "Who the hell are you?!" roared Captain Britlar. Good question.

A couple of soldiers had grabbed the reins so the rider wasn't going anywhere. Seeing the uniforms seemed to reassure him though, he stopped trying to resist and allowed himself to be pulled from the saddle. Didn't have a lot of choice, really.

I sauntered over to eavesdrop on the conversation between him, Captain Britlar and the lady. It made interesting listening. I wasn't really surprised to hear Magic's name. He'd done the impossible again.

Shortly afterwards, the rider remounted and went back the way he had come, again at great speed. Britlar had us all regroup and start walking. I moved back and forth up the line spreading the news I'd overheard.

It seems when Magic left our camp, he took the sacred objects. He is a sneaky, devious man. With Smiley and Meataxe, he walked non-stop to the capital city. Non-stop! This was an amazing feat considering he had been walking without sleep for almost three days. After depositing the religious goodies with the local guard and some priests he talked the interested parties into mounting a rescue mission. He had come back for us, this time with a mounted troop as escort. The fellow we had encountered was a scout, sent ahead to see how desperate our situation had become.

I suppose seeing us all lounging around had given him a poor idea of our straightened circumstances. Still, I thought, I could live with someone's low opinion of us. Better than being dead.

We hadn't travelled far when we were met by the main rescue force. They congratulated Captain Britlar and the lady on a job well done, made a few jokes at our expense and then allowed me to see

Magic. He was pretty wrecked but he gave me a smile as I walked up, "Good to see you, slacker," he said. The man must be made of iron.

"You're looking a bit crook, Magic. Something you ate?" I asked. We shook hands and then he slid gently to the ground, unconscious.

No one from the NightWatch had actually died in all this upheaval. That's not a bad way to finish.

We spent the night camped around Magic. He seemed to have made a strong impression on the folks in the capital. I don't know how he does it, people trust him, integrity reeks off the man. His escort, the mounted force, were very solicitous of his health and fussed over him to a great degree. Fuss, fuss, fuss. Charles would have been dreadfully embarrassed, pity he was too whacked to enjoy it. I made a promise to myself to tell him all about it, over and over again.

Next morning most of us, except Magic, were feeling a whole lot better. After a few more days of lazy walking, we trundled off down the road and slowly made our way to the capital, a great, rambling, sprawling city. As we came over the last hill it lay spread out before us, the main gates in their high walls were about an hour's march away.

As we walked the last part Magic and I shared news, gossip and our opinions. He told me why he took the Holy Artefacts. "We were dead on our feet, Val. After you knocked that assassin on the head, I thought it was only a matter of time before we got into more trouble. I took off to get help. I knew no-one was going to listen to me without some sort of credential, that's why I took the artefacts. Smiley was needed as a translator so we didn't get killed right off the bat. And Meataxe, well, he's just too horrible to be stopped by a little thing like total exhaustion. Besides, someone had to carry the gear and I'm management."

"Go alright?" I asked. I had never doubted Magic. You bleed with a man a few times and you know he's solid.

He smiled and said, "They loved me."

"I hate you," I said.

The gates were open, it was mid-afternoon and the sun was shining. Talk about your happy endings. The cavalry had bolted ahead to spread the news because that's what cavalry does, gets in first with the good news and gets all the girls. If the news is bad, you don't see the cavalry, they're all in the next country and still running. I don't like cavalry.

"You brought back cavalry," I said.

He punched me on the shoulder, "Get over it, you big wus." We walked through the gates and Magic waved for the NightWatch to follow him. The rest of the little cavalcade went straight up the main road but we turned right and eventually entered a little park. We were allowed to camp here. Without too much fuss we were soon tucked into a nice cosy atmosphere of fires, food and leisurely conversation. Again with the green grass and gently waving trees. Personally, I was sick of it. Country living and camping out is not one of my favourite pastimes. I'm a city kind of guy.

Magic gathered everyone together and told us all about his actions and thanked us all for hanging it all together. "I want you all here tomorrow at noon, gathered right here," he said. "Bit of a surprise. You'll like it."

As we walked back to our bucolic life, I raised a point which had been worrying me for some time, "Say, Charles" I said. "Got a bit of a problem."

"What would that be, Val?" he said.

"We've got, or had, six months to get to the other market, right?" I asked.

"Correct," he said.

"Okay," I said, "We're stuffed. We've taken this long to get here, how on earth are we going to get all the way around the rest of the world? Even on a sailing ship we might take months. When we set out, you had a plan, right? Tell me you had a plan?"

We walked through our campsite. I saw an inn loom ahead, a good sign, I thought.

"Yeah, I had a plan. I planned for something to turn up. Of course, I didn't have a plan. All I could do was hope," he said. "Val, if we stayed where we were, we'd all be dead. Well, I think we would be dead, can't be sure. Anyway, I decided to have a go and see what happened."

"And what's happened, Charles?" I asked, following him into the inn.

"Been a bit grim, Val, no denying that." Magic signalled for a few drinks and don't stop them coming. I could deal with that. "In fact, we had no chance to reach that other Drop Market. We were toast."

"You say 'were' like it means something, Magic. We're still stuffed. I've spoken to a few of the locals with Smiley and I know we have a whole ocean between us and the next continent. A whole ocean, Charles. Not a lake, not a small inland sea but a whole, entire, complete and huge ocean. Now, Charles, I am dead loyal, you know that. But tell me true, are we stuffed or what?" I took a long pull on my drink and looked at him. Smug mongrel gave me a cheesy grin.

"See you, tomorrow, at noon, Val" he said.

I never liked senior management.

Chapter 55

After a few more drinks I was feeling no pain. When Wallace and H'nuth slipped into the chairs opposite with another bottle to share I was in no position to object. We chatted a while, I quite liked Wallace and was warming to his devilish friend, they knew the rules for keeping a man company. Not a lot of talk, just companionship. "How'd you go with Lucky?" I asked, "Get him into the Military?"

Wallace took a drink, said, "Working on it," then drank again and scratched his bicep.

The action caused me to look at his tattoo again, "So you're a *Deathsman*, eh? One of the heavy hitters?" He was wearing a sleeveless leather jerkin, worn and scarred, a bit like him. His face was weather beaten but strong, a competent, tough man. No idea why he had sought out my company, I would have thought Willem or Horse would be more of a match. He was too intelligent for Meataxe and not intelligent enough for Right Honourable. As for Teddy Boy, he and Wallace could compete for Most Taciturn Thug of the year.

He leaned back in the chair and looked down at his tattoo, "Not a *Deathsman*, THE *Deathsman*." Stretching out his arms to relieve the fatigue he finished, "Only one, me." This was new, I thought, I'm drinking with a mob's top hit man. It was quite a surreal experience, sitting in that noisy tavern across from the sort of man I normally avoid, usually by running away. The air was full of smoke and stench, men argued, lied, shouted or drank alone. Mum would not have been impressed with the company I was keeping.

"What happens now?" I asked. "Do you wait for a caravan back to your home?" I couldn't help myself, Wallace had sparked my curiosity, I wanted to find out more about his history.

"Nope, this was my last job. Wanted to ask you about this Watch thing."

"Watch thing?" I asked. He wasn't making a lot of sense.

"Could someone like Lucky join?"

I groaned, "No, definitely not." I thought some more, over time we have had our share of loudmouthed, useless people. The more I thought about it the more I realised this description fitted most of us. "Maybe. Probably get himself killed early." We had another drink.

"I thought he was joining Military School or something. What about that plan?" I asked. We finished that bottle, I brought another. It seemed to be the decent thing to do.

Wallace grew more relaxed, he poured us each another drink, "Don't worry, I've got him lined up for a place in the cavalry. Starts tomorrow. Just wanted to see your reaction." He leaned back and drank. I did the same. Lucky cavalry, I thought.

We talked on and off about places we'd been, people we'd seen. In Wallace's case it sometimes involved people he'd killed. Top night, I think I sang a bit.

I do remember climbing on top of a table and claiming I could beat anyone in the bar before being proved comprehensively wrong.

Next day I woke up crook. No denying it, cheap drink will do it to a man. And I think there was a stage last night where I decided that anything in my glass was a good drop. Probably an error, I felt as sick as two dogs. People may say that they are as sick as a dog. I was as sick as two of them. I was hung-over at the cellular level. Life hated me.

Wallace and H'nuth, the ugliest, scariest pair I have ever seen,came by and checked on me, told me about my challenge to the bar. I didn't like the way they laughed when Wallace said it but I thanked him for pulling me out before I had taken more than a couple of hits. I had a few more nicks and bruises which I would feel when they got their turn.

Just before noon Meataxe brought me to the little park and popped me on a rock. If Meataxe was feeling sympathy for me then I was definitely at death's door. Noon came and that's when I saw the damndest thing.

A lot priests trooped in, all dressed in their best clothes and carrying the Sacred Artefacts on a special litter. Some sort of religious ceremony happened and then the High Priest gave the nod to a flunky. This little guy rolled onto the green, green grass and stuck his hand into the ground. Later Magic told me that he had one of the artefacts and he plugged it into a recess in the earth. But from where I sat, or swayed, all I saw was some skinny dude stick his hand in the ground and then a shimmer appear in the air. Of course, by then a shimmer in the air was not something I trusted since a lot of my air shimmered. Still, sick or not this was a pretty good deal.

Magic came over and shook my shoulder saying, "What do you reckon about that, Val? It's a portal, a gateway to their High Temple. They use it to go to and fro during the season of worship. And get this, Val. Anyone can use it for the next month. Anyone. How good's that?" I think I threw up on his shoes before passing out. Can't be sure because the next time I came to we were on the other side of that amazing portal. Of course, I missed the lot, but Right Honourable told me all about it. In detail. While eating some sort of greasy meat. I hate him, too.

Sometime mid-morning next day I surfaced. Teddy Boy was sitting on a crate and said, "Welcome to the sub-continent". Then he walked off. I groaned and rolled over, swearing off drink for good.

I had awoken in a tent pitched on a lovely flat plain. This grassy plain was surrounded on one side by the sea, on another by high mountains and on the last part by another large city. Oh, yes, quite some distance off was a hill and on this hill was the other Drop Market. Blow me down.

Magic had done it again, pulled us out of a mess into safety. We had another meeting and goodness knows I love a good meeting. Can't get enough of them, I say. With us were some of the bigwigs, the Lady and her shadow, Captain Britlar. Father Dale was in attendance, looking a bit out of place in this group. The High Priest with a bunch of flunkies and then all the gang from the Watch. I noticed Wallace and H'nuth leaning against a tree at the back.

Magic spoke about our gratitude for the Empire's assistance in securing our safe passage. He went on at some length, I don't normally give a lot of thanks to Empires but, hey, it was Magic. The High Priest responded, thanking us for delivering their artefacts safely for the ceremony. Interestingly, the Lady spoke next, on behalf of the Emperor. Seems she was something of a diplomat, a trouble-shooter for the crown.

The journey from our crash site had certainly given us better group cohesion. Right Honourable was still giving daily quarterstaff lessons. After all this time the new Watch members were pretty good. In fact, they scared the daylights out of civilians, especially when they did some synchronised drill as a demonstration at the start of the meeting. Right Honourable has always been a show-off. Veteran NightWatch sensibly avoided drill.

The meeting finished, we returned to our campsite to pack for the last leg of our journey. We still had to travel across the plain to the Market but we felt we could make that little stroll. The Lady asked if she could join us for the walk. She seemed pretty interested in having a look at our spaceship thingy. Personally, I think it was to hang around Magic a bit more. I can spot young love and she had it. Judging by the number of quiet chats they had been having I was pretty sure Magic was also smitten. Go, Charles, I thought.

Wilks found me gazing at the portal, he offered to explain how a primitive society had such advanced technology but I frankly didn't care. He spluttered a lot when I said I was willing to accept it as magic.

"Nonsense!" he foamed. "It's perfectly understandable science!" but I'd already wandered away.

Next morning, we joined a caravan heading over to the Market. A collection of wagons and beasts were all laden with the luxuries of an entire world. Spices, jewels, anything small and of high value. The merchants wanted to impress their off-world visitors with a great display before bringing out further loads of food, furs and bulky items.

This first caravan and all its goods were the property of the Emperor. If he was satisfied about the deals then a tent city would develop around the Drop Market for any other merchant. Britlar was in command and had final say over the goods in the caravan. He was the man to impress.

I also suspect the Emperor and the High Priest both wanted to make sure we got home without any more hiccups. Britlar stood in his saddle shouting orders, the gates opened and out we went.

Chapter 56

I used the time to turn over all the strange events from this journey, something was picking away at me, tickling my Watchman's sense. After an hour I sent runners to a few Watchmen, I wanted a meeting. The trek to the market would take about three hours, should be enough time for me to scratch my itch.

Magic was on point but I didn't include him in the meeting, I wanted a shot at this myself. I was dawdling towards the back of the column, better to keep an eye on things. One by one Right Honourable, Teddy Boy, Horse, Meataxe and Willem dropped back. Soon we were walking, chatting, just a bunch of friends out for a stroll. The landscape was open, rolling grassland on all sides, visibility was clear up to the Market, the city gradually receded behind us but we could see the high walls easily enough.

"What's on your mind, Val?" asked Right Honourable. "I can't believe I just said that," he finished.

"I need to explain all the deaths," I said. "Not the accidents, not the fights, just the murders. The newbies in the village, Hells Bells! I don't even know their names! Stomach and Large, Father Dexus, probably others."

"Why us, Val?" asked Willem, "It's just us here, what about Father Dale and Smiley. Bit of a hole in our knowledge base."

He was right, I hadn't included them in this little debrief. But this group had been around for a long time, we'd put in a lot together. I knew them, knew when to listen and when to ignore them. I didn't feel as comfortable with the others. I guess I just did not know enough to trust them. I tried expressing this to them, when I'd finished trying to explain my misgivings it was Horse who said, "It's 'cause we're your mates, dimwit. Get to the point."

Fair enough, I thought. "The deaths started after the priests joined us, they're the common factor. The crash and its aftermath didn't set off any closet psychopaths in our group except for Santini and I think that was resolved. He seems to have settled into some sort of pastoral role. God help us. Anyway, he was only interested in offing H'nuth, I can't see him doing fellow Watchmen. So, I'm betting the killer wasn't one of us. I include Wilks as 'one of us.'" This set of a few groans from the team.

Willem exploded, "Wilks! If I never hear his 'Willem, just one thing...' again I will die happy." The others chipped in with similar feelings, seems I was not the only one he drove mad.

Teddy Boy said, "Leonard and Ruth, their names were Leonard and Ruth." Ted always knows the right stuff. I thanked him, our dead had names. We kept walking.

"It all points to one of those Deacon guys, one who was with us from the start," commented Willem. "Either one or both could have been Black Ones. Could have done all the killings."

Right Honourable asked, "All of them? How does that work?"

Willem stared ahead, I could see his eyes lose focus as he thought it through, "Give me a minute, I'm making this up as I go. Okay, let's call the killer 'Dominic' after our old Archbishop."

"How appropriate," muttered Meataxe. He hadn't said much so far, this was a bit too serious for him but he was happy for us to talk on.

"Right," Willem went on. "So Dominic kills the two newbies, sorry, Leonard and Ruth."

"Why?" asked Right Honourable.

Willem shrugged, "Don't know. Practice, maybe, see how hard we were to kill. I'm just trying to see if it works. Later, Dominic drugs Stomach and Large by coating their weapons with one of those potions. Slips into their room at night and does that sarengo stuff. Goes back to the temple where he later kills Father Dexus and gives Father Dale a kick in the head. After we leave town, he kills the new Senior Priest."

This sounded possible, "And then swims the river to catch us and creeps into camp to retrieve some of the artefacts," I said.

"Yep," said Willem. "Val, you might be the guy who killed 'Dominic.'"

"By the Saints!" I muttered. Could that be it? Had I, almost by accident, killed a serial killer and solved the problem?

Teddy Boy brought us back to reality, "Still got the 'why'." He was right, of course. Before we got any further the column stopped for a break, Magic wanted a squad leader's meeting before we arrived at the Market.

I asked the lads to keep quiet about our discussion as we moved up to the head of the stationary column. Along the way we passed Father Dale, giving him a wave. He was standing at the back of a wagon from the temple, the priests were sending out a delegation to set up a tent church at the market site. Father Dale was back in his role as flunky, fetching and carrying. I gathered up Smiley and Wilks on the way, just wanted them standing by in case we needed our own flunkies.

H'nuth and Wallace stood next to one wagon. Wallace gave us a little wave as we walked past. I wondered why Wallace was still with us.

The Market was about an hour's walk ahead. We came up to Magic and his new girlfriend as they stood gazing at the huge structure. It would be an intimidating sight, plonking itself down outside your doorstep. I asked Wilks, "Why would they land so far away from the city? Trudging over here and back takes a full day. Wouldn't it make more sense to sit it down just outside the gates?"

"Well," he responded, visibly growing with all the attention, "It's a bit complex but I'll try to break it down using non-technical terms." Meataxe groaned, I don't think Wilks noticed, he just continued. "We consider all of the variables such as planetary rotation, mass of the object to descend – in this case a Market –

initial Ship velocity and, well, a host of other data. The calculations are quite intricate and take a bit of doing, but we can plot where the Market will be at the point of separation from the Ship."

"It'd be outside the door, wouldn't it?" Meataxe asked.

"Well, not quite," answered Wilks. "It's actually moving on a pre-planned arc of entry into the atmosphere. It has, after all, mass and velocity but I know it appears simplistic to the untrained. This trajectory has been calculated accurately. We know exactly where the Market will be until it impacts atmosphere. Then the on-board crew, someone like me," he gave a modest cough, "assumes control. Positioning thrusters compensate for trajectory deviations due to turbulence or other extraneous influences."

I had given up trying to follow him, my attention wandered over to the Market. Amazing, I thought, we stepped out of a big hunk of metal like that after it had plunged down from space. Looking up into the blue sky I was again astonished at our survival. I tuned in again to hear Wilks say, "The parachutes bring in too many variables to allow for precise positioning, we always program in a suitable margin for error in case the Market overcompensates into a life threatening location. We wouldn't, for example, send a Market to a coastal environment. Too high a probability of an aquatic immersion. It's always an inland location, away from large bodies of water."

He finished up with, "I hope this has given you the necessary background. Anything else you need?"

Magic looked around, a puzzled look on his face, "Anyone help me out here?"

"They kick the Market out the door, it falls like a rock until the parachutes deploy. Then it goes anywhere so it's kept well away from towns. Wouldn't do to squash the future customers." Ted has a brain back there.

"Thanks, Ted, okay, that explains why it's so far away. Now, how are we going to do this approach, gentlemen?" I saw what he was getting at. It would be a bit of a surprise for the crew of the other market if we just strolled in. "Have a look at us," he finished. "We've let ourselves go a bit".

We certainly had, our once new and clean overalls had gradually been torn or destroyed by the travel. Each of us had augmented the slowly shredding garment with native garb until now we could pass for locals on a cursory examination. Except for one thing, I noticed that each of us had their shoulder patch exposed, the little Security emblem which told we were the NightWatch. I'd be willing to bet that all of our survivors had done the same. Thinking back I remembered some had rescued the patch from a torn sleeve and sewn it on the new clothing.

The Lady spoke up, "Also, we are the first major caravan to come to your Market. We have a Holy Month just prior to the opening of the portal during which no major commercial business may be transacted. When the portal opens there is a flow of goods both ways, what we have behind us will form the start of a small tent city to facilitate trade."

"Thanks, Kate," said Magic. It seems she had a name. "We've been down for over two months, what sort of contact would they have had with the city before the Holy Month started?" he asked.

"Some," she answered, "I have been told there were small visits before Holy Month from the Market traders, probably to learn our language through your Translator Beads. But there was minimal trading, all the merchants would have been preparing for Holy Month. Since then, nothing at all."

"They must be feeling a bit confused," said Right Honourable. "They land, establish contact, learn the language and get set for the big trading session. Then nothing. No more visitors, all contact cut off. Bit of a laugh, really."

We stood a while in thought, mulling over the state of mind of those in the Market. Meataxe spoke up, "Must be wetting their pants trying to work out what they've done to upset the locals. And we're going to waltz in all fat and sassy. Can't wait."

"Well, you might have to wait a bit longer," Magic spoke in his command tone. "Kate, I'd like you and right Honourable to make the first approach. The rest of us, including the caravan, will wait back."

I saw Captain Britlar step forward and clear his throat. "Excuse me?" he said, very quietly.

I think he felt a bit put out, he was the man in charge of the caravan, not Magic. Kate was only a private citizen after her successful hunt for the now dead Black One. Britlar was a high-ranking Temple officer, just the man to lead the first caravan of the season. He and Magic traded looks, Captain Britlar went on, "Could I just remind you all that I am the senior officer here. Magic and I will step aside and he may make suggestions." He leaned on the word 'suggestions'. "Then I shall make decisions about how to proceed." He and Magic walked ahead on the road, stopped and chatted.

We couldn't hear anything but it was an interesting conversation to observe, not a lot of visible emotion. It started with a speech from Britlar while Magic stood looking contrite. He made a few comments back to the Captain, and then they stood quietly for a few moments. After a pause they continued chatting softly, back and forth. They finished up by smiling at each other, shaking hands and returning to the rest of us.

Britlar announced, "Do whatever Charles says. He's in charge."

Right Honourable nudged me, "How does he do that?"

Magic told us he'd had a change of plan after talking to Britlar. They both beamed at each other when he said this, the sneaky dogs were up to something. Magic informed us that the initial approach would be made by him and me.

Shortly afterwards, Magic and I approached the main entrance to the Market. On the way he said, "Val, ask me to negotiate for you."

"Charles," I said, "will you negotiate for me?"

"No problem," he answered. The Market door opened and an obvious guard stepped out. A Tharl. We stopped and I said, "How are you doin'?"

It was my old friend, Captain Chayla. Big, ugly and definitely unfriendly. He pulled out a blaster, pointed it at my head and said, "You are a dead man, cur."

Chapter 57

Magic held up a hand and yelled, "Stand!" I stood there with my mouth open, out of the corner of my eye I saw he was holding a blaster! Did everyone except me have one of these things?

Our little tableau held while the door behind Chayla opened and the Senior Market Trader came out, he was recognisable by the insignias on his jacket. "Stand down, Captain Chayla. Let us hear them out."

Chayla slobbered something incoherent but put away his weapon. He turned and called out some reinforcements, shortly a squad of Tharls emerged, all with blasters and poor attitudes. Our old Market wasn't looking so bad right about now. Magic holstered his weapon, caught my look and said, "Got it from Ted. Thought it might be useful."

The Senior Market Trader identified himself as Trader Blatz, he stood looking at both of us for a while and finally said, "I had heard you were all dead."

"People keep trying, no doubt about that," I said. "How did you know what happened to us?"

He gave me the once over, assessing my worth or threat level. Again, I failed. This wasn't doing my self-esteem any good. He responded, "We have a radio, of course." Turning to Magic he asked, "How on earth did you live. The last we heard you had a severe malfunction at the start of the drop with no chance of survival. Where is your Market, more importantly, where are the Trade Goods?" He had all the right questions.

"Long story," replied Magic. He looked at me and said, "Why don't you and Captain Chayla go and have a quiet talk, Val, find out what else you've done to upset him?" Chayla objected but was overruled by his trader. I think Blatz could pick up that Magic wanted to have a private talk. Lucky me, I got to have a heart to heart with one of my biggest fans.

"Come on, Chucky, let's go and play while the grownups talk," I said and moved away from the group.

Chayla followed, grabbed me by the shoulder and spun me around to face him, "My name is Chayla, Captain Chayla, and you are less than scum." I was regretting plucking his useless hide from the Inquisition. Ungrateful sod, I thought. Pretty sure he was only held from killing me then and there by his need to be obedient to Trader Blatz. I was going to have to be very nice to the trader.

We stood there a while, me trying to make small talk and him ignoring my presence. Tharls are big and impressive, Chayla stood cloaked in disgust, his weapon harness drawing my eye more and more. After I finally gave up with the chat he turned and spoke. Moving so that his body blocked me from Magic and the Trader he stepped in close and said, "You dishonour me by being alive. I hold you responsible for every barbaric act done by my captors on your lice ridden planet." Obviously, we had a difference of opinion about the whole rescue concept.

"Give it up, Chayla, our Drop Market was sabotaged." I was in his face now, angry as hell. Nostrils flaring, I was spitting words out through clenched teeth. "We were all meant to die, someone from Security must have done it, someone who hates us. That could be you, ugly, did you try to kill us all?" I was ready to go one-on-one with him. Not the best career move I had ever made.

He continued to exhale bad breath and threats, "On the ship you killed someone I cared about a great deal, scum. Like you, she was human, one of your own kind. She was of my clan. We had adopted her and you cut her down without a thought. If I ever have the chance I will take your life in an instant. I am interested only in your death, just you. Others are responsible for the sabotage. Incompetents, obviously. Know this, to me and my brothers, you are the embodiment of disgust." Having finished his piece, he moved off and joined his troop of fellow Tharl guards. I looked at them and they stared hatred back at me.

Do I know how to win friends, or what?

Drifting back to the Trader I heard Magic ask, "Has the trading been good for you here? Doing well, are you?" I looked at him, he knew the answers to these questions but I knew enough to shut up. I waited in silence, exchanging dark looks with Chayla and wondering at his level of animosity. Still, a lot of people don't like me, I'm used to it.

Trader Blatz was a worried man, he told us how they landed successfully, established contact with the locals, had enough language to enable the Translator Beads and then nothing. They were ostracized, no one spoke to them, no contact for the last month. All his sales targets were evaporating. When the Market was collected, he would be demoted. "Not one sale," he moaned. "Not one!"

Magic filled him in on our travels but I don't think the Trader took much in. All he saw was a blank ledger. We sat on the grass together. The Tharls continued to stand and look threatening. "Perhaps I can help," Magic said, almost as a passing thought. "That caravan has trade goods. I know the owners. I think they will talk to me if approached the right way. Perhaps I could ask what has happened, even negotiate for you."

Blatz leaped at the opportunity, "That would be most kind of you."

"I've never been involved in a Market before," said Magic. "Tell me, would you normally expect to sell everything you have in the six months you are on the planet?"

Blatz shrugged, "That's the goal but it's rarely achieved, those few Traders who achieve such a notable feat gain great standing. Of course, the value of the trade must be significant. it is dishonourable to sell without a profit. But to sell all with a high margin, it is the stuff dreams are made of...," he drifted off, thinking of scaling the heights of glory.

"Indeed," said Magic. "How do you know the value of the goods in the Market? How does one calculate the value of goods from a planet? Surely this is difficult?"

It was like watching a master at work, Magic looked completely at a loss. Blatz gave him a pitying look, "It is difficult, Captain, that is why we have Traders. I can look at goods and know within a whisker what its value might be. I appreciate your kind offer of negotiating for us but understand you will be cheated. You are a guard. You should not be placed in a position where you are out of your skill area. Still, I would value any effort you are able to make. I would rather return with a small loss than go back with nothing to show. My shame would be great."

Magic asked, "How much would you value everything in your Market? Roughly speaking, I mean. What would you need to go back and show a healthy profit?"

I saw a change come over Blatz, it was no longer Blatz the shipmate but Blatz the Trader talking, "That depends," he said. "We have many very valuable commodities, some very small, almost priceless items. A figure for the entire contents of the Market, hmmm, it would be very high." He paused a minute, gazed at nothing while doing some deep thinking, looked around, counted on his fingers and put on quite a show. Finally, he gave a figure to Magic.

"That's a lot of money;" said Magic. I mentally whistled at the amount before Magic continued, "I can see why you don't want to go back without a profit. I could talk to the owners of the caravan but to be honest I'll never do as well as you in a trade." He stood up. We began moving back towards the caravan.

"Is there any way I could see their goods?" blurted the Trader. "I could give you some advice, perhaps we wouldn't be cheated so much." There was definite pleading in his eyes.

Magic said, "I'll see what I can do. In the meantime, my people need looking after. Without being in fear of their lives." He looked meaningfully at Captain Chayla. Blatz turned to the Tharl and issued instructions for us all to be cared for. Then he joined Magic in another stroll, hammering out a deal, no doubt.

I left the kids to play.

Some hours later I was sitting in the shade, washed, fed and watered. Tents had sprung up to serve as bargaining stalls, there was even a shelter strung over an assortment of tables and chairs where some enterprising souls sold food and drink.

Feeling very satisfied, I was enjoying watching the ebb and flow of people. Wallace sat at a table, alone, but not for long. As I lay there, I saw Captain Chayla approach him quite purposefully. He stood and looked down at Wallace, they spoke for a time. I couldn't hear what they were saying but it looked serious. Then Chayla sat down and they talked some more. It looked like Wallace was being asked a question, Chayla's gestures were vigorous but I felt certain he was trying to get Wallace's agreement on something.

The Tharl stopped talking and looked earnestly into the slaver's eyes, after a beat Wallace nodded and they clasped arms.

Something was going on.

Chapter 58

Magic came over, sat down and asked, "How is everyone, Val?"

"We're good, Magic. Have a look at their shoulder patches, they've all shaded them in. The deadly NightWatch! Not a bad idea, we need a bit of symbolism. Something to hang on to, our City seems a long time away, Charles." After a pleasant sociable pause, I asked, "Want to tell me what's going on?"

"Not sure what you're getting at, Val," he responded, sitting down beside me. "We're just a bunch of security goons, doing our job."

"Give me a break, Charles. You had everyone leave the caravan after displaying the goods. I saw you escort Blatz all over the stuff while the locals kept their distance. You've got a scheme going, you crook."

"Fair go, Val. I had Wilks check the regulations, we're allowed to buy and sell trade goods. That's all we're doing, a bit of buying and selling. You even asked me to negotiate," he said.

"What are we buying and selling, we haven't got anything to trade?" I asked.

"Britlar thought we'd done the Empire a bit of good so he gave me some credit," he answered.

"What'd we buy, Charles?" I could tell he was enjoying this, the old dog.

"To be quite honest, Val," he spoke over my snort of disbelief, "Britlar sold me the entire caravan. We own the lot! Got a good price, too."

I sat up. "Saints Above, Charles! The whole caravan! Who are we going to sell that to ... oh, you low, scheming guardsman, you." I had finally worked it out, Charles had brought the caravan. He would sell it to Blatz for a nice little profit. "Where's the money going? Who keeps the cash?"

He stood up, dusted his new coveralls off and gave me a hurt look, "Give it a rest, Val, if this works out the NightWatch will have its own source of funds. Could be useful for paying off those debts back on the spaceship."

I stood up and shook hands with him, "Well done, mate. You're always looking after us, a bit of cash will certainly help with all that graft and corruption on the ship."

He didn't move off, I had an uneasy feeling he had more to say, "Anything else, Charles?"

"Yeah, well, I may have got a bit carried away with all this wheeling and dealing, Val," he sounded a bit anxious. When Magic sounds anxious, mere mortals flee in terror.

"You only brought the caravan, right?" I asked.

"Yep...sort of..." he said.

"And?"

"I, uh, bought the rest of the Market from Blatz. The whole thing, every bit, just got a bit carried away. We've run into a bit more debt until we sell it all. Actually, a lot of debt."

We were debt free for a few moments there, between the time he sold the Emperor's caravan and the moment he bought the Drop Market. I sighed and asked, "What do we have to do, Charles?"

He had the grace to look embarrassed, "Just sell everything, Val, everything in the Drop Market. We've still got time, if everyone pitches in and runs a stall, we could do it. Probably... maybe." He was giving me his most winning smile but I wasn't having any. Now we were so far in debt to the spaceship we would be slaves to them forever.

Before I could explode, we were arrested by Captain Chayla's security team.

Magic's heart was in the right place, I kept telling myself. We were sitting on the floor of one of the isolation cells in the Market, Magic against one wall with me facing him. "What?" he said.

"You bought the Market, Charles, the whole Market! What were you thinking?" I asked.

"Look, Blatz was happy with the deal. Ecstatic even. He goes back having sold everything and at a good price. Once he saw the trade goods on offer he was drooling. Especially some of the spices and jewellery, apparently it's good stuff. All we have to do is sell the rest of the Trade goods from the Market, Britlar will help us. Trust me," he smiled.

I stood up and went to the door, peering through the grill I asked, "So why are we here? What have we – and when I say 'we' I mean 'you' – done wrong? Does Blatz know the only reason he couldn't sell to the natives was because they were having a religious holiday?"

"He does now," responded Magic. "Look, it was a bit of a swiftie but I didn't hide anything. I told him about the Holy Month, had Britlar come in and talk to him, all above board. The three of us worked out a very fair little deal. Britlar said he would only authorise the NightWatch to be traders because he knows us, he trusts us. Plus, I think he feels this world owes us for rescuing their artefacts. Blatz is happy because he is guaranteed a good price, including a healthy profit. The Church here gets a slice of the action. We get some change for ourselves. Everybody's happy"

Tugging at the bars in the grill I commented, "I'm not all that happy, Charles." Leaning against the door I said, "We still don't know why we are locked up."

Magic came and stood next to me, "Anything to do with you and your old buddy, Chayla? What's going on there, Val? Anything you want to tell me? Did he set up the crash?" He leaned against the wall, his arms folded.

"He says no and I believe him. He just wants me dead. He does know the Market was sabotaged, just claims it was done by some other incompetent. He says I killed someone dear to him, a human.

Could have done, I suppose. But he seems to be really taking it to heart."

"Who'd you kill?" asked Magic. "What about that girl in the storeroom, the thief. Could she be the one?"

"Probably," I said, "who could tell? But why would Chayla be so cut up about the death of a sneak thief?"

"You said she had a tattoo, one from the great families on the ship, ask him," said Magic.

"Yeah, right, Charles. I'll just bring it up in casual conversation the next time he's spitting at me." I went and sat back against the rear wall. "Okay, let's accept the fact I've made an enemy, he said he'd kill me any chance he gets. Same goes for his boys. Looks like I won't be making the return trip without a few extra holes." I felt tired right to my bones, it seemed every time I turned around there was another problem. When would it all stop?

Shortly afterwards one of this Market's guards unlocked the doors allowing Blatz to enter. "Gentlemen, I do apologise. Charles, one of your men, Technician Wilks, showed me a regulation which meant I had to arrest you."

I groaned, Teddy Boy may have to shoot Wilks for me, I thought. "What's the regulation, Trader Blatz?" asked Magic.

"Loss of a Market," responded Blatz. "You must be placed under arrest until a court of inquiry sits to judge your part in the affair. It's a little-known regulation; I'm surprised he knew of it." I wasn't.

Blatz went on, "As much as it grieves me, I must hold the leadership of the NightWatch to account. The rest of your people are fine, they are all trading their hearts out, but you two have to be arrested. If I didn't do this after Wilks informed me of the rule, I would also be culpable. I'm so sorry, Charles. Your squad leaders want to see you to make sure things are on the level. We only have a couple of months to go until pick-up, we have to stay together, Charles, please don't incite things. Can I get you anything?"

"Get me Wilks and something pointy," I said.

Before we could go any further Britlar burst in, "Charles, get out here. There's been another *sarengo*!"

Chapter 59

It was the Lady, Kate. She was spreadeagled in front of the altar of the tent church set up by Father Dale. He was sitting beside her, holding one dead hand and crying his eyes out. Magic staggered like he was hit when he saw the body. He ran down the aisle, knelt beside his fallen love and cradled her head. I ripped a cloth off some crates to drape over the body, she was mutilated the same as Stomach and Large.

Dominic was still with us.

I slumped in a chair, watching over Magic. There was nothing to be done for Kate, my concern was the living. He kept stroking her hair, murmuring words she would never hear, talking his way through the grief. Charles was a widower, he didn't give his heart away, didn't play up with the girls like some of the younger ones, he loved seldom but he loved deep. I sat near my friend, watching the tears score scar lines into his heart. After a while I sat on the floor beside him and put my hand on his shoulder. He would know he was not alone.

Right Honourable questioned Father Dale, I listened. He and Britlar had come in to ensure everything was ready for the church to begin services. A more senior priest was due the next day. And there she was.

The day passed, squad leaders looked after things, giving Charles support, ignoring me. Chayla stopped by and spoke words of consolation to Magic, but Charles didn't hear anything. I was surprised by the Tharl's thoughtfulness, our eyes met over the body and I nodded my head in silent thanks. His top lip curled into a snarl, his eyes speared distaste and he left us to our mourning. No change in our relationship, then.

As night fell Father Dale brought me some food and drink. I wandered away to sit alone under a tree. Dominic was with us again, killing. I felt totally inadequate, Magic was incapable of giving us a direction for a time, I knew people would need me but I wanted to go away and hide. I was fed up with keeping everything running, with being a rock. I wanted to step down, resign and just be one of the grunts. Let someone else pull it all together, it was too much for me. I fell asleep.

When I awoke, I was pegged out on the ground, arms and legs stretched wide. Father Dale squatted beside me, humming a little tune as he rolled some silver nails in his hands.

Opening my mouth I croaked, "Hello, Dominic."

The next bit wasn't nice. Dale gagged me and made sure it was tight before slicing me a bit with his knife, nothing too deep but enough to hurt. He told me the pain was for my own good. As an unbeliever I should consider myself fortunate to have been singled out for the *sarengo*, it would ensure my salvation.

After a bit more cutting of my flesh, I blacked out. He removed the gag to dribble some water into my parched mouth. That's what I saw when I came to, Dale leaning over me being very solicitous, hoping I wasn't dying. We still had a lot to do, he said. I couldn't wait.

"I may cut out your tongue next," he said. "But if you promise not to scream, I will leave it in. As I bless you with the holy pain you may come closer to salvation by saying one of the Anointed Chants. Would you like that? Would you like to chant? Or shall I cut out your tongue now? Hmm? What would you like?"

"Why are you doing this?" I croaked.

"Oh, no! No questions! The time for questions has passed. Did I not give you ample time to ask questions on our journey? Yes, I did. Many, many times. But you never asked! You are Unbelievers, all Unbelievers! Unbelievers must face pain. Only then may they know true glory. You lucky, lucky man!" He cut off a little toe, I stifled a scream, not wanting to lose my tongue.

"Tonight, you will begin your march to Glory. You will pass all of those others who could not be washed in pain. The first two suffered only a little because I did not know how your bodies worked. And the big ones, oh, dear me, the big ones. Well, they suffered not at all! Nothing! You will pass them easily on your road. They slept through it all, too much potion on their weapons. Dear me, so unworthy, too much." He began to scrap the skin on my stomach with his blade. Bits of flesh curled around his knife blade, the pain washed over me like fire, I blacked out again.

He was still there when I awoke. "Good man! Strong man! Your road to Glory is just beginning. You must walk it all night.All night! And then, in the morning, as dawn breaks, I will help you to Salvation. You will be able to watch me place the sacred Pins into your unworthy body! Such Bliss!" He was standing over me now, his knife dripped bits of skin and blood onto my chest as he waved it around. "That wicked woman, so unworthy! I did not let her suffer. She did not deserve it! A woman! But you, you can carry the pain!"

He stretched up, knife now high, his eyes bright in the glow of the little fire. My head ached, my throat was parched and the pain from my stomach was so intense I trembled.

There was a bright flash off in the night and I saw the strangest thing. The front of Dale's chest glowed for a moment and then just disappeared leaving a fist sized hole through which I could glimpse his bone and lungs. The priest's face had enough time to express surprise before life fled from the insane eyes. His body began to fall forward, it would land heavily on me, a true dead weight.

His hand opened, dropping the knife. I watched it spear towards my right eye.

I pulled my head to the left as far as I could and turned my face away from the descending blade. The point slashed my neck at the same time as Dale's body hit my chest causing me to expel all breath, his lifeless hand flopping onto my face. Some days it doesn't pay to get out of bed.

As I passed out again, I heard Right Honourable say, "Nice one, Ted.

Wilks saved me, I couldn't believe it. When I wasn't found the squad leaders had a crisis meeting. They left Charles out of it. No one had noticed Dale missing, no one ever noticed Dale, but I was needed, I had to be found.

Our Translator Beads have a tracking device in them, it only works over a short distance. We never knew about it because, well, it's technology and too much of this sort of information makes our heads hurt. But Wilks knew about it and explained it was used to keep tabs on people on a ship. Or in situations like this when you have been kidnapped by a psychopathic priest.

When Wilks found I was missing he suggested to Willem that he use the Market's tracking device to find me. Then he had to explain what he was talking about. It took some hours to eliminate all the beads from the search, the regular security troops have their gear logged in against their name and so the tracking can link to a specific person. We never bothered with that piece of excellent planning; we picked up whatever Translator Bead was lying around. We even swapped them about when needed. All this generated a dog's breakfast of names and Translator beads. We may have to change that practice in future.

Wilks gradually eliminated all the tracking points until he was left with just a few. Mine was bleeping at a little walk from the camp. I may marry Wilks.

I awoke in a clean bed, my face heavily bandaged. A small tent was over my stomach, when I peeked under I saw a patch of raw muscle the size of my hand covered in what looked like a clear gel. I recognised it as a fast-healing unguent used for burns. Beside me was Right Honourable, he called through the open door, "He's awake!"

Shortly afterwards the lads filed in. I was in one of the interior rooms in the Market, plenty of empty space after all the trading. We chatted for a while, they left when I dozed off.

Britlar concluded that Dale was another Black One, probably killed Father Dexus and arranged for another of his brethren to clean up after him. Dale was trying to steal the artefacts. If the Black Ones controlled them, they controlled the Empire. We felt he was going to turn the artefacts over to the guy sneaking into our camp. Of course, I messed up that plan when I killed him. No wonder Dale was cross with me.

Next day Teddy Boy dropped by. When I asked him how things were going he said the trading was going well. The NightWatch would probably sell everything in the Market and still have some time before the retrieval rocket. It looked like we could have some much needed peace and quiet for the remainder of this tour.

When I said as much Ted vaguely agreed and said, "Yeah."

He paused and then went on, "Val, we need you out there. The Tharls are becoming more and more surly. Chayla's constantly throwing insults, something's coming. Don't know what but I feel a bad time ahead."

Chapter 60

When a guardsman of Ted's experience feels uneasy, I listen. I asked him to help me dress but when I sat up the stitches on my neck started to bleed. The pain from my raw stomach was so intense I collapsed back onto the bed. Ted refused to help me for at least another day, he put me back under the covers and gave me some more painkillers.

The next time I surfaced the room was empty except for one visitor, Wallace. He sat in the only chair, arms folded, legs stretched out. We looked at each other for a few moments before he broke what was becoming an uncomfortable silence. "Going to have a nice scar on that neck," he said.

"Let's hope that's all I get out of this." I looked at him, his gaze never dropped, eyes like ice. "So, what's the deal, Wallace? I saw you talking to Chayla. Did you accept a new contract? On me?" My arms were under the sheets, I was helpless.

He unfolded his arms and stood up. I tensed but he only moved to the foot of the bed where he stood with his hands in pockets. "Chayla wants a cut of the money you are making from all the trading. He tells me he's part of a syndicate on your ship, a powerful one. The girl you killed, the one he's so upset about, was his niece."

"But she was human, couldn't have been his niece," I responded.

"I don't know how that works either, but that's what he claims. They have the same sign, did you see a tattoo like this on the girl?" he asked, taking a piece of paper from a pocket. He unfolded it and I recognised the same sign as on the girl whose head I had removed.

"Okay," I said. "Somehow, they're linked. He hates me. I got that. But what's all this about him being part of a syndicate?"

He placed a small recorder on my bed. "It's all in here. I was talking to Wilks, he showed me this thing and how to use it. Guy's a jerk but he knows stuff. Chayla and I became quite close after I agreed to do a small job for him." He reached into his jacket and took out a knife.

I tensed. Not a lot I could do, for some reason I didn't think to cry out. We had to finish this ourselves. If he came close enough I was going to be able to get a couple of good hits in before he stuck me with what I am sure was the biggest blade in the world.

"Come on," he said. "Let's go. When Chayla sees me leave the Market he's going to signal his team to kill or capture the rest of the NightWatch. I get to keep the survivors as slaves. Sort of a bonus." He was waiting by the door, looking at me expectantly.

"You're helping?" I asked. "Not going to kill me?" This was all going a bit fast for my poor drug-soaked brain.

He pulled open some drawers and found my clothes, throwing them onto the bed. "Not today, Val. Now get up, I only found out about Chayla's plan before coming in here, he seemed keen to brag about how he was going to finish the job started up on the ship."

He wasn't making a lot of sense but at least he hadn't killed me. I managed to get my pants on but the shirt was impossible, my stomach screamed. I had to do this, I had to keep moving. Wallace put my shoes on while I sat on the bed and clamped my teeth together. Standing up I staggered a step, he gave me a worried look and cracked the door open.

As he peeked out a blaster poked him in the teeth. Wallace had seen what these weapons could do. He stopped and backed into the room. Pushing him was Ted, the barrel of his shooter pressed into the slaver's mouth.

"You all right, Val?" he asked when he saw me.

"I'm fine, Ted. Wallace is on our side. I think. What are you doing here?" Ted looked at me a while, Wallace stood very still, jaws wide over the blaster still thrust deep into his mouth. Eventually Ted was satisfied I had suffered no harm, he pulled his weapon out carefully, nodded at Wallace and said, "I saw our friend sneaking in, thought I might do the same."

To Wallace he said, "We going to have any trouble over this?" he indicated the barrel of the blaster and Wallace's mouth.

"No," said Wallace, "I'm good." He stretched his jaw a few times, seemed satisfied everything was in order and went on, "You sure no one else saw you come in?"

Ted wiped the barrel and made the weapon disappear. "I'm sure. I'm especially sure no Tharl spotted me." He checked my stomach, grimaced, then clucked over my neck. "You're going to have a beaut scar there, Val. Have to call you zipper-neck."

"Thanks, Ted, you're a real comfort. Wallace was just telling me about Chayla's plan." I stayed near the bed, whenever I spoke it was through clenched teeth. The pain was making me sweat. "Keep going, Wallace."

"When I leave here that will be a signal to Chayla and his team that you are dead. They plan to attack your people, killing or capturing everyone. They have a story ready for the Trader about treachery. Your treachery."

"What treachery?" I found more painkillers, swallowed a handful with some water.

Wallace cracked the door a little and peeked out. "He's going to say he has proof the other Market didn't crash, that you deliberately sabotaged it. He will claim you landed successfully and stole all the contents. He says he can convince Blatz that you planned to kill us all here, including the Traders. And you intended keeping the goods for yourself."

Ted nodded, "That'd do it." It probably would, too. The Traders seem to take theft of their wares very seriously.

"Where are the Tharls now?" I groaned.

"Scattered throughout the encampment," said Wallace. "They've all got blasters. When they see me come out, they are to open fire on all the NightWatch. You won't have a chance."

"Magic?" asked Ted.

Wallace shut the door, turning back into the room he shook his head and said, "No, he's locked up good and tight. They plan to keep him that way, bring him back to the ship as a trophy. He's safe, but we can't get to him."

This wasn't looking good. If Wallace went out the slaughter would begin. I was in no shape for a running battle. That left Ted, but what could he do. I looked at him, sitting beside me in silence. His NightWatch patch was darkened, I could see the sweat and blood on it, he'd carried that badge a lot of places. He looked back at me with a slightly expectant face, waiting for me to come up with a plan. I wasn't good at plans. Magic did plans, I just hit people. The silence lengthened. How could we warn the NightWatch, tell them of the ambush. We needed a silent signal, one that would not alert the Tharls and pre-empt the killing.

A silent signal. "Wallace," I groaned, "give me your knife." He placed the ugly blade into my hand, I told Ted to sit still while I cut the sleeve off his shirt, the sleeve emblazoned with the NightWatch patch. I slit the sleeve and made a bandana, gave it to Ted and said, "Put it on, wrap it around your head so that the patch is visible at the front."

"What's up?" asked Wallace.

Looking at Ted I said, "Do you know?" The tablets had taken the edge off the pain, I was still sweating and weak but I could think and move a bit more.

Ted stood up, bandana firmly in place, a big grin spread across his face. "Too right!" To Wallace he explained "We had a situation back in the City, had to get through lots of uniforms and run away. We needed a way to tell who was on the home team in case a fight broke out. Day Watch had the same uniform as us so we needed something just for us. The Man in Black had us tie our scarves around our heads. Anyone not in a scarf was a bad guy. Worked a treat."

I hoped it would work again. I hoped the NightWatch veterans would see Ted walking around and remember how we ran through that long ago night. I also hoped all the newbies were still taking notice of the veterans. "Give Ted five minutes, Wallace, then you go out. After that we pray."

I lay back down on the bed, panting a little.

Chapter 61

Ted left, Wallace waited five minutes and then slipped out. He had me keep his knife in case I had any visitors but I wasn't waiting. As soon as Wallace shut the door behind him I got up and left the room. I must have been quite a sight, dressed only in pants and boots, clutching a knife with my raw stomach glistening wetly. Down the corridor I slunk, before I had gone more than a few steps I heard the sounds of blasters, cries of pain and the chaos of battle.

Emerging into the main loading bay I watched the fight through the big open doors. I was inside the Market while all the fighting was outside, my aching body preventing me from taking any action. As I leaned against the huge, open doors I saw a lot of dead and dying from both Tharls and the NightWatch. Ted's signal had worked. The Tharls were a beaten force. They had expected no resistance, they had not considered we would fight back.

But we were not the same oafish mob who had fled the City. Now we were vicious, now we fight back.

Men and women wearing our patch were tearing into the stunned Tharls with any weapon that came to hand, they struck with a ferocity which appalled the onlookers. I saw a Tharl standing with a look of disbelief as a female member of the Watch leaped at his face and bit a large piece from his cheek. She spat it out before picking up a bottle and ramming it into his eye. He collapsed while she stood, glaring with a manic intensity as blood trickled down her jaw.

The remaining Tharls broke and ran, at their head was Chayla, leading them back to the Market. I staggered to my feet as they burst into the loading bay, Chayla slapped the emergency door mechanism and the metal doors slid into place. This was a safety device, meant to lock the bad guys out in case the Market was ever attacked.

Turning to survey his remaining troops, Chayla saw me. He stopped and smiled, "Well, well, there is a god."

I pulled out my knife and slumped into a fighting stance. Behind Chayla the door to the control room opened as Wilks entered, "Who closed the doors?" he said. He couldn't see what was going on as I frantically tried to think of a way to take the big Tharl down. "I'll need to see some good cause, people, these things don't just shut themselves. Hefty fines for misuse. Val, you're up and about!" Then he saw us all, realised bad things were happening and went very quiet.

I had started to fill the silence with a series of low moans. The Tharl captain instructed his squad to enter the control room and climb the stairs to the weapon turrets. These were more insurance against native attack. With the doors shut and the four blaster turrets manned the Market could hold out for months, a fact I am sure the Tharls intended to exploit. I saw all of them disappear into the control room with Wilks rapidly retreating ahead of them.

I was alone, except for the monster intent on my death.

Chayla swatted my knife hand away and punched me in the stomach. Oh, God, it hurt. He knew where I was injured, everyone did, I was lit up down there like a light bulb, a red, drippy light bulb. The pain wrapped around my torso like a blanket of fire, an incredible, all invasive burn. I took some small pleasure in holding on to the knife, little good it was going to do me.

He started telling me how he was going to cause me a lot of pain before I died. Boy, had I heard that before. He also took perverse delight in telling me about his syndicate and what a nuisance the NightWatch had been. So much so that the leader had devised a plan to get rid of us. That plan I knew, dump us out the airlock in a dodgy Market and watch us die. He told me all about it, every detail.

While he gloated, I sucked in air. I was bent at the waist, trying to think a coherent thought.

While I was doubled over he smacked me with an open hand on the side of the head, neatly targeting my new stitches. They burst open and I started to bleed some more as I fell to the floor. He laughed and stood over me, grabbing my hair to pull my head up. He slowly pulled and pulled, dragging me erect until I was looking him directly in the eye. My feet were off the ground, the only thing supporting me was the huge hold he had on most of my hair, I think I felt the strands start pulling out but on the scale of pain I was in it barely registered.

The Tharl's eyes bored into mine, "You killed my niece, you pile of offal. She was adopted by the syndicate and given to me for training. She was a good girl, brave and strong. She would have come back to us after having her fling with those vermin. She wore our badge." He slapped me twice, back and forth. More hair came out. "I asked for your head, but they thought of a better fate. You could all die while your Market crashed. And now, you will all die!" He punched me in the stomach again.

My eyes were watering, arms flailing, brain gibbering. Then I felt the knife, it was still in my hand. Survival instinct, I suppose; never let go of a weapon. I took a firmer grip on the handle, spat at Chayla to distract him and slammed the knife as hard as I could into the elbow of his arm. The arm holding me up by the hair. It sank into the back of the elbow, all the way in up to the hilt.

He screamed, dropped me and staggered back with the knife jammed into the joint of his elbow. I curled into a ball and wept, slowly pulling myself up to my feet. My stomach was raw, bruised muscle but if I didn't keep going I was already dead. I lurched into Chayla and swung a punch, but not at him, I didn't have the strength to cause a full grown Tharl any harm.

Instead of his face, I swung at the handle of my knife. I put all I had into it, I was swinging for my life. The handle snapped off. The blade was embedded in his right elbow.

Now I've always thought I was a good screamer but the noise that came out of his throat was world class, absolutely outstanding.

He kept his right arm straight, I guess the blade had lodged in the joint preventing any bending. His left arm was still good and it caught me on my good ear, sending me tumbling across the floor.

At this point I didn't know where I was, my head was ringing and most of my body ached, throbbed or bled. Lifting my head off the metal deck I saw Chayla scrabbling for his holstered blaster. Since it was on his right side he was forced to reach across his body with his left hand, the butt of the weapon pointed backwards. He was trying to twist his left hand enough to snag the handle. He kept his right arm at full extension, well out of the way.

If he got that blaster out then it was all over. I lunged and we wrestled. Well, he wrestled, I just hung on to the trigger mount and fought his good hand for possession. To let go was death, to hang on wasn't much better. I had no spare arms or legs, everything was busy, my whole focus was on that blaster.

In all the confusion he brought his injured arm down closer, so I rammed my head up into the joint. He yowled some more and relaxed his grip on the butt. The blaster was still strapped into the holster but now I could cram a finger into the pistol guard. I pressed the trigger and hung on some more.

The muzzle blast took out the end of the holster, creased his pants and burnt off his right boot, complete with enclosed foot. We fell to the deck, I wasn't hearing much of anything now, between his screams and mine we pretty much filled all the available space. He rolled on top of me, a huge angry weight, and continued to punch my face with his good hand. His right hand was resting on the floor; I guess the burnt foot took his mind off the elbow.

My hands were trapped between our bodies but I didn't mind. In the struggle I had managed to pull his blaster out of the holster; I am, after all, a devious bastard. It was squashed between my chest and his stomach. I let the rest of my body fend for itself and concentrated on turning the barrel as far into his gut as I could.

I smiled through the punches and pulled the trigger.

The shot took out his stomach and most of his back. I kept the trigger pressed until there was no flesh resting against the barrel. I melted a hole through his body, my hands eventually rested in a neatly cauterised circle.

I wriggled my fingers waiting for the rest of his squad to find me under the body of their boss. They were going to be seriously steamed with me but I didn't mind. I had run out, there was nothing left in my tank. Death would be a nice improvement.

I felt the weight go as someone pulled the body away. I lay looking through the now open doors, gathered around were the NightWatch, looking down at me with a wide array of amazement. I was pretty amazed, too.

"Having a bit of a lie down, are you, Val," said Willem.

"You're a messy bloke, Valentine," said Horse. "Place stinks of burnt Tharl."

"Why aren't you dead yet, Val?" asked Meataxe.

Good question, I blacked out. Again.

Chapter 62

It was Wilks. He had done it again, this time saving us all. When the Tharls raced up the stairs to the turrets he went to the control panel and shut the access doors at both ends. They were trapped on the staircase and surrendered when Right Honourable gave them the old ultimatum. Give up or we'll kill you.

One Tharl had run down to kill Magic, our Captain was alone and unarmed, should have been easy meat for a vicious Tharl. He opened the door and was met by H'nuth who plunged a knife into his left eye. Talk about surprised. Wallace had shared his conversations with his new best friend so H'nuth had finally finished his report on us. I guess we had passed.

We also had several taped conversations between Wallace and Chayla incriminating them in a range of misdeeds. These included the biggest crime of all, theft from the Traders. To top it all off we had Chayla's ramblings as he taunted me during the fight.

"A syndicate, eh?" mused Magic, newly released from his locked storeroom. "Wonder how the investigation's going back on board the ship. We might just tread carefully when we return, see how the land lies."

I fell asleep back in my recovery bed, Magic and Trader Blatz continued to talk in low tones about the politics of ship life.

By the time the recovery rocket came down I was fully recovered, I had some new scars even if I was missing a toe. I've got plenty of spare toes. The NightWatch made a killing as traders, we would be able to pay off our debts and have some left funds left over.

Magic used the time to grieve, he was surrounded by those who wished him well and our gentle comradeship pulled him back from whatever abyss he had confronted.

Wilks manned the radio and sent the appropriate signals, he also sent up a recording of all the nasty conversations. The other technician was a casualty of Chayla's violence.

My stint as Sergeant was almost done, when we returned to the ship, I could kiss goodbye to all the worry. The Man in Black would take up his role as our captain and Magic would again be the sergeant. Strangely, this didn't make me feel all that happy; I liked to be up the big end of town.

Right on schedule the shuttle came down. The trip up let us use the couches with their blue glow. I don't think I was alone in having a little shudder as we strapped in, this time we took a bit of time and trouble locating the right command couches. Magic and I still had to face charges over losing a Market but we weren't too worried, all the evidence implicated someone back on the ship, not the NightWatch.

Docking took a bit of time, we used it to form up in the large open area of the Market, shifting all the couches and their blue glows against the wall. Magic and I stepped out through a small door onto the deck of the ship to make our initial report while the squad leaders finished this task. Blatz came with us.

Standing in front of the big Market door was the Man in Black. A little behind him were the rest of the Trading Council and Senior crew members. What's up, I thought?

"Hello, Charles, welcome back," said the Man in Black.

"Evening, Franz, you're looking well," responded Magic. Eyeing the people behind our leader Magic said, "What's all this then, Franz?"

"Been a few changes, Charles, your little recording stirred things up quite nicely. Seems like I'm the one person all the factions can trust." The Man in Black gestured over his shoulder at the other big wigs. "I've been promoted, no-one trusts the Tharls anymore, so I'm the new Head of Security. I'll be looking after the entire ship."

Standing behind Magic I watched the faces of all those opposite us. I was looking for the hateful glance, the guilty look. The council, the officers, all looked stern and grim. The Man in Black had another surprise, "Reckon you better stay on as Captain of the Watch. That all right with you?"

They shook hands. Magic had been a good Captain, we were lucky to have him. Looking at me the Man in Black asked, "I don't know about young Valentine, though. What have you done with him, Charles? He looks like he's gone ten rounds with a feral pig. You might need someone with a bit more experience for Sergeant. The Watch has some hard cases in need of a firm hand."

I felt confused and a little hurt. Then again, I understood what he was saying, too many times had I watched Magic handle situations with an ease I would never possess. He was made of the right stuff. I was just a fill in sergeant, a hitter not a thinker.

Magic looked at me, "Yeah, Franz, I reckon you're right, he acts without thinking, bit of a wild card. And you know what people say about his gentle nature."

"Now cut that out!" I said, "I am a nice guy."

They both smiled. "And a mean animal in a fight," stated Magic. "On the other hand, Val, you are far too ugly to be in the ranks. I suppose we've gotten used to your little ways. No, we better keep him as Sergeant." I felt better after this affirmation. At least, I think I felt better.

The doors to the Market opened revealing the NightWatch, in all its glory. They slouched, stooped, chatted, had no sense of drill, dressed in a wide variety of native cloths and did not look like they could keep order in a playground. I saw Wallace and H'nuth in the front row; Wallace must have snuck aboard, running from a past life. A closer look revealed he was wearing a NightWatch shoulder patch, seems we had picked up another recruit.

Blow me down, H'nuth was wearing a Watch patch, too. We had our very own devil.

Right Honourable took a pace forward. In his best parade ground voice, he commanded, "NightWatch! Attent-ion!"

They ignored him.

THE END

Valentine and the NightWatch will return to battle pirates and space zombies.

If you enjoyed this book, please consider leaving a review on the Amazon website, even if it's only a line or two.

And tell your friends, word-of-mouth is crucial for any author to succeed.

Terry may be contacted at hornbywriting@gmail.com

Don't miss out!

Visit the website below and you can sign up to receive emails whenever Terry Hornby publishes a new book. There's no charge and no obligation.

https://books2read.com/r/B-A-ZYBAB-KMCNC

BOOKS 2 READ

Connecting independent readers to independent writers.